love among the recipes

Carol M. Cram

New Arcadia Publishing

www.newarcadiapublishing.com

ISBN-13: 978-0-9810241-9-6

Cover Design: Bailey McGinn – www.baileydesignsbooks.com

Printed and bound in the United States of America

Praise for *Love Among the Recipes*

"Cram's passion for Paris is apparent on every page, and the book is chock-full of rich descriptions of famous landmarks like the Louvre and mouthwatering dishes...Genna is an intriguing hero: a woman who has experienced motherhood and switched careers midlife, leading her to the place she's always wanted to live, with surprises around every corner and an open mind to receive them."
– *Kirkus Reviews*

"A delicious feast for foodies and Francophiles ~ Paris has never tasted better!" – Patricia Sands, Author of *Drawing Lessons*

"A perfect escape. This romantic and engaging story has a wonderfully humorous touch. Cram's lovely writing brings Paris and its many treasures to life. I truly felt like an armchair traveler...what a delight!" – Amy Maroney, Author of *The Miramonde Trilogy*

"Take a dash of travel, stir in some flirtation, and add a pinch of sparkle to a woman's life after she leaves her husband to write a cookbook on the other side of the world. Set in the bustling bistros of Paris, this book adventures into the deep cauldrons and heady filled chalices of true love." – Cathleen With, award-winning Author of *Having Faith in the Polar Girls' Prison*

"It's a wonderful, fluid and beguiling read, a marvelous book, which made me laugh out loud." – Martin Lake, Author of *Cry of the Heart*

For Gregg and Julia, who have accompanied me on so many Parisian adventures and who keep me sane

one

April 2015 – Paris

Basic Macarons
A circular meringue-based confection with a rounded top, smooth filling, and flat base

Without looking, Genna stepped off the curb and narrowly escaped being lobbed from the bumper of a speeding Citroën when a man grabbed her elbow and yanked her back.

"Gardez-vous, madame."

Genna swung around and collided with the man's other arm, sending his phone clattering to the pavement.

"Merde!"

"Désolée!" Genna's heart twanged like an unbound bungee cord at the near miss.

Ignoring her, the man stooped to retrieve his phone and then cradled it between both hands.

Chiseled features, a South of France tan, dark hair speckled with gray, pushing fifty. He looked like he belonged on the cover of *L'Urbane Parisien: Watch Him Smolder – Mature Edition.*

Mais oui.

Wonder replaced terror. Genna could count on the fingers of one hand how often in recent years she'd been within ten yards of a man who had made her little heart flutter.

Actually, she didn't need any fingers.

"*Merci beaucoup!*"

Still ignoring her, Monsieur Hottie looked down at his phone. The screen flickered. Sighing with relief, he bent low over the display, almost planting firm lips on the mirrored surface.

"*Merci,*" she said again. "*La circulation . . .*" The traffic.

"*Ah, oui.*" The man let loose a stream of French presumably about the dreadful state of the traffic in the nation's capital. Genna pasted on her trying-to-understand-French smile, but only the odd word penetrated—*voiture* was car, *extraordinaire*—obvious, another *merde*—the one French swear word she knew.

The man cocked his head toward the pedestrian light, which was still green. After making a good show of looking both right and left, he started across the road. Genna followed a few paces behind, her heart still hammering, acutely conscious of how ridiculous she must look to him—a woman pushing fifty in sensible running shoes and with a purple daypack slung across one shoulder.

When they reached the safety of the other side, the man glanced back.

"*Merci!*" Genna said breathlessly. She smiled, and for a second, the man's eyes widened, his lips twitching with amusement.

"*De rien, madame.*" It is nothing.

He raised one hand in a wave, then turned left into the narrow Rue de Grenelle. As Genna watched him go, an adrenalin-spiked elation flooded her. She felt like throwing her head back and laughing up at the sharp blue sky. She was in Paris! Everything was going to be fine so long as she watched where she was going. She'd been *so right* to come.

Genna carried on to Rue de Sèvres and from there along Rue Bonaparte to her apartment, steps from the Boulevard Saint-Germain and directly across the street from the fabled Café Les Deux Magots. As soon as she found a way to get online, she'd email Nancy and describe the dishy Frenchman who'd just saved her from Death by Citroën. Nancy was convinced that Genna had gone to Paris to find a new man.

Nancy was dead wrong, but no matter how many times Genna explained why she'd chosen Paris, Nancy had refused to believe her.

"Don't be ridiculous," she'd said the day before Genna left. "After what you've been through? Besides, you can't spend every minute of your day cooking."

Oh yes, she could! Genna wrestled open the heavy wooden door to her building, crossed the quiet courtyard, and started up the circular staircase. Five flights later, her chest heaving, she rounded the last twist to come forehead to toe with two scuffed shoes.

"*Bonjour, madame.*"

She looked up to see a man who had long since bid *au revoir* to the back end of eighty.

"*Ah, bonjour.* Um . . ."

"Gustav Leblanc," he said, raising one hoary eyebrow.

"Yes? Oh! I'm sorry. I mean, *désolée.* Please, come in."

Genna squeezed past him, her shopping bags clanking. Monsieur narrowed his eyes. She unlocked the door and ushered him into the dingy apartment, feeling embarrassed about the hideous art, stained walls, and shabby furniture until she remembered that as the owner of the apartment, Monsieur Leblanc could hardly object to its decor.

He planted himself in the middle of the living room and stared as she deposited the bags on the couch. He exuded a feral, gnome-like quality wrapped in body odor laced with the stench of stale Gauloises.

"You are comfortable." It was not a question.

"The apartment is fine. Thank you." The attendant at the rental agency where Genna had picked up the key had told her that the owner was a recluse whom she'd likely never meet.

And yet, here he was.

Monsieur shuffled to a heavy sideboard next to the table, pried open a drawer, and extracted several sheets of paper. "You see?"

"Ah, no." Genna walked toward him.

"Rules!" Monsieur Leblanc barked. "*Les règles*. Four languages! *Anglais, allemand, italien, et, bien sûr, le français*. Please to read them. This place, this *appartement*, belonged to my *grand-mère*."

Genna wondered if old Grandma Leblanc had been responsible for the five-foot-wide needlepoint reproduction of *La Grande Odalisque* by Ingres fastened with steel pegs to the wall above the couch. The figure of the nude courtesan resembled Ingres's painting in size, shape, and subject, but the resemblance stopped there. Checkered patches in three shades of pinky-orange wool made the courtesan's skin look like a sunset on acid.

She started to read the faded, uneven type of Monsieur's rules. The subject of water, or, more accurately, its lack, occupied the entire first page. Long hot showers were not something Monsieur countenanced for tenants, nor for himself, evidently.

"Thank you. *Merci*."

He grunted. "*Bon*. Now, you see books?" He gestured to a dust-choked bookshelf under the window. Most of the books were English paperbacks and Parisian guidebooks, with spines showing dates in the eighties, almost three decades earlier. There was even one from the year she was born. The Beatles might still have been together.

"Books are for you, but please . . ." He wagged his finger under Genna's nose. "Do not take them from the *appartement*. I have a list!"

"No, of course not."

"And cooking."

"What about it?" Genna edged in front of the shopping bags, hoping Monsieur wouldn't notice the stainless-steel whisk slithering out of its bag and threatening to bounce across the threadbare carpet.

"*Le gaz*. You know how to use?"

"I have gas at home."

"Do not use too much."

She wondered what constituted too much. Now was probably not the best time to tell him she planned to cook a great deal during her stay in the apartment and that her shopping bags bulged with cooking utensils. Genna needed a well-equipped kitchen for the work she planned to do in Paris. The only cooking equipment in the dusty kitchen was a frying pan caked with the muck of a thousand dinners, a battered saucepan with its coating long stripped, and one knife warped into a corkscrew.

"*Eh bien.*" Monsieur grinned, showing brown teeth that tightened her stomach and made her glad she hadn't eaten for several hours. He handed her a creased card. "I run the *tabac* on Rue de Grenelle. Come see me if you need anything. My son also. He is *un avocat*, a lawyer. He helps me when he can."

"How lucky for you."

He closed his mouth and shrugged, as Gallic a movement as any Genna had yet seen in Paris. "The rent . . ."

"Yes? I paid the first two months as agreed in the contract, and then the terms are week to week."

He looked at her blankly and then flapped one gnarled hand. "*Oui, oui, mais,* but—the rate, *vous savez,* you know, it is reduced because you stay so long."

"I realize that. It seems reasonable." Truthfully, it was exorbitant compared to what she'd pay back home, but compared to other apartments in the neighborhood, it was a deal for someone with plenty of money.

Unfortunately, she wasn't someone with plenty of money.

"*Eh bien.*" He shifted from one foot to the other. "It is lower."

"Yes, I understand." How grateful did he need her to be?

"So, *l'électricité, les lumières, vous savez,* the lights."

"Yes?"

"Not too much."

"You want me to use less electricity because the rent is lower?"

Monsieur peered up at her through sharp black eyes. "*Oui.*"

"Oh."

Monsieur cocked his head toward the door to the bedroom. Without a word, Genna went into the bedroom, snapped off the bedside light, and returned to the living room.

"*Bon.*" He moved toward the door.

"Ah, *monsieur?*"

He paused, a scowl on his face. "*Oui?*"

"I need to use the internet, but I can't figure out how to get online. Do you have the Wi-Fi password?" She pronounced it *wee fee* in the European way.

Monsieur Leblanc could not have looked more shocked if she'd stripped and jiggled her breasts in front of his red-veined nose.

"The internet?" He shook his head as if trying to rid himself of appalling thoughts.

"I want to be able to check my email and do some research."

"Email?"

Genna was beginning to wonder if a lifetime of penny-pinching had unbalanced him.

"You know about the internet," she said, hoping she didn't sound patronizing. "*Pour l'ordinateur.* For the computer."

"*Oui, oui, je le connais, je le connais. L'internet. L'ordinateur.*" He sucked in sallow cheeks and then let out a long sigh. "No internet."

"But . . ."

"*Non.*"

She decided that asking him to fix the television, which so far had emitted only static, was tantamount to throwing herself off the top of the Eiffel Tower.

"*Au revoir, madame.*"

After the door shut behind Monsieur, Genna sank onto the hard couch. The complete isolation of no internet and no television for six months generated a rush of panic. What was she thinking coming to this city of two million souls — ten, if you counted the suburbs? Not one person knew her or cared whether she lived or died.

"Get a grip, Genna," she said out loud.

The sound of her voice brought her back to reality. Her phone had the cheapest data plan available, but that didn't need to be the end of the world. If she wanted to go online, she could find a café with Wi-Fi or, better still, a place with computers and internet access.

Big deal.

It also occurred to her that no Wi-Fi meant she could get Drew's emails at one sitting every few days, and then delete them all at once.

Smiling again, Genna kicked off her runners and lay back on the couch. The weeks stretched ahead with delicious unpredictability. Paris was waiting for her to explore, and she couldn't wait for the adventures to begin.

two

Mango Macarons
*Filled with spicy mango jam and drizzled with bitter
chocolate*

On her master list of Parisian sites, Genna placed the Eiffel Tower
in the top spot followed by each of the museums, gardens, and
monuments she thought had potential. Drew liked saying that
Genna had a list for everything, and that if death wasn't on her list,
then it couldn't happen.

He exaggerated, of course, but it was true that Genna loved to
make lists, the more elaborate the better.

After spending three days equipping her kitchen for serious
cooking and familiarizing herself with the food shops and markets
in the neighborhood, Genna struck out on a warm April morning
for the Eiffel Tower. She headed west along the Boulevard Saint-
Germain for several blocks before angling north through quiet
residential streets toward the Seine.

A sense of calm enveloped her when she stepped onto the
cobbled walkway bordering the river. The smell of river water
mingled with wet stone stirred memories of the Capilano River
near the house that she and Drew had purchased sixteen months
earlier.

Her former house, she reminded herself.

She walked quickly in an attempt to squelch the memories and
burn off the excess calories she'd consumed the night before.

Already, the waistband of her skirt pinched uncomfortably. These days, cookbook authors couldn't afford to look like they ate what they cooked. The rawboned Julia Child figure was no more, which was a shame since Genna tended more toward Julia Child than Julia Roberts. Most of the biggest cookbook authors (big in terms of sales, not girth) looked like movie stars.

Genna's new cookbook (her sixth) was to be called *Eat Like a Parisian* and would be her first crossover cookbook/guidebook. Sara Banks, her editor at Gowan Publishing, had been enthusiastic about Genna's pitch.

> *Eat Like a Parisian combines a passion for travel with a love of cooking to produce a new kind of travel cookbook. Intrepid travelers can use the book as a jumping-off point for their own explorations of Paris, while adventurous cooks will enjoy creating the tasty, bistro-style dishes. With names like Eiffel Tower Duck, Steak Musée D'Orsay, and Mona Lisa Crème Caramel, each dish offers a playful homage to a Parisian site.*

Genna got the idea for the book a few months before her second Christmas without Drew. By March, she'd received a modest advance on royalties from the publisher and a promise from her financial-advisor guy that by June he'd top up her account with the proceeds from several surefire investments.

With the money and a visa that allowed her to live in France for six months, Genna was prepared to devote herself to eating and sightseeing, cooking and writing. She had to make it work. The alternative was to go back to her basement suite in North Vancouver.

No way.

The tip of the Eiffel Tower was just visible above the high wall of the embankment. Genna was sure she'd soon be mounting the stairs to the street at the base of the tower. But after another fifteen minutes of brisk walking, she didn't seem to have moved an inch

closer. The sun that earlier had warmed her face with the softness
of an early April morning now blazed across the river, bouncing off
the water, searing in its intensity. She kept walking, her feet hot
now with a blister just starting to form on the ball of her right foot.
She tied her sweater around her waist, took a swig of water from
the bottle in her daypack, and trudged on.

"It can't be much farther. Look at the map." A woman's voice,
the accent broad New York.

"I don't need the map to tell me it's miles away. Can't we just
get a cab?" An older couple passed Genna going in the same
direction, the man's eyes fixed disconsolately on the cobblestones.

"It's a waste of money," his wife said. "We've *got* to stick to our
budget. We're already ten euros over and it's not even nine
o'clock."

"But we're wasting *time* with all this walking. Come on, here's
a stairway. I bet we can hail a cab at the top."

"We'll be broke at this rate."

"At least we won't be crippled."

"Ha, ha." The woman glanced back at her husband, her
expression a mixture of exasperation and affection.

With a sharp stab of envy, Genna recognized the bickering as
the back-and-forth of a marriage that had settled over the decades
into comfortable predictability. The woman worried about money;
the man grumbled at the first sign of physical discomfort. The
pattern would continue for the rest of their lives together.

Why couldn't she have had that? What had she done wrong?

She watched the pair climb the stairs to the road and decided
the man had a point. Walking had its place in the grand scheme of
sightseeing, but not when it began resembling the Death March of
Bataan. Genna reached the road just in time to see the couple
disappear into a white taxi. Within minutes, she flagged down her
own.

"*La tour Eiffel, s'il vous plaît.*"

The driver glanced back at her, bushy eyebrows raised above
eyes veined red with exhaustion. He looked like he would kill for a

soft bed and a respite from stupid tourists. "*C'est près, madame.*" It's near.

She shrugged, he shrugged, and seconds later they screeched into the traffic.

The Eiffel Tower *was* close, and it was enormous. The driver dropped her off across the street, so she had a good view of the tower's four massive pylons enclosing a huge square across which snaked long lines of hot tourists. She crossed the street and joined one of the lines. Ahead surged a large group of boisterous schoolchildren. She moved to a different line that was longer but consisted of docile-looking seniors led by guides holding umbrellas aloft. Several of the poor dears looked as if they'd much prefer a nice sit-down and a cup of tea to shuffling toward what was essentially an elevator ride.

The line moved quickly, the wait just long enough for Genna to gaze up at the crisscrossed underbelly of the *premier étage* — the first level — and contemplate the feat of engineering it represented. Built in 1889 for the Paris World's Fair, the tower was meant to be taken apart a year later. Was a structure built well over a century ago sturdy enough to carry an average yearly load of six million tourists up its gray-gold girders?

It didn't bear thinking about.

Genna rode straight to the second level along with a gaggle of seniors that, from the sound of them, hailed from the north of England.

"Eeee!" exclaimed one as the elevator lumbered skyward. "It's a good thing that breakfast we had was so sparse."

"Aye, I'd have murdered for a fry-up."

"I've a mind to complain. Imagine! Five bloody euros for a glass of juice and a bit of bun."

"It's a disgrace."

"Aye."

Squashed into an outside corner, her face turned to the view, Genna thought fondly of her Yorkshire-born granny.

"Mabel's got the gout, did you hear?"

"No! Mind you, it's to be expected."

"She's always been one for the rich food."

"Aye."

One of the ladies elbowed her way in front of her companions to stand next to Genna. "She'd have been well chuffed with this," the woman said. She smelled of lily of the valley and face powder.

"With what?"

"This here. The view."

"Aye. Champion."

"Do you think there'll be somewhere to sit up top? Me poor feet are howling."

"You shouldn't have worn them shoes."

"Aye, well, serves me right then."

Genna resisted the temptation to give the woman a hug. She'd have thought she was mad, but what a story to tell when they got back home! Genna's grandmother had dragged her grandfather on bus trips all over the continent and never remembered what she'd seen.

The elevator juddered to a stop at the *deuxième étage*. Genna detached herself from the tour group and found a place to sit overlooking the view.

Two young women strode past.

"I told Joy she must leave him before it's too late."

"Did she?"

"Of course not! Joy's so stubborn, she's . . ."

The two women looked to be in their thirties, both tanned, sleek, and North American. Before Genna was able to find out more about Joy's stubbornness, the women turned the corner to continue their conversation without so much as glancing at the view.

"I told you to put that away!"

"Mom!"

A young woman stopped near Genna and dropped to her knees before her sniffling child, a boy of about six. One chubby hand clutched a video game.

"This vacation is costing us a fortune," the mother hissed. "You can play your game in the hotel and that's it."

The venom in the woman's voice was so palpable that Genna flinched. Her reaction was not so much distaste at the mother's behavior as recognition of her own. She heard the same frustration she remembered feeling with her own children when they hadn't done something she wanted.

The little boy's face was crimson, his eyes teary, but his grip on the video game defiant. What did he care about a bunch of rooftops?

"Do you hear me?" the mother demanded.

The boy nodded tearfully. "But, Mom, I'm bored."

"Bored? You're in Paris!"

"I want to go to the hotel."

The mother saw an inroad and, to Genna's relief, regained control of herself.

"All right," she said, her voice softening into the universal tones of parental wheedling. "How about you put away the game for now and we'll look through this nice telescope? Then you can play the game while we're having a snack."

The little boy looked up at his mother and then beyond her to the telescope. Genna could almost see the wheels grinding as he weighed his options. Slowly his fingers softened their hold on the video game. His mother took out a tissue and wiped his face, and then suddenly clasped him to her chest. She turned toward Genna and smiled sheepishly.

"It's a lot for little ones to take in," Genna said. "I remember needing to make time for breaks when my children were young."

The mother nodded. "I'm starting to realize that."

"But they grow up so fast. The next time you come, he'll be chasing the French girls."

The mother managed a weak laugh as she stood up and took her son's hand. "Have a nice day," she said.

"You too."

The woman led the boy to a telescope where she was joined by a man and a girl of about ten. The girl was reading the descriptions of the skyline that circled the ledge and giving her father a bossy commentary.

The two children looked to be the same age apart as Genna's two children. At twenty-seven, Becky was making a success of her first real job as a junior curator at Vancouver's anthropology museum, while Michael at twenty-three was . . .

Genna despaired of her son's lack of direction, although she wouldn't put it past him to figure out a way to show up in Paris. The prospect of free accommodation and his mother's cooking might prove irresistible. All he'd need would be the fare, and he'd find a way to get it if he wanted to. Michael might not be ambitious, but he was resourceful.

As Genna watched the family walk off, the idea for her Eiffel Tower dish popped into her head. She'd pair it with *steak haché et frites*—fried hamburger and french fries, the lowliest dish on any Parisian bistro menu, always reserved for the *menu enfant*, the children's menu.

The summer when she'd traveled around France for six weeks with Drew and the kids, eight-year-old Michael had eaten *steak haché et frites* almost every day. One beef patty, grilled and crispy, accompanied by a mound of light, hot, salty, and crunchy french fries—the best fries in the world. *Steak haché et frites* was as basic as cooking got in France.

The Eiffel Tower, arguably the most important tourist site in Paris, should be paired with the all-time favorite of parents traveling with children and desperate to get something nutritious into their stomachs.

Genna took out her notebook and began to write.

If you're traveling in Paris with young children, the Eiffel Tower will be high on your list of must-sees. The size and shape of the soaring tower, its elegance undimmed in well over a century, captivates even young children. And the ride up the elevators to the troisième étage —

the third level — has the power to excite children brought up on video games and Disney theme parks.

Just remember that the end result of the ride is a view, which for most children is as appealing as broccoli. Minimize your time at the viewing platforms and head instead for the souvenir stands at the first and second levels. Here, you'll find plush Eiffel Towers sporting tiny red berets and Eiffel Tower–shaped earrings, backpacks, and paperweights along with T-shirts, caps, puzzles, mugs, and even underwear emblazoned with images of the Eiffel Tower. What child can resist? To keep the peace, consider allocating a small portion of your budget to letting them buy one item.

Steak haché et frites shows up on every children's menu in every bistro in France. Cooked in the French bistro way, the humble hamburger patty is slightly charred, meaty, and melty. For the real bistro flavor, pair this dish with homemade mayonnaise or a grainy béarnaise sauce.

Good start! Genna snapped the notebook closed, shoved it into her daypack, and stood up for a stretch, then strolled around the viewing platform encircling the second level. On the trip with the kids, she'd taken them up to the very tippy-top. Even now, she shuddered as she remembered the terrible vertigo that had gripped her when the tiny elevator shot skyward from the second level and hurtled toward the impossibly slender apex of the tower.

The rooftops of Paris had blurred into a gray mass with only the solid black monolith of the modern Montparnasse Tower to the south keeping pace with the elevator's skyward momentum. At the top, she'd glued her back to the wall, too frightened even to go to the barred edge of the viewing platform. That evening, she'd needed a good half liter of wine to recover.

Genna descended the two levels to the ground and walked a few blocks east to find one of the bistros on her list. At 1:00 p.m., the place was crowded. Unsmiling servers weaved and twisted their slim bodies around earnest businesspeople as intent on their food as on their conversations. She ordered a carafe of house white, a thick slice of quiche Lorraine, and a tossed salad from the reassuringly traditional menu. For dessert, she indulged in a single boule of mango ice cream sprinkled with toasted coconut.

After lunch, she walked back to the apartment and prepared *steak haché et frites* for dinner (it was wonderful!). Then, feeling pleasantly full, she took a walk along the Seine, this time to the east as far as the Île de la Cité. At an open area near Notre-Dame Cathedral, inline skaters swept with dizzying speed around a series of plastic pylons. Genna spent an entertaining half hour watching them and thinking about her son. He'd have been right at home with the skaters, speed being one of his favorite things.

She remembered Drew complaining with a mixture of pride and exasperation about Michael's fearlessness when at the age of six he'd ridden his bike at breakneck speed down one of the steepest hills in West Vancouver. Drew was not a daredevil himself—far from it. Many times, Genna had taken Michael's side in clashes with Drew, not because she wasn't worried about her son (she was), but because she admired his confidence. Drew liked to play it safe and Michael did not.

On the other hand, Genna knew Michael would never be capable of doing what his father had done.

Genna walked slowly home, dodging the swarms of young people in the tiny streets leading from Boulevard Saint-Michel. This part of the Left Bank was her favorite—a bit seedier than the posher area around Rue Bonaparte, the smells of cheap gyros and hot dogs heavy in the air. She missed Michael and Becky. Well, of course she did. But she couldn't regret for a minute coming to Paris.

With her first week behind her, a workable daily routine was becoming set—sightseeing in the morning, lunch at a bistro, writing and cooking in the afternoon, and then sampling the results for dinner before enjoying a walk in the evening air.

That night, she snuggled her head into the pillow and drifted to sleep, the very picture of contented womanhood. She could not let thoughts of Drew and their life together get in the way of what she'd come to Paris to accomplish.

three

Lemon Macarons
Tart, smooth, buttercup yellow — sunshine on a plate

Gris. That was the only word for it, and it was the perfect word. Gray in English, *gris* in French. Both versions captured in a single syllable the flat hopelessness of a day when no sun penetrated the monochrome.

On a *gris* day, everything in Paris was gray — the buildings, the pavement, the Seine, the faces of the people hurrying to work while dreaming of holidays in Provence. Notre-Dame's towers viewed from the small window on the landing outside Genna's fifth-floor apartment resembled two dead, gray pillars piercing a flat, gray sky.

On this her eighth day in Paris, Genna had planned to visit Sainte-Chapelle, but since a sunny day was essential to exposing the true glories of the chapel's stained glass windows, she adjusted her master list. Sainte-Chapelle swapped places with the Musée National du Moyen Âge — the National Museum of the Middle Ages, known also as the Cluny Museum.

She'd happily spend the morning prowling past exhibits of old stone and religious relics and have lunch at a bistro near the museum.

As she dressed for the weather in an oversize knit shirt, a rain jacket, and her sensible navy blue travel skirt with its hidden pockets to thwart *les voleurs*, thieves, Genna wondered what recipe to pair with a museum that specialized in the Middle Ages. As historical eras went, the medieval period was her favorite. She loved thinking about the thousands of artisans who had thrived during the period, many helping to build the great cathedrals of Europe.

Her visit to Notre-Dame Cathedral the day before had been a great success, yielding two recipes for *Eat Like a Parisian: Notre-Dame Lemon Sole* and *Rose Window Strawberry Tart*.

A visit to Notre-Dame Cathedral takes you into the heart and soul of France. Emerging from a recent cleaning, the cream-colored stone glows in the spring sunshine, much as it did when it was first built a millennium ago.

The cathedral sits on an island in the middle of the Seine, until modern times the principal artery for commerce. For centuries, fish from the river nourished the well-fed clerics who kept the great cathedral running.

From soul to sole, this recipe for grilled lemon sole swims in a light cream sauce made tart by thin slices of melted lemon. Serve with a fluffy rice pilaf studded with pistachio nuts for a heavenly experience.

The Cluny Museum was within easy walking distance of Genna's apartment. Since the route would take her near the *tabac* owned by her landlord, Monsieur Leblanc, she decided to stop in and ask about the puzzling matter of garbage disposal. After a week, the receptacle under the sink was overflowing. Monsieur's instructions had not mentioned garbage. Perhaps Monsieur did not approve of garbage.

The tiny, old-fashioned *tabac* looked out of place on a street that in recent years had sprouted shops selling designer fashions, upscale *objets d'art*, and high-priced real estate. Genna pushed open the door, wrinkling her nose at the blast of stale air that made her wonder how often a customer came in.

"*Bonjour?*"

Nothing.

She walked to the counter behind which rose a wall of cigarette packages, most coated with dust. A display of pipes looked undisturbed since the time when every fashionable wag in town wore a top hat.

"*Bonjour?*"

Behind the counter, a door flew open.

"*Oui? Qu'est que vous voulez?*" What do you want?

Genna gulped. The man was not only gorgeous, but to her surprise, he was the same man who had saved her from the speeding Citroën the week before.

"Um . . . *Je suis Genna McGraw.*"

He didn't appear to have recognized her. That was good.

"*Oui?*"

"Er . . . *tu*, I mean *vous*, um, *vous êtes le fils?*" Genna wanted to fall through the ancient floorboards. She'd just asked him if he was the son.

"*Le fils?*"

"*Désolée.* Um . . . Monsieur Leblanc. *Il est ton*, I mean *votre, père?*" She cursed her high school French teachers who had insisted students use the familiar *tu* form in mock conversations instead of the more socially acceptable *vous*.

"Ah!" He laughed and then, to Genna's infinite relief, switched to charmingly accented English. "You are the tenant at the Rue Bonaparte *appartement.*"

"Yes. *Oui.*" Genna stuck out her hand. "Your father asked me to come here if I had any questions or needed anything."

His hand was dry, firm, and strong, and he held hers a little longer than necessary.

"*Enchanté, madame. Je suis Pierre Leblanc.* My father has gone out for a while. May I assist you?"

"My garbage!" she blurted.

"Garbage?" One elegant eyebrow rose.

"Uh, I mean my garbage *disposal*. I mean, I can't find where to place my garbage."

"Place?"

Genna was beginning to suspect he was enjoying himself, no doubt well used to the effect he had on women, particularly North American women who had little experience with such a delicious package of easy sophistication.

"You know what I mean." Her tone sharpened. Now he'd think she was one of those entitled women who were forever asking to see the manager. That was not the impression she wanted to make.

The smile disappeared. "Forgive me, madame. I presume you wish to know where you should dispose of your, ah, garbage. In French, we say *les ordures*."

"Thank you. Yes. I couldn't find any garbage cans in the courtyard."

"That is understandable," he said. "Look for the blue bin in the small passageway at the far end of the courtyard. There is where you may place your, ah, *garbage*."

"Oh." Genna willed herself to appear mature and confident. The man no doubt had a wife and several children. If he didn't, he'd have his pick of elegant French females—or males, for that matter.

"Is there anything else I may help you with, madame?"

"Ah, no." She didn't move. The last time she'd felt this awkward, Michael Jackson's "Beat It" had been playing at the school sock hop.

"You are enjoying the *appartement*?"

"Oh, yes, of course. It's very nice."

"It is appalling," he said and then laughed. "Do not worry. You will not offend me if you agree. For years, I've been trying to get Papa to make *les rénovations*."

"Why hasn't he?"

"Money, of course. Papa cannot see the point of spending money on making the *appartement* more presentable. If he did that, he'd get more tenants."

"But isn't the whole point of running a holiday rental to get tenants?"

"For most, yes, but for my father?" He shrugged, now looking uncannily like Monsieur Leblanc senior, but with better personal hygiene. "Papa would be happy to keep the place empty forever."

"And forgo the rent?"

"Ah yes, well, it is complicated." The suave exterior fractured just enough for her to want to see more.

"I'm sorry," she said. "It's none of my business."

He inclined his head. "We are, of course, committed to making sure your stay is comfortable."

"I've brightened the place up a bit."

"Oh?"

"I bought some new cushions, a tablecloth, some prints. I hope you don't mind. I plan to stay for six months if all goes well."

"If all goes well?"

"Well, you know . . ."

He shook his head. "What needs to go well?"

"It's a long story."

"Complicated?" he asked with a hint of a smile.

"Not as complicated as the story you don't want to tell me." He looked confused again. "About your papa? Why he doesn't want tenants?"

"*Ah, oui.* As you say in English, point taken." He put his elbows on the counter and leaned forward.

"I should be going."

"Of course. This place"—he gestured at the grubby racks of magazines—"is not for the telling of one's life story, *n'est-ce pas?*"

"Perhaps not."

"Would you consent to meet me later this afternoon for *un café?*"

"Pardon?"

"*Un café*, a coffee at Café de Flore."

"I'm sorry, I know what *un café* means. I was just a bit surprised."

"Why should you be surprised?" He had a way of asking questions that made Genna believe her answers were the most interesting in the world.

"Ah, no reason."

"It is *un café*," he said. "To welcome you to Paris."

"Yes, of course. I'd love to meet for a coffee. The Café de Flore is around the corner from my apartment. But, of course, you know that."

"Shall we say five o'clock?"

"That would be fine. I'll see you then." She turned to the door, wrenched it open, and fled into the busy street. What was she thinking? She'd accepted an invitation for coffee with a strange man in a city where she knew no one except the strange man's father. Well, so what? Pierre Leblanc probably owned a share of his father's apartment and wanted to protect his investment by making sure Genna wasn't going to skip out on the rent or throw wild parties.

Had he been flirting with her? No, of course not. He was a Frenchman. Being charming was his birthright. And obviously he hadn't recognized her. She glanced down at her white running shoes and pink ankle socks.

Quelle horreur! Had he noticed?

Genna started walking rapidly in the direction of the Musée National du Moyen Âge. How appropriate! She could be the star attraction in a museum devoted to middle age. She arrived expecting to find grimy chunks of stone and a few religious relics. Instead, she found a sumptuous display of tapestries, jewelry, wood carvings, icons, and Gothic sculptures.

The thoughtfully arranged objects slowly worked their magic on her. She circled through the dark rooms, lost in wonder at the beauty created by medieval artisans so many centuries earlier. The fluttering in her chest subsided. She had *not* come to Paris to risk her hard-won independence on a handsome French *avocat*.

Never. No way. *Jamais.*

The museum's main attraction was the series of enigmatic *Lady and the Unicorn* tapestries from the fifteenth century housed in its own specially constructed room. Five of the six tapestries depicted a different sense—sight, taste, smell, hearing, and touch. The sixth and final tapestry was called *A Mon Seul Désir*, translated as "*by my desire alone*," "*by my will alone*," and several other versions that added to the delicious obscurity of the tapestry's meaning.

The center of each tapestry depicted a beautiful young woman, her elaborate medieval gown picked out in fine threads of gold, royal blue, and scarlet. To one side of her squatted a lion and on the other side sat a white unicorn, its horn long and slender. Both lion and unicorn gazed adoringly at the woman, their faces childlike in their purity.

In the "Hearing" tapestry, the woman played the harp, but her gaze was faraway and distracted, while in the "Taste" tapestry, one hand trailed across a tray of sweetmeats offered by a kneeling servant. In the "Sight" tapestry, the front legs of the unicorn rested on the lady's knees while it contemplated its reflection in a mirror she was holding.

But it was the "Touch" tapestry that revealed what those medieval tapestry workers were really all about. The young woman looked toward the lion, which sat docile and obedient. Her right hand grasped a tall flagpole and her left hand wrapped around the horn of the prancing unicorn.

Ah oui!

The symbolism was unmistakable, proving again, if proof were needed, that sex had preoccupied humans in every era.

Genna stared at the tapestries for over half an hour before getting an idea for a recipe to match with the Cluny Museum.

* * *

"Duck confit?" Pierre stirred his espresso, his second since Genna had arrived to find him waiting for her at an outside table overlooking the Boulevard Saint-Germain. "Intriguing choice. How does it relate to a museum that exhibits artifacts from the *Moyen Âge*?"

They'd been talking for over two hours. The Café de Flore was filling with sleek-looking French businesspeople stopping for a coffee or an apéritif before heading to dinner. She found in Pierre an attentive listener who effortlessly put her at ease. She told him about *Eat Like a Parisian*, and he thought it was an excellent idea, even giving her the names of several bistros that he assured her were *merveilleux*. Marvelous.

"My inspiration was the *Lady and the Unicorn* tapestries. You know them, of course?"

"*Mais, bien sûr.*" Of course.

"I wanted a dish that represents all five senses, like the tapestries, and that is also somehow exotic, like the unicorn. Duck is still rather an exotic dish in North America, and duck confit is difficult and time-consuming to make."

"It was one of my mother's favorites," Pierre said, a thoughtful expression in his eyes as he stared past Genna at the busy street. "It's a specialty of Gascony, where my mother was from. She'd make duck confit in the winter and store it for many months before we ate it. You know, of course, that *confit* means preserved?"

"Yes. But the people who buy my cookbooks won't want to cure the duck legs in salt, poach them in fat, and pack them in more fat for several weeks. I need to develop a version that retains the flavor but is much less work."

"Even my mother made it only once a year," Pierre said. "But you must include it in your cookbook. It is a bistro favorite. Now, I can understand how it incorporates taste and smell, but what of the other three senses?"

"Think of a serving of two legs. Now imagine them balanced together to form a kind of arch, like the lion and the unicorn supporting the lady. That's sight."

He nodded. "The presentation of any dish is *très important*."

"Exactly. Now hearing. Most foods are not noisy."

"But the skin of duck confit is, how you say it, brittle?"

"Crispy. Each bite of duck confit should crackle in the mouth."

"And touch?"

"Touch is why I chose duck confit. It's one of the few dishes that you can pick up to eat."

"Not in France!"

"But my book is for North Americans, and picking up what is essentially a drumstick is like a cultural right. People would look at you funny if you ate a drumstick with a knife and fork."

"Duck confit is not like some crumb-coated horror from the Colonel!"

"You have Kentucky Fried Chicken in Paris?"

"*Malheureusement, oui.*" Pierre shook his head sorrowfully, reminding Genna of how Monsieur Leblanc had looked when she'd asked him about an internet connection. "It is a travesty. Of course, as a chef yourself, you would object to *le fast food*."

"I'm not a chef. I write cookbooks."

"But you must cook, *non*?" He looked puzzled.

"I test each recipe in my books, but I trained as a teacher, not a chef."

"*Une professeure?*"

"More like an *instructrice*. I taught high school home economics for ten years before I decided to write cookbooks."

"Home economics? I am not familiar with this."

"I don't know what the course is called in a French school, but you must have something similar. At the school where I worked, we had two types of home economics courses—cooking and sewing. I taught cooking."

"Did you enjoy it?"

"For the first few years, but then I got bored of teaching the same curriculum over and over."

"You like to make changes, no?"

Genna laughed. "I suppose I do. My husband . . ." She paused as he again raised his eyebrows—both of them this time. "I mean, my soon-to-be-ex-husband, used to give me a hard time because I was often so restless."

"And your restlessness has taken you away from him." Before she could reply, he picked up her hand in both of his and held it. "He should not have let you go."

To Genna's horror, tears pricked her eyelids. She *never* cried. Well, almost never. And certainly not when an elegant Frenchman in an historic Parisian café was holding her hand.

Although, come to think of it, her experience in that regard was limited to never.

She slipped her hand from his grasp. "I must go."

"Why? Do you have another *rendezvous*?"

"I'm quite tired after my day at the museum. I'd like to get home and have a light supper and an early night."

"But you must let me take you to dinner. There's a wonderful little bistro near here I'm sure you will not have visited yet."

"I don't think so," she said, scrambling to her feet so quickly the coffee cups rattled.

He also stood. At a shade under six feet, he was tall for a Frenchman and much taller than Drew. Genna felt small and petite—an unfamiliar sensation for someone who was five foot seven in her stocking feet and not exactly a winsome sprite. He moved toward her. Was he going to kiss her, right in the middle of the upscale Café de Flore?

When he again took her hand, she couldn't decide if she was disappointed or relieved.

"*Au revoir.*"

"Yes, *oui, au revoir.*"

He released her hand. Her accent was probably still horrific, but at least he was polite enough not to wince.

"Another evening, perhaps?"

"Ah, sure. I mean, *oui. Merci.*"

He leaned forward so his mouth was inches from her ear. "Take care in the traffic," he whispered. *"La circulation est très dangereuse, n'est-ce pas?"*

"Pardon?"

He smiled and shrugged, palms up.

"You do remember me!"

"Mais, bien sûr. You are not a woman who is easy to forget, Madame Genna McGraw." He paused. "What is Genna, by the way? Is it short for something?"

"Geneviève, but only my French grandmother called me that. She's been gone for many years now."

"Mais, c'est belle! Geneviève." The lilting way in which he said her name put her in danger of melting into a glistening puddle of middle-aged desire.

Not good.

Not good at all.

"Um, *merci?*" she stammered before turning and almost running out of the café. She sensed Pierre's eyes burning two holes in her back, but she resisted the urge to turn around as she darted to the corner and crossed the Rue Bonaparte to the door of her apartment building. The courtyard was already dark. She waited in the shadows for several minutes until she was sure Pierre had left the café and then reemerged onto the street. She needed to pour her heart out in an email to Nancy. If it hadn't been for her best friend's encouragement, Genna might still be languishing in her basement suite.

Genna made it to a small place on Rue Mignon that offered cheap computer access and printing services. She plunked herself onto a plastic chair in front of a free monitor, logged on, and began to type.

```
Hi Nancy

You know how you said I should find a sexy
Frenchman to fall in love with? Guess what? I
found one! But don't worry, I have no intention
of falling in love with him or anyone else. Mind
```

you, if I were so inclined (I'm not. Honestly!), he'd be the perfect candidate.

His name is Pierre Leblanc and, get this, he's the son of horrid old Monsieur Leblanc, my landlord that I told you about. He looks to be in his early fifties, tall, snappy dresser, speaks perfect English, loves art, and as far as I can tell, he's on his own.

What's surprising is that he seems to like me. Okay, that sounds as if I'm in Grade 9. What I mean is that he appears to be interested.

I met him when I went to his father's *tabac* shop to ask where to dispose of my garbage. We got to chatting and he asked me to meet him for coffee later in the afternoon. We ended up talking for ages. He suggested dinner, but I balked. How lame is that? But when was the last time I dated a man who wasn't Drew? Don't remind me about Fun Gordon. He doesn't count.

I'm sure Pierre must think I'm a complete idiot the way I ran out of the café when he invited me to dinner. It was silly of me to panic. After all, as I keep trying to convince myself, I'm a grown woman. But I'm so out of practice!

What should I do if he asks me out again? Part of me wants to be left alone, but the other part, well! Write back soon!

Love Genna

Genna clicked Send. Still buzzing from all the coffee she'd consumed with Pierre, she paid the attendant, then wandered back along the Boulevard Saint-Germain toward the apartment. A crowd of young people spilled out onto the sidewalk up ahead, and a distinctly American odor assaulted her.

Her stomach clenched with hunger. She slipped through the thronged restaurant to the counter at the back. A young woman took her order for *le Big Mac avec pommes frites et un Coca-Cola*.

What the hell, even cookbook authors needed a night off once in a while.

four

Orange Macarons
Filled with tart marmalade and dark chocolate

At 9:30 a.m., after almost two weeks in Paris, one coffee date with a sophisticated Frenchman, and five new recipes for *Eat Like a Parisian*, Genna followed the crowds through the tunnels under the massive Châtelet Métro station to Line 1, Direction La Défense. A few stops brought her to Champs-Élysées Clemenceau.

She was on her way to her first French language class. Five years of high-school French a few decades earlier were enough for Genna to keep herself fed, caffeinated, and lubricated with the occasional glass or two of wine.

What she couldn't do was hold a conversation in French that lasted longer than two minutes. Also, Genna had to admit that she wouldn't object to the odd encounter with human beings who were not waiters or shop assistants. Her time with Pierre at the Café de Flore had been pleasant but not repeated. He'd made no attempt to contact her again.

And why would he? She'd given him *le brush off* and he didn't seem like the kind of man accustomed to rejection. Did she even *want* to see him again? Her friend Nancy had scolded her, telling her that if he did contact her again—and it was a big if—she was to be considerably more forthcoming. After all, Nancy wrote, what was she afraid of?

As a two-time ex-wife with generous alimony and a steady stream of boyfriends, Nancy had perfected the art of the no-strings relationship. She spent her days either shopping or flitting from upscale charity to upscale charity with names like The Friends of West Vancouver Poodles Society and Save Our Views. She was hardly in a position to provide reliable advice when it came to men.

The address of the language school belonged to a modern doorway that opened onto a linoleum-covered foyer and a steep staircase. Genna scaled the four flights of stairs to a blue door advertising "L'École Javert." She hoped the intermediate class that she'd optimistically signed up for wouldn't be a variation on *Les Miz* for hapless foreigners.

She opened the door to a reception area enclosed in taupe walls adorned with posters of French beauties of the scenic landscape variety, not the svelte, pouty-lipped waifs Genna passed on the streets.

"You are Madame McGraw?"

Speaking of pouty lipped and svelte. The receptionist reminded Genna of the women who worked at the cosmetics counters in department stores. Flawless makeup, perfect hair, and an exquisitely cut beige suit molded around petite curves.

"Yes. I'm here for the ten o'clock class. I'm a bit early."

"*Non, non, non!*" the woman exclaimed, gold earrings flashing. She bustled forward and took Genna's arm.

"*Français seulement! Alors, encore!*" French only. Again!

"Oh, uh, *désolée*. Um, *oui. Je suis ici pour la classe de dix heures.*" I am here for the class at ten o'clock.

The woman barely disguised a shudder at Genna's accent.

"Um, *Je suis . . .*" Genna paused. What was "early" in French? She searched the part of her brain containing all the French she'd ever learned. It didn't take long to discover that the French for *I'm a bit early* was AWOL, if indeed it had ever existed. She flashed back to those stilted conversations in French 11. No one was ever early.

Come to think of it, no one ever said anything useful. Conversations revolved around saying your name and that you were a student at Point Grey Secondary School in Vancouver, British Columbia. *Je suis une étudiante à l'école secondaire de Point Grey de Vancouver.* The curriculum presumed every student would remain sixteen years old forever.

The woman indicated the black leather couch. *"Asseyez-vous, s'il vous plaît. Nous attendons les autres étudiants. Dix minutes de plus, je pense."*

Genna was pleased she understood most of what the receptionist said. Something about sitting, ten minutes, and students. She took a seat and glanced at her watch: 9:50. In ten minutes the other students would arrive. Right.

The magazines piled on the end table next to the couch were French travel magazines—easy to enjoy in any language. She picked up one with a picture of lavender fields on the cover and turned to a story about Provence, illustrated with sumptuous photographs of sunflowers and slumbering medieval villages, bowls of ripe tomatoes and slick, black olives.

She leafed through the pages, gratified to recognize many of the places she'd visited on a family holiday to France. Drew had inherited a windfall from his grandmother and had agreed to spend it on a trip to Europe. They'd driven around France and wound up their trip with a five-day stay in Paris—a city Drew loathed and Genna loved. But at least he'd enjoyed their time in the country.

She remembered him browsing the antique shops in L'Isle-sur-la-Sorgue in Provence, his ridiculous khaki shorts displaying too much white leg, his face beet red from the strong southern sun. The kids had been bored and were starting to whine, but he'd insisted everyone wait while he picked through a pile of old corkscrews.

Genna had used the antique corkscrew he'd bought that day to open the last bottle of wine they'd shared before her world fell apart. She'd made chicken fricassee soaked in a mushroom cream sauce laced with sherry. Drew told her it was one of her best, and she thanked him. They smiled at each other across the shiny dining room table set into an alcove overlooking the view in their new home. They were contented with their lives and with each other. The future looked bright.

Chicken fricassee soaked in a mushroom cream sauce laced with sherry was one dish that would *not* make it into *Eat Like a Parisian.*

The door crashed open.

"Hi!" called a young woman as she strode into the small office. "I'm here for the ten o'clock class. Marsha Renfrew?"

The receptionist went through the whole "*Non, non, non, français seulement*" routine with the newcomer who rolled her eyes in Genna's direction and then repeated her greeting in what sounded to Genna like flawlessly accented French.

What the hell was *she* doing here?

"*Cinq minutes,*" the receptionist said, gesturing to the couch. "*Attendez, s'il vous plâit.*"

The woman plunked herself down next to Genna. "Are you here for the ten o'clock class too?"

Genna nodded. "Your French is very good."

The young woman tossed a head of crinkly black hair. "It's not bad, but I need a brush-up. I've just moved back to Paris with my boyfriend and I can't believe how rusty my French has gotten."

"Back to Paris?"

"Oh, sure. I was here, gosh, about ten years ago when I was a student. I took classes at L'École des Beaux-Arts." She held out her hand. "Marsha Renfrew."

"Genna McGraw."

"Nice to meet you."

Genna liked the look of her new classmate—compact and wiry with an open, friendly face. Like many Americans Genna had met, Marsha had a knack for making whomever she was speaking with feel comfortable and interesting. Genna was about to ask more questions, like what Marsha was doing now in Paris, when the door opened again to admit the third member of the ten o'clock class, a man in his forties. He approached the receptionist and introduced himself in halting French. His reward was a brilliant smile and an offer of *café*. Marsha and Genna looked at each other and grinned. The receptionist hadn't offered *them* a coffee.

"*Crème?*"

"*Ah, oui, merci,*" the man said. He nodded at Marsha and Genna before taking the coffee and seating himself on a hard chair near the door. She wondered what he did for a living that gave him time to take French lessons two times a week during the day. Since he hadn't spoken English yet, she couldn't even be sure of his nationality. He might be American or possibly German. He looked well fed and confident.

"Where are you from?" Marsha asked.

"Vancouver."

"Oooh! I've been there! You have great skiing!"

"Yes," Genna said, pleased to hear her hometown praised. "Whistler has some of the best skiing in the world."

"No kidding! It's fantastic, and I'm from Colorado so I ought to know. Do you ski?"

"I used to, when I was a teenager." That wasn't quite true. She'd wanted to keep skiing after she married, but all her skiing friends had moved away, and Drew hated nature. Man-made stuff attracted him—old furniture, things made of wood by craftsmen long dead, that sort of thing. Genna's attempts to get him into the mountains rising from the doorstep of their first home in North Vancouver had been fruitless. He'd consent only to the occasional walk around the neighborhood to see which houses were for sale.

"That's a shame," Marsha was saying. "So how come you're in Paris?"

"I'm working on a cookbook slash travel guide."

"You're a writer? That's amazing! What's a cookbook slash travel guide?"

"I'm combining recipes for French bistro dishes with descriptions of Paris sights."

"Sounds fascinating! I'll bet my boyfriend would be interested. He's British."

The arrival of two more students—a mother with a young woman who looked to be her daughter—saved Genna from asking what being British had to do with anything. The daughter, who looked to be around twenty, stared at the floor while the mother spoke English to the receptionist, who, of course, replied with rapid French that Genna guessed were directions to follow her.

Genna stood and moved with the rest of the students around the front counter and into a room with ceiling-high windows overlooking the street. Several upholstered chairs on castors clustered around a large table. The receptionist seated herself at the head of the table and gestured for the students to join her.

Genna soon discovered that the receptionist's curvy little frame encased a will of iron. She transformed into Mademoiselle Deville, a formidable *instructrice* who, within minutes, succeeded in turning Genna's insides to mush. By the time the class was over, Genna hoped to never hear another French word for as long as she lived.

How could she have thought herself qualified for the intermediate class? Marsha conversed like a native and the man— a German named Helmut—was at least able to put together a sentence without dissolving into a flame-faced, stammering boob. Denise and Tessa from England were also able to hold their own.

More than once, Genna heard Denise sigh, and saw Helmut drum his fingers on the table when it was her turn to speak. Marsha threw her sympathetic glances every so often, but Genna was too upset to feel grateful.

Trying to spit out one sentence was agony. She had to confine herself to the present tense and managed only the most mundane of pleasantries. When called upon to state what she did for a living, she managed to say she was an "*écrivaine*," a writer, but she had no clue how to say that she wrote cookbooks.

Les livres des cuisine? Who knew?

After the class, Genna waited until the other students had left before confronting Mademoiselle.

"Excuse me," she said in English. Her head was pounding, her palms sweaty.

"*En français.*"

Genna shook her head. "I'm all out of French. Is there another class I could join? I don't belong in the intermediate class."

The instructor nodded her agreement and motioned for Genna to follow her to the front office, where she sat at her desk, tapped a few keys on the computer, frowned at the screen, and then shook her head.

"*Ce n'est pas possible,*" she said. "The beginners' classes, they are filled." She scrolled the mouse with a fingernail lacquered the color of ripe plums. "*Non!* This class is the only class until, ah, *un moment, juillet.*"

"But that's almost three months away!"

"*C'est dommage.* You stay here. I give you materials." She turned to a bookcase above the computer and started pulling out books. "You read and practice."

"I don't think I can keep up. I'd like to withdraw."

"You can drop out of the class, but no refund. You signed a contract."

"But that's ridiculous! What if I were ill?"

"You are not ill," Mademoiselle Deville pointed out. "And as the *instructrice*, I say you must stay in the class." She smiled, a hint of pity in her perfectly lined smoky eyes. "It will be okay. You just need confidence."

Genna was too tired to argue. She scooped up the books and headed out the door. On the landing, she found Marsha waiting for her.

"She didn't let you out, did she."

"None of the beginner courses are available until July and she won't give me a refund. I guess I could insist, but I'm worn out. That was brutal!"

"Oh, come on, it wasn't *that* bad. I was watching you. You were able to follow most of the conversations. It's when you had to speak that you clammed up. That's just a lack of confidence."

"So Mademoiselle Deville tells me."

"Well, Mademoiselle Deville is right." Marsha grinned. "Let's go get a coffee and I can help you practice. I know a good place not far from here."

Genna wanted nothing more than to return to her apartment and hide her throbbing head under the colorful new pillows, but Marsha was already halfway to the second floor and suddenly an hour or two of female companionship—in English and without strings—didn't seem like such a terrible prospect.

The April sun was warm enough for them to sit outside at a café on the Champs-Élysées. They ordered café crèmes and settled into two chairs set side by side at a small round table facing the street. A parade of Parisians passed in front of them, some strolling, a few hurrying, almost all talking on their phones. Tourists—in pairs and in large groups—also flowed past, eyes swiveling, phones snapping.

"Do you really think I'll be able to keep up with this class?" Genna asked. "I feel like an idiot. I can understand most of what you and the others say, but when the instructor talks, I get one word in ten. Even that would have been bearable if she'd have just let me listen. But is it just me or was she *trying* to humiliate me by calling on me so often?"

"She called on everyone about the same amount. It seems like a lot because there's only five of us." Marsha turned sideways to look at Genna. "You did fine. Sure, you were nervous, but nobody minded. We're there to learn."

"Yes, and having a complete dunce in the class doesn't help anyone."

"Let's forget about French class. We'll have our coffee and get acquainted. Then, we can make plans to get together later to practice."

"You're not working this afternoon?"

Marsha's smile faded and she shifted her eyes to her coffee. "Well, no, not today. I'm on hiatus right now." She looked up. "Yes, that's it. A hiatus. That's why I've got time for French classes."

"A hiatus from what? You said you went to L'École des Beaux-Arts. Are you an artist?"

"Designer. But I wanted to be an artist—a painter, to be exact. The next Berthe Morisot, maybe. But I found out pretty fast that a girl's got to make a living. There wasn't much call for my paintings back in Denver, so I moved to New York and talked myself into a job at a design firm. The rest is history."

Genna laughed. "Let me guess. You rose through the ranks in the design firm, came to the attention of the suits, and got yourself posted to the Paris branch. Am I close?"

"Close enough." Marsha paused as if trying to decide how much to tell Genna, then shook her head ruefully. "The truth is that I don't have a job. I came to Paris because of my boyfriend." When Genna didn't reply, she rushed on. "I can tell what you're thinking, and, I know, it's such a cliché. It's the twenty-first century! I'm not supposed to follow my man halfway across the globe."

"You wouldn't be the first."

"I know. And he *is* wonderful! I met him in New York about two months ago. He's from London, but he was in New York doing some consulting work with the company I worked for. We kind of hit it off right away, and before I knew it, he was asking me to come to Paris with him."

"Sounds like quite the whirlwind romance."

"You sound like my mom." Marsha laughed at the frown on Genna's face. "Don't look like that! I wasn't comparing you to my mother. And besides, I agree with her. It *is* going pretty fast."

"Are you all right with that?"

"Oh sure. Colin's great. I've had a few duds in my time, believe me. But when Colin came along, I got the feeling, you know, that he's the one."

"I'm sure he is." Genna smiled at Marsha and drained the last of her café crème. "It's been lovely chatting, but I need to get going."

"To visit one of the places you want to include in your book?"

"The Orangerie. I want to see the Monet water lily paintings. *Les Nymphéas?*"

"Can I come with you? I've got nothing on this afternoon until six when Colin and I are going to view an apartment." Marsha wrapped both her hands around her cup and stared into the last bits of foam, her eyes hooded. "I'd appreciate it."

Genna wanted to say no. She liked Marsha. Who wouldn't? But the constant chattering would kill the solitude she counted on to uncover a connection between Monet's water lilies and a recipe.

"Please." Marsha eyes brightened. "We can practice French. And I've never been to the Orangerie."

"You haven't? But you're a designer! How can you not have seen Monet's water lilies?"

"I know, it's inexcusable. But I was waiting to go with Colin. He's a Monet nut."

"I'm glad to hear he has good taste, but if you go with me, what will Colin say?"

"Oh, he'll be okay because I won't tell him. Please, Genna. Let me come with you. I can't bear another afternoon in our apartment. It's ghastly."

Genna relented. Saying no to Marsha would be like stomping on a puppy. "Right," she said. "Let's pay and get going. We can walk from here."

"Wonderful! Here, I'll get this." Marsha scooped up the bill before Genna had a chance to protest. "I'm enjoying a financial boon right now and I'm determined to enjoy it."

"I thought you weren't working."

"I sold my apartment in New York before coming to Paris. Colin helped me find the buyer. He said I'd be a fool to pass on the offer, and I made a bundle on it. Colin wants me to put the money into an apartment here."

"Colin wants you to buy an apartment in Paris?" Genna couldn't help thinking about how Drew had convinced her to sink most of their savings into an overpriced home that she'd ended up living in for only two months.

"He's right, of course," Marsha said as she led the way out of the restaurant and turned left toward the Tuileries. "Colin is good at business. He says the market in Paris is red-hot and that we need to get into it as soon as possible."

Genna was itching to ask if Colin would also be contributing to the cost of the apartment.

"Colin says it's silly to keep all the money in the bank if we're going to settle in Paris."

"What if you change your mind?"

"I love Paris! I can't see going back to New York once I get a job."

Genna bit back the impulse to ask what Marsha planned to do if she didn't get a job in Paris. "I'm sure everything will work out fine," she said instead, then wrapped her arms around her chest, shivering in the sudden stiff breeze. April in Paris, so beloved by poets, romantics, and songwriters, could so quickly turn chilly. Genna thought back to her long, hot trudge to the Eiffel Tower two weeks earlier. Where had *that* weather gone?

The walk down the Champs-Élysées, across the Place de la Concorde to the Orangerie took a good twenty minutes, during which Marsha kept up a steady stream of conversation, confirming Genna's fears for the afternoon. No way would she be finding a recipe for *Eat Like a Parisian*, which meant she'd need to return another day, stretching her already-thin sightseeing budget.

The two women approached the neoclassical Musée de l'Orangerie separated by a wide, tree-lined walkway from the Jeu de Paume opposite.

"I can't believe you've never been here," Genna said.

"Nope. And when you meet Colin, which I hope you will soon, promise me you won't tell him about today? He'd be mad."

"I promise." Genna bit back what she really wanted to say, which was that Colin sounded like a jerk and that Marsha deserved better. On the other hand, who was she to talk?

After buying tickets, Genna and Marsha skirted the water-lily-infested gift shop and walked through the spare white vestibule into Salle 1, the first of the two rooms displaying the eight canvases of *Les Nymphéas*. Marsha walked a few steps into the room, stopped dead, and swayed. Genna rushed forward to catch her.

"Oh my God!" Marsha gasped, her limbs barely able to support her as she let Genna settle her onto the single oval-shaped bench in the middle of the room. "It's unbelievable. I think I'm going to cry."

Genna patted Marsha's shoulder and then turned to examine the paintings. In her experience, extreme art appreciation required privacy. She began walking around the room, inviting the paintings to envelop her with their calm blues and greens. Each of the four massive works molded to the curved walls. She imagined a hot, hot summer day, the sun flooding the waters of the pond, deep shadows and blazing expanses, lilies of pink, white, and creamy yellow.

The promise of coolness in the midst of heat.

"Vichyssoise," she murmured. Next to her, a young man contemplating the brushwork scowled at her. What business did she have talking about food in this most sacred of art palaces?

But to Genna, food and art were equally necessary. Without food, life was not possible, and without art, life was not possible to live well. But the young man looked undernourished and cross, so Genna turned away and entered Salle 2.

Whereas in Salle 1, one of the four paintings glowed with golds, reds, and pinks, an anomaly in the blue world, all four paintings in Salle 2 pulsed with infinite shades of blue lightened here and there with touches of light pink and white and the looming shadows of several black tree trunks. Genna was walking into a fairy world of vast subterranean lakes illuminated by crystal-studded walls. She had an overwhelming urge to spread her arms wide and twirl around the room, enfolded in a calm oasis unattainable in the real world. But, of course, her arms stayed at her sides as she backed into the metal bench, sat down, and pulled out her notebook.

Made with tender young leeks, pale yellow potatoes, heavy cream, and black pepper, a bowl of chilled vichyssoise on a hot summer day will transport you to Monet's world, where your soul receives the solace that only nature can supply.

That would do for a start. Including oranges as a nod to the Orangerie was another option, but vichyssoise felt more suitable for the Monets. Genna leaned back on her elbows and gave herself over to contemplating the paintings and the people looking at them. She wondered if Marsha had recovered enough from the Stendahl effect induced by Salle 1 to venture into Salle 2. Genna had always liked the notion of the Stendahl effect and had felt it on her one trip to Italy, where Stendahl had experienced it.

According to legend, Florence's astounding art treasures had so entranced the great French novelist that he'd swooned in ecstasy, suffered palpitations, and been in danger of collapsing in a heap of fried brain cells onto the marble floor of the Uffizi. One line from Stendahl's memoirs stuck with Genna.

I reached the point where one encounters celestial sensations.

She liked the sound of celestial sensations. Great art could take her to new heights and wouldn't let her down.

Not like people could.

Marsha wandered into Salle 2, glanced vaguely at Genna, and then began slowly examining the paintings. Her body was all compact curves that in later years would likely tend to chubbiness. She looked as ready to go for a brisk hike in the mountains as she did to sip champagne in a candlelit bistro.

Genna liked her very much. Marsha had an appealing enthusiasm and, when she wasn't talking about Colin, was smart and fun. She hoped Colin appreciated her.

With a start, Genna realized that her only friend was an ocean and a continent away. How had she let her stock of female friends get so low?

five

Red Wine Macarons
A splash of Merlot swirled through buttercream filling

Cooking always relaxed Genna. She put on music, donned an apron, and pulled her hair into a rough ponytail. The blank counter was her canvas. She paused, savoring the emptiness before arranging her knives, the heavy new cutting board, several platters, and a small container for scraps. Everything was clean and neat, the calm before the storm. Methodically, she began gathering her ingredients from the fridge and cupboards.

She worked with careful precision, wasting little energy as she chopped garlic and onions, beef, and thyme. Building the *mise en place* was her favorite part of cooking. She loved to see the platters fill with shiny red peppers ready for roasting, garlic chopped into translucence, solid chunks of red steak marbled with creamy fat.

She was making bœuf bourguignon for her first dinner party in Paris.

Since their afternoon together at the Orangerie, Genna and Marsha had shared three lunches after French class. With Colin at work during the day and not inclined to socialize when he got home, Marsha admitted to Genna that she was lonely.

After their latest lunch that stretched to an entire afternoon and included a wander through the Louvre's cavernous rooms of decorative objects from the seventeenth- and eighteenth-centuries, Marsha had agreed to come to Genna's for dinner the following week and to bring the elusive Colin.

The day before the party, Genna had visited the Musée Delacroix on Rue de Furstenberg around the corner from her apartment. The idea for bœuf bourguignon came to her as she was touring rooms that once housed Delacroix's living quarters and studio. When she thought of Delacroix, she thought of clutter and heat, of fallen soldiers and distressed maidens densely painted in browns and ochers and reds. Delacroix's large canvases were too big, too full, too heroic—and a good match for the richness of a well-cooked bœuf bourguignon.

Genna hummed as she chopped. The day would end well with the apartment filled with the fragrant red wine scents of the stew and, she hoped, the laughter of her guests.

During one of their lunches, Genna had told Marsha about Pierre Leblanc.

"He's interested in you," Marsha said. "Why else would he ask you to dinner?"

"Pity?"

"Oh, please. You have to stop thinking of yourself as some dried-up middle-aged matron."

"Aren't I, though?"

"Bollocks, as Colin would say. You're lovely looking and you're funny and you're interesting. And to Pierre Leblanc, you're quite exotic."

"About as exotic as a cheeseburger."

"Stop it! Pierre will show up again, and when he does, you're not to turn him down."

"I'm not looking for romance."

"Everyone's looking for romance," said Marsha.

Genna scooped a mound of chopped onions onto the *mise en place* and started on the carrots—slim and crunchy from the market. Marsha was wrong about everyone looking for romance.

A year ago, after four months on her own and with her anger at Drew still carving her heart like a hot knife through marzipan, Genna had agreed to go on a date with Gordon Wadsworth.

When Nancy set her up, she insisted that an evening with Fun Gordon was just what she needed, that an evening with Fun Gordon would take her mind off Drew and the house and the money and her future. Genna hadn't been on a date since the year before she married Drew almost three decades ago.

According to Nancy, Fun Gordon sold luxury cars by day and had been married twice. "You'll have plenty in common. When he's not selling Ferraris to gangsters, Fun Gordon is an avid bird-watcher."

"I don't know anything about bird-watching."

"So what? You can learn. And Gordon also likes food."

"Everyone likes food."

"You know what I mean. He and his second wife used to take foodie tours to Europe. You'll have *tons* to talk about."

"Why's he called Fun Gordon?"

"You'll see!"

The evening started well enough. Gordon (Genna refused to call him Fun Gordon, even in her head) chose a seafood restaurant in Vancouver overlooking the boats moored in Coal Harbour. Knowing she wrote cookbooks, Gordon gallantly suggested she order for both of them. She chose the West Coast Platter for Two, which consisted of a tasty selection of lobster, snow crab, scallops, prawns, and wild sockeye salmon served with *pico de gallo* and drawn butter.

Drew was terribly—life-threateningly—allergic to seafood. Eating seafood while on a date with another man wasn't as satisfying as force-feeding it to Drew, but it would have to do.

Genna savored the first few bites of butter-slick scallops and was starting to relax when Gordon morphed into the Birdman of Alcatraz, but without the table manners.

He talked nonstop—often with his mouth full—about his latest foray to the Reifel Bird Sanctuary, an hour's drive south of Vancouver toward the US border.

"Being April, a lot of the birds are starting their mating rituals. You have to see it! Did you know that sandhill cranes mate for life? Well, they do, and there's a residential pair at the sanctuary that have been together for *years*. Of course, they're not mating anymore, but at this time of year they're naturally protecting their nest."

"Naturally."

"Exactly! And they can get incredibly aggressive. You really want to see them."

Genna smiled tightly. The sandhill cranes yielded to the mallards and then the Canada geese and the robins and the woodpeckers and the chickadees and . . .

Eventually, she gave up trying to listen. Fortunately, Fun Gordon didn't appear to notice, which left her plenty of time to inwardly curse Nancy.

When Genna complained over coffee the next morning, Nancy told her she was being too picky. She needed to give Fun Gordon another chance to show how, well, fun he was. Genna said no. Offended, Nancy never again arranged a date for Genna, which suited her just fine. For almost another year, she lived alone in her basement suite, lying low on some days with such deep loathing of both herself and Drew that sometimes she wondered about the point of doing anything.

Thankfully, she also had good days and on one of them she put together the proposal that brought her to Paris.

Genna hoped Colin wouldn't be a bore. Someone as smart and engaging as Marsha was bound to have an interesting boyfriend. She hated to think he'd be one of those fair-haired, carelessly aristocratic Brits with a cutting sense of humor and all the right opinions.

* * *

"You say that this dish . . ." Colin drawled.

"Bœuf bourguignon."

"Quite. You will pair it with the Musée Delacroix? You mean his studio—the one around the corner?"

"Yes. I went there yesterday."

"And thought of bœuf bourguignon."

"Yes."

"Ah."

"It's not an exact correlation," Genna said. "None of the pairings are."

"I think it's fascinating," Marsha said. She was smiling, but the knuckles of the thin fingers holding her wineglass gleamed white.

"I can imagine the correlation must sometimes be exceedingly slim."

"Right, well, it's all in good fun anyway."

Genna was determined not to let Colin get to her. He couldn't be more than a few years older than her daughter, Becky.

"The cookbook is designed to be a kind of amusing homage to Paris," she said. "I combine a bistro-style recipe with a specific Parisian site, such as the Eiffel Tower or the Tuileries Gardens. I guess you'd call the book a crossover—a cookbook within a guidebook, or vice versa."

"How very postmodern," Colin said.

Genna said nothing, but refrained from taking a sip of wine, fearing she'd snap the glass with her teeth.

"But it's a gimmick, right?" Colin persisted.

"If you want to call it that, but in my business, gimmicks sell, which I'm sure is true in any business."

"Not in the case of *my* business."

"Design?" Genna knew she was getting close to insulting a guest, but he'd started it. She felt a twinge of regret at the prospect of upsetting Marsha, but it couldn't be helped.

Her boyfriend was an ass.

"Very much so," Colin said. "Fashions come and go, I grant you, but when all is said and done, there are constants in design that, well . . ."

"Don't change?"

"Quite." Colin put down his fork and took a sip of wine.

At least he couldn't object to the wine since he'd brought it himself. And Genna had to concede that it was an excellent choice—a full, robust Côtes du Rhône that paired superbly with the bœuf bourguignon. But that was to be expected. An hour before they were due for dinner, Marsha had called to inquire about the entrée so they'd be sure to buy the right wine.

Colin may be an ass, but he was a cultured ass.

As the evening progressed, Genna learned that Colin had his future with Marsha mapped out. After buying an apartment in a fashionable Parisian neighborhood, they would get married, pop out their first child, acquire another property in a trendy part of southern France, and then round off with a second child. Of course, they'd have one of each—a boy first and then a girl.

Colin's London drawl—part royal family, part pretentious cockney—set her teeth on edge. She wondered why he'd stooped so low as to get involved with an American when he seemed to consider anything associated with the New World, as he called it, beneath contempt. On the other hand, having a green card and the option to work in New York might come in handy should the European economy go sideways.

And Marsha herself had indicated she had substantial cash from the sale of her New York apartment.

At the end of the evening, after brandies were drunk and goodbyes said, Genna flopped onto the hard couch under the needlepoint *Odalisque*. She glanced up at the picture, its planes flattened by the angle, but its fuzzy texture untamed.

Her favorite part of the dismal evening had been the look on Colin's face when he'd first entered the apartment and seen the needlepoint. His jaw dropped open, then shut, then open again in rapid succession, rather like the large and ugly grouper fish Genna remembered seeing on a long-ago Caribbean holiday. She'd wondered if she should rush forward with the offer of a stiff vodka. But Colin was British, and he did have manners. He clamped his jaws shut and smirked as he held out the wine.

"How lovely!" Genna trilled in her best hostess voice. Her third book, *The Comfy Entertainer*, devoted several pages to the subject of welcoming guests.

As hostess, your prime responsibility is to make your guests feel like their arrival in your home is the best of all possible events. But sincerity is key. A gushing welcome can put people off, making them uncomfortable, as if they had walked into a vat of oversweet fruit rather than the calm and comfortable warmth of your living room.

If guests bring a present, such as a bottle of wine or a houseplant, take it, admire it, and make sure it plays a role in the evening. If wine, drink it at the appropriate time. Never stash it away, no matter how inferior it may be to the wine you planned to serve.

Thankfully, the forty-euro price tag still stuck to the bottom of the wine that Marsha and Colin brought beat out the wine Genna planned to serve by thirty euros.

Genna heaved herself off the couch and went to bed. The evening had not been a total waste. She was happy with her bœuf bourguignon and it had been pleasant to have people to talk with, even if one of them had been Colin. The solitariness of her new life was mostly bearable, but there were moments, like in the quiet after guests departed, when she missed her old life.

She and Drew would sit together on the couch and drink mugs of steaming milk to blunt the booze. They'd talk about their guests, chuckling at foibles, comparing notes about who said what. They almost always agreed, their laughter shared and natural, their mutual contentment unspoken but always present.

Genna had trusted Drew with her heart and with her life.

She bit back a sob, chiding herself for ruining an already dubious evening with regrets about the past. Before she'd left Vancouver, her cousin George, who owned the basement suite she'd fled to, told her that one day she'd need to forgive Drew.

Never.

δix

Coffee Macarons
Studded with coffee beans and filled with milk chocolate

The next morning—a sunny Friday—Genna set off down the Boulevard Saint-Germain toward the Odéon Métro stop. The ten-minute walk got her blood pumping and head cleared from the effects of too much wine and too much Colin the night before.

She knew she should feel happy for Colin and Marsha. They were just starting their lives together, full of hope as they launched into an adventure that for Genna had turned out to be a good thirty years shorter than she'd signed up for.

One of the last times she'd seen Drew was the previous October at their third open house. As soon as he appeared at the door, his face dropped into hang-dog remorse, the expression he adopted whenever she was within hailing distance.

"Hi, Gen. Come in."

She walked past him without saying hello, fighting the impulse to run upstairs to check the bedroom.

"Is the agent here?"

"Not yet."

Genna turned into the living room and wanted to weep. Dirty mugs stuck to the side table, old newspapers and library books covered every other surface, and a ragged brown stain spread across the middle cushion of the cream couch. She knew the rest of the house would look even worse. The agent would have a fit and probably refuse to continue representing them. Genna could hardly blame him.

"You're determined to sabotage any chance we have of selling this place."

"I wouldn't call it sabotage."

"How about obstruction? Or severe blocking behavior? Or just plain being an asshole?"

"Come on, Gen, don't be like that. I've said I'm sorry a thousand times."

"Sure." She started collecting mugs. In the half hour before the open house she could at least make a stab at tidying the place.

"I think we're wrong to sell now," Drew said as he followed her around the room. "The market's not good."

"House prices in this neighborhood have gone up twenty percent this past year." Genna kept her back to him as she cleaned. They had had this conversation too many times. She could recite it in her sleep.

"If we sell, neither of us will be able to afford to buy another place in this area."

Genna waited for the next line. It was always the same.

"If we stay together, we could buy something else around here. You know, make a fresh start."

Predictable as ever. In fact, Drew had been predictable every day of their married life until the day he'd been unpredictable.

"I have no desire to buy anything in this neighborhood," Genna said. "I want my half of the money out of the house so I can get on with my life."

"Where will you go?"

"Paris."

And as soon as she said it—her hands full of chipped mugs crusted with the furred dredges of two-week-old coffee, in a house she'd lived in for only two months, Genna knew it was true. She would go to Paris.

"You can't go to Paris!"

Genna turned to him, honestly surprised. "Why not?"

"How will you live?"

"I have money."

"From where?"

She stared across the room at Drew. His hair was streaked with gray and his body, though chubbier than when they'd married, was well toned. As usual, a slight pall of sawdust hung around him, an occupational hazard of his work as a custom furniture maker.

"I'll be fine." She didn't know *how* she'd be fine, but she knew without an ounce of doubt that going to Paris was exactly what she needed to do. And as for money, well, she'd just have to get creative until Drew finally sold the house. The publisher was asking for a new cookbook. She'd whip up a proposal that had something to do with Paris. How hard could that be? Paris and food went together like eggs and soufflés, or Roquefort cheese and walnuts, or macarons and café crèmes.

She almost laughed out loud, feeling more alive than she had for months.

"What about me?" Drew's voice took on the plaintive tone that irritated Genna to the point of wanting to murder someone, preferably him. "You can't just up and leave."

"I already did."

"Yes, but this is just temporary." He smiled and walked towards her, his arms outstretched.

"It's not temporary."

"Of course, it is. I guess I can understand why you needed to get away for a while, but it's been, what, ten months now? You can't *still* be mad at me. Don't you think it's time you came home?"

"No, Drew, I'm not planning to come home. This isn't my home anymore."

"You can't keep this up forever."

"Keep what up?"

"This tough-girl act. It's not you."

Tough-girl act? Genna felt about as tough as a mashed banana.

Or at least she used to. Now, it was a sunny day in Paris and she was on her way to the Père Lachaise Cemetery, the final resting place of many of the world's greatest musicians and writers, from Chopin to Oscar Wilde to Jim Morrison. Maybe a visit to a graveyard was appropriate. The death of a marriage shared a lot of similarities with the death of a person.

If only a dead marriage could go away and find a nice quiet tomb in which to rot. But things weren't so easy. For a start, there were the kids. Becky had been particularly upset by the breakup, although she didn't know the real reason, and Genna wasn't about to tell her. Some things were best kept secret from one's strident and opinionated daughter.

Michael had been a little more sanguine. He was busy living the ski-bum life up at Whistler and was much more interested in his own sex life than that of his parents. So long as they occasionally helped him with loans that he didn't need to repay, Michael was happy.

Genna had not expected to miss Becky and Michael so much. It wasn't like she spent much time with either of her children when she was at home, but at least she could see them if she wanted to. Now that eight thousand kilometers separated them, Genna felt bereft, as if a limb had been severed. She saw their faces in the faces of passing young people. When she spied a Canadian flag sewn on a backpack, she wondered for a moment if one of her children had arrived in Paris to visit her.

Genna put thoughts of home out of her mind and instead focused on where to stop for her morning coffee and croissant before catching the Métro up to Père Lachaise across the river in the twentieth arrondissement.

At Odéon, she passed a Starbucks. As always, Genna marveled at the inroads that so many American chains had made into the sophisticated Parisian cityscape. She could not understand why Parisians preferred prefab coffee and corporate decor to the warmth and soul of a traditional café. In her opinion, no chain could compete with white-aproned, somber-faced waiters, tiny round tables, and red upholstery. Yet plenty of the chains did, and very successfully, judging by the lineup snaking to the door of the Starbucks. Across the street, the Parisian café with its row of tables facing the sidewalk was almost empty.

The contrast between the bustling chain and the sleepy café annoyed Genna. She sped up, intending to cross the narrow side street to the traditional café. Damned if she was going to support the multinational corporate giant. She stepped off the curb, plunged one foot into a steaming mound of dog *merde*, shot forward, and fell flat on her face, inches from yet another speeding Citroën. The driver honked and gesticulated and then revved his engine for a two-tire turn into the Boulevard Saint-Germain.

Genna lay still, her entire body vibrating with shock and shame. She didn't feel any pain, so she was sure she hadn't broken anything. Her left hip, shoulder, and cheek had absorbed most of the fall. She tasted grit and smelled the exhaust of passing cars, heard French voices surrounding her, the volume rising with true Gallic drama as they discussed the problem of what to do with her.

"*C'est qu'elle est morte?*" Is she dead?

"*Je ne pense pas.*" I don't think so.

The pavement under her cheek was already warming in the spring sun. All she needed was a few more moments to recover. She extracted a few words from the babble of voices.

"*Secours! Dommage! Oh là là . . . !*"

This last comment made her smile even as she stifled a groan. One of the most surprising things she'd discovered in Paris was that people really did say *Oh là là*. In times of extreme provocation, she'd even heard the occasional *Oh là là là là*, which seemed excessive, but perfectly captured excess outrage or surprise.

She sensed a presence near her head and then heard the rhythmic beeping of a phone grow louder as whoever was dialing it knelt beside her. A rush of French, a pause, a decisive "*Oui, merci.*"

"Madame?"

The male voice was full of concern. Genna's face reddened as she imagined the effect her prone body was having on her rescuer, not to mention the other people gathered above her. She hoped her navy cotton skirt still covered her backside.

"Is she okay?"

The English startled Genna so much that she rolled onto her bruised side, gasped, and then rolled back to her other side.

"*Je ne sais pas*," said the male voice belonging to the phone. I don't know.

"She looks like a tourist." The new voice belonged to another male, but this one much younger and with an accent Genna wasn't able to place.

The humiliation was too much. With a determined grunt, she struggled to her hands and knees and from there to her feet. She began to sway. The man with the phone and the young man with the accent positioned themselves on either side of her.

"Careful, ma'am," said the younger one. "That was a nasty fall."

"*Je suis* okay," Genna said with as much dignity as her bruised face and burning elbow would allow. She looked around at the gathering crowd. "*Je suis* okay," she called. "*Merci. Désolée.* Sorry."

Désolée was fast becoming Genna's most used word behind *merci* and *bonjour*. It seemed that she was forever sorry about something, from stepping on someone's toy poodle to saying *la* when she meant *le*.

"You sit down," said the phone man in careful English. "*Vous avez eu un accident.*"

"*Oui. Je suis désolée.*"

"Don't bother too much about the *désolées*," the young man said cheerfully. "You slipped in dog shit. The main thing is that you're all right. Here's a napkin. Scrape the worst of it off your shoe and come inside. I'll make you a coffee."

Genna nodded, realizing that the young man was an Australian. Her eyes were starting to focus again, and she saw that he looked exactly how she imagined a young Australian male should look—tall, blond, tanned. She realized she was still leaning against the phone man. "*Merci beaucoup. Vous êtes très gentil.*"

The man had his phone out again to make another call.

"Did you call for help?" Genna asked.

He looked at her and then at the Australian, who translated in surprisingly good French with an Australian twang that made the man grimace. He shook his head and explained in rapid French that he had been finishing a call to a business associate when he saw Madame fall. Genna was at least glad to be spared an ambulance siren interrupting the swish of traffic on the boulevard. She realized with relief that she really was okay. She'd have a few colorful bruises, but she'd survive. The thought that the fall could have been so much worse frightened her.

Although she rarely let herself think about the price of solitude, there were times, and this was one of them, when she realized how alone and vulnerable she was. If she were injured or even killed, her family might not find out for days, even weeks. Neither Pierre Leblanc nor her father had paid her any more visits, and the only other people who knew where she lived were Marsha and Colin. She hoped that at least Marsha might miss her at French class and come to investigate. No one in Paris had her phone number.

"Come on! Let's get you inside." The young man took her elbow and steered her into the Starbucks where he pointed to the toilets at the back. "How about you wash up and then we'll have a coffee."

"Oh! Well, I guess a medium latte would be nice . . . um, a grande?"

"That's okay," said the young man. "We don't use the American sizes here." He grinned. "I barely know the difference between a grande and a venti."

Genna headed to the toilets at the back of the store. She gave her hands a good scrubbing, checked in the mirror for bruises, and wiped a smudge of gravel off her chin. When she emerged, the young man was behind the bar preparing her coffee. He waved at her as she settled into a padded leather chair. It was green and comfortable and reminded her of home.

Her throat tightened and her eyes prickled. The rush of homesickness was as upsetting as it was unexpected. She shook off the sensation. It was understandable, but that didn't mean she should let herself start pining for the snowcapped mountains and ancient cedar forests of her homeland. As soon as she finished her latte, she'd be on her way and could forget all about the humiliation of falling flat on her face in front of a Starbucks on the Boulevard Saint-Germain.

"Here's your coffee."

She took the cup from the young man. He stood above her, so she had to crane her neck to see him.

"Thank you."

"No worries," he said. "Are you sure you're all right now?"

He squatted down next to her chair, a thoughtful act she appreciated. Now that she had the chance to really look at him, she realized that her first impression had been bang on. He had curly blond hair that sprouted like fusilli pasta, blue eyes, a scraggly beard, and a smile that could melt the hearts of every woman under forty who came into the place. Even if she hadn't already heard him speak, she'd have known he wasn't French. He looked like a poster boy for a surfboard company, the very image of an Australian surfer dude.

"Can I buy you a coffee?" Genna asked, then regretted it when she saw his eyes widen. Did he think she was trying to pick him up? He was a child, younger than Michael, and surely not inclined to waste more time talking to a middle-aged woman who had trouble crossing the road without falling into it.

"Sure," he said. "I was about to go on my break anyway. Hold on a sec—I'll get Marcel to make me something."

He walked to the bar and placed the order in French.

"Thanks," he said when he returned and placed his coffee on the table between them. "I could use a bit of time off my feet." He grinned. "Feeling better?"

"Yes, thank you, but also very foolish."

"Ah, no bother. You didn't hurt yourself, that's the main thing. So, what's your name and what are you doing in Paris?"

Genna almost laughed out loud. For such a young man, he was remarkably self-possessed. "Genna McGraw. I'm a cookbook author and I'm living in Paris for as long as I can afford to."

"Nice to meet you, Genna McGraw." He leaned forward across the table and shook her hand. "My name's Tyler. I'm studying art history at the Sorbonne."

"And working as a barista?"

"Yeah, well, a bloke's gotta make a living! Not that it's much of one, but it helps pay the rent."

"You speak French well."

"Yeah, my mum made me learn it. She never made it to France but she always wanted to. She took tons of classes and everything." His grin faded as he sucked down the top layer of foam from his cappuccino.

"Do you like Paris?"

"I love it! Don't you?"

"Of course."

"Yeah, but not everyone does. I have a few mates from back home who complain all the time about the noise, how expensive everything is, the way people rush about."

"All true," Genna agreed. "But, still, it's a wonderful city. I wish I could stay forever."

"You wouldn't miss home? Where is home? I'm guessing somewhere in the States?"

"Vancouver."

"Oh yeah, I've been to Vancouver," he said. "A few years back, I spent a winter at Whistler."

"My son lives there."

"Ah, lucky bloke."

"He thinks so."

"You're not so keen?"

"Michael's twenty-three and he still thinks his mission in life is to play."

"Sounds about right to me."

"I guess I sound kind of old-fashioned."

"Kind of, which is too bad because you're not old."

"Not young either." Genna put down her cup and struggled out of the chair. A strong arm gripped her elbow and heaved. She popped up and just missed grazing his chin with the top of her head. He held on until he was sure she was steady on her feet.

"There you go, Genna."

"Thanks. You've been kind. "

"No worries. And now we've gotten acquainted, come back for a visit. I want to hear all about your cookbooks."

"You do?"

"Sure! Since I moved here, I've been getting into the food thing. I don't have much of a kitchen, but I've learned to cook all sorts of stuff." He laughed. "My mum would be proud."

"I've written a cookbook for students," she said. "I'll bring you a copy." *Campus Cooking* had been a modest hit with the college crowd.

"Beaut! Thanks, Genna." He walked her to the door and held it open. "G'day."

Genna left in a cheerful mood despite a few twinges along her thigh, a slight burning on her shoulder, and the occasional stench of dog dropping wafting up from her shoe.

She was ready to tackle the cemetery.

seven

Hazelnut Macarons
Filled with toasted hazelnuts in a mocha cream ganache

Marsha's prediction that Genna would see Pierre again came true the next day. Late in the afternoon, Genna emerged from the Saint-Germain-des-Prés Métro stop and rounded the corner from Boulevard Saint-Germain into Rue Bonaparte. Directly across from her on the opposite corner, chic Parisians and wide-eyed tourists filled the tables on the terrace outside the Café Les Deux Magots. She glanced toward the café and then continued down Rue Bonaparte to her apartment. The prices at the famous place were too rich for her to indulge very often. Already, she needed to increase her budget, limit bistro meals to no more than four a week and visit cafés only in the morning to get her daily café crème and croissant.

"Geneviève!"

Her stomach lurched. Across the street at the café sat Pierre Leblanc at a table facing the sidewalk. He wore a plain blue shirt, open at the neck, and a dark brown leather jacket. A pair of sunglasses perched on top of his head.

He looked like a movie star.

Genna, on the other hand, was wearing a navy skirt paired with an oversize pink blouse and running shoes. Her hair was windblown and her face bare of makeup. Her palms started to sweat. Rue Bonaparte was a narrow one-way street, and she was only a few feet away from him.

Reminding herself yet again that she was not some silly teenager but a grown woman with two adult children and a life of her own, she crossed the street.

"*Bonjour!*" he said. "Please, sit down. I've been waiting here hoping to see you."

"Hello," Genna said, sitting down and tucking her purple daypack out of sight. "This is a surprise."

"You have had a good day?"

"Very nice, thank you." She smiled. "I have been to the Parc Monceau, and yesterday I visited Père Lachaise Cemetery."

Pierre nodded at a passing waiter, who stopped and waited while Genna ordered *un verre de vin rouge.*

"Did you make any connections for your cookbook?"

"I'm still working on it. Père Lachaise is proving to be a challenge."

"Oh?"

"It's not suggesting anything yet. I'm not sure food and death go together."

"Food is about life, *non?*"

"*Mais bien sûr!*"

"*Bon!* Your accent is improving."

"*Merci.*" She took a quick gulp of wine. "So, how is your father?" It wasn't her best line, but she couldn't think of anything else to say, and it would take several more glasses of wine before she had the confidence to speak more than a few words of French to a Frenchman.

"He is the same as usual," Pierre said. "My father is, ah, a character. He is happiest when he is saving money."

"I'm sure he's a very kind man."

"Don't let him hear you say that! But, yes, he is a kind man who has not had the easiest life."

Genna wondered what kind of life the senior Monsieur Leblanc had led. He looked to be old enough to remember the war, maybe even old enough to have been a teenage member of the Resistance. Had he risked his life on these streets, dodging the Nazi occupiers? She was dying to ask but sensed that her romantic notions of wartime Paris were just that—romantic notions that bore no resemblance to what must have been a grim reality.

"My father was a teenager when he fought in the Resistance," Pierre was saying as if he'd read her mind. "He lived in your *appartement* with his *grand-mère*."

"Where were his parents?"

"Killed. They, too, were in the Resistance, but they were not so lucky as Papa."

"I'm so sorry."

"They were shot." Pierre was silent for a few moments. Then he smiled sadly and shook his head. "This is a poor beginning. The war, it was a long time ago. One day, I will show you the plaque with my grandparents' names. But not today. I was waiting for you because I have a proposition."

A proposition? Genna's mind raced through possibilities. Did he want her to be his temporary mistress? After all, he was a Frenchman.

"What did you have in mind?"

Oh, for God's sake. She sounded like Mae West.

"Tomorrow is Sunday."

"Yes . . . ?"

"The fountains will be playing at Versailles. Did you know they are turned on only on weekends in the spring and summer?"

Genna had to laugh. "Yes, as a matter of fact, I did. I was planning to go to Versailles tomorrow to see them."

"Ah!" Pierre exclaimed and clapped his impeccably manicured hands. Genna didn't think Drew even knew what a manicure was. His nails were always encrusted with sawdust.

"*Ah*, what?"

"We can go together, of course. I came here to ask you to accompany me to Versailles for the day. And I discover you are already planning to go." He stopped. "Or do you already have an escort?"

As if.

"No, I'll be going alone." *So now she was Greta Garbo?*

"Would you prefer it? To go alone?"

"Oh, no. I mean, I'd be delighted to accompany you to Versailles."

She sounded like the Queen. Would she ever get it right?

Pierre leaned forward. "I, too, am delighted. You wait. The fountains of Versailles are one of the great wonders of France."

As far as Genna was concerned, she was already looking at one of the great wonders of France. She smiled and sipped her wine while thinking about what to wear. When packing for her Parisian sojourn, she had neglected to include a going-out-with-a-gorgeous-Frenchman outfit.

Several hours and a few glasses of wine later, Genna stood naked before the narrow oval mirror inside the wooden wardrobe in her bedroom. The prognosis was not good. The clothes hanging on the lopsided rail looked about as sexy as the hall closet in an old folks' home. Her entire wardrobe consisted of several large shirts, three pairs of black pants, two practical navy skirts, and a variety of knit tank tops in bright colors designed to coordinate with all the bottoms. She would win points with packing gurus who insisted that everything match everything, but that was the only positive thing about her wardrobe.

How could she have come to Paris with a stack of clothes fit for her mother? No, that wasn't true. Until the day she died at the age of eighty-two, Genna's mother had maintained two closets full of stylish clothes and had been a welcome regular at several of West Vancouver's most fashionable shops.

Genna had only herself to blame for her appalling lack of style. She'd never been much of a fashion plate, but after she left Drew, she just kind of gave up. What was the point of dressing to kill when she felt half-dead?

But this was an emergency. Genna picked up her phone and called Marsha. The odds that she'd be available to help her, considering it was Saturday night in Paris, were less than nil, but she had to try.

Marsha answered the phone on the first ring. "Hello, Colin? Oh, honey, I'm so sorry."

"It's Genna."

"Oh! Genna. Hi!" Marsha forced a laugh as brittle as cracked ice. "I thought it might be Colin. He went out with friends and he said he'd call when he was on his way home. But it's only eight o'clock so I guess I was kind of surprised when the phone rang."

"You're all alone?"

"Sure, but it's okay. I'm happy here with my book."

"Have you eaten?"

"I'll make myself a sandwich."

"You're coming out with me. I haven't eaten either and I need your advice."

"But I told Colin I'd stay home tonight."

"You said he was out with his friends."

"He is, but he might decide to come home early."

"Then let him come home early. Come on, Marsha. You shouldn't be alone on a Saturday night."

Silence.

"I *really* need your advice. Pierre was waiting for me at Café Les Deux Magots when I got back to the apartment this afternoon."

That did it. An hour later, Genna and Marsha were ensconced in a steamy little bistro a few blocks from Marsha's apartment in the Marais.

"Scarves!" Marsha pronounced after Genna described the pathetic contents of her closet. "Do you have any?"

"Just one that I use for my hair when it's windy."

"Color?"

"Um, sort of whitish beige?"

"You don't know?"

"Not really."

"Never mind. After dinner, we'll go back to my place and I'll find you a few things to dress up your basic skirt-and-shirt look."

"Really? That's very kind of you. I have to admit that I need the help."

"And we can also do a quick bit of work on your makeup."

"I don't wear much makeup."

"So I see."

"It's just that I can't be bothered." Genna swallowed a forkful of tarte Tatin made with caramelized apples and sprinkled with toasted hazelnuts. The taste and texture combination worked well. She made a mental note to include toasted hazelnuts in one of her recipes.

"Well it's time you *started* bothering."

She looked up. "Hmm?"

Marsha laughed. "Could you tear yourself away from swooning over your dessert for two seconds to acknowledge that giving nature a *little* help isn't a crime against feminism?"

"All right. How was your coconut cake?"

"It was too sweet. Come on, let's get out of here." Marsha motioned for the waiter and again insisted on taking care of the bill despite Genna's protests.

"Please, let me. I need to feel like I've got *some* control," Marsha said.

Talk about feminism. How could a woman like Marsha feel like she had no control over her life?

"Are you sure you're okay?" Genna asked when they were out on the street.

"I'm perfect! Why wouldn't I be? I'm in Paris, I have a wonderful boyfriend, and I didn't get a chance to tell you, but we've found an apartment!"

"Why didn't you say so sooner? That's wonderful news!"

"I hope so."

"Is it near here?"

"It's in the neighborhood. But I don't want to talk about it yet, not until everything's definite. Tonight is all about getting you ready for your hot date tomorrow."

"It's not a hot date."

"You're spending an entire day in the company of a man you describe as drop-dead gorgeous. I'd call that a hot date." Marsha unlocked the front door of her apartment building and ushered Genna into the dark courtyard.

"I'm sure he just wants to show me the fountains."

"Oh, he wants to show you the fountains all right."

"Marsha!"

Their laughter bounced off the walls of the apartments enclosing the courtyard.

"Shh! We might wake up the neighbors."

"It's only ten."

"They're early-nighters."

"What are they, monks?"

They burst into another round of giggles as Marsha led Genna up a dark stairwell to the fourth floor and down an even darker corridor. The ancient building reeked of stale food mixed with the damp smell of old stone.

"Here we are," she whispered as she unlocked a door, started through it, and then stopped so abruptly that Genna collided with her.

"*Merde.*"

"Huh?"

"Nothing. Come on in. It looks like Colin's home already. Hello, darling!"

"Marsha?" The voice was rough, not at all like the cultured voice Genna remembered from the dinner party. "Where the fuck have you been?" He held up Marsha's phone. "I've been trying to call." His looming presence made Genna want to step back onto the landing.

"Sorry, I must have forgotten to put it in my bag. I've got Genna with me," Marsha said. "See, here she is." She grabbed Genna's arm and pulled her forward.

"Hi, Colin. Sorry to disturb you so late. Marsha said you'd still be out."

"Obviously." Without another word, Colin threw the phone on the hall table and stumped into the living room.

Marsha steered Genna in the opposite direction toward the bedroom. "I'm lending Genna a few clothes," she called over her shoulder. "Won't be long."

Marsha closed the bedroom door and went to work pulling scarves out of drawers and rooting through various jewelry boxes.

Genna sat on the bed and watched Marsha's rushed, almost frantic movements. Although small and cramped, the bedroom showed evidence of a designer's touch. A crisp and creamy bedspread of padded silk paired with lavender cushions evoked long, hot summers in the South of France. During a typical damp and dreary Parisian winter, the room would be a welcome oasis. A wardrobe and battered dresser, along with mismatched bedside tables, gave the room a pleasingly lopsided air echoed by the skewed corners and a ceiling rippled with age.

"Is everything okay?" Genna asked. "Colin seems annoyed."

Marsha kept her face away from Genna. "Oh, no, he's fine. It's just that he was surprised to see you. Here, this will go with that green tank top you wore to class the other day. A scarf can do wonders for even the most mundane outfit."

Genna wrapped the turquoise and emerald toned scarf around her neck. Marsha stepped forward and with a few deft turns knotted the silky material so the ends trailed over one shoulder.

"There. Tie it like that and you'll look fantastic." Marsha pulled Genna up and turned her toward the mirror. Both faces were reflected for an instant. Marsha's was dead white. She ducked out of sight and opened the bedroom door.

Genna took the hint and followed Marsha to the front door. "I appreciate your help," she said. "I'll call you tomorrow night."

Marsha shook her head. "No," she whispered. "I'll call you or I'll see you if I make it to class on Monday. We're going to be super busy for the next few days. You know, with the new apartment and all. Good night. Have a wonderful time at Versailles."

Before Genna could thank Marsha for dinner, the door was shut in her face. She stood still on the tiny landing and listened, sure she'd hear Colin start to shout, afraid she might also hear Marsha cry out. What was she expecting? Did she think he'd harm her? The man might be rude, but that didn't make him a brute. Still, Genna waited a few seconds longer. Hearing only the low murmur of voices, she breathed a sigh of relief and descended the creaking staircase to the courtyard. She reached the street just in time to flag down a passing taxi. The driver sped through the twisting streets of the Marais down to the Quai des Célestins and the brilliantly lit Seine, the Eiffel Tower glittering in the distance. They shot across the Pont Neuf and minutes later lurched to a stop in front of Genna's apartment on Rue Bonaparte.

Any excitement about spending the next day with Pierre had long since evaporated. Genna crawled into bed and wrapped her arms around the spare pillow.

All of a sudden, Paris didn't feel so wonderful.

eight

Honey Macarons
Kicked up a notch with a spicy ginger jam filling

Sunday morning dawned with reassuring loveliness. Genna dressed carefully, tied Marsha's green scarf around her neck but was unable to get it to lie flat, then spent ten minutes rooting through her tiny makeup bag. The end result was less than optimal, but it would have to do.

The face peering back at her from the cloudy bathroom mirror was open and glowing pink from the spring sun and a hot shower. She looked wholesome. Not sultry, not sophisticated, not sexy. She looked like the girl next door who had morphed into the woman next door. If someone were to point Genna out in a crowd, they'd say, *That lady with the friendly smile and a few extra pounds.*

On her way out, Genna grabbed her notebook. Pierre or no Pierre, she wasn't going to let a day at Versailles pass by without some attempt at recording it. Several options for recipes to pair with one of the world's most sumptuous palaces had already occurred to her.

Pierre was to pick her up at ten to drive them to Versailles, and Genna was looking forward to the break from buses and the Mètro. She pushed open the heavy door to the sidewalk just as a sports car roared up to the curb. The top was down, and Pierre sat at the wheel, resplendent in white scarf, sunglasses, and leather gloves.

"I'll be right back!" she called before turning around and rushing back up the stairs. She knew a little something about sports cars. Her only boyfriend before Drew had driven a vintage 1972 TR6 convertible and she remembered what a spin in it had done to her hair. She dashed up to the apartment, grabbed her white-beige scarf, and tied it Marilyn Monroe–style around her head. There was no way she was going to arrive at Versailles looking as if she'd stuck her head into a tumble dryer.

"*Bonjour, Geneviève,*" Pierre said as she slid into the front seat of the low-slung car. It was dark red with coffee-brown leather seats and a polished wood instrument panel. "You look beautiful this morning."

He leaned over and brushed her cheek with his lips. Just in time, she remembered to swivel her head to catch the return journey to her other cheek.

"Hi!" She settled back into the soft leather. "This is quite some car."

"I am glad you like it. It's not often I get a chance to drive out of the city. You do me a favor to accompany me today."

Pierre put the car in gear and roared down Rue Bonaparte to the Quai Voltaire. They crossed the Seine at the Pont de la Concorde and proceeded in grand style up the Champs-Élysées to the Place d'Étoile.

Genna felt like a sleek jetsetter with millions in a Swiss bank account, a yacht anchored off Nice, and taut thighs. She glimpsed herself in the side mirror and almost laughed aloud. There was no getting around it. Even in a fancy sports car with a fancy Frenchman, she was still a nice girl who liked to cook and didn't know the difference between toner and moisturizer.

They skirted the Arc de Triomphe and then veered off down the Avenue Foch to the Boulevard Périphérique. Up ahead, the Eiffel Tower pierced a sapphire sky. The wind whipped at Genna's scarf and made her eyes water. She felt as if she were flying away from her old life and toward a new one, not knowing what it could bring, and, for once, not caring.

The day progressed in a series of marvelous moments. In the spectacular Hall of Mirrors in the palace at Versailles, Genna was transported to a time of powdered wigs, fine lace, and intrigue. The fountains sparkled in the sun and the long promenade stretched into a hazy distance. After touring the palace, she and Pierre wandered the grounds, ending up on the clipped lawn in front of the Petit Trianon. The small palace had been given to doomed Marie Antoinette by her husband, the also-doomed Louis XVI. But before those two had been doomed, they'd certainly known how to eat cake.

The delicate, honey-colored facade of the Petit Trianon glowed in the spring sunshine.

"Do you know the story of the Petit Trianon?" Pierre asked.

Leaning back on her elbows, Genna shook her head.

"It was originally built for Madame de Pompadour, the mistress of Louis XV."

"Ah," she said.

Why did he mention mistress?

"Poor Madame got to enjoy it for only four years before she died."

"*C'est dommage.*"

"*Oui.* And then her place was taken by Madame du Barry, another of Louis's mistresses."

"He was a busy man."

Pierre laughed. "I suppose he was."

Genna stared up at the sky, now washed pale blue in the midafternoon sun. "This place is stunning. No wonder your country had a revolution!"

"I am pleased you like Versailles. Have you had any ideas yet for your book?"

"Hmm," she said. "Getting there."

"May I help?"

"Sure." Genna sat up. "The whole process is kind of mysterious, but I start by brainstorming words about the site that eventually lead me to thoughts about food."

"What words?"

"Descriptive ones. What words come to mind here?"

Pierre settled back onto his elbows and closed his eyes. Genna enjoyed the opportunity to study his profile. A few deep wrinkles furrowed his brow and cheeks, but they made him look rugged and distinguished rather than old. His strong jaw was only slightly softened with age, his neck smooth, his skin still tanned from his recent trip to Morocco. Pierre had told her about his fascination with North Africa, which he visited whenever he could get away from his law practice.

"I think of royalty," he began.

"Good start."

"And green."

"Sunlight," Genna added.

"Clipped."

"Golden."

"Luscious."

"Oooh! Good one." Genna laughed. "Creamy."

"Creamy?"

"Look at that facade," Genna said, gesturing to the trim, neoclassical Petit Trianon. "Have you ever seen more beautiful honey tones?"

"*C'est bon.* How about formal?"

"Sumptuous."

"Luxurious."

"Got it!" Genna sat up and spread she arms wide. "Caesar salad!"

Pierre pondered the connection with Versailles, and then nodded. "*Mais oui, je comprends.* Versailles was the home of our French kings, our Caesars, if you will."

"And what could be more welcome at the start of a memorable meal than a leafy, creamy Caesar salad studded with croutons, capers, and anchovies? A Caesar salad fit for a king!"

"*Vous êtes très amusante.*"

"I hope that's a compliment."

"Oh, very much so. You are also an interesting lady, Geneviève." He sat up and slipped one arm around her waist, then pulled her toward him.

She caught a whiff of spice mixed with soap—clean, sharp, and very male. She wanted to sink into his embrace, right there on the grass in front of the Petit Trianon, like they were a couple of teenagers with more hormones than brains. His breath was warm as his lips trailed up her neck. A strong hand cradled the small of her back.

Like the heroine of a bodice-ripping romance, Genna considered swooning, or at least getting her bodice ripped off. Too bad her light green top had no buttons.

And then without warning, a sick dread twisted her stomach. She leaned back and neatly slipped out of Pierre's grasp. For a moment, he looked a little foolish as he bent to kiss air, but then he quickly regained his composure and sat back.

"I'm sorry, Pierre," she stammered. "But I don't think I can."

"You object to a little romance?"

"I don't know. No, it's not that. I mean, I'm sorry."

She sounded like a total idiot.

What was the matter with her? Pierre Leblanc was hardly Fun Gordon, the birdwatcher with no table manners. On the contrary, Pierre Leblanc was smart and kind and spectacularly good-looking—and like no man she'd ever met.

She didn't want to admit it, but the truth was she hadn't a clue what to do with him. Well, okay, she knew what to *do* with him, but having a relationship?

"Ah, Geneviève. You cannot be sorry. It is of no matter. We are having a beautiful day. I merely wanted to make it more beautiful."

Although he smiled, Genna noticed the slightest shadow of hurt pass across his eyes.

"I guess I'm not ready," she said.

He sat back on his elbows again. "You are hard upon yourself, Geneviève. I have known you for a short time, but already I see you are not as confident as you like people to think. You are a bit frightened, *non?*"

Genna fixed her gaze on the grass, not daring to speak.

He sat up and reached for her left hand. She watched as with one long finger he stroked the faint white line on her third finger. The warmth of his touch soothed more than excited her. She'd forgotten how much she missed being touched.

"How long ago?" he asked.

"Over a year now." She laid her open palm on the grass, sighing at the velvet coolness. She still missed the garden she'd been obliged to give up along with her husband. Collateral damage. "More like sixteen months. You'd think I'd be over it."

"I do not think that is a long time," he said, his voice soft with sympathy.

"It was a few days before Christmas."

Her heart squeezed at the memory of that terrible day when, too shocked even to cry, she'd retreated to a cheap motel room out by the airport.

Both her children had announced that they planned to be away for Christmas, which hadn't bothered Genna at the time. She'd looked forward to spending a quiet day with Drew, opening a few presents, enjoying a simple meal instead of cooking a turkey—no fuss, just the two of them in their lovely new home.

Instead, she'd spent that Christmas Day in the motel eating lukewarm take-out Chinese food. Even the fortune cookie had conspired against her.

You and your partner will be happy in life together.

Someone, somewhere, had a sense of humor, but at the time, Genna had been in no mood to appreciate it.

"So, you came to Paris to escape?"

"Perhaps."

They said nothing for a few moments.

"Come," he said, standing and pulling her to her feet. "This is too lovely a day to get so serious. We have a long walk back to the car. Let us enjoy it and talk of other things." He picked up her daypack and put his arm around her shoulders. "We can come up with more recipes. What about the Petit Trianon? Can it have its own recipe or are you allowed just one for the whole of Versailles?"

"*Ah, mais non!*" Genna laughed, relieved that Pierre wasn't taking her refusal seriously. Maybe one day he'd ask again and maybe one day she'd say yes. But not today. "I make the rules, which means I can have a recipe for every one of the fountains of Versailles if I want."

"You make the rules?" he asked. "*Oui,* I will agree to that."

They spent the rest of the afternoon wandering around the grounds of Versailles. Those French kings had not stinted on land acquisition. The entire Versailles complex, including the massive palace, a canal, two lakes, and hundreds of fountains, was spread over eight hundred hectares.

They drove back to Paris with the setting sun at their backs and stopped for dinner at a restaurant in the swishy sixteenth arrondissement.

Since coming to Paris, she had confined her culinary investigations to small neighborhood bistros serving the flavorful and unpretentious dishes that would populate the pages of *Eat Like a Parisian.* Her budget did not run to the three- and four-star restaurants where chefs impaled themselves on their boning knives if they lost a star and *l'addition* required a second mortgage.

By Parisian standards, the restaurant Pierre chose was not at the temple-of-gastronomy, two-hundred-euro-a-plate level, but it was much, much higher up the fiduciary scale than Genna had ever been. Each dish was expertly prepared and presented. Each mouthful was an orgasmic explosion of taste and texture.

Genna was in heaven.

Between the food and the company, she didn't think she'd ever enjoyed an evening more. When Pierre excused himself to visit the toilet, she tried to remember the last time she and Drew had treated themselves to a nice dinner.

To be fair, money had been tight after they bought the House with the View, as they liked to call it (capital letters proudly implied). But they'd agreed it was worth sacrificing a few comforts so they could make a large down payment. For those first two months, Genna had loved every minute of being in her new home overlooking the water.

It was their dream home, the home they planned to grow old in, the home where they'd welcome grandchildren and wake up every day together in the same bed.

The last time they'd eaten out was in late January over a year ago, just a few weeks after Drew's plunge off the edge of the marriage pool into the deep end. He'd convinced her to meet him at a local Italian restaurant. The veal piccata had been less edible than a rubber eraser and the lemon and caper sauce was separated and oily.

And that was the best part of an evening that had ended disastrously with Genna fuming and Drew tight-lipped with frustration.

With Pierre, the evening passed with measured grace. The unobtrusive service was paced to allow them time to savor each course and explore new avenues of conversation.

As they had at the Café de Flore, they talked of art and food and travel. In his youth, Pierre had backpacked through India and Southeast Asia and even Australia. Genna tried and failed to imagine Pierre swatting flies in the outback.

After dinner, Pierre drove her back to her apartment, bestowed the regulation two-cheeked *bise*, and waited while she fumbled for the key to the heavy front door. She carefully mounted the five flights of stairs to the apartment, her balance not quite what it should be thanks to the excellent wine Pierre had ordered.

When she snapped on the living room light, the *Odalisque* on the wall over the couch was, as always, looking over her shoulder, her gaze inscrutable, as if she had mastered the art of being in the world without making judgments.

Naked and exposed, but not in the least embarrassed, the courtesan seemed to say, *Look at me. I'm as good as you are. We are equals because we are human.*

"It's you and me," Genna said to the picture. "Two chicks on their own in Paris."

nine

Caramel Macarons
Filled with pumpkin puree flavored with cloves

"You went home by yourself?" Marsha's eyes widened as she stirred sugar into her café crème. "From the way you were talking about Pierre, I was sure you'd jump at the chance for a bit of extracurricular snuggling."

"I don't think he had snuggling in mind."

"Aha! I knew it! Come on, Genna, what are you waiting for? How often have you met a man like Pierre?"

"I *am* still married, you know."

"And that's the reason you said no?"

"Maybe?"

"You're crazy. Here you are in Paris, footloose and fancy-free, and with a gorgeous Frenchman on your tail, so to speak."

"Marsha!"

"What's holding you back?"

Genna shook her head. In the warm glow of the May sunshine flooding their favorite café on the Champs-Élysées, her doubts seemed misplaced. And besides, the situation was totally different. She hadn't pledged her *life* to Pierre.

"Do I have to be with Pierre just because he asks me?" she asked.

"You know that's not what I'm saying."

"What *are* you saying?"

"You're on your own for pretty much the first time in your adult life, right?"

Genna nodded. "Drew and I married when I was twenty-two, so, yes, you could say I've never been on my own until now, except for my years at university."

"Then it's time you loosened up and had some fun."

"I'm loose."

"No, you're not. This cup is looser than you are. You do know there's more to life than cooking."

"Of course, I do!"

"Then why didn't you invite Pierre back to your apartment?"

"He can't be interested in someone like me."

"Didn't you say he tried to kiss you at Versailles?"

"He probably felt sorry for me."

Marsha put her cup down with a sharp *crack* on the marble tabletop. "Listen to yourself! If I said that, what would you think?"

"But it's different for you. You're young and you're beautiful."

"And you're not?"

Genna laughed. "I'm not young. Anyway, suppose we drop it for now. We're not getting anywhere in this conversation."

"Rather like your love life," Marsha said and then grinned. "All right, I'll drop it. But when Pierre calls again . . ."

"I'm pretty sure he won't."

"*When* he calls again," she repeated, "I want you to consider that he might like you."

"Sure."

"Genna!"

"All right, I'll give him another chance. *If* he calls, which I doubt he will. Why would he?"

"And now you're fishing for compliments."

Genna changed the subject. "Tell me about your new place."

"There's not much to say."

"Where is it?"

"I told you already. It's in the Marais, not far from our current place."

"And?"

Marsha opened her large handbag and rummaged for her wallet, then threw down some cash and scrambled to her feet. "I've got to get going now. Have a wonderful afternoon. What are you visiting today?"

"I'm taking the day off."

But Marsha wasn't listening. With a distracted wave, she inserted herself into the throngs of pedestrians surging past the café and was gone.

Feeling more concerned than hurt, Genna drained her coffee and left the café, walking in the opposite direction. Something was bothering Marsha, and Genna felt somehow responsible. Should she *say* something about Colin? Isn't that what a real friend would do?

Suddenly, the prospect of descending into the bowels of the Métro and heading straight home made her feel claustrophobic. Genna needed fresh air and time to think. She set off on the forty-minute walk back to the apartment. Whatever was going on with Marsha would sort itself out, and, in the meantime, maybe she was right about Pierre. He was handsome and well-spoken and interesting and cultured, and they were both adults.

But so what? She was in Paris to write a book, not muddy the waters with fascinating Frenchmen.

* * *

For the rest of the week, Genna applied herself to writing. After French class on Wednesday, Marsha left in a hurry instead of joining Genna for coffee.

Her only reminder of Pierre came in an email from Nancy. She, of course, thought Genna was being ridiculous, but that was to be expected from Nancy.

Genna!

You have *got* to be kidding me about Pierre. If he's everything you've said, why didn't you at least kiss the man? Are you telling me you want to spend all your time in Paris alone? Cooking isn't *that* exciting, even for you.

Don't you think you deserve to let your hair down after all you've been through?

Things here are the same as usual. You're not missing much, believe me.

Enjoy Paris and write back soon!

Nancy

Nancy's email made Genna laugh, even if she had no intention of following its advice.

On Friday morning, almost a week after wandering the byways of Versailles with Pierre, Genna awoke late to a bedroom flooded with morning sun, the day stretching before her, full of promise. Everything was working out just the way she'd hoped. True, the money from her advance was starting to run low, and she didn't know what she'd do when her six-month visa expired, but for once in her life, she was content to take each day as it came.

After French class, she planned to visit the Musée Rodin, one of the few places in Paris that Drew had liked. He'd visited the museum many years ago on a student trip to Europe before he met Genna.

The Christmas she was pregnant with Michael, she surprised him with a coffee-table book of Rodin's work. She remembered sitting on the couch in front of the fire on a rainy west coast Boxing Day, leafing through the color plates while Drew pointed out his favorites. The book lay across her enormous stomach and they laughed at how convenient a shelf it made.

Genna sat up, rapping her head against the iron bedstead. In twenty-eight years of marriage, had Drew *ever* treated her with half the attention that Pierre had lavished on her at Versailles? Well, okay, he'd had flashes of sweetness, and whenever she was sick, he brought her chai tea and borrowed stacks of travel documentaries from the library that they watched together.

Her phone rang. She scrabbled for it on the bedside table, sure it must be Nancy. It was like her to follow her email with a direct attack.

"Hey, you!" Genna said.

"Hello?"

"Oh! Sorry. I mean hello. This is Genna."

"Righto! Hiya!"

"Tyler?" Since her first meeting with the Australian barista the day she fell, Genna had dropped into the Starbucks a couple of times for a latte and a quick chat with Tyler about their mutual love of food. She'd given him her number so he could call when he had cooking-related questions.

"That's me! Good on you. How're you doing this morning?"

"Uh, good. Did you have a question about cooking?"

"Is tonight one of your going-out nights?"

Tyler knew all about Genna's master list and how she tried to visit a different restaurant four times a week.

"I think so." She threw off the covers and padded into the kitchen to find her list. "Let's see, it's May eighth, right?"

"Yep, Friday."

"I've got Le Margolis down for tonight. It's in Montparnasse."

"Sounds brilliant." He paused and Genna wondered, with a start, if he was angling for an invitation.

"I have a favor to ask you. It's about my dad."

Genna sat down on the wooden kitchen chair, her bare bottom squelching against the rough wood. "Okay?"

"He's just arrived from Sydney."

"That's nice. I'm sure he's glad to see you."

"Yeah, but the problem is, see, I have to work tonight. He's never been to Europe and he's a bit nervous about going out on his own. He doesn't know any French and, well, you know."

Genna did know, and she sympathized. Paris was a splendid city, but it could be quite daunting for the first-time visitor. She shifted her weight, one cheek popping off the chair and subsiding again. The last thing she felt like doing with her evening was entertaining an Aussie stranger.

"Genna? You still there?"

"Yes, sure."

"Would you mind?"

"No, not at all. I would love to meet your father. Le Margolis is a great first restaurant to visit in Paris. He'll love it."

"Well, I'm not too sure about that. Dad's more of a steak-on-the-barbie kind of guy. But he'll pay."

"That's very kind of him," she said. "How should I meet up with him this evening? Oh, and what's his name?"

"It's Bill, Bill Turner." Tyler paused. "Since my mum passed, Dad's gotten used to being on his own, but I don't think he likes it much."

His mother was dead?

There was still time to get out of it. What if Bill Turner was even half as good looking as his son? Genna did not need *two* men in her life. One man had already been more than enough.

At the rate she was going, her solitary sojourn in Paris was turning into beach blanket bingo.

Whoa, Nelly! She was letting herself get carried away. It wasn't as if she'd be welcoming him into her boudoir. Besides, she didn't have a boudoir. The poky little bedroom with its saggy mattress and dull brown furniture had little to recommend it as a love nest.

"I'm sorry about your mother," she said.

"Yeah. It's been rough. She died about two years ago. I stayed home as long as I could, but I needed to get on with my life. Coming to Paris to study was my big dream. You'll help me a lot by taking Dad out tonight. He's kind of lonely."

Great, a lonely Aussie widower in Paris. What could go wrong?

"Yes, I can understand that. How about I come by tonight around seven? We can walk through the Luxembourg Gardens to Montparnasse. What time are you off work? Will you join us later?"

"I'm off at midnight, so you can drop Dad back at Starbucks on your way home. He'll be happy as long as he's got some English newspapers to read."

"Tell your father I'd be happy to introduce him to a good French restaurant. You can tell him that Le Margolis used to be one of the hangouts of Simone de Beauvoir and Jean-Paul Sartre."

Tyler laughed. "My dad wouldn't know Simone de Beauvoir if she hit him with a stick. Class is starting. I'll see you later."

Genna put down her phone and tried hard not to sigh. What was she thinking? An evening with a man who knew nothing about literature or history and with steak-on-the-barbie tastes? Bill Turner from Sydney was bound to be a beefy, red-faced Aussie with a loud voice and even louder opinions.

She threw on a skirt, matched it with a purple top, then left the apartment and walked to the Métro for the trip under the river to French class. When she got there, she was surprised to find Marsha absent and the class subdued. The other three students combined could not light up the room the way Marsha did. Helmut, the fortyish businessman from Munich, spoke French with such a strong German accent that none of them, except Mademoiselle Deville, who clearly had a thing for him, could understand him. Denise and her daughter spoke quite passable French, but only Denise made any voluntary contribution to the class. She'd been born in Martinique and so had spoken French as a child before emigrating to Britain as a teenager. Her daughter, Tessa, spoke only when the instructor called upon her and then in such a quiet voice that everyone needed to lean forward to hear her. After class, Genna asked Mademoiselle if Marsha had called in, and received a curt shake of her head. Genna gathered the instructor was not pleased by Marsha's unexplained absence.

Once out on the street, Genna gave Marsha a call. She barely recognized the voice that answered.

"Marsha?"

"Hi, Genna. Sorry I didn't make it to class. I hope Mademoiselle wasn't too annoyed."

"She'll get over it. But what about you? Are you all right? You sound exhausted."

"I'm okay."

"You don't sound okay."

"I'm fine, Genna. I've been busy getting things sorted out with the new apartment. I'm on my way to the lawyer's right now."

"Will you be long? We could meet for lunch."

"No!"

"Oh, well, that's okay."

"Sorry. It's just that I'm super busy right now. Um. I've got to go." Just before the line went dead, Genna heard a male voice.

"Get off the phone, Marsha. We can't be . . ."

Genna threw phone into her daypack and walked briskly toward the Métro.

The Musée Rodin was the worst place she could visit on a day when her head was spinning with thoughts about men. Pierre, Drew, Colin, the unknown Bill Turner? She could do without the lot of them. She should stick to cooking. A good recipe never let her down. All she had to do was follow the directions and, voilà, she had something great to eat. If she made a mistake, she could start over, eat the result, or order pizza. Unlike in life, mistakes in cooking often led to amazing taste combinations.

She descended into the Métro at Champs-Élysées Clemenceau and headed south to Varenne, then strolled through the quiet residential streets in the seventh arrondissement to the Musée Rodin, a lovingly restored seventeenth-century mansion tucked behind a high wall. Once through the gate, she found herself in a sun-warmed garden with clipped hedges, formal flower beds, and the massive statue of *The Thinker*.

She remembered pictures of *The Thinker* from Drew's book, but she was not prepared for the power of his bowed head and shiny black limbs silhouetted against the clear blue sky. Like many visitors before her, Genna wondered what *The Thinker* was thinking. Was it some great philosophical construct that so furrowed his brow and made his fist clench with concentration? Was he a writer imagining himself into the skin of a new character? Or was he trying to remember where he left his keys?

Inside the mansion housing the Rodin collection, Genna wandered through room after high-ceilinged, gorgeously corniced room, gazing at sculpture after sculpture. Rodin certainly had a way with marble. He also had a way with sex. The famous statue of *The Kiss*—the two lovers embracing with unselfconscious sensuality—glowed in the middle of one room. Nothing and no one existed for them but each other.

A pang of loneliness darted through her. Would she ever again be that enamored, that bonded to another person?

She was a fool to turn down Pierre. He was offering a chance at unfettered romance—a quick romp, no strings attached. She turned away, only to be arrested by the sight of several small sculptures lining the room around *The Kiss*, each more sensuous than the last, some making *The Kiss* look like a high school smooch.

Oh là là indeed.

Genna walked out onto a balcony overlooking the magnificent expanse of formal gardens that stretched behind the mansion for several city blocks, ending in a perfect, round pound.

Crème brûlée.

Of course!

A silky crème brûlée topped with a sheen of caramelized sugar cracked open by one smart rap of the spoon made the perfect ending to a meal. It combined hard and soft together in one dish, like one of Rodin's sculptures. The cold marble came alive with the heat generated by the two bodies wrapped around each other.

What looked solid became malleable and alive.

Genna left the museum in a much better mood than when she'd entered it—so good that on the way back to her apartment, she stopped at a dress shop and gave her credit card a workout. Maybe Marsha was right about giving nature some help. Also, Le Margolis was a cut above her usual restaurants, more like the one Pierre had taken her to. She'd felt self-conscious then in her drab skirt and green top.

Although she wasn't remotely interested in Tyler's dad, even if he looked like an older version of Tyler, it wouldn't kill her to perk up her habitual look.

She put her life into the hands of the shop assistant, a woman about Genna's age, who spoke English well and sympathized with the havoc wrought by inconvenient bulges. In less than an hour, she had Genna looking better than she'd looked in years.

The new outfit—a plain black dress, scoop-necked and fitted, under a loose turquoise jacket that matched her eyes—skimmed her hips and flattered her curves. A necklace and earrings of chunky blue stones set in silver completed the ensemble.

"Now you must have your hair done," the assistant said. When Genna started to object, she held up one elegant hand while with the other she tapped a number into her phone. "There is still time before your *rendezvous* tonight. I have a friend who runs a salon close to here. I will see if she can fit you in."

Genna had already told Madame that the new outfit was for a *rendezvous* that evening. She had not mentioned that the meeting was with a man, but the woman was French, and so of course she put *deux et deux* together. Genna was not likely spending over a hundred euros to dress for tea with her maiden aunt.

An hour in the salon transformed her blondish hair into a blown-out halo that framed her face perfectly.

After the salon, she had just enough time to get back to the apartment, change into her new outfit, dig out a pair of black flats to replace her usual running shoes, and throw on some makeup before she was out the door and heading for the Odéon Starbucks and her evening with Bill Turner.

ten

Cherry Macarons
Filled with a vanilla and sour cherry ganache

Tyler's eyes widened when he saw Genna enter the Starbucks. For a moment, she felt like turning around and walking out. Would he think she'd dolled herself up to meet his father? He knew she was on her own and could also add two and two and come up with an answer that cast her in the role of aging femme fatale.

Too late.

A solid mass rose before Genna and extended a beefy hand.

"This is Genna McGraw," Tyler said. "Genna, my dad, Bill Turner."

A thatch of thinning hair topped a square-shaped face ripened in the antipodean sun to a rosy brown that reminded Genna of a sliced-open cedar tree back home. The man was about as opposite from slim, graceful Pierre as it was possible to be and still be the same gender.

"Pleased to meet you," she said, returning his handshake. His hand was strong and smooth and was quickly followed by another hand that enveloped hers in a two-handed shake that made her knees feel the teeniest bit rubbery.

"Tyler's told me all about you," he boomed. "You're the cookbook lady."

"I write cookbooks, yes," she said weakly as she disengaged her hand. "Are you interested in cooking?"

His bark of a laugh startled everyone in the café. Several heads turned, and Genna felt like sinking through the floor.

"Hear that, Tyler! Me cooking! I'd like to see the brave bloke who'd eat what I cooked. Course, these days I'm on my own and I'm having to cook a bit, but believe me, you wouldn't want to know. I'm hopeless in the kitchen."

"I could teach you."

What? She'd just met the man and already he'd confirmed her worst fears. He was a big, brash, loud Aussie who looked as much at home in the Parisian Starbucks as a kangaroo at a cocktail party. She didn't even want to imagine how he'd look at the chic French restaurant she'd picked for the evening.

"Well, there's an offer I might take you up on! But you've got your work cut out for you and that's no mistake. My Marjorie couldn't get me to boil water."

At the mention of his mother, Tyler smiled. "No, Dad. But Mum would never have let you in the kitchen anyway."

"Aye, true enough, my boy!" he laughed. "True enough. She would not at that."

For a few moments, both men were silent. Genna could almost see the grief hanging like a dark veil between them. She shifted her feet, wondering if it was too early to say anything and deciding it was.

"Tyler tells me you've just arrived from Sydney. How was the flight?"

"Too bloody long, it was," Bill said, obviously relieved by the change of subject. "I was glad to be in first class, I can tell you that. Those poor buggers at the back—I can't fathom how they stood it."

"Did you get an upgrade?"

"Ah, no, I wouldn't have wanted to depend on that. I said to myself when I decided to come visit Tyler that I was going first class or not at all."

"I've never flown first class."

91

"Then you've been missing out. But no mind, let's get going and leave Tyler here to get to work. All good, son?"

"No worries, Dad. You have a nice dinner, and I'll see you back here later."

"Shall we?" Bill held out his arm for Genna.

The gallantry surprised her. Bill Turner didn't look like the kind of man who paid much attention to social niceties. Although dressed in a suit—a well-cut suit, she noticed as she took his arm—Bill looked like he would be much more comfortable in boots and jeans. If *he* were to stride through the outback, he'd be right at home, his weather-beaten face shaded by a hat with a snakeskin band.

That's the thing with clichés: they often turned out to be true. And as Genna discovered during the evening, she hadn't been that far wrong about Bill. Although he'd been to the outback only on holiday, he did spend the bulk of his time outdoors.

"Landscaper," he responded when she asked what he did for a living. They were seated at a corner table at Le Margolis, a superb bottle of red wine from the Loire Valley already open and poured, and their orders given. Genna was having duck with a cherry and port sauce and Bill—somewhat predictably—had ordered steak and *pommes frites*.

"Do you do residential work?" she asked. "Or commercial?"

"Bit of both. It depends on the branch."

"Branch?"

"Of the business. Turner Landscaping. There are eight branches around Australia and two in New Zealand. Some specialize more in commercial work like condo complexes, office buildings, that sort of thing."

"Your company has ten branches?"

"Yeah, well, I got carried away about fifteen years back. Started expanding like crazy. But all that's behind me now. I've sold the business to travel the world." He smiled across the table at Genna, looking like an overgrown boy.

Her stomach lurched.

What the hell?

"I'm a bit of a gardener myself," she said, aware her voice sounded an octave higher than normal. She took a quick gulp of wine and returned his smile. "Where I live—I mean the house where I used to live—had a large garden." Why did she mention the house? It was surrounded by a mature garden, a garden with "good bones," according to the realtor. Just after buying the house, Genna had spent the day before Halloween on her hands and knees in the damp autumn leaves, planting bulbs for the spring.

At the time, Genna could not have imagined that when the tulips sprouted from the black dirt, she'd be living in a basement suite with a view of a weed-choked backyard, or, even more unlikely, that a year after that, she'd be sitting in a discreetly lit Paris restaurant with crisp tablecloths, red leather chairs, and an Aussie landscaper.

"You've got some wonderful gardens up there in British Columbia," Bill said.

"You've been there?"

"A few times. My brother lives downtown near that big park."

"Stanley Park."

"That's it. When Tyler went to Whistler, my brother found him a place to stay and a job. He runs a helicopter sightseeing business, so he's back and forth to Whistler a lot."

"You're quite the outdoorsy family."

"Too right about that! We spent most of our youth outdoors. We grew up on a farm outside Sydney, had about seventy-five acres of fruit trees—apples, plums, apricots, cherries. My dad had us working as soon as we were able to walk."

"You must have loved it."

"Aye, I ended up making plants my living, so I guess I did."

He had the kindest eyes she'd ever seen in a man—deep blue, almost indigo, but sparkling with good humor. For the next several hours, he entertained her with stories about all the deadly critters he'd encountered in three decades of landscaping. By the end of the evening, he'd convinced her that the entire Australian continent was one writhing mass of venomous beasts all hell-bent on murder.

In return, Genna told him about her cookbooks, her current project in Paris, and her plans for future books. Not once did either of them refer to their spouses, but their presence hovered in the background of the conversation, unseen but not forgotten for a second.

By eleven o'clock, Bill's jet lag kicked in and they made their way somewhat unsteadily from the restaurant to a taxi. As they were pulling up outside the Starbucks, Bill reminded Genna of her promise.

"I'm here in Paris for a few weeks to keep an eye on Tyler, but since he's working and at school a lot, I'll have plenty of time on my hands. You've promised to teach me cooking and I'm going to hold you to it."

"Tyler has my number. Call me when you'd like a lesson."

"I'll do that, make no mistake." He patted her clumsily on the shoulder. "I've had a smashing evening. Thanks so much for taking pity on me on my first night in Paris."

"My pleasure."

He handed the driver twice the fare showing on the meter, then heaved himself out of the taxi and waved as the driver executed a perfect U-turn across the Boulevard Saint-Germain, mercifully free of traffic at the late hour, and seconds later dropped Genna in front of her apartment.

"*Bonne nuit*," he said cheerfully.

The warmth suffusing her as she settled into bed might have owed something to the bottle—two?—of wine she'd shared with Bill, but she wasn't so sure. She compared her evenings in the company of two very different men. With Pierre, the conversation had revolved around art and history and had maintained an understated formality. Bill, on the other hand, had her laughing out loud.

Smiling, Genna fell into a deep, wine-steeped sleep that was thankfully dreamless.

eleven

Green Melon Macarons
Filled with whipped cream cheese and pineapple mint

The next day, Genna left the city streets to stroll the tangle of secret pathways in the Parc des Buttes-Chaumont in the nineteenth arrondissement. Created in the 1860s with the help of Baron Haussmann, the architect largely responsible for the grand boulevards of Paris, the romantic park featured a large rocky cliff topped by a replica of a Roman temple and a waterfall plunging into a circular lake.

Genna had visited the Parc des Buttes-Chaumont once before on the family trip. Drew had read about it in a guidebook called *Off the Beaten Path Paris* and had insisted they see it. Drew loved exploring sites overlooked by the average tourist. Genna suspected it made him feel superior.

As she lounged by the side of the lake, Genna considered what recipe to pair with the park. For all its interesting landscaping and faux structures, the park felt like a neighborhood hangout, a place for people to relax on weekends. The recipe needed to be something simple and popular, something an average Parisian family would eat when they returned to their homes to cook their evening meal.

A mother duck waddled past, a phalanx of yellow fluff balls in her wake. As the duck ushered her chicks into the pond, the perfect dish popped into Genna's head. She scrambled to her feet and headed for the Métro and home. She'd pick up the ingredients in the market near the apartment and then treat herself to what had been one of Drew's favorite meals, although she wouldn't hold that against it.

Her cookbook would be lean to the point of emaciation if she left out everything Drew liked. One thing she could say about him was that he always ate whatever dish she served. He was certainly no gourmet and answered all her queries about taste and texture with a grunted "It's good," but at least he never complained. Once, she even overheard him bragging to one of his clients about what a great cook his wife was, how she even wrote cookbooks that won awards. Genna remembered flushing with pleasure. Drew wasn't one for overdoing things in the praise department. He always said she didn't need him to stroke her ego.

The local *boucher* listened soberly to her halting French, then selected and wrapped a specimen that just days before had clucked happily in an idyllic enclosure somewhere in the Loire Valley. It likely even had a name.

Cécile or Monique or Clotilde.

Genna was almost to the fourth floor of her building when she heard a rustling on the landing above. Was it Pierre? Bill Turner? Her heart did a quick two-step at the prospect, although she couldn't say for sure which man she'd prefer to see. What surprised her was how much she'd enjoyed the company of both. Just as she made up her mind which of the two men she'd *most* prefer to see, her nostrils twitched at the distinctive reek of Gauloises.

"*Ah, madame! Bon!* I wait for you."

Genna's hopes for the evening crash-landed. What had she done to warrant a visit from Monsieur? Had he received a bill for the electricity? Had he decided that having no tenant was better than having one who used too much *gaz*?

"*Bonsoir, Monsieur,*" she said, edging past him to the door and setting down the carrier bag bulging with the fixings for Chicken with Forty Cloves of Garlic. To North Americans, adding forty cloves of garlic to a single dish sounded impossibly pungent, but as soon as most people tasted it, they became firm converts. Few things in life equaled the texture and taste of garlic roasted in chicken juices and then mashed into a thick paste and spread liberally across hunks of warmed baguette.

The translucent white flesh of the chicken peeked from the top of her bag.

"You are cooking *le poulet*?" Monsieur asked.

"Ah, yes. Roasting it. *Poulet aux Quarante Gousses d'Ail*. Do you know it?"

Monsieur's black eyes widened, and he swayed forward, gripping the railing to keep his balance. Genna feared he was about to have a stroke, but he just nodded and said, *"Oui. C'est bon."*

She unlocked the door and indicated he should lead the way inside. To her dismay, she noticed that she'd left the kitchen light on. That would never do. But Monsieur didn't seem to notice. He stood in the middle of the living room and squinted at her improvements.

"You make changes."

"Ah, yes, *oui*. I hope it's all right? Your son said you wouldn't mind so long as I put everything back when I leave."

"You plan to leave?" He regarded her with surprise.

"Oh, no, not for many months yet, I hope. Do you need the *appartement*?"

"Non, non! Ne vous inquiétez pas." Don't trouble yourself.

"Oh." Genna tried to think of something to say. Monsieur seemed in no hurry to go and she needed to get the chicken started if she hoped to have it roasted in time for dinner at a reasonable hour.

"You are cooking *ce soir*?"

"Oui."

"My son, he told me that you are a chef?"

"Not a chef, no."

Monsieur's face fell. *"Non? Mais . . ."*

Finally, the euro dropped.

"Aimeriez-vous rester pour le dîner?" Would you like to stay for dinner?

His face broke into a huge grin. *"Oui! Merci! Je suis enchanté."* He went on to tell Genna in rapid French that he'd heard all about her cookbook writing from his son and that he was impressed to learn she was a chef and that he would not intrude for the world, but . . .

Genna laughed with relief. Higher bills for excess *gaz* usage were no competition for the demands of his stomach. After all, he was French.

"You are most welcome, monsieur." She took her bags into the kitchen, then handed him a bottle of wine and a corkscrew. "Please, open this while I get to work."

Although lacking the charm of his handsome and freshly pressed son, Monsieur most certainly did not lack an appreciation for good food. By the time Genna's Chicken with Forty Cloves of Garlic emerged crispy and steaming from the oven, they had already made short work of an excellent country pâté she'd made the day before (not yet paired with anything, but a girl always needed a good pâté). After the chicken, they enjoyed ramekins of Musée Rodin Crème Brûlée.

Monsieur didn't cook for himself, but he was well informed about the affairs of the stomach. Genna gathered that his beloved *grand-mère* and then his wife, God rest her soul, had both been superb cooks.

As the wine relaxed him, he became positively voluble about the relative merits of the saucissons on offer at the neighborhood *boucheries*, the many uses for *épinards*—spinach—in a good quiche, and the best places in Paris to buy melons so crisp and flavorful, they'd make a grown man sob.

Genna recognized in Monsieur a true kindred spirit.

At the end of the evening, she invited him to return in a few days for another meal. His quick agreement confirmed her suspicion that since the death of his wife two years earlier, Monsieur had not been eating well. Few cooks can resist serving a willing and knowledgeable food lover, and Genna was no exception.

But after Monsieur left the apartment, she opened all the windows to air the place out.

twelve

Kiwi Macarons
Jade green and filled with guava and coconut cream

A few days after her dinner with Monsieur Leblanc and six weeks to the day since she'd arrived in Paris, Genna stood beneath the Arc de Triomphe and gazed up at the stone rosettes on its underside, marveling at the size and grandeur of the arch, not to mention the ego of the little Corsican who had ordered it built.

She heard them before she saw them—Denise and Tessa, the mother-daughter duo from French class.

"Listen to this, Tessa!" After decades living in Britain, Denise's accent still retained its Caribbean lilt overlaid with a hint of Home Counties. "The Arc de Triomphe was begun in 1809 to celebrate Napoleon's victory in the Battle of Austerlitz. That's in Austria."

"I know, Mum." The voice was so soft Genna barely distinguished it over the rustle of Denise's guidebook.

"The arch is one hundred sixty-four feet tall by one hundred forty-eight feet wide," Denise continued. "And listen, this bit's interesting. Way back in 1919, someone flew a biplane right through the arch!"

Genna debated whether to walk away before they noticed her. She'd been on the verge of finding a good dish to match with the Arc de Triomphe. Interrupting the process to make small talk with

Denise might drive any spark of a connection right out of her mind. And as for Tessa, Genna had never heard the girl speak outside class. With her face half-hidden behind a curtain of thick black hair and her perpetual slouch, Tessa was hard going.

"And look! Here's the Tomb of the Unknown Soldier," Denise was saying. "It represents all the men lost in all the wars."

"Is there a body in there?"

"Apparently so. Or more likely bits of one."

"Gross!"

"Come on, let's go up to the top."

"Hang on."

Genna turned to see Tessa standing before the eternal flame that cast shifting shadows on the smooth marble expanse of the tomb. Her head was bowed as if she was trying to imagine the unknown soldier, as Genna had a few minutes earlier.

Who was he? Had he come from Paris or the countryside? How old was he when he was killed? Likely no older than Tessa. He was a young man who had been cut down and buried at the epicenter of France beneath the symbol of its past glories. How much better for him if he'd been allowed to grow old, to live his life in obscurity, and then be buried beneath a plaque that at least recorded his name.

Her Arc de Triomphe recipe popped into her head and she smiled.

Perfect.

"Come on, love," Denise said impatiently. "The queue for the stairs is getting longer."

"Yeah, in a minute."

"Tessa!"

"Hold on a sec. Look over there. Isn't that Genna from French class?"

Denise bustled toward her, waving the guidebook. She was a woman of comfortably generous proportions with an open, friendly face.

"Hello! Fancy meeting you here!"

"Hi. Lovely day."

"That it is. Have you been up top?"

Genna shook her head and looked around Denise. "Hello, Tessa. What do you think of the Arc de Triomphe?"

"Okay," mumbled Tessa. She was looking back over her shoulder at the tomb.

"It's a powerful monument, isn't it?"

"Huh?" Tessa turned back. "Oh yeah, I guess."

"I always think the poor young man is caught in limbo somewhere, yelling his name. Something like *I am Jacques Amiel, private, French Army, born March 18, 1899, killed April 15, 1918. I was nineteen and I didn't want to die.*"

Tessa looked at Genna like she was insane, but then her face softened, and she nodded shyly. "Maybe."

Genna turned back to Denise. "I'm going up too. Come on. Let's go together."

From the viewing platform, the azure sky of a flawless May day curved high over a picture-perfect view of Paris. The famous landmarks and boulevards fanned out below like a giant 3-D map.

"This is the best view in Paris," Genna said. "Much better than the view from the Eiffel Tower, don't you think?"

"We haven't been up the Eiffel Tower," Denise said. "We're on a bit of a budget. Besides, as you say, this is a good view, and it's covered by the Museum Pass."

Genna tried again. "See that modern blue building over there?" She pointed southwest. "That's the Pompidou Centre. Have you been?"

"Not yet. I'm not sure we'd like it."

"You must go! The twentieth-century collection is one of the best in the world. All the greats are there. Picasso, Magritte, Miró . . . you name it."

"We're not much for art that doesn't look like something."

"What about you, Tessa?"

"Me?"

"Are you interested in modern art?"

"Um, well . . ."

"Tessa thinks like I do about modern stuff. Neither of us are that bothered about art in general. We only lasted an hour in the Louvre. To be honest, I'm not sure what all the fuss is about. We finally found the *Mona Lisa*, but there were so many tour groups all gathered in front of her and she was covered in glass, so we didn't see a thing. And then we walked and walked and walked! I didn't think there were that many pictures in the world. And if you ask me, most weren't worth looking at, right, Tessa?"

Tessa kept gazing at the view, her thin shoulders so rigid Genna saw the outline of her bones under her thin pink T-shirt.

"There's no lack of pictures at the Louvre," Genna said cheerfully. She wasn't going to find much common ground with Denise on the subject of art. But she liked her. What you saw was what you got with Denise, and Genna suspected there was more to Tessa than met the eye.

"What are you two doing for dinner?" Genna asked suddenly.

Tessa's head snapped up and her body tensed even more. She reminded Genna of a small bird balanced on a wire, trusting gravity to keep it from plummeting to the ground.

"We haven't made plans yet," said Denise. "Usually, we open a can of something. We've got a hot plate in our apartment."

"Whereabouts are you staying?"

"Near the Luxembourg Gardens. It's lovely and quiet."

"You're not too far from me. That settles it. You must come to my place for dinner tonight."

She saw Tessa's shoulders fall a few inches.

"Oh no!" Denise exclaimed. "We'd be such an imposition."

Tessa turned away from the view and leaned sideways against the railing, her back to Genna.

"You'd be doing me a huge favor," Genna said. "Before we met, I decided on the dish to pair with the Arc de Triomphe for the book I'm writing. I told you about it in class? Anyway, I'd love to share it with you."

"You'd have to go to so much trouble."

"No trouble at all. I was planning to work on the recipe anyway, and if you join me, you can make suggestions." Genna reached out and touched Tessa on the shoulder.

"Do you cook?"

"Um, no," she mumbled, without turning around.

"She can burn toast." Denise laughed. "I've never yet got her to take an interest in it."

"Well, it's time she learned!"

Tessa finally looked over her shoulder. Her face was almost invisible behind the hair, but Genna detected a flash of white teeth, a glimmer of a smile.

Genna had another brainstorm. "Why don't you come over early, Tessa, and you can help me with the prep?"

"Dear me, no!" Denise said, laughing. "She'd only be in your way."

"Not at all. And I need the help. How about I expect Tessa at five, and, Denise, you can come around seven and we'll serve *you* dinner?"

"Well . . ."

"I'll take that as a yes," Genna said. "Now, ladies, if you'll excuse me, I need to get to the shops." She rummaged in her pack for a notebook and pen, and then ripped a page from the notebook and scribbled her address. "I'm on Rue Bonaparte a few doors down from the Church of Saint-Germain-des-Prés. Ring the bell at the front door for number six."

"That's kind of you," Denise said. "But are you sure you want Tessa to come early? As I said, she's not much of a cook."

"Don't worry about that," Genna said, winking at Tessa. "I'll find plenty to keep her busy."

"Well, if you're sure." Denise turned to Tessa. "What do you say to Genna?"

Tessa mumbled something that Genna took as a thank-you.

"Good. See you at five." Genna descended the stairs to the Place d'Étoile and set off for the Métro. Hopefully, the *boucherie* still had some good cuts.

* * *

Three hours later, Genna had Tessa chopping garlic for Arc de Triomphe Braised Lamb Shanks with Caramelized Onions. Tessa worked carefully, her anxiousness to please touching. Genna had the feeling that Tessa was rarely asked to do anything and so was determined to prove she wasn't as useless as her mother would have people think.

"Good start with the garlic. Let me show you how to cut it even more finely." Genna took the knife and expertly reduced Tessa's careful slices to a thick paste.

"This is minced garlic," she explained. "We'll use it in the sauce."

Tessa nodded and to Genna's surprise spoke the first full sentence since arriving thirty minutes earlier.

"You make it look so easy."

"I've had lots of practice!"

Genna sensed Tessa was bursting with questions she was too shy to ask.

"Do you cook at home?" Genna asked.

"Oh, no!" Tessa looked genuinely shocked. "You heard Mum! And besides, she don't like anyone messing about in her kitchen. She says I'll learn to cook quick enough when I get a family of my own."

"Your mother has a point. I was lucky to have a grandma who taught me a lot about baking when I was young, but I didn't really learn how to cook meals until I got married."

"You didn't?"

"Nope. But we lived near a cooking school in Vancouver and I started taking classes. Over the years I got into it more and more until I ended up teaching at a local high school and finally writing cookbooks."

"Do you still teach?"

"I gave it up about ten years ago. All I do now is cook and write about it."

"Can you teach me?" Tessa asked so softly Genna had to lean closer to hear.

"I'd love to, but aren't you and your mom leaving Paris soon?"

"In about three weeks."

"Well, three weeks isn't long, but it's a start. If you like cooking, you could find a school near your home and get some proper training."

Tessa's head shot up, her dark eyes hopeful. "You mean train to be a chef? Like on telly?"

"Sure, why not?"

Genna could almost see the light bulb flickering above Tessa's head as she digested the image of herself dressed in a chef's tunic, mincing garlic in a steamy, bustling kitchen far away from her mother. It was as if the girl had suddenly got hold of something to believe in, something to make her unique in the eyes of the world and, more important, in her own eyes.

"What were you planning to do when you got home?" Genna asked.

"Probably get my old job back. I worked in a pub." Tessa made a face. "Didn't much like it. Or I might go to college. Mum says I should take some kind of practical course. She likes nursing. Her mum was a nurse when she first came over from the West Indies back in the sixties. Mum says those days were hard, but that Granny was determined to give her kids—my mum and her brother—a good education."

"What does your mother do now?" asked Genna. She tried to imagine what profession allowed Denise to take time off for an extended stay in Paris.

"She works for a TV production company. Helps her posh boss with his appointments and such. Mum's always on about him."

"What do *you* want to do?"

Tessa glanced up and grinned. "Not nursing."

"Would your mom let you go to a college that offered a chef training program?"

"They have programs like that at college?"

"Probably not at every college, but I'm sure you can find plenty that do. You live in London, don't you?"

"Outside London, in Reading."

"I'm positive you'll find colleges nearby that offer cooking courses. Check the internet. Here, peel these kiwis and then slice them. We'll use them as a garnish for the cream tarts."

Tessa said nothing as she reached for a kiwi and began peeling. Genna winced as she watched Tessa mangle it. Whatever was going on in her head was being transferred to her hands, but Genna didn't have the heart to correct her. She sensed that thoughts of momentous import were coursing through Tessa's brain and that it wasn't accustomed to the sensation.

By the time Denise puffed up the five flights of stairs, Genna and Tessa were on their second glass of red wine and fast becoming friends. As the wine loosened Tessa up, the questions poured forth. She asked about Genna's book and cooking for a living and how she chose ingredients. It wasn't often Genna had such an eager audience, and she was enjoying herself.

"You made all this from scratch?" Denise asked as she surveyed the platters laid out on the table. In addition to the lamb shanks, Genna had prepared a vegetable tian of zucchinis, onions, and tomatoes layered with olive oil and thyme, and topped with shredded asiago cheese and lightly grilled. Under her supervision, Tessa had prepared Versailles Caesar Salad, and Genna completed the meal with the kiwi-topped cream tarts and baked *madeleines*, the quintessentially Parisian butter cookies known for their distinctive scalloped shell shape.

"Tessa was a great help."

"She didn't get in your way?"

"Not at all. We've had a great time, haven't we, Tessa."

A shrug. "Guess so."

Genna served Denise a generous helping of lamb shanks topped with several spoonsful of caramelized onions. "I hope you like lamb."

"Never much had it," Denise admitted. "We don't eat a lot of fancy stuff. My mum taught me all sorts of dishes from back home, but over the years I've gotten out of the habit of cooking, what with bringing up the kids and all." She grinned. "Thank goodness for takeaway, right?"

"I certainly had my share of takeout when my kids were younger," Genna said. "But, you know, lamb shanks aren't fancy. In fact, they can be a low-budget meal. They need a lot of braising to get tender. Before you leave, I'll give you the recipe."

Denise looked dubiously at her plate, and then with good humor speared a forkful of lamb and popped it in her mouth. Her eyes widened as the red wine sauce flavored with rosemary worked its magic. "That's bloody marvelous!"

"What's this lamb got to do with the arch?" Denise asked after a few more forkfuls.

"The idea came to me when I was looking at the Tomb for the Unknown Soldier. I thought about how all the pomp and splendor depended on the sacrifice of millions of young men."

"Bit depressing, that."

"I know, but I couldn't stop thinking about all those dead soldiers. Most of them wouldn't have been much older than my son."

"So you chose lamb." When Genna nodded, Denise sat silent for a moment and then smiled. "I get it."

"What?" Tessa asked.

"I was remembering an expression from the Bible," Genna said.

"Tessa wouldn't know much about the Bible," Denise laughed. "I was brought up pretty religious, although I'm not much of a churchgoer anymore. But I see what you're getting at. *Lambs to the slaughter*, right?"

"That's it. Do you think it's too dark?"

"Well, it's not exactly sweetness and light, but I don't think you should change it. For one thing, this lamb's too wonderful to leave out of your book, and for another, well . . ." Denise's smile faded as her eyes filled suddenly with tears. Tessa jumped up and circled the table to squat next to her mother. "It's okay, Mum," she whispered. "It wasn't like that for our Jared."

"I know it," she sniffed, "but I was thinking about all them wars and how Jared would have loved this food. He was always one to try new things." Tears leaked down her cheeks.

Tessa patted her mother's arm and then looked across the table at Genna. "Sorry," she mumbled. "It's my brother, Jared. He was killed about a year ago."

"Killed? Oh dear, I'm so sorry."

"He was going to be a soldier," Tessa said, suddenly looking very young. "But just before he was to go for his training, he was killed in a car accident." She shook her head. "He was twenty-two."

"Oh."

Denise looked up. "Sorry about that. You've made us such a lovely meal and here I go all blubbering."

"Please, don't even think about it. And I'm so sorry about your son. You must be so proud of him."

Denise nodded. "At least I can be grateful he was killed instantly—drunk driver on the motorway."

Genna thought of her own Michael, a year older than Denise's son, and shuddered. Losing him was unthinkable.

"I'm all right, love," Denise said to Tessa. "Finish your meal. Genna's gone to so much trouble."

Tessa rose and returned to her seat. She glanced over at Genna and smiled shyly. Genna nodded back, more determined than ever to find a way to help Tessa learn to cook.

The girl needed a bit of joy in her life.

thirteen

Apple Cider Macarons
Pale orange and filled with apple-nutmeg compote

"Thanks for taking Dad out last week," Tyler said as he prepared Genna's morning latte. She'd given up going to the more authentic café across the street. Chatting with Tyler was more fun than sitting alone and being served by a waiter who barely glanced in her direction.

"We had a lovely time."

"I heard."

"Is your dad enjoying Paris?"

"To be honest, he's pretty bored. I haven't the time to take him sightseeing, and I think he's feeling neglected." He handed Genna her latte. "Um, I don't suppose you'd mind taking him with you today?"

"I'm going out to Giverny to see Monet's garden."

"That's perfect for Dad."

"Yes, I thought you'd say that. Tell him to meet me at the internet place over on Rue Mignon in about half an hour. I need to check my email and then I plan to catch the 9:26 train from Gare Saint-Lazare."

"You know you can use the Wi-Fi here on your phone," Tyler said.

"I know, but I'd rather type on a keyboard, and I don't have internet access in my apartment."

Tyler looked so horrified that Genna had to smile. "It's okay. I kind of like being unplugged most of the time."

"To each their own," he said cheerfully. "Anyway, no worries. I'll send Dad over. And thanks, Genna."

Genna wondered if she was a candidate for therapy. Bill Turner was a nice enough guy, but she wasn't sure they had enough in common to spend an entire day together. What if they ran out of things to say halfway through the train journey to Giverny? Or, worse, what if he droned on so much about the plants in Monet's garden that Genna had no hope of finding a recipe connection?

When would she learn to keep her mouth shut?

At the internet place, Genna snagged a free computer and logged on. An email popped in from Drew. She'd taken to deleting his emails without reading them, but for some reason, her curiosity got the better of her. Was there anything Drew could say to change her mind? She doubted it, but maybe she should read at least one of his messages.

Gen!

Are you EVER going to reply to my emails? I must have sent a dozen since you left. I've lost track. This is getting ridiculous! You going off to Paris makes zero sense. You know you can't stay there forever. I checked and the longest visa you can get is for six months. So then what? You'll have to come home.

I want us back together again, Genna. I haven't changed on that score since, you know, what happened. I'm sorry! How many more times do I have to say it and write it? One of these days you'll have to forgive me, so what are you waiting for?

The realtor's useless, by the way. Total jerk. He keeps on at me to get the house cleaned professionally before a showing. Waste of money if you ask me. The view sells the place, but the guy hasn't brought over any decent prospects for weeks.

Maybe it's a sign that we shouldn't sell the house at all. I know how much you like to put stock in signs. And you love the house! Please come back and let's get on with our lives. We've always been good together. You know we are.

Genna sighed and pressed Delete, then opened a new message window and addressed it to Nancy.

Hi Nancy

You won't believe it, but I'm going to spend the day with Bill Turner, the Aussie man I told you about. I'm taking him up to Monet's gardens at Giverny. His son asked me to, and what could I say?

I can guess what you're thinking and no, I'm not attracted to him, or anyone else, not even Pierre. Okay, I was flattered, but that's it. The last thing I need is a new man.

What's happening at home? You haven't written for ages. I just read one of Drew's emails. Pathetic! He keeps saying he wants me back. Forget it.

The house still hasn't sold, which is a huge drag. My money is running out much faster than I expected. Paris is such an expensive city. I'm hoping my financial guy will have some good news for me soon, but if he doesn't, and if Drew can't sell the house by July, I'll have to come home early. I really don't want to do that.

Paris agrees with me, but I always knew it would. And being here on my own without Drew has been wonderful. I get to see whatever I want

without him moaning about some imagined ill or
other.

"Tyler said I'd find you here." The deep voice filled the tiny
storefront that was also crammed with printers and mailboxes. Two
backpackers, the only other people using the computers, hunched
farther down in their plastic chairs, eyes fixed on their screens. It
would take a nuclear explosion to shift them.

"Hi, Bill! I'm almost finished. Can I meet you outside?"

"Take your time."

Bill's just arrived so I've got to go. Write me
soon!

Love Genna

She clicked Send, paid the attendant for the time, and met Bill
out on the sidewalk.

"Did Tyler tell you where we're going today?" Genna stepped
to the curb and hailed a taxi.

"Some gardens an hour or so outside the city? That suits me
fine. I'd enjoy a spot of greenery."

"There are plenty of parks in Paris."

"Sure, but they're not much fun to visit on my own. I appreciate
you letting me tag along. Tyler tells me these gardens are world-
famous."

"That's an understatement! I read somewhere that over a
million people a year visit Monet's gardens at Giverny. There's big
business in water lilies."

The taxi dropped them at the Gare Saint-Lazare, with minutes
to spare before the train left.

"How do we get to this gardens place from the station?" Bill
asked as the train pulled out. They were seated across from each
other by the window. A middle-aged businessman with a nose that
put de Gaulle's to shame sat in the aisle seat next to Genna. The seat
next to Bill was empty.

"There's a bus that meets every train, but I was planning to rent
a bike. Giverny is about three kilometers from the station. Are you

fine with cycling?" Bill didn't look like a cyclist. The thought of him in tight black cycle shorts made her smile.

"What's so funny?"

"Nothing."

"You were thinking that I don't look much like a cyclist," he said grinning, "and you'd be right. My Marjorie was forever trying to get me out on a bike, but she never had any success. I think bikes are best left for youngsters."

"Come on, you're not too old to ride a bike."

"That's what my Marjorie used to say."

"We can take the bus or a taxi if you prefer."

"No, no. If you were planning on renting a bike, I'm not about to cramp your style. I'm pulling your leg. When I was younger, I cycled from Brisbane to Sydney in twenty-four hours."

"Really? Wow!" Then Genna remembered her geography. "Wait a minute! Isn't Brisbane hundreds of kilometers from Sydney? A friend of mine said it took her a day and a half to drive it."

"Ah, you're too smart for me. I can see I'll need to keep my wits about me."

Genna burst out laughing, causing the man next to her to shift in his seat and rattle his newspaper. Bill winked, and Genna almost choked in an effort to swallow another laugh. Perhaps the day would turn out well after all. He was certainly an easy man to spend time with.

They got off the train at Vernon and crossed the street to the row of rental bikes outside a bar. The waiter helped them pick out two, and they headed off on the path to Monet's gardens at Giverny. Genna led the way, smiling at the good-humored stream of commentary that Bill kept up as he rattled along a few feet behind her. The only time she'd gone cycling with Drew around the sea wall at Stanley Park, he'd complained about the wind, the sun in his eyes, the soreness of his legs, the alignment of Mercury with Venus. Whatever.

Needless to say, they never again went cycling together.

Bill, on the other hand, admired everything—the sun on the river, the houses they passed, the birds, the view of a distant church spire. All of it delighted him.

At the gardens, Bill proved to be the perfect companion. As a landscaper by trade, he recognized a great garden when he saw one. They wandered the twisting pathways and explored shaded nooks. He knew when to talk about the trees and the flowers and when to keep quiet. By the time they emerged onto one of the famous green Japanese bridges spanning a lily pond, Genna felt as if she'd known and liked him forever.

Before her stretched the real-life version of the water lily paintings in the Orangerie. A huge weeping willow dominated the far corner. Clumps of lily pads lay scattered across the still waters of the pond, which reflected a turquoise sky studded with white clouds.

She sighed deeply. "Heavenly."

"Too right." Bill joined her at the bridge railing, his strong arms inches from hers. If he shifted his body ever so slightly, they'd touch.

Green and cool, light, airy, a hint of complexity, melt in the mouth.

"Asparagus soufflé."

Bill nodded sagely, still gazing out over the pond. "That would be your recipe?"

"What do you think?"

"As I told you, cooking isn't my thing. Isn't a soufflé made with eggs?"

"Yes, and it's tricky to make well. One false move and the soufflé falls into an eggy puddle that you have to scrape off the bottom of the dish."

"Sounds charming."

"But when it works, a soufflé is a taste of heaven, like this place." She nodded dreamily at the view. "And the asparagus gives it some greenery."

"I like the nod to plant life. You can't go wrong with vegetables, and I'm particularly fond of asparagus."

"We could start your cooking lessons tonight with the soufflé, if you like." She paused, blushed. Had she just invited him to dinner?

"Sounds good." He leaned closer, his bulk a comforting presence that made her feel safe. The word *solid* came to mind.

Nice and solid.

She grinned. "All right. Come on, let's get some lunch. There's a place near here that I've read serves wonderful food."

"Suits me. I was wondering when you'd mention lunch. I've been perishing this past hour." They turned away from the view and crossed over the bridge.

"Why didn't you say something?"

"And rush you through a place like this? Naw, that wouldn't be on at all. You should have seen your face when you were looking out over the pond back there. I wouldn't have wanted to cut short your time here by a second."

Genna didn't know what to say, so she said nothing. But she couldn't help thinking that Marjorie Turner had been one very lucky woman.

They settled into a corner table inside Le Restaurant Baudy, situated a few minutes' walk from the gardens. According to the guidebook, the restaurant had been frequented by the likes of Renoir, Cézanne, Sisley, and Mary Cassatt. There was seating available outside, but Bill took one look at the dense foliage surrounding the terrace and asked that they sit inside.

"I'm nervous about the wasps."

"Wasps?"

"I know, bit of a problem for a landscaper, but I'm highly allergic. One sting would lay me out cold." He winked. "Now, tell me what's good. The menu's all in French."

Genna scanned the menu and recommended the *terrine de foie de volaille* to start, followed by the *omelette Baudy*.

"I know what an omelet is, but what's the first one?"

"The *terrine de foie de volaille* is a chicken liver pâté that usually includes cognac. You won't be disappointed. And I see here that the omelet contains confit of duck." She looked up anxiously. "Do you like duck?"

"I can't say I've tried it all that often, but I'm game if you think it's good."

"It will be good. And if you're still hungry, you must have the apple tart for dessert. After all, we're in Normandy where the best apples are grown."

"Are you up for some wine?" he asked, opening the wine list with practiced ease. Genna was beginning to realize that Bill Turner only pretended to be a hick from the Aussie outback who gnawed raw lizards for breakfast. He was probably able to read the French menu as well as she could. But his willingness to let her take the lead was endearing.

"I'm always up for wine."

"That's my girl!"

A warm glow spread through Genna. She was hardly his girl, and yet . . .

The waitress arrived and listened patiently as Genna gave the order in French. When she finished, Bill pushed the wine list across to her and indicated his choice with one thick finger. Genna tried to appear nonchalant. The price of the bottle was considerably more than the two lunches combined.

"Are you sure?" she asked when the waitress left.

"About what?"

"That wine's expensive."

"I think we're worth it. Don't you?"

All Genna could think about was Drew's almost pathological fear of spending money, unless it was on wood for one of his projects. He would never, not in a million years, order anything but the cheapest house wine.

"You're looking serious," Bill said. "We can change the order, but I must confess that I have a weakness for good wine."

Genna could think of worse failings.

"No, no, I'm sorry. It's not the wine." Frantically, Genna tried to think of a plausible excuse for the sudden downturn in her expression. Her father used to tease her that she'd make a lousy poker player. Her face reflected every thought, good or bad.

"Um, I was thinking about your cooking lesson," she said.

"I hope I won't be a bother."

"Of course not! I'm looking forward to it. When we get back to town, we'll go to the market and pick up what we need. Let's hope we can find fresh asparagus, but if we can't, I can substitute spinach or some nice roasted vegetables."

"I'm all yours," he said. "Whatever you think is best will be perfect with me."

They dawdled for two hours over lunch, so the place was empty by the time they finished. The staff didn't appear to mind. The waitress even leaned toward Genna when Bill was distracted with his Visa card to whisper, "*Votre mari est très gentil. Vous avez de la chance.*" Your husband is very nice; you are lucky.

"*Oh, non! Il n'est pas mon mari!*" He is not my husband.

"*Mais il est très gentil!*"

Genna had to agree with her there. Bill *was* very nice. Very nice indeed.

On the journey back to Paris, they got seats next to each other. Within minutes of pulling out of the station, the fresh air, good food, and even better wine took their toll. Genna's eyes grew heavy and her neck took on a life of its own. An hour later, she awoke to find her head nestled into the crook of Bill's solid shoulder.

She couldn't remember the last time she'd felt so safe. She also felt embarrassed. What if she'd drooled all over his arm? She snapped her head upright. "Sorry!"

"No worries," he said. "You needed the rest."

"Right, well." She fumbled for her daypack and extracted a wad of Kleenex. "Looks like we're almost in." The ugly back end of Paris ground past as the train crept toward Gare Saint-Lazare. She looked down at the ring finger on her left hand. Weeks of wandering the streets of Paris in the spring sun had obliterated the faint white line. She was sure she'd mentioned her children at some point, but she was equally certain she'd said nothing about their father. Bill would likely conclude she was available, which was more or less true. But did she *want* him to think that? What did *available* mean?

"I think I'm too tired for cooking tonight," she said, turning to face him. "Can we reschedule?"

"Sure, if that's what you want." He smiled, showing even white teeth and crinkly blue eyes. "But I'm disappointed."

Genna's heart did a quick cartwheel, but she sternly ignored it, turning to stare out the window so she didn't have to look at those damn crinkly blue eyes. "Sorry," she mumbled. She suspected that he didn't believe her story about being too tired but thankfully had the grace not to press her.

When the train pulled into the station, they got off and walked in silence to the exit.

"I'll grab the Métro from here," Genna said. "It was a wonderful day." She nodded toward the road. "You'll find lots of taxis out there."

He leaned forward, his bulk filling her vision. She smelled expensive aftershave and warm wine. Something peculiar was happening to her knees. If she didn't walk away *right now*, they were in danger of buckling.

"Bye," she said, then ducked around him and ran down the stairs to the Métro, not daring to turn around to see him standing alone in the middle of the crowded station.

Rush hour had started and the Métro was packed with black-suited businesspeople and tired tourists. Genna gripped the overhead railing and fixed her gaze on the stations whizzing past. People flushed in and out of the car like oiled sardines. What was wrong with her? Bill didn't deserve such treatment, not after the wonderful day they'd spent together. And she *liked* Bill. He was kind with lovely, warm eyes and he made her laugh. Spending time with him was easy.

Too easy?

She was being ridiculous. She's been out with Bill twice and barely knew him. He liked her, that much was clear, but so what? She liked him too.

And that, Genna concluded, as she swayed with the movement of the train, was the problem.

On the way back to the apartment, she picked up a bundle of young asparagus and a dozen eggs from a small supermarket. She may as well test the soufflé recipe for herself, although in her current mood she'd be amazed if it puffed.

She found Monsieur Leblanc waiting on the landing. He tapped his watch. "Today, seven. It is now fifteen minutes past."

She'd completely forgotten that she'd invited Monsieur for dinner. It was a good thing after all that she hadn't brought Bill home. How would Monsieur react to her entertaining a man in the *appartement*? Think of the extra *électricité*!

"*Désolée, monsieur,*" she said. "*Entrez-vous, s'il vous plâit. Aimez-vous les œufs?*" Do you like eggs?

"*Ah, bon,*" he said, following her into the apartment. "*Merci.*"

fourteen

Pomegranate Macarons
Rich vermillion shells filled with peppery jelly

"That's sweet of you to take such an interest in Tessa," Marsha said.

After over a week away from French class, Marsha finally showed up and consented to join Genna afterward for lunch at a bistro in the Marais. The place had been on Genna's list ever since Colin recommended it. She might not like the man as a boyfriend for Marsha, but she respected his taste buds. The other two bistros he'd recommended had been superb.

"Tessa's only twenty," Genna said. "And she's been through a lot since her brother was killed. Denise told me that her husband took off about six months ago. He couldn't handle what had happened to their son. So now she's on her own with Tessa and I sense she doesn't really know what to do with her."

"What brought them to Paris? She's never said in class."

"Her boss is some kind of bigwig in TV. Apparently, he lent them his studio apartment near the Luxembourg Gardens."

"Nice boss."

"Denise thinks so. Anyway, she told me she had some money put away and she decided it would do them some good to get away from England for a few months. They're set to go home in June."

"Denise has her hands full."

"She does." Genna sensed that Marsha's thoughts were far away from Denise and Tessa. "Did you buy the apartment?"

"Yes."

"That's amazing! Congratulations!"

Marsha continued picking at a *salade verte* studded with tiny spheres of peppered goat cheese and pomegranate seeds. Genna made a mental note to include a similar salad in the book if she could find a match. The Jardin des Plantes, which she'd yet to visit, was a possibility, although the connection was a bit obvious.

"You don't seem excited," Genna said when Marsha made no effort to elaborate.

"Of course, I'm excited." Marsha looked up, her eyes flashing as she stabbed at a piece of arugula.

"Why didn't you tell me?"

"We've been talking about Tessa, and, besides, there's not that much to tell. It's an apartment."

"It's an apartment in Paris, Marsha. Come on, you can't tell me you're excited and not give me some details. Where is it?"

"On Rue Charlot, not far from the Musée Picasso."

"And . . . ?"

"What do you want me to say?" Marsha sounded like she was talking about a piece of furniture she'd found abandoned in the street rather than a piece of real estate probably costing a million and a half euros. Apartments in that part of Paris did not come cheap.

"When will you move in?"

"Pretty much anytime now. I got the key yesterday."

"That's fast! When can I see it?"

The skin under Marsha's eyes was a dark indigo that contrasted starkly with her pale skin. She looked like she hadn't slept for a week. She sighed. "You can see it now if you want."

"I'd love to!"

Marsha nodded at the waiter, who floated over, tucked the bill under a saucer, and removed the plates. She barely glanced at the bill before tossing thirty euros on the table and motioning for

Genna to follow her out of the restaurant. They were a few blocks from the Rue Charlot.

"Have you found a dish to match with for the Musée Picasso?" Marsha asked as they passed the Rue de Thorigny, the street where the museum was located.

"Yes, I visited about a week ago."

"A lot of people think it's the best small museum in Paris."

"I decided on bouillabaisse."

"Isn't that a specialty of Marseilles?"

"Sure, but most of the dishes in the book come from other parts of France. Paris doesn't have its own indigenous cuisine. Go to any bistro and you'll find dishes from Brittany, Provence, Gascony, you name it. Adding bouillabaisse isn't a problem. And it's totally appropriate for the Musée Picasso."

"Why?"

Genna was glad for the opportunity to take Marsha's mind off whatever was worrying her.

"Bouillabaisse is a true mélange of the traditional and the contemporary, which is kind of like the Musée Picasso. You've been there, right?"

"When I was a student, I went there at least once a month."

"I think I love the building even more than the collection," Genna said.

For the first time, Marsha smiled. "The Hôtel Salé?"

"I read that it was built in the seventeenth century by a man who made his fortune collecting the salt tax."

"And bouillabaisse can be pretty salty given that it's packed with ingredients from the sea," Marsha said. "Is that what you're thinking?"

"Yes, and also the nature of Picasso's work. He experimented with just about every painting style of the twentieth century. That variety reminded me of how you can make bouillabaisse with all sorts of fish and seafood."

"True, and Picasso was born in Málaga on the Mediterranean."

"You got it."

"Let me know when you need a taste test," Marsha said. "I may have grown up in Colorado, but I love fish."

"I need more than one or two people to test the recipe on," Genna said thoughtfully. "Bouillabaisse is a dish best made for a large group of people. It's perfect for a party."

"So, let's have a party." Marsha turned to Genna, her eyes shining. "Let's have a party for everyone in our class. Helmut, Denise, Tessa."

"And Mademoiselle?"

"Sure. Why not? She can flirt with Helmut!"

"My apartment's too small for a party."

"It'll be fine. I can lend you a few extra chairs. We should be able to squeeze the six of us around your table. You could serve a whole meal from your cookbook, including the bouillabaisse. By now you must have a recipe for every course."

"I suppose I could put something together," Genna said.

"You said that Denise and Tessa are leaving in June which is when our course ends. Why don't you throw a farewell party?"

Genna stopped walking and groped in her daypack for her date book, then thumbed through the pages for May. Their last class was June 5, and the sixth was a Saturday.

"You can get Tessa to help you."

"Good idea, and I might invite Tyler, too, you know, the young guy who works at the Odéon Starbucks?"

"Sure."

"I've been out with his father a couple of times." Genna laughed at the expression on Marsha's face. "But I'll get to that later. Tyler could meet Tessa and, you know . . ."

"You want to play matchmaker?"

"Well, no, not exactly. But Tyler's already said he likes to cook and Tessa's thinking she might like it and, well . . ."

"What do you think will happen? They'll fall for each other over the mashed fish heads?" Marsha asked.

"No! And I'm not putting fish heads into my bouillabaisse. But it would be nice for Tessa to meet someone her own age. And Tyler is a good guy."

"What about the father?"

"I'm not sure. I sort of abandoned him the last time we were together, which was kind of mean, because he's a nice man."

"So why did you?"

Genna shrugged. "I wish I knew. I guess I got scared."

"Of what?"

"I don't know, getting involved maybe? He's only here for a few weeks."

"You sound upset."

"I'm not upset."

"Sure."

They turned into the narrow Rue Charlot and Marsha strode ahead.

"Marsha!" Genna ran to catch up. "I'm *not* upset."

"And Pierre? Are you going to ask him too?"

"I don't know, maybe?"

"You're doing pretty well for someone who came to Paris to be on her own." Marsha said. She stopped abruptly next to a solid black door and fished for her key, elbows akimbo, her movements jerky like her head had forgotten how to connect with her hands.

Genna felt the sting of the remark but decided to let it go. It wasn't like Marsha to be so sharp. Something was up, and it wasn't good.

"Here we are," Marsha said, leading the way across a cool cobbled courtyard to a small foyer, where she pressed the button for an ancient elevator. "We're on the top floor."

"I didn't *plan* to meet either of them."

The elevator, just big enough for the two of them, clanged to a stop and the metal doors creaked open. The women squeezed in.

"No, but do you *plan* to give either of them a chance?"

"What's *that* supposed to mean?"

Marsha fixed her gaze on the floor numbers flashing slowly past. At the fourth floor, they stepped onto a tiny landing with only one door. Marsha unlocked it and ushered Genna into a spacious apartment with high ceilings, whitewashed walls, oak floors, and dazzling sunlight.

All thoughts of Bill or Pierre or indeed any human being flew from Genna's mind as she walked across the enormous living room to a bank of floor-to-ceiling windows overlooking the rooftops of Paris.

"It's stunning!" Genna exclaimed.

Marsha burst into tears.

Genna whirled around. Instinctively, she held out her arms. Marsha rushed into them, her body trembling like a child's. For several minutes, wrenching sobs were the only sounds echoing in the elegant space. Genna thought of the very few times Becky had cried in her arms. The memory squeezed her heart with longing as she made soft cooing sounds and desperately tried to think of something helpful to say.

"Shh, come on," she whispered when finally, the sobs subsided into wet gulps. "Let's sit over there and you can tell me all about it." Genna led Marsha through an archway to a wide window seat next to the kitchen. Stainless steel appliances shone in the sunlight pouring through a skylight. A marble countertop at least three meters long extended from the window to the archway. Six people could easily sit there, sipping wine while the cook prepared a meal. It was a kitchen worthy of a chef. Genna made a Herculean effort to focus on Marsha and resisted the urge to check out the massive cutting board inlaid into the counter next to a sink as big as a bathtub.

"He's furious with me!" Marsha wailed. She let go of Genna and sat back against the window. "What am I going to do?"

Genna clucked sympathetically although she couldn't help feeling relieved that Colin might finally be out of the picture. But she knew better than to minimize Marsha's pain.

Better than most, Genna understood how it felt to have her future laid to waste.

"What happened?"

"He walked out on me! He said that if I was going to be a selfish bitch, then I didn't deserve to be in a relationship."

"He said that?"

"He's angry about the apartment. After I bought it, he wanted me to put both our names on the title."

"And?"

"I said no. And now he's gone."

"You own all this?"

"I bought it with the money I got from selling my place in New York. Colin said we should invest all of it in the apartment, and that an apartment in Paris will always be a good investment."

"The apartment's in your name only?" Genna still couldn't get her head around it.

"Yes. That's the problem. Colin wants me to make him half owner and I refused."

"Good for you!"

"What?"

"If you bought the apartment with your money, then why should he be half owner? You're not married."

"No, but we will be."

"He proposed?"

"Yes, no. I mean, he wants to, or at least he did. And now I don't know what to do."

"You do," Genna said, getting up and passing back through the wide arch to the airy living room. The apartment had been skillfully renovated to highlight the best features of its nineteenth-century roots while ensuring twenty-first-century comfort. She was itching to see the rest of the place.

"You are protecting your interests, and quite rightly," she said, turning to look at Marsha who was still sitting at the window. "Colin should realize that."

127

Marsha joined Genna in the living room. "But what if Colin's right, and I'm just being difficult?"

"You're being smart."

"And look where it's gotten me. I've got a great place to live and no one to share it with."

"Sounds like he was just having a temper tantrum." Genna remembered what Colin had been like the night she went back to Marsha's apartment to pick up a scarf. He struck her as someone capable of elevating moodiness to a performance art.

"At first I thought he was. He's gotten angry before and threatened to leave me. Sometimes, he's even left for a day or two, but this time he's been gone for five days! And I don't know where he is."

"Did he take his clothes?"

"Most of them."

"Is he still going to work, or did he go back to England?"

"I called his office, but they wouldn't put me through to him and they wouldn't say where he was. And he's not answering his phone. So, yes, he might have gone back to London. He was so mad at me, Genna. You can't imagine what he was like. I shouldn't have made him go."

"*You* didn't make him go. You stood up for yourself."

"I can't be on my own. Not now."

"Why not? You're not pregnant, are you?" Genna peered at Marsha's flat stomach.

"No!" Marsha looked so horrified that Genna had to smile. "No, nothing like that. But I'm thirty-two! How many more guys are there out there for me?"

As someone who had married at twenty-two and had a baby a year later, Genna had never experienced the agony of the ticking clock. By the time Genna was Marsha's age, Becky was in Grade 4 and Genna was starting the teaching career she'd abandoned to get married. She wished she knew what to say to comfort Marsha, but all she could think about was how gorgeous Marsha would make the apartment, with or without Colin.

Genna walked to the windows overlooking the narrow street. The building opposite was newly painted a pale gray that contrasted lusciously with a profusion of red geraniums tumbling out of window boxes. The apartment really was the most incredible find.

"Most of the time, Colin's great," Marsha was saying. "You don't know him like I do. And when he gets mad, it's because I've done something stupid. It's not his fault."

Genna winced. "Do you want him back?"

"Yes!"

"And if he comes back, will you put him on title?"

"*When* he comes back. And yes, I should. After all, we're getting married."

"I thought you said you weren't sure about that. And besides, if you're this reluctant to share ownership of the apartment with him, then maybe it's not such a great idea to marry him. Not that I'm saying you *should* sign over half the place even if you do get married. But you obviously have doubts."

"When we were in New York together, Colin was fantastic—so attentive and with that dreamy accent. But since coming to Paris, and with all this fuss about the apartment and the money, I'm not sure what to think anymore."

Genna knew exactly what to think, but with a valiant effort, she kept her mouth shut.

"If I really loved him, I wouldn't care, would I?" Marsha asked. "I'd be happy to give him everything he wants. Didn't you feel that way when you got married?"

"When Drew and I got married, neither of us had anything. We were very young."

"Yes, and I'm not so young."

"So you think you should stay with him because you're afraid you might end up alone?"

"I wouldn't be the first woman to do that."

"No, and you wouldn't be the first woman to end up out on her own with a couple of kids and a lot of unpaid bills." To Genna, the solution was clear. Marsha was the one in a position of power. All she had to do was get on with her life. And she certainly had a wonderful apartment in which to start.

"I'm sorry," Marsha said.

"For what?"

"For making such a fuss. I mean, it's probably just a misunderstanding. How about we get out of here? You must have better things to do than to sit around listening to me sniffle and whine."

"I don't mind," Genna said. "I wasn't planning to do much today except visit the Pompidou. I haven't come up with a dish to pair with it yet."

"Why don't you go there now and see if you can think of something? It's not far." Suddenly agitated, Marsha started pacing back and forth across the polished hardwood floors. The herringbone pattern looked original, but impeccably restored. Genna imagined ladies in bustles gliding across it, fans cocked, gentlemen in breeches bowing.

"What are you going to do?" Marsha's tears had dried up and her mouth was set in a determined line.

"Don't worry about me. I've got plenty to do."

"Why don't you come to the Pompidou and help me think of a dish? You know much more about modern art than I do."

"No."

Marsha strode to the door and opened it, leaving Genna no choice but to follow her to the landing. The elevator had returned to the ground floor, but Marsha didn't wait for it. She started down the narrow circular stairwell. Out on the street, Marsha gave Genna an absentminded hug and promised she'd call. As Genna watched her go, she had the feeling she was watching Marie Antoinette in modern dress make her way to the Bastille.

Genna chided herself for being overdramatic. Marsha was a smart woman. She'd figure out her priorities. Genna just hoped Colin stayed out of the picture permanently. Sighing, she turned in the opposite direction and walked along the Rue Charlot to the

Place Stravinsky and the jumbled pipes and girders of the inside-outside Pompidou Centre. Immediately before her rose the whimsical Stravinsky Fountain—a favorite of her children on their family trip to Paris. Sixteen sculptures, including a treble clef, a pair of swollen red lips, and various brightly painted amorphous shapes, rotated, swiveled, and shot water at odd angles. Genna defied anyone to stand next to Niki de Saint Phalle's extraordinary creation on a hot summer's day and not smile.

She sat on the concrete wall surrounding the fountain and waited for it to work its magic on her, to erase the feel of Marsha's body shaking in her arms. Why was Marsha wasting herself on the wrong man? She had so much energy and passion to offer the world.

Was that what she had done?

Genna shook her head. Her situation was different. The years with Drew hadn't been terrible, not by a long shot. She remembered how charmed he'd been when they'd first seen the fountain. They'd laughed with the kids at the multicolored snake slithering skyward, water spouting from its mouth. Next to it, a blue bowler hat turned in slow circles. Genna shifted her gaze to the rotating red heart, its childlike design reminding her of the art projects the kids had made when they were little.

When they'd been packing to move to the House with the View, she and Drew had laughingly agreed to ditch several boxes of the artwork and forget to tell the kids.

Their life together had been comfortable, predictable, easy.

Genna focused her attention on the massive bird man that dominated the fountain, its beaked head haloed by a six-pronged golden crown, its body painted in a crazy mix of reds and yellows, blues and greens.

The perfect dish came to her. What could be better at mirroring the color and spirit of the Stravinsky fountain than an artfully constructed fruit flan?

Slices of yellow peaches, green kiwis, and creamy white pears, glistening blueberries, and rosy-red strawberries and raspberries and cherries would be arranged in perfect spirals on top of a custard filling spread over a crunchy sugar crust, the whole creation bathed in a glaze of equal parts sherry and Cointreau.

If only she could fix Marsha's life as easily as she could put together a fruit flan, Genna thought as she left the fountain and headed for the Métro and home. The Pompidou Centre would have to wait for another day.

On the way back to her apartment, Genna stopped in at the Starbucks on the off chance she'd find Bill there. She owed him an apology. He'd done nothing to deserve her abrupt exit at the Gare Saint-Lazare the day before.

A line of customers stretched out the door. She peered over the heads to see if Bill was inside, but everyone in the place looked under thirty. The line shuffled forward toward the counter where Tyler was working efficiently to fill the orders. He saw Genna and waved.

"Dad left this morning," he said when she made it to the counter.

"But he never said anything about leaving!" Genna felt curiously bereft.

"He only decided to go last night. Coffee?"

"Large latte. How was he able to get a flight so quickly?"

"Sorry," Tyler turned back to Genna. "I wasn't clear. Dad took the train to London. He's gone to visit relatives."

"Oh."

"Three euros, please."

"Right." She handed over the money. "Do you know when he'll be back?"

Tyler shook his head and looked around her to the next customer. She had the distinct feeling that Bill had shared something with Tyler about her graceless exit. He definitely wasn't being his usually friendly self.

She picked up her latte and left the store, then walked along the Boulevard Saint-Germain to Rue Bonaparte. As she dodged the swarms of pedestrians, the incessant honking from the traffic ringing in her ears, she felt for the first time since coming to Paris that she was in the middle of a very, very large city.

Her green-and-blue land of water, trees, and mountains was so impossibly far away. Leaving it might not have been the smartest thing she'd ever done. Drew was still there. The House with the View was still there. Her life was still there if she wanted to take it back.

To take Drew back.

Genna stopped abruptly, earning an indignant *Madame!* from the man walking behind her. She moved aside and leaned against the iron palings enclosing the churchyard of Saint-Germain-des-Prés steps from her apartment.

Life would be so much simpler if she just gave up on Paris and went home. Drew was no prince, but he also wasn't a pompous ass like Colin.

Sure, he'd screwed up. Badly.

But maybe he deserved a second chance.

Did he?

She hadn't a clue.

fifteen

Lime Macarons
Jade green shells filled with marshmallow cream

Genna spent the next day virtually comatose on her hard couch.
She felt encased in concrete, too exhausted to even move her head.
Whoever said it was easy to walk away from one life and embrace
a new one had almost certainly never tried it.

Her mind cycled through a montage of past hurts, an endless
loop where she was forever the injured party. One minute, anger
wrapped iron bands around her chest, and the next, sadness
loosened the pressure only to leave her feeling even more drained.
A cocktail of grievance as toxic as rat poison spiraled through her.

Why had he done it? How could he have betrayed her? What
had *she* done to deserve it?

Nothing. She'd done nothing. They'd been happy, or at least
contented.

Genna gazed into an abyss so dark and lonely that she wished
she could go to sleep and not wake up until the past had lost any
power to hurt her.

In the end, it was food that restored her resolve. By six o'clock,
after ten straight hours on the couch, the gnawing in her stomach
compelled her to her feet. She left the apartment and walked to her
favorite Breton crêperie near Odéon where she ordered a galette—

the savory, buckwheat crêpe from Brittany. It came stuffed with andouille sausages, onion confit, and melted camembert. The place was crowded and noisy, the comforting smells reminding Genna of her French grandmother who had first instilled in her a love of food. As Genna let each bite of the galette work its magic, she felt her mood improve. What was it that her grandmother used to say?

"Food is like love, Geneviève. You must welcome it into your life and then work with it to make it good."

Genna finished her meal with a simple dessert crêpe flavored with lime and sugar accompanied by a glass of cider. Feeling comfortably full, she left the restaurant and walked to the river where she nabbed the only bench not occupied by an entwined couple.

The grand bulk of the Louvre rose above the opposite bank of the Seine, gleaming in the setting sun. The sky turned a deep, satisfying blue.

Genna gazed at the view and then down at her clasped hands — strong, capable hands she relished using to turn food into something good, something that made people happy. She let her hands fall to her sides and sat back on the bench, lifting her head and inhaling the warm spring air.

The floodlights switched on, bathing the bridges and monuments of Paris in soft gold. A couple next to her smiled and pointed.

Something inside her shifted. Just hours before, her future had felt cold and hopeless. Now, she envisioned a new future, one that glowed with the promise of fresh beginnings.

For the first time since leaving home, she realized that Drew had done her a favor.

She jumped to her feet and returned to the Quai de Conti, then dodged the crowds of tourists and locals enjoying the evening on her way to the internet place. Ten spams, another email from Drew, a reminder to renew her subscription to *Time* magazine (no point), and three newsletters from stores back home scrolled by, and then — bingo! Nestled between a personal message from the prince of an obscure African kingdom and an exhortation to sign a petition to fight climate change was an email from Becky.

Finally!

Genna opened the message and settled herself for a good read. Becky was famous in the family for her long emails.

Hi Mom

I hope you're doing well in Paris. I know how much you love the place, although I must admit I can't understand why you want to be there for so long. Were you serious when you said you'd stay until the fall? That's a long time to be away from Dad, don't you think?

Speaking of Dad, I've been over to see him at the house a few times. He's not good, Mom. He really misses you. He also told me that he's emailed you loads of times but that you haven't replied. That seems a bit mean if you don't mind me saying so.

Sighing, her good mood shattered, Genna closed the email without reading the rest of it. Once Becky got riled up, she could write a novella full of vitriol. And besides, the store was closing.

"You all right?" asked the attendant as Genna paid him. He sounded American, from the South, she guessed. Texas maybe.

Would she ever learn to keep a straight face? She might as well wear a neon sign that flashed, I'M UPSET in rainbow colors.

"I'm okay," she said as she accepted the change. "Someone back home's mad at me. You know how it is."

The young man nodded. "I hear you. My mom emails me every week to ask when I'm coming home. She wants me to go back to school and do something useful with my life."

"And what do *you* want?"

"Not to be told to do something useful with my life."

Genna laughed. "I think that's what we all want. To be left alone to make our own decisions, even if they're the wrong ones."

"For sure." He ushered her toward the door. "Have a good night."

"You, too."

She arrived home to find a note from Pierre.

Please accompany me tomorrow to the Parc de la Villette. I must show you modern Paris. I will be outside at ten.

She made herself a cup of tea and retrieved her battered guidebook. A scant half page was devoted to the Parc de la Villette, the third largest park in Paris and located in the nineteenth arrondissement in the northeast corner of the city. Bisected by the Canal St. Martin, the park housed an enormous complex of museums and entertainment venues along with a whimsical clutch of themed gardens that intrigued Genna with names such as Mirror, Dragon, Dune, and Balance. Since its creation in the 1980s, the Parc de la Villette had become a popular destination for Parisians and largely ignored by tourists.

Genna put down the guidebook and thoughtfully sipped her tea. What would Becky think if she knew her mother was spending a whole day in the company of gorgeous Pierre? Knowing Becky, she'd be incensed because Becky generally operated on only two cylinders—incensed and infuriated. But Genna couldn't really blame her daughter for taking Drew's side. She didn't know the truth and Genna wasn't about to tell her.

Her thoughts cycled back to earlier in the evening when she'd realized that maybe Drew had done her a favor. If he hadn't cheated, she'd still be back home, still living her quiet, easy, uncomplicated life.

No Pierre. No Bill Turner. No Paris.

A jolt of excitement about the next day made her smile. She resolved to enjoy herself with Pierre, and with any luck, she'd find a good dish to pair with the Parc de la Villette.

She couldn't lose sight of why she'd come to Paris.

sixteen

Toasted Walnut Macarons
Golden brown shells filled with creamy blue cheese

The next morning Pierre whisked her through quiet Sunday streets toward La Villette in the northeast corner of Paris. As he drove, they chatted about the progress she'd made with her book, a new bistro he'd discovered, and her plans for future sightseeing.

"You will meet many people who consider the Parc de la Villette an abomination," he said, "And yet every time I took my boys there when they were young, the fields and gardens were crowded. Parisians love to complain about modern Paris, and then they are the first to enjoy it."

"Like the Pompidou?"

"Precisely. I well remember the furor when they built it. You would not have believed it."

"Back home, people don't get too bothered about new buildings. I guess because that's pretty much all we have."

"Your city is young, no?"

"Very." Despite her resolve to leave the past behind, a spasm of homesickness darted through her, bleak as freezing drizzle in November. As the endless blocks of gray buildings flashed past, she thought of the dense green conifers standing guard over her backyard in West Vancouver, of the wide view from her living room of mountains and sea. It was mid-May, and the rhododendrons would be flowering all over the city. Massive blooms in magenta, purple, scarlet, and white covered bushes reaching heights of twenty feet and more, their dark, glossy leaves glowing in the spring sun. Few places on earth were as beguiling as Vancouver on a sunny day in May.

"And now I have made you sick for home?"

"Homesick. And yes, I am a little bit. May is a beautiful time of year in Vancouver when it's not raining, and even when it is. Everything is green. But tell me about the Parc de la Villette. Why do you think I'll like it?"

"I have not an idea if you will like it. It is nothing like Versailles. Many years ago, the whole area was filled with slaughterhouses."

"Delightful."

He laughed and told her about the history of the park as they drove through neighborhoods new to her. After parking next to the Canal Saint-Martin, they set off across a pedestrian bridge to the park entrance. All around them swarmed Parisian families, the children dancing ahead, excited to be out on such a beautiful day.

The sprawling park's capricious design enchanted Genna. One minute, she stood with Pierre beside a huge expanse of green teeming with soccer players, and the next they were staring at one of the many follies dotted around the park. Each one was painted fire engine red and had a clunky, half-constructed look with assorted beams jutting at odd angles that reminded Genna of Michael's Lego projects. The small, themed gardens intrigued her with their quirkiness. In the Garden of Trellises, ninety bubbling fountains erupted through eight terraces of climbing vines, while in the Garden of Islands, a black-and-white marbled path wound through oak and pine trees.

Her favorite garden was the Garden of Childhood Fears, where a walkway broadcasting eerie music crossed over a forest of blue spruce and silver birch trees. They ended their circuit of the ten gardens in the Garden of the Dragon, where children played on a giant eighty-meter dragon-shaped climbing apparatus and slide.

"Do you have a connection yet?" Pierre asked as they took advantage of a convenient bench overlooking the canal to sit and rest their feet.

"Nope."

He looked disappointed.

"It's not your fault!"

"Yes, but I remember how easily you came up with Caesar Salad at Versailles. I was hoping this place, which is dear to my heart, might also inspire you."

"Why is it dear to your heart?"

"I brought my boys here almost every weekend for many years. They never tired of the place, and I never tired of watching them."

"Where are your boys now?"

"Both are grown and gone. I do not see them much. When their mother remarried and moved to Switzerland, naturally the boys accompanied her."

"How old are they?"

"André is nineteen and Claude is seventeen. They left about five years ago. I see them sometimes in the summer, but not as often as I'd like. They forget soon about their papa."

"No, I'm sure they haven't forgotten you."

"Perhaps not. But their mama does not help much. She and I did not part as friends. She did not like that I was, as she put it, too set in my ways."

"What did she mean?"

"That I do not like making changes, that I am stuck in the past."

"Are you?"

"What is wrong with the past? I was happy when my boys were young."

"I'm sorry."

"No, it is I who should be sorry," Pierre said. "I should not have talked about my wife. We were not suited, and it was no one's fault."

Together, they watched a barge glide past on the canal. Genna's stomach growled. Pierre stared at her, horrified, and then burst out laughing.

"*Le déjeuner!* You must think me a brute! Enough of this—what is it you say? Gloom and doom? We must eat!"

"I thought you'd never ask!" Genna let him pull her up. They stood close together for a few milliseconds, and then, as if they read each other's minds, they crossed the line from potential lovers to firm friends.

Pierre Leblanc was the most handsome, suave, and gentlemanly man Genna had ever met, but when push came to shove, chemistry ruled. The air between them pulsed with comfortable, cozy ions that let them enjoy long chats in stylish bistros. But the static electricity needed to generate passion was absent, at least for Genna.

He nodded, his smile rueful—a touch regretful? Then, with a shrug worthy of Monsieur Leblanc senior, he took her arm, and they crossed the pedestrian bridge to the parking lot.

Pierre drove them around the top of Paris and south into the tangle of streets and hills of Montmartre. Genna had already paired the colorful and touristy Place du Tertre with a recipe for the crispy, chewy, and gloriously colorful macarons that took pride of place in every French patisserie. Pierre took her to a bistro far enough away from the tourists to feel authentic, but not so far away that it didn't have staggering prices.

"Still nothing for the Parc de la Villette?" Pierre asked as they tucked into their first courses—buttery bundles of crisp phyllo pastry stuffed with sautéed mushrooms, shallots, and creamy goat cheese for Genna and an endive and Roquefort salad with toasted walnuts for Pierre.

"I think it's too disparate."

He frowned at the unfamiliar word.

"Too varied, too much stuff. All those red sculptures were interesting, but they are so angular and kind of sterile. Food has warmth and curves. It's not hard and geometric."

Pierre speared a walnut and looked at it critically. "Yes, but what about the order that a chef brings to food when he wishes to serve it? Your little bundles of phyllo, for example. You do not find them in nature."

Genna took another forkful of the mushroom mixture and savored the hints of cognac and something else. She paused. *Anise.* Yes. It was an unusual combination, but it worked. A great chef successfully fused ingredients that often had no business going together. A recipe to pair with the aggressively manufactured follies in the Parc de la Villette needed to combine opposing elements.

"You are thinking." Pierre laughed. "You should see your face."

Genna shook her head. "Sorry. I was considering the relationship between the natural areas of the park and the strange angular follies. There's such a juxtaposition of the natural and the man-made."

"I believe that was the point."

"Yes, I can understand that, but how does it relate to food?"

"That is a question that you must answer."

"Or I could leave the park out of the book."

"No!" he exclaimed with mock horror that carried an undercurrent of real emotion. "You cannot leave out my favorite park where I spent so many hours with my boys."

Genna's next forkful included some of the phyllo pastry, still hot from the oven and crackling with flecks of pepper and roasted garlic. A perfect blend of crunchy and smooth exploded in her mouth. Life couldn't be all bad when filled with such moments.

"Got it!" she said so loudly that the other diners swiveled their heads to look. A few disapproving clucks echoed through the quiet restaurant.

"*Oui?*"

"A layered terrine of pork pâté with roasted red peppers and a layer or two of nuts all pressed into a perfect rectangle. When you cut the terrine into thick slices, all the layers are exposed."

"Like the structures of the park in nature."

"Exactly!" She put down her fork and grinned at Pierre. "You are an amazing inspiration, Pierre. That's the second good connection I've made, thanks to you."

"It is my pleasure."

After more than six weeks in Paris, Genna was no stranger to great bistro meals, but her lunch with Pierre certainly deserved a place on her list of the best lunches of all time, and not only because of the food. She and Pierre talked about their lives and a little about their loves. Pierre also described his flourishing law business and how he wanted to spend more time decorating his new apartment in the elegant sixteenth arrondissement across the river from the Eiffel Tower.

"I have many ideas," he said, sipping a glass of crisp Montrachet from the Côte de Beaune in Burgundy. Its almond and honey notes made a perfect complement to the plain grilled fish he'd ordered for the main course. Genna drank a divine Médoc from Bordeaux. The sommelier assured her it would easily hold its own with the rich flavors of her rabbit in mustard sauce. He was right.

"And?"

"*Malheureusement*, I do not have the eye. I think I know what I want, but I don't know how I can make it happen."

"You need someone to help you."

"I have no luck with the designers I have engaged so far. One of them wanted me to make everything in the room red."

"That would be like living in the pit of hell!"

"*Exactement*. And another, she was most insistent that I rip out my fireplace even though it is from the eighteenth century. She said that my sentimental attachment to the past was symptomatic of the—how did she say?—the enervating malaise that keeps Parisians frozen in time. Or something like that. She made me feel older than my papa."

"Sounds awful!"

"Yes, and frustrating. I am near despair that I will ever find someone who can help me."

It was rather like a successful marriage, Genna reflected, the matching of a client with a designer. Little upsets and misunderstandings were inevitable, but in the end, an essential grounding of mutual respect and acceptance should prevail.

"I'm sure you'll find someone,"

"I hope you are right." He smiled, the double meaning hanging in the air.

Genna wasn't sure where to look. Fortunately, the waiter arrived with dessert, giving her an excuse to devote all her attention to the lightest, most divine lemon mousse she ever hoped to taste on this earth.

They ended the evening with a promise to get together for another outing in a week or two.

"Thank you for a wonderful day, Pierre," she said after their parting two-cheeked kiss.

"My pleasure, Geneviève. I am happy we can be friends."

"I am too."

Back in her apartment, she began roughing out a recipe for the pork terrine with roasted red peppers and hazelnuts. As she wrote, she reflected that her life in Paris had the virtue of being *her* life in Paris. Instead of wife and mother, she was Genna the cookbook author living on the Rue Bonaparte in an apartment dominated by a hideous needlepoint reproduction of Ingres's *La Grande Odalisque*.

She looked up from her writing. The courtesan's over-the-shoulder gaze, enigmatic and yet bold, seemed to say *You've got this*.

Genna raised her cup of tea in a silent toast.

seventeen

Apple Pie Macarons
*Flavored with cinnamon and topped with marbled
caramel frosting*

Monday dawned dull and humid, another Parisian *gris* day. Genna dragged herself out of bed, stopped by Starbucks for a coffee, only to be disappointed that Tyler was off work, and then rode the Métro to French class.

To her surprise, the class was almost enjoyable. She stumbled through several sentences in a row, and once, for a fleeting second, she swore that Mademoiselle Deville smiled. It was a tight, constrained smile to be sure, but a smile, nonetheless. Genna's confidence soared.

After class, she invited everyone to a dinner party at her place in two weeks' time. They all accepted, even Mademoiselle. Helmut looked particularly gratified at the prospect of meeting Mademoiselle outside the classroom. Although his preference for her was unmistakable, it didn't appear as if he'd done anything beyond staring adoringly at her during class and then finding excuses to linger afterward for extra coaching.

Tessa and Denise were both eager to accept, especially Tessa.

Genna took her aside after class and made her promise to come early on the day of the party to help with the preparations. She also invited her for a few more cooking lessons. Tessa almost glowed.

Genna caught up with Marsha out on the street. She agreed reluctantly when Genna asked her to join her for a coffee.

"You'll come to the party, won't you?" Genna asked once they'd squeezed into an alcove by the window in their favorite café. The grayness of the day, although warm, made sitting outside too gloomy. Inside, the red velvet upholstery and polished brass would cheer up the most determined grouch.

"Yeah, I suppose." Listlessly, Marsha stirred her coffee, then took a tentative sip. Loud laughter erupted from three women at a nearby table. Marsha jumped, spilling her coffee. "American tourists! When will they learn that in Europe people keep their voices down in public? It's embarrassing."

Marsha saw Genna's surprised look and blushed. "Sorry. That wasn't kind. But I get fed up with my countrymen sometimes."

"You don't know they're Americans."

"They sound it."

"They might be Canadians."

"No, they don't have your accent."

"I don't have an accent!"

"Yeah, right, eh? You just go *ooot* on your *rooof.*" Finally, Marsha smiled. "You're as Canadian as cheddar cheese and hockey."

"Well, you couldn't look more 'Middle America' if you tried. I'll bet you were a cheerleader in high school."

"Squad captain. Colin was appalled when I told him." Like a light going out, Marsha's smile disappeared. She picked up a napkin to blot the spilled coffee.

Genna nodded toward the women, two of whom were gesturing madly for the waiter who was taking great pains to ignore them. "Listen."

Marsha obligingly leaned forward to listen. The delicate skin under her eyes was an even darker purple than it had been when

Genna saw her the week before. Now she looked as if she hadn't slept for two weeks.

"Chicago. No question."

"I'm not convinced."

"Ask them."

"All right." Genna was looking for any excuse to get Marsha smiling again. "I will." She stood and walked up to the women.

"Hi!" Genna said. "Enjoying Paris?"

"We love it! It's so French!" one woman chirped.

What did she expect? Lithuanian?

"Where are you from?" Genna asked.

"Toronto!" they chorused.

"In Canada," one of them added helpfully.

"Oh!" And before she could stop herself, Genna said, "I'm from Vancouver."

"You're kidding!"

As Genna knew they would, the women acted as if they'd never met another Canadian in their lives. She'd often noticed that when Canadians traveled, they treated every Canadian they met as their long-lost cousin fresh in from a spell on the tundra.

"Have a great trip," Genna said as she turned back to her own table. She wasn't in the mood for the inevitable conversation comparing the weather in Toronto with the weather in Vancouver. Another tendency of Canadians meeting abroad was to discuss the relative merits of the weather in their hometowns. The conversation always ended with the rueful admission that nowhere in Canada had a great climate, or even a moderately okay climate, except possibly Vancouver for the few days a year when it didn't rain. And then they'd laugh and declare they were still darn glad to be Canadian. Further investigation would also reveal that each one of them carried a miniature maple leaf secreted somewhere about their person or affixed to their luggage. No Canadian left the country without one.

It was kind of a law.

When Genna returned to her table, she found ten euros and no Marsha. She hurried out of the café and looked up and down the busy street, but Marsha was long gone. She was small and could cover a lot of ground on her former-cheerleading-squad-captain legs.

Genna regretted not asking about Colin. Had he come back yet? Had Marsha started preparing for the move? Tomorrow she'd *definitely* call Marsha and *make* her say what was going on. As her friend, Genna owed it to Marsha to interfere.

Genna set off toward the river. She had the Tour Saint-Jacques on her list, a brisk two-kilometer walk that would take her along the grand Rue de Rivoli past the Boulevard de Sébastopol in the fourth arrondissement. At least her fitness level had improved. Her thighs were stronger, and the waistbands of her skirts were loosening. Since coming to Paris, she'd made more friends than she'd had since the children were born. What with raising them and working and taking care of their lives, there had been little time for a social life.

Truth be told, she had only Nancy, who wasn't always the most reliable of friends. They'd met fifteen years ago when their sons had been in Grade 2 and she and Nancy had taken charge of the boys' Cub Scouts troop. They'd spent hours planning outings, coming up with useless craft projects for the boys to create and break, and thinking up games to promote social responsibility while keeping the boys occupied.

One of the happiest days of Genna's life was the day Michael announced that he would never—and he meant never— return to Cubs, no matter what his mother or anyone else on the planet said. She'd made a show of insisting he take responsibility for seeing things through, etc., etc., but her heart wasn't in it. Calling herself Akela and pretending she cared about all the *Jungle Book* nonsense gave her a migraine.

Genna and Nancy had remained friends over the years, even as their boys grew apart and Genna plugged along first with teaching and then with writing cookbooks. She could usually count on

Nancy to go for lunch or take a walk along the seawall when she wasn't busy with one of her boyfriends or causes.

Genna arrived sweaty and slightly out of breath at the Square de la Tour Saint-Jacques. According to her guidebook, the tower had been built between 1509 and 1523 in the Flamboyant Gothic style. Flamboyant for sure, Genna thought, as she gazed up at the masses of delicate stonework encrusting the tower from halfway up to the top where gargoyles, two for each corner, thrust into the gray Paris sky. On a *gris* day, the dull beige of the newly cleaned tower blended into the gray-white sky. Genna sat on a convenient bench and let her mind wander.

Sausages came to mind almost immediately, which wasn't surprising given the shape of the tower and that the Tour Saint-Jacques was the only remaining part of the church of Saint-Jacques-la-Boucherie. Back in the day, the wealthy butchers of nearby Les Halles had supplied the money to build the church.

Genna liked the contrast of the ornate tower with the lowly sausage, a dish perfect for an everyday dinner. She could include directions for making the actual sausage. A homemade sausage made from freshly ground meats in the cook's own kitchen and blended with a rich mix of seasonings was surely one of life's great gastronomic pleasures. It reminded her of the story she'd read about the famous philosopher Nicolas Flamel.

She pulled out her notebook and began to write.

Nicolas Flamel, the legendary 15th-century alchemist, was said to have learned how to turn lead into gold and then parlayed that knowledge into a date with immortality. He is believed to have died in 1418 at the age of 80 and buried in a tomb of his own design at the base of the Tour Saint-Jacques. But not long after his death, a grave robber in search of gold found his tomb empty, thereby lending credence to the legend that neither Flamel nor his wife, Pernelle, had died, but still wander the streets of Paris to this day. If so, they'd feel at home in the vicinity of the Tour Saint-Jacques, where you'll find a Rue Flamel and a Rue Pernelle.

Sausages made in the home kitchen are the gastronomic equivalent of the alchemical transformation of lead into gold. From the inauspicious beginnings of ground meat comes the gold of a flawlessly cooked sausage – the outside crispy, the inside exploding with flavor. In the eyes of your family, these sausages will make you immortal.

Not a bad start, she thought, as she closed her notebook. She glanced at her watch. Almost four o'clock—time to get home and start cooking for Monsieur's arrival at seven for what had become his twice-weekly feed. She looked forward to their dinners together. Unlike her shifting relationships with the men popping up all over her life, not to mention the relationship with the man she'd left behind, her relationship with Monsieur Leblanc was refreshingly uncomplicated.

She cooked, he delivered his gastronomic verdict, and they both drank copious amounts of wine.

At Le Châtelet Métro, Genna caught the Line 4 direct to Saint-Germain-des-Prés. She would have liked to test her Tour Saint-Jacques sausage recipe on Monsieur, but before she made the recipe, she'd need to buy a good meat grinder that included an attachment for stuffing sausages. She did a quick mental inventory of the food in her fridge and came up blank. Then she remembered Monsieur mentioning how much he enjoyed fish. She continued to the Rue Jacob to find the *poissonerie* on Rue de Seine. Stacks of fish from all over Europe and beyond glistened on mounds of crushed ice. She chose two firm fillets of tuna. Fresh tuna, pressed in cracked pepper and seared so the insides shimmered a delicate pink, would be a real treat for Monsieur. She doubted his parsimonious habits allowed him to spend double-digit euros on the main course.

Her own habits could use a bit of parsimony, she reflected, as she paid for the fish and tried not to think about her dwindling bank account. If only Drew would sell the house. But so far, nothing. The realtor had even threatened to stop representing the property. Every prospective buyer he brought left in a hurry, trailing sawdust from their shoes.

Genna made it home with an hour to spare before Monsieur lumbered up the stairs, his taste buds on high alert. She prepared a simple spinach salad with sliced pears and black Moroccan olives, then set out two plates with homemade crackers and generous slices of the Parc de la Villette pork terrine with roasted red peppers and hazelnuts. She knew Monsieur was fond of pâté and had strong opinions regarding how it should be made. His dear wife, Collette, had made the best pâté in Paris, and hence the world. Genna looked forward to his verdict on her terrine. She didn't expect to reach the heights of Collette, but she held out hope for Monsieur's ultimate commendation—a gruff nod and a grudging "*Bon*."

"You get better," he said after finishing his last forkful of apple tart flavored with cinnamon. He leaned back in his chair and surveyed his clean plate. "*Les patates*. What did you do?"

"I added crème fraîche."

"Humph. *Pas mal*."

"More wine?" She reached for the chilled bottle of Chardonnay she'd picked to go with the tuna.

"*Bien sûr*."

They drank in easy silence, both happily full.

"Yesterday, you spend the day with Pierre, *non*?"

"*Ah, oui*. He took me to the Parc de la Villette."

"Pfftt. I do not like. But Pierre, he . . ." He stopped, his English failing him.

"He used to take his boys there," she said. "He told me."

"*Oui. C'est dommage. Sa femme* . . ." He shrugged. His wife.

"*Je comprends*," Genna said. I understand.

"*C'est la même chose pour vous?*" Is it the same for you?

Genna shook her head. Was it the same for her? Pierre had said that he and his wife were not friends. For years, she'd considered

Drew her best friend. She took a hasty sip of wine, hoping Monsieur hadn't noticed her bright eyes.

"Do you see the boys?" she asked. *"Les garçons?"* His grandsons.

"Non."

"C'est dommage."

"Oui."

Silence descended again as Genna contemplated the vagaries of relationships that severed children from their *grand-père*. What harm was there in Monsieur? Sure, he didn't have the best personal hygiene habits in the world — or any hygiene habits — but he had a heart broken by the death of his dear Collette. He didn't deserve to have his grandchildren kept from him. Genna knew Pierre was an only child and that his children were Monsieur's sole connection to the next generation.

"Pierre," he began.

"Oui?"

"Il est solitaire." He is lonely. Monsieur looked sharply at Genna, his black eyes undimmed by several glasses of Chardonnay. *"Vous savez?"* You know?

"Oui, je sais," she said. How was she to tell his father that she wasn't the woman to make Pierre less lonely? *"Il est mon ami."* He is my friend.

"Ah." Monsieur sighed. *"C'est dommage."*

He drained his glass and pushed himself away from the table. She joined him at the door as he prepared to leave. Normally, he stuck one hand out for her to shake. This time, he clasped her to his concave chest and bestowed a vigorous kiss first on one cheek and then on the other.

"Bonne nuit, ma petite."

A lump rose in her throat as he detached himself and turned to leave. Her own father had died five years ago. Monsieur was an unlikely replacement, but what did that matter? It wasn't as if she got to be a petite anything these days.

She wasn't going to knock it.

eighteen

Roasted Fig Macarons
Tinged purple and drizzled with alfalfa honey

The next morning, Genna walked across the river to the Louvre and treated herself to a few hours wandering through the exhibits of Greek, Roman, and Etruscan artifacts in the Sully wing. She adored the vast stretches of the Louvre where few tourists ventured. While the Denon Wing, home of the *Mona Lisa*, heaved with frantic tour groups intent on checking Mona off their list of must-sees, most of the rest of the Louvre was nearly empty.

She trailed past glass cases brimming with cooking pots and spear tips, wrought gold bracelets and bronze helmets. Her attention was arrested by a roughly hewn terra-cotta piece showing a row of figures seated at a bench, kneading what appeared to be dough. Thanks to her progress in French class, she easily deciphered the description. The object represented bakers making bread. The preparation of food was rarely represented in art, and almost never in the art of antiquity. Genna tried to imagine the artisan who had sculpted the little piece and for what reason. It was neither well-formed nor beautiful. A child with Plasticine could have done better. But at over 2,500 years old, the piece was remarkable.

No French meal was complete without bread. In keeping with the spirit of the humble row of bakers, she decided to pair the Greek and Roman Antiquities displays at the Louvre with a heavy country loaf made from stone-ground wheat and studded with walnuts and figs, bread made for mopping up a thick stew on a frosty night.

She walked out of the Louvre and into the sunny central courtyard. She skirted the Place de la Concorde, on high alert for speeding Citröens, and descended to the Tuileries, where she found a metal chair alongside a lavishly planted flower bed. She sat, closed her eyes, and sighed with pleasure.

She thought of Marsha, so young and so full of potential, and yet torn to shreds by her fear of being alone. And Pierre! He was a kind man who deserved love. Life was not always fair.

Genna's eyes flew open. Of course! Why hadn't she realized it before? Marsha and Pierre had to meet. Marsha was the perfect person to decorate Pierre's new apartment. And Marsha deserved someone so much better than Colin.

She barely got her phone to her ear after dialing before Marsha answered.

"I'm sorry!"

"It's Genna. And you don't need to apologize to me."

Silence.

"Marsha?"

"I can't talk right now."

"Are you okay?"

"Yes." Marsha said the word precisely, as if confirming a reservation or responding to a survey.

"You don't sound okay."

"I'm fine, Genna." Her voice grew stronger. "We'll talk later. Colin's back."

Merde.

"Is that good?" Genna asked.

"Of course! I'm ecstatic."

She didn't sound ecstatic. She sounded like she was battling a particularly virulent sinus infection. "Where are you?"

"At home."

"I can be there in twenty minutes. Will you wait for me?"

"No, Genna, I can't. Colin and I are going to see the lawyer." Before Genna could say anything, Marsha plowed forward, her words tumbling over themselves. "Forget what I said about Colin, I got it all wrong. He left for a business trip to England and I got all mixed up and thought he was leaving me."

Marsha trilled a laugh that was as authentic as a plastic Eiffel Tower key chain.

"You said he'd taken most of his clothes."

"I was exaggerating. But everything's perfect now. We've set a date for the wedding."

Oh. Was Genna supposed to congratulate her? Where in the etiquette books is advice on how to respond to news that a friend is marrying a jerk, especially after holding said friend's hand a week ago while she sobbed her heart out?

"Why did you say you were sorry when you answered the phone?" Genna asked. "What's happening, Marsha?"

The silence lasted so long that Genna was sure she'd lost her.

"Marsha?"

"I'm here. But I should go. Colin might call."

"Colin can call back. When are you meeting the lawyer?"

"Four o'clock."

The fact Marsha was still talking boded well. Genna pressed her advantage.

"Remember when you promised to lend me some chairs?"

"For the party?"

"Yes. I know it's two weeks away, but can I come and get them now? It's only 2:30." Genna held her breath, waiting for another excuse.

More silence, and then "Okay."

"Great!" Before Marsha had a chance to change her mind, Genna hung up, then set off for the Place de la Concorde, dodging the phalanxes of tourists desperate to find a place to rest their aching feet after the rigors of the Louvre. A passing taxi responded to her wave, swerving across two lanes of traffic, and slamming to a halt next to her. She gave the driver Marsha's address and settled into the back seat.

She stared out the window at the jumble of traffic and rushing people that made Paris so entertaining. Every nationality in the world streamed past—teens on a school field trip, a gaggle of Japanese tourists wearing identical hats, women in hijabs, old men in flat caps, stately men dressed in flowing African robes, dark-skinned men with phones clamped to their ears, sour-faced deliverymen, and tall, thin Parisian girls leaning back ever so slightly so their angular hips led each step. Their faces were masks of sophisticated unconcern—pouting, sharp cheekbones, flawless makeup, scarves artfully draped.

Back home, the chance of seeing women on the street who looked ready to model the latest creations by Dior or Saint Laurent was slim. Here, even the older women looked as if they'd stepped out of one of the fashion houses, either as models themselves or as customers. French women had a special air about them that was impossible to imitate. They appeared sure of their right to exist in the world and took their beauty for granted even as they took careful pains to enhance it.

The only sloppy women Genna saw on the streets of Paris were tourists.

The taxi stopped at a traffic light. Crossing the street in front of them was a perfect Parisian family. Both *Maman* and Papa were in their early thirties and had given great consideration to how they presented themselves to the world as parents. The baby rested serenely in an enormous pram shaded by a glacially white lace parasol. *Maman* wore tight black jeans, a short leather jacket in a rich shade of aubergine, a nipped-in pale pink silk top that showed plenty of breastfeeding cleavage, and knee-high boots with three-inch heels. Her hair was swept up off her face in a twist of blonde highlights; her eyes bore witness to a thorough but tasteful session with an expensive brand of eye makeup; her lips were formed into a pout glistening with the perfect amount of gloss. She looked like she'd never known a moment's distress since popping out her adorable offspring. Genna saw no evidence of spit-up on her jacket lapel, no dark circles, no saggy bits. She was toned, sleek, and dazzling.

Almost as dazzling as her husband.

He leaned forward across the pram and adjusted the coverlet, smoothing it over his gurgling child. His hair was expertly cut and styled short, but not too short, coiffed but not effeminate. Two hundred years ago, his ancestors would have been resplendent in powdered wigs, satins, and lace. He wore a tight ocean-blue sweater over a striped shirt, the tails of which peeked fashionably below the sweater's hem. Jeans faded to a perfect blue to match his sweater, topped casual loafers that screamed Gucci.

The light changed and the gorgeous family was soon lost in the crowds surging toward the Pont des Arts. Genna wondered if they were headed to the Louvre. Perhaps wee Monique or Michelle or Mimì was about to enjoy her first exposure to great art. How wonderful to bring up a child in this city! She pictured ten-year-olds comparing Raphael's composition to the figure modeling in a painting by Rubens.

As the taxi crossed the river and turned east toward Marsha's apartment, Genna's butterflies—or rather, *papillons*—reasserted themselves. In either language, the beating wings brushed the lining of her stomach, again leading her to question what she thought she was doing.

Marsha greeted Genna at the door, wearing short orange shorts and a stretchy purple top.

"Come on in. Colin just called. He'll be here any moment. I have to get changed."

She turned and disappeared into the bedroom, leaving Genna to find her own way to the compact living area. It was the first time Genna had been in Marsha's living room and she was charmed by its understated elegance. Genna could live a thousand years and never have half the decorating smarts that Marsha had in her little finger. Tall, narrow windows overlooked a tiny, cobbled street. Even on a sunny day, the room received little sunlight. It should have looked dreary, but Marsha had transformed it into a cozy space that radiated its own light from the artful combination of what looked like twenty shades of white and pale yellow. Where the bedroom had been a Byzantine mix of richly textured jewel tones, the living room was pure light that was as cheerful and welcoming as a summer dawn.

Genna had to convince Marsha to meet with Pierre.

"Here you go!" Marsha's voice was bright again. She stood at the door, looking cool in white linen trousers and a coral blouse that complemented her masses of dark hair. In each hand she held a folding chair. "They're not terribly comfortable, but I'm sure no one will mind for an evening. Will two be enough?"

"Better make it four."

"Who else are you planning to invite?"

"I'm not sure, but I'm one of those hostesses who likes to overprepare. Those chairs look light. I think I can manage four in the taxi if you have them."

"I have them!" She disappeared down the hall. Genna returned to contemplating the living room. She couldn't wait to see what Marsha would do with her new apartment if she was able to accomplish so much with such an unpromising space.

"Thanks!" Genna said when Marsha re-emerged with two more chairs. "When are you moving?"

"I'll start packing in the next few days. We're moving on the fifteenth."

"And the wedding?" Genna hated to ask, but to not ask would look like she didn't care. And she did care. Very much.

"September fifth. Colin wants us to get married in England so all his friends and family can be there."

"What about your family? Will your parents come over?"

"I'm not sure. They haven't said, but probably not. My dad isn't well and my mom won't want to leave him."

"Even to come to your wedding?"

"Mom will be disappointed, but she'll understand." Marsha moved away from the door, clearly anxious for Genna to leave. "Do you need help with the chairs?"

"I'll be fine." Genna rose from the couch and followed Marsha down the hall. She knew she should just take the chairs and go, but she couldn't help herself.

"Marsha, are you sure you should put Colin on the title to the apartment? You know, it might be hard to get your money out if something happens between you."

"Nothing's going to happen between us," Marsha snapped. "Colin loves me."

"I'm sure he does, but it makes sense to protect yourself."

"I don't need to *protect* myself from Colin. He'll be my husband in three months."

"Who's your lawyer?"

"Someone Colin knows who does the legal work for his firm. Colin says he knows what he's doing."

"Yes, but will he represent your interests or only Colin's?"

"Both, of course."

Genna edged further out on a treacherous limb. "Marsha, would you consider postponing the meeting for a few days?"

"Why would I want to do that?"

"You need a lawyer who will take care of *your* interests."

"Colin's taking care of my interests. He'd be livid if I postponed the meeting."

"I could ask Pierre."

"*Your* Pierre?"

"He's hardly my Pierre, but, yes, I told you about him yesterday. He's a lawyer and I'm sure he wouldn't mind talking to you. Even if he doesn't do real estate work, he's bound to know someone who does. Marsha, it's too much money to fool around with. You know I'm right."

"But Colin says I'm being immature and that if I really cared for him, I wouldn't have made such a fuss about the money."

"What do *you* think?"

"I wish we'd never bought the apartment in the first place." Marsha shook her head. "I mean, this place isn't perfect, but it's cozy enough. I'd much rather spend my time getting back to work."

"As you should. I also wanted to tell you that Pierre is looking for a designer for his new apartment. You two would get along beautifully."

"Oh, well, I probably shouldn't be thinking about taking on new work."

"You just said you wanted to get back to work."

"Did I? Sorry. Colin says I shouldn't worry about working, that I'll have my hands full organizing the move. He has a bunch of business trips over the summer and so he won't be able to help much. And besides, the design world is super competitive, especially in Paris. I don't have a client base yet and Colin says it would be too stressful for me."

If Genna heard Marsha say "Colin says" one more time, she was likely to vomit all over the twenty-toned living room. That Marsha had talent as a designer was apparent to anyone with eyes, except Colin. Genna wished there were something she could bite to prevent herself from screaming.

Colin's arm would work well.

And with that image foremost in her mind, she heard the unmistakable British tones of the man himself on the landing outside the door.

"Marsha! Open the damn door. I've got my arms full."

Genna caught Marsha's arm as she started for the door. "Please, just put him off for today. I'll say you have to help me and that you can't get out of it. You *have* to talk to Pierre."

Marsha stared at Genna, her eyes huge with either fear or anger. Genna couldn't tell which. Then, to her relief, Marsha nodded. While she ran to the door to open it, Genna searched her brain for a plausible reason why Marsha should go with her and skip the lawyer's meeting with Colin.

"Genna's here!" Marsha said as Colin shoved himself through the door, his laptop case narrowly missing Marsha's shoulder as he swung around to see Genna.

"Hello, Colin."

He dumped the case at Marsha's feet and pushed past Genna into the living room. "We need to get going," he said over his shoulder. "Monsieur Molyneux won't appreciate being kept waiting."

"I just phoned Monsieur Molyneux and canceled our appointment," Marsha said.

She lied with such clarity and conviction that she almost convinced Genna.

"You did what?" Colin popped back into the hall, a scowl creasing his smooth forehead. "But he squeezed us in today as a special favor to me because I promised to look at designs for his dining room. You can't be serious."

"He was very understanding," Marsha said. "I told him something urgent had come up and that we'd reschedule."

Genna could see Colin was making a huge effort to remain calm. She sensed her presence in the apartment was the only thing standing between Marsha and a full-blown temper tantrum.

"I need Marsha to help me this afternoon," Genna said.

"*Une crise de cuisine?*"

"Something like that."

"I'll tell you all about it later," Marsha said. She stood on tiptoe and kissed Colin's smoothly shaven cheek, then grabbed her purse from the hall table.

"But I left work early for this meeting," he sputtered.

"I know, darling, and I'm sorry, but there's nothing I can do. Monsieur Molyneux was so nice. He said to book another appointment with him in a few weeks when he gets back from vacation."

Genna almost laughed out loud at the expression on Colin's face.

"I have to go with Genna now, but I can meet you at Le Jèmrod for dinner. I'll call." She turned to Genna and hissed. "Grab the chairs."

Genna picked up the chairs and followed Marsha down the stairs to the ground floor and out onto the street.

"What was all that about?" she asked when minutes later they were in a taxi heading for Genna's apartment.

"Don't ask me questions yet," Marsha said as she punched numbers into her phone. *"Allô? Monsieur Molyneux, s'il vous plaît. Oui. J'attends. Merci."* She glanced sideways at Genna and grinned. "I've got to cancel the appointment with the lawyer before Colin takes it into his head to phone him."

"Monsieur Molyneux? C'est Marsha Renfrew. Oui." She winked at Genna and then switched to English. "I am extremely sorry, monsieur, but Colin and I have to cancel our meeting today." She nodded. "Yes, that's right. Something has come up." Another pause. "Yes, I understand you are leaving for vacation in a few days. No, please don't worry about it. I will make another appointment with your secretary for after you return. *Merci, monsieur. Adieu.*"

"Nice work."

"Colin is going to kill me."

"I doubt that."

"But he'll be furious."

"He'll get over it."

"And if he doesn't?"

"Then you'll have to come up with another lie. You're obviously very good at it." The two women burst out laughing, causing the taxi driver to swear as he swerved to avoid an oncoming truck.

"Désolée!" they chorused and then broke into another fit of laughter.

"Do you do that often?" Genna asked when she stopped laughing.

"Do what?"

"Lie so convincingly to Colin. I almost believed you myself."

"I don't like to think of it as lying, exactly."

"What would you call it?"

"Survival? Sometimes it's easier to lie than to argue."

Funnily enough, Genna did understand what she meant. In her years with Drew, she'd been known to stoop to the odd lie herself in the interest of keeping the peace. Was there such a thing as a completely honest relationship?

"I'll call Pierre. He might be able to meet us at Les Deux Magots."

"I shouldn't have done it," Marsha fretted, her bravado suddenly dissipating like a flock of startled pigeons. "I should call Monsieur Molyneux back. What if Colin takes off?"

Then you'd be well rid of him, Genna thought, but didn't say.

"You made the right decision back there. And all you're doing is delaying things for a few weeks. If Colin can't handle that, then too bad."

"Are you sure?"

"Marsha! You've said yourself that lying to Colin isn't new for you. If you're fine with that, then give it a rest."

"Okay." Her voice sounded small but firm. Even so, Genna kept an eye on Marsha's phone. If necessary, she'd dash it from her hand and out the open window to be crushed beneath the wheels of another speeding Citroën. Good thing there were so many of them in Paris.

Genna pulled out her own phone and dialed Pierre's number. He answered on the third ring. *"Allo, ici Pierre."*

"Hi, Pierre. It's Genna."

There was the briefest of pauses and then Genna could swear she heard him smile, if such a thing were possible.

"Ah, Geneviève. I am glad to hear from you. Have you had a pleasant week?"

"Very pleasant. And you?"

"Malheureusement, busy," he said. "Work — it is too much."

"I was wondering if you would do me a favor."

"But of course. Anything."

"I have a friend who needs a lawyer to represent her interests in the purchase of an apartment. Do you know anyone I could call?"

"I can meet with her if you wish."

"That would be amazing. Would you have time to meet us at Les Deux Magots?"

"I would be delighted. Shall we say in an hour"

"Perfect. And thank you, Pierre. I appreciate it."

"I am honored to help."

"He'll meet us in an hour," she said to Marsha.

"I should have gone along with Colin," Marsha said. "He'll never agree to me having my own lawyer. He'll see it as a betrayal."

"And that doesn't worry you?"

"I don't know. Should it?"

"It's up to you, but if you want my opinion . . ."

Marsha turned her head away to stare out the window. The taxi driver shot across the Pont Notre-Dame and on to the Île de la Cité, then turned right and drove alongside the Seine. He reached the end of the island and turned left to cross the Pont Neuf. Dense traffic brought the taxi to a stop. Marsha's hand rested on the door handle and for a moment Genna was worried she'd open it and run through the traffic to the other side of the street and then catch a taxi back to her apartment.

"Marsha?"

The taxi inched forward.

"Doesn't every relationship involve some kind of compromise?" Marsha asked, still not looking at Genna.

"It does, but . . ."

Finally, Marsha turned, her eyes glistening. "How do you *know*, Genna?"

"Know what?"

"That you've done the right thing? That you've made the best decision?"

The taxi rolled forward several more feet, and then the driver put it in gear and sped toward the turnoff to the Quai di Conti.

"That's the sixty-four-thousand-dollar question, as my dad used to say," Genna said, relaxing as Marsha removed her hand from the door handle and settled back in her seat.

"What do you mean?"

"You can't ever really know," Genna said. "All you can do is trust that your heart isn't steering you wrong."

"My heart?" The bitterness in Marsha's voice didn't sound right coming from a woman who professed herself in love.

To their right, the long expanse of the Louvre sped past as they headed west toward Rue Bonaparte. Genna thought about how much she'd enjoyed her time at the Louvre a few days earlier. She loved being free to wander wherever she wished, to stop and enjoy whatever exhibit caught her fancy.

She hadn't been lonely for a second.

nineteen

Raspberry Macarons
Ruby red with white chocolate filling

The taxi dropped them off in front of Genna's apartment. They hauled the chairs up the five flights and stashed them in a cupboard in the bedroom. Marsha peered at the peeling wallpaper and threadbare bedspread.

"I know," Genna said. "It's pretty grim."

"It has a lot of potential. Look at the beautiful old windows, and you have wonderful high ceilings. You could take down these horrible green curtains and put up something light and gauzy. And this floor is probably the original. See the grain? A bit of work with a sander would bring it up."

"It's a rental, Marsha."

"I should have a chat with your Monsieur Leblanc. With a little effort, he could make this apartment high-end."

"I can barely afford the rent now, and Monsieur reduced it because I said I'd stay six months. I think he only rented to me because I'm staying a long time. This apartment belonged to Monsieur's *grand-mère*. He lived here as a boy during the war."

"Hmmm." Genna could tell Marsha wasn't listening. Instead, she was scratching at the wallpaper with one sharp fingernail.

"Lots of layers here. But if you stripped it all off, I'll bet you'd get to the original wall. Whitewashing would do wonders."

"No whitewashing, Marsha."

"Sorry? Oh, right." She pulled her gaze away from the wallpaper and turned to face Genna. "Should we go meet your Pierre now?"

"He's not my Pierre."

"So you keep saying. But are you sure? He sounds wonderful."

"He is wonderful."

"But?"

"We're friends."

"No chance of anything else?"

"Nope." Genna led the way out of the bedroom.

"You'd rather be alone?" Marsha asked as she followed Genna to the landing and waited while she locked the door, then started down the spiral staircase.

"At the moment, yes," Genna said as they rounded the first spiral, amused by how Marsha's question so closely mirrored what she'd been thinking about in the taxi. She glanced up at Marsha. "I'm not looking for the hassles of a new relationship. At least not with Pierre."

"Aha! I knew it. You're thinking about that Aussie guy, aren't you? Tyler's dad?"

Genna shrugged in unconscious imitation of Monsieur. "It won't do me much good. He's taken off to England."

"But he's coming back, right?"

"I don't know. And even if he does, I'm not sure he'll want to see me."

"Why not?"

"Remember I told you I kind of gave him the cold shoulder the other day after we went to Giverny?"

"Oh? Sorry. I don't remember. Why did you give him the cold shoulder?"

"I guess I got nervous."

Was that the reason?

167

They reached the ground floor and set off across the cobbled courtyard and into the darkness of the entrance area. Genna groped for the bolt that secured the heavy old door, slid it open, and pushed it into the sunlight. They stepped from the quiet of the courtyard into the jangle of Rue Bonaparte.

"You might find this hard to believe, but I'm not looking for romance," Genna said, more to convince herself than Marsha.

"Everyone's looking for romance."

"Is that what you have with Colin? Romance?"

Marsha flounced across Rue Bonaparte ahead of Genna and snagged an outside table at Les Deux Magots.

Genna followed in her wake, angry with herself for upsetting Marsha again. But, honestly, who was Marsha to make pronouncements about romance when she was planning to pledge her troth to the world's most pretentious arse?

"Is Pierre here yet??" Marsha asked.

"I don't see him." Genna lowered herself into the chair next to Marsha and signaled the waiter. He ignored her, but glided over when Marsha raised one finger.

"*Oui?*"

"Wine?"

Genna nodded. "Please."

Marsha ordered two glasses of red wine in rapid French before turning on Genna.

"You don't think much of Colin, do you?"

Genna had two choices — lie and say he was charming and that whatever Marsha wanted was fine by her, or tell the truth. Fortunately, she was saved from doing either by the arrival of Pierre.

"*Bonjour, Geneviève!*" He stooped to kiss her on both cheeks and then turned to Marsha. "And this must be your beautiful friend." He inclined his head.

"Marsha Renfrew. Please, sit down."

With one elegant hand, Pierre slotted a chair into the narrow space between the edge of the round table and the street. He gazed at Marsha with frank Gallic admiration. Although a shade too old for her, he was certainly a better bet than Colin.

No, Genna would *not* stoop to matchmaking. That was *so* beneath her.

"Marsha is in need of legal advice," she said.

"As you told me on the phone. But, please, tell me what is going on."

Marsha was not able to resist Pierre's charms for long. He had a way of making whomever he spoke to feel special, particularly if they were female. Genna watched with amusement as he turned his charm on Marsha. She imagined he rarely lost a case.

Marsha told him about the apartment and the agreement to make Colin half owner. Pierre listened gravely, only occasionally taking a sip of wine and asking a question.

Meanwhile, Genna occupied herself by enjoying the view of the Church of Saint-Germain-des-Prés across the street. She'd read that a church had existed on the site for over 1500 years. The current version dated from the twelfth century, but with numerous changes, including the distinctive spire added in the nineteenth century.

Genna glanced at Marsha and Pierre. They'd switched to French. Marsha looked more relaxed than Genna had seen her in weeks. Whatever Pierre was saying to her—and his French was far too fast for Genna—was definitely cheering Marsha up and hopefully encouraging her to rethink her allegiance to Colin.

Genna turned her attention back to the church and focused on coming up with an appropriate recipe. Most of the church was in the Romanesque style with round arches and thick columns. She needed something heavy and traditional, yet flavorful and rich. The original church hosted the corpses of the Merovingian Kings and, allegedly, the heart of René Descartes, the French philosopher.

Heart, antiquity, solidity, round.

The words swirled around in Genna's head, bumping into ingredients as she searched for connections.

"French onion soup!"

Pierre broke off his conversation with Marsha, smiling at Genna's interjection. Marsha rolled her eyes, but also smiled.

"*Absolument*," he said. "You cannot leave out France's national soup! But with what site?"

Genna nodded toward the church.

"Ah! L'abbaye de Saint-Germain-des-Prés." Pierre regarded it, eyes narrowed, for several seconds. "*Bon.*"

Genna beamed. Pierre was so much his father's son. "Thanks. What have you two been talking about? Your French is too fast for me."

"Pierre has been telling me about his apartment," Marsha said. "He would like me to see it."

"Marsha has given me some excellent ideas already," Pierre said. "I think I've finally found someone I can work with."

Genna knew it! In a flash, her mind fast-forwarded to Marsha surrounded by wallpaper books and fabric samples in Pierre's apartment as she effortlessly transformed it into an oasis of sophisticated calm.

"Well, we'll see," Marsha said.

"See what?" The voice was unmistakable.

In unison, the three of them looked up to see the man who had spoken standing in front of them on the sidewalk.

Merde.

* * *

The next morning, Genna described the scene for Nancy.

```
Hi Nancy

Remember me telling you about Marsha and her
awful boyfriend, Colin? Well, today things came
to a head. Colin showed up while Marsha and I
were talking with Pierre at a café. You should
have seen the look on his face! If this had been
the 18th century, he'd have challenged Pierre
to a duel.
```

As it was, he just nodded coldly at Pierre when I introduced them and then waited for Marsha to get up and go with him. I was hoping she'd stay put, but no such luck. She turned beet red and walked off with Colin without even saying goodbye. I felt embarrassed for her, but Pierre didn't seem to mind. He just shrugged, so like his father, and ordered more wine.

We had dinner together at a place over near the Eiffel Tower and then went up the tower to see the lights (amazing, btw). I wish I knew how Marsha's evening turned out. She's a different person around Colin. It's painful to watch.

Drew still emails me, but I don't read them. If he sells the house, the agent will let me know.

What's up with you? How's your love life?

Write soon. As you can see, I've changed my email address, so please use this one from now on. I'm tired of emptying my inbox of Drew's emails. I'll get back in touch with him when I'm ready.

If I'm ever ready!

Love Genna

Genna emerged from the internet café into a late spring morning vibrating with life. A babble of languages—French, English, Arabic, German, Japanese, and many more she didn't recognize filled the air.

She stopped in front of a patisserie to admire the neat rows of macarons and other confections, from luscious tarts to tall wedges of multi-tiered cakes to eclairs, mousses, custards, cookies, and dozens more confections she didn't even have names for. How could so much beauty be packed into so small a space?

Genna turned sideways to check her reflection in the window, then shrugged and entered the shop. She emerged several minutes later with a white box containing a raspberry tart, a slice of millefeuille gateau, a small chocolate cheesecake, and three macarons.

When in Paris . . .

twenty

Blueberry Macarons
Deep indigo with citrus buttercream

A few days later, Genna stopped by the Starbucks on her way to Sainte-Chapelle. She told herself she wanted to say hello to Tyler, but the truth was she wanted to find out if Bill had returned from England. She'd enjoyed his company during their day at Giverny and especially liked how he made her laugh. She also owed him an apology.

He hadn't deserved her running out on him at the Gare Saint-Lazare. They were adults and they could be friends. It wasn't as if she'd be following Bill to Australia and adding recipes for fried platypus and broiled kangaroo steaks to her cookbooks. On the other hand, kangaroo steaks were apparently both lean and tasty.

It must be all that hopping.

Genna smiled to herself. They were just two people on their own in Paris. Friends. No strings.

But when she entered the Starbucks and spied Bill overflowing a deep leather chair in the middle of the café, she was taken aback by the violent flip-flop in her stomach.

She glanced over at Tyler who waved. She waved back and then turned to leave. Bill was reading the newspaper and had not yet seen her.

"Dad!"

Bill looked up, startled, and then seeing Genna, smiled warily. "Well, hello there!"

"You're back," she said, her voice higher than normal.

"As you see."

"How was England?" She sat down quickly, not trusting her legs to keep her upright.

What was going on?

"It was wet."

"The weather here's been wonderful. Sunny and dry."

The weather? They were talking about the weather?

"I heard." With large hands, he deftly folded his paper. A cascade of croissant crumbs drifted down the front of his mulberry-colored shirt.

Genna's stomach did another quick sashay. Was he glad to see her or still annoyed that she'd abandoned him after the Giverny trip?

"Did you visit relatives?"

"My sister. She lives up in Durham. In the north."

"Yes, I know Durham. Lovely cathedral."

Her lines were getting inaner by the second.

"It is at that." He continued to stare at Genna, but his mouth was starting to soften, and his eyes looked more welcoming.

"I'm off to Sainte-Chapelle today," she said.

"Yes?"

"Do you want to come with me?" The words tumbled out like she was fourteen and asking a boy to the school dance.

"Well, Genna," he said, and then paused as he appeared to collect his thoughts. Her heart thumped. Here comes the brush-off. And she had only herself to blame. He had every right to be angry with her.

"I'd actually love nothing better than to come with you."

"Really?"

"Of course. I've been sitting here hoping you'd show up. Tyler said you usually come in around now."

"You were waiting for me?"

"Yep." He pawed ineffectually at the croissant crumbs. "Why should that surprise you?"

"I just thought, well . . ."

He leaned forward and took one of her hands in a two-handed grip. "That's your trouble, Genna. You think too much." He stood and pulled her up. "Let's get out into the sunshine. Back home, I'm used to being on my feet all day long. Since coming to Paris, I've spent most of my time sitting on my duff, reading the paper. I've had enough of world politics, I can tell you."

"Why don't you do some sightseeing?" Genna asked as he ushered her to the door and out into the street.

"It's no fun alone."

He came alongside her, and at the next light, they crossed the Boulevard Saint-Germain and headed into the tangled warren of little streets that wound through the Left Bank toward the Seine.

They walked in silence, Genna not sure what to say next, and Bill looking thoughtful. She wondered if he was already regretting coming with her.

"My Marjorie loved Paris," he said suddenly.

"Oh! Did she visit often?"

"Naw, never. She wanted to, but the business took so much time, and then there were the kids. But Marjorie read books about Paris and brought home travel videos from the library. We promised ourselves that when the last one left the nest, we'd go abroad. But when the time came, it was too late."

"I'm sorry. You must miss her terribly."

"She was everything in the world to me," he said, his deep voice cracking. "I almost went mad those months after she passed. Tyler was dead worried."

They turned right into a narrow street lined with shops brimming with art, antiques, and designer clothes. Genna wondered who shopped there, or, more accurately, who could afford to shop there. What would Marjorie Turner have made of it?

"How did you get through it?" she asked.

"Time. Just plain old time. Every day was a struggle, but as the months went on, things slowly got easier. Marjorie would have hated to see me the way I was after she was gone. That was her worst fear, you know."

"What do you mean?"

"That I'd fall apart. She knew how much I depended on her. People who knew us thought I was the one with everything figured out." He shook his head. "But it was all my Marjorie. If it hadn't been for her, I'd still be selling cherries by the roadside back on the farm. She gave me the kick in the pants I needed to launch the business, and after it started growing, she made sure I got the right people on board. Marjorie chose every one of the branch sites."

"Living without her must be hard. I can't imagine."

Bill looked sideways at her. His pace slackened as they came to a corner and waited side by side for the cars to pass. "You've had a loss too."

"Yes, but mine was voluntary."

"That doesn't make it any easier to bear."

"I suppose not." She lapsed back into silence.

Bill took her arm as they crossed the road. "This is a gloomy way to start the day! Come on, lead the way to your saint chapel place."

"Sainte-Chapelle."

"Whatever you say."

They emerged onto the Quai Anatole France. The late May morning was glorious, all pink and golden and light green. They started across the Pont des Arts and then stopped at the same time in the middle to lean against the railing. Spread before them was one of the best views in Paris. The Île de la Cité dominated the center of the river directly ahead, the two towers of Notre-Dame Cathedral shining butter yellow in the sunshine.

"What's so special about this chapel place you're taking me to?"

"You'll see."

They crossed over to the Right Bank and walked another fifteen minutes along the river to walk over the Pont Marie to the Île de la

Cité. Bill entertained Genna with stories about landscaping challenges in Australia. At the entrance to the precinct containing the Sainte-Chapelle, they submitted to the airport-style security check before crossing the courtyard to the chapel entrance. Once inside, Bill looked dubiously around the deep blue-and-gold vaulted ceilings of the main floor and the cluttered souvenir kiosks.

"Very nice," he said.

"Yes, but this isn't what I wanted you to see. We need to go upstairs." Genna led the way to the steep, cramped spiral staircase, its walls slick with the touch of a million hands over eight centuries. A few steps before the top, she stumbled, anxious to step into a space she remembered thinking looked exactly like her concept of heaven.

A large hand pressed against the small of her back. For a few seconds, she let the warmth flow through her. The touch was sturdy and capable. Not for a second did Genna believe Marjorie Turner had a monopoly on the strength in the family.

"Watch yourself." His voice sounded soft, gentle even. She shivered in the dank stairwell, but not from the cold. Then, with a deep, sharp breath, she stepped into the impossibly light and airy second level of Sainte-Chapelle and turned quickly so she could watch Bill's reaction. He was frowning with concentration as he turned sideways to ease himself through the narrow space while watching his footing on stairs worn to treacherous ruts.

He glanced up and stopped dead, almost knocking the young woman behind him back down the stairwell. He took a few steps forward, his jaw slack with astonishment that morphed rapidly into a massive grin.

Just in time, Genna stopped herself from sinking into his arms. Instead, she started to cry. Big fat tears splashed down her cheeks. She covered her eyes with her hands, her shoulders heaving. Her throat caught on the smell of old stone toasted by the sun streaming through the stained glass. She thought about her first visit to Sainte-Chapelle with Drew and the kids—Drew in a funk, the kids whining for ice cream.

177

While Genna had gasped with the wonder of the space, Drew had grumbled about the long wait to get in just to look at a bunch of stained glass. He'd wanted to leave almost as soon as they arrived, but Genna insisted he stay with the kids while she walked slowly, reverently around the small space, her head thrown back to admire the windows. Sainte-Chapelle had been built in only six years over a ten-year span between 1238 and 1248 — an unheard-of pace. Drew flopped into one of the folding chairs lining the two sides of the chapel, scowling, a kid on either side of him. Later, he chided her for dragging them to yet another church. They argued in fierce whispers so the kids, walking ahead of them, wouldn't hear.

Fifteen radiant windows of stained glass, each containing four vertical panels, rose to Gothic points far above their heads. Impossibly thin bundles of colorfully painted stone columns as slender and insubstantial as strips of balsa separated each window. The lush blues and reds and yellows of the stained glass soaked the room in multicolored glory.

No amount of reading about the architectural advances that led from the solid Gothic mass of Notre-Dame in the eleventh century to the gossamer miracle of the thirteenth-century Sainte-Chapelle could capture the reality. The architect who had designed and executed the chapel was a direct descendant of the angels.

A pair of thick arms enveloped Genna in a bear hug, right there in the middle of one of the most celestial spaces on earth. "Hey, no worries. You're all right. That's it."

Despite all that had happened since she'd left Drew, Genna had never cried, not *really* cried. Many times, she'd tried to, had sat alone in her car and hoped for tears, her throat catching, eyes blurred. But never once had her chest exploded with full, deep, hopeless sobs. Never once had she really let herself go.

And now that she finally had, she was in the middle of one of her favorite places in Paris with a man she barely knew. The other visitors to the chapel flowed around them, some staring at her, most with their attention on the windows. Genna closed her eyes and inhaled the mingled scents of laundry soap and aftershave. Bill kept holding her close, shielding her from curious eyes.

Slowly, the constriction in her chest eased and the sobs turned to gulps. Blindly, she felt in her daypack for tissues. Bill took her hand and from his pocket brought out a folded white handkerchief and handed it to her. Genna almost started sobbing again. The last man who had handed her a real cloth handkerchief had been her father. She'd been six and brokenhearted by the death of the family dog.

"I'm sorry," she gulped.

"Come on. Let's sit down." He led her to the folding chairs. She wiped her eyes, too embarrassed to look at him. He sat comfortably next to her, his solid presence reassuring, his gaze fixed on the stained glass. She knew he was giving her time to recover herself and felt foolish and grateful at the same time.

Genna raised her eyes to the beauty soaring to the golden-ribbed ceiling. The muted buzz of voices and the beeps of cameras faded as she let the light and color wrap around and through her.

Slowly, the heaviness in her chest eased. Her shoulders fell and her muscles relaxed, relief flooding her. Had the tears finally washed away the past? She closed her eyes and imagined it receding—slowly and gently, but finally, leaving her open and free.

After many minutes during which Bill stayed silent, she took a deep breath, put her hands on her knees and stood up. "Let's go."

"Sure thing."

Bill followed her down the exit stairwell and back out to the busy street. He didn't try to get her to talk, ambling along next to her like an oversize Saint Bernard. But instead of offering her a cask of brandy, he took her to a restaurant on Île Saint-Louis and ordered an expensive bottle of Bordeaux.

Genna needed two glasses of the wine and an excellent lunch before she was finally able to talk about what had happened to her back at Sainte-Chapelle. To his credit, Bill listened with a quiet, solid sympathy and not a hint of judgment. She told him about that afternoon in December when she'd come home early from a book tour.

"You're still angry, aren't you?"

"I don't know. Some days I am and then other days . . ."

"You're just sad."

"How did you know?"

Bill topped up her glass. "Let's not talk about that now. Are you starting to feel better?"

"I am, thanks."

The lunch had restored her equilibrium. As always, she marveled at the healing effects of good food and wine. The three-course lunch started with a *salade de lentilles du Puy* topped with a perfectly poached egg, followed by a creamy mushroom risotto that would have moved Genna to tears if she hadn't already wept enough for one day. For dessert, she chose a Pavlova—dry, white meringue filled with a mélange of strawberries, raspberries, and blueberries.

"This is it," she said as she swallowed a mouthful of meringue.

"Your dish for Sainte-Chapelle?" Bill looked up from his chocolate profiteroles. "Let me guess, it has something to do with light? The meringue is like a cloud filled with shards of stained glass."

"Nice!"

Bill grinned. "I'm getting the hang of this."

"You are."

They spent the afternoon walking around the streets of Paris, from the Île Saint-Louis to Place des Vosges in the Marais, and from there to the Pompidou. Genna had thought of Bill as the kind of guy who wouldn't "get" modern art, but she was wrong. It turned out his son's aptitude for art had not come from nowhere.

"Oh, aye, I studied art history in uni. For a time, I wanted to be a painter."

"You did?"

"That surprises you?"

"Yes, I mean, no." Genna shook her head. "All right, fine, I didn't have you pegged as an art lover."

"You still think I'm an Aussie hick, don't you?"

"Of course not!"

"Liar."

Genna laughed out loud, causing a few heads to turn. They were on the fourth floor of the Pompidou, where so much of the great art of the twentieth century was displayed. Bill knew most of the artists and pointed out his favorites. To her delight, Genna discovered they shared a fondness for the work of Max Ernst and Jackson Pollock. Drew never had much patience with modern art. He liked old things that he could pick up and handle.

The day progressed in a series of easygoing activities—strolling to Les Halles and catching the Métro back to the Left Bank, enjoying coffees while watching the world pass by, and then stopping for dinner at a restaurant on the Left Bank not far from Genna's apartment. She chose a braised tomato tart studded with olives for the starter and a melt-in-the-mouth lamb confit for the main course. For dessert, they shared a slab of Grand Marnier cheesecake fit for the gods.

After dinner, they strolled along the floodlit Seine, hand in hand. Couples surrounded them, many sitting with their feet dangling over the river, all wrapped in passionate embraces— living Rodins in the most romantic city on earth. By the time they trailed up the Rue Bonaparte, Genna's head on Bill's broad shoulder, his arm around her waist, the conclusion to the evening was inevitable. Genna led the way through the cool, dark courtyard of her building and up the stairs to her apartment. Bill stopped at the window on the top landing.

"You have a view of Notre-Dame Cathedral from here."

"Yes, beautiful, isn't it?"

"Stunning," he said, but he was no longer looking out the window.

Gently, he took the key from her hand and drew her toward him. He was a good head taller than she, his size reassuring, dependable. His arms encircled her waist and she reached up to touch his face. His breath, warm with wine, fluttered across her cheek. His first kiss was soft, almost apologetic.

She wanted to draw back, her mind at war with her body. What if he didn't like what he saw? On the other hand, when was the last time she'd experienced such a delicious jolt of desire?

But if she gave in . . .

"Stop thinking," Bill whispered. He kissed her again, this time with more insistence. They melted together, the heat leaving them no choice but to go forward into a world foreign to both of them, and at the same time too thrilling to push away.

Bill reached one arm around her and unlocked the door. Together, they tumbled into the living room, laughing now, giddy with new discovery.

Light from the overhead fixture flooded the apartment. Surely Genna hadn't left it on all day. What would Monsieur Leblanc say?

"Hello, Mom," said the last voice Genna expected to hear in Paris. "Who the hell is *that?*"

twenty-one

Brandy Macarons
Filled with chocolate ganache infused with mulled spices

Genna was glad to see her, of course. She could hardly say otherwise, although Becky's sense of timing left something to be desired.

After an awkward introduction during which Becky's sullen acknowledgment of Bill made Genna squirm with shame, she ushered Bill out to the landing. He dropped a quick kiss on her cheek and promised to call. She watched him disappear around the first twist of the staircase.

Sighing, she returned to the apartment to unruffle the outraged feathers of her firstborn.

"I emailed you a week ago to tell you I was coming. Why didn't you answer?"

"I don't have internet access here."

"You send emails to Nancy."

"I've sent her a few, but not for several days. I also changed my email address, but I guess I forgot to tell you. Sorry about that."

At that moment, she didn't feel particularly sorry.

"Busy?"

"Yes, Becky. I *am* working."

"You're writing a cookbook. That's hardly enough to keep you chained to your desk twenty-four seven."

"How did you get into the apartment?"

"I charmed your French boyfriend."

"Pierre?"

"How many have you got, Mom?" Becky glared at Genna. "The guy that just left is an Aussie, isn't he?"

"From Sydney. And we're friends.'

"It looked more than friendly from where I was sitting."

"Cut it out, Becky. How did you get the key?"

"As I said, I got it from that Pierre guy, at his shop. You told Nancy about him and she remembered the name of the place, although it would have been nice if she'd also given me your new email address. You've certainly been more forthcoming with Nancy than you have with your own family. Dad's going crazy trying to get in touch with you."

"Is that why you came? For Dad?"

"Partly."

"So, you went to the *tabac* and got Pierre to give you the key. Why would he do that? You could be anyone."

"Come on, Mom. He only had to look at me to see I was your daughter."

That was true. Becky and Genna did look a great deal alike, give or take a few decades. They both had the same wavy cap of blonde hair and the same blue eyes. Becky had her father's chin, but that was pretty much all she'd inherited of the Watson genes. When Becky was a baby, Genna's mother hung Becky's picture next to a picture of Genna at the same age.

They looked identical.

"It's late. Let's get some sleep and tomorrow I can show you around Paris. How long are you staying?"

"Two weeks. That's as much time as I could get off work."

"Lovely. We can cover a lot of ground in two weeks."

Sure, lovely.

Genna thought of Bill and couldn't help feeling regretful. The touch of his hand on her arm, his lips on hers, the clean soap smell of him. Bill was due to leave for Sydney about the same time Becky was returning to Canada. What were her chances of sneaking away for some alone time?

Next to nil, if Genna knew Becky.

* * *

Fortunately, Becky was in a much better mood the next morning. Genna took her for coffee and croissants (but *not* to Starbucks), and soon the charms of a late-spring day in Paris worked their magic on her. She chatted about her job, her flight, and the places she wanted to visit in Paris. Thankfully, she didn't mention her father. She was even interested in Genna's book and listened attentively to her description of the progress.

"I love it! How much more do you need to write?"

"I'd say I'm about halfway through in terms of collecting dishes and sites, but I've still got a lot of testing to do."

"You can finish it when you get home."

"Home?"

"You can't be thinking of staying here much longer."

"When the money I'm waiting for comes through, I'll have enough to last until the end of September. Of course, if your father sold the house, I wouldn't have to worry about money, in which case I'll apply to extend the visa. The French government just needs me to prove I can sustain myself financially."

"September! That's over three months away."

"I told you when I left that I was planning to stay in Paris for six months. I got here in April and now it's the beginning of June. Why are you surprised?"

"That's what you *said*, but I didn't think you were serious."

"Why wouldn't I be?"

"But you *have* to get back home to Dad."

"Why?"

"You can't stay in Paris forever."

"I have no plans to leave."

"But I was counting on you coming home with me!"

"Did you consider asking me first?"

"I *am* asking you."

"No, Becky, you're telling me, and the answer is no, I'm not going home with you." Genna paused a few beats. "Maybe I'll never go home."

That sounded a trifle overdramatic, even for Genna, but Becky's presumption that Genna would see the error of her ways and jet home with her tail between her legs irritated her.

Who did her overbearing, pushy daughter think she was?

"You're being ridiculous," Becky said, sounding a lot like her father. Drew loved telling Genna how ridiculous she was for waxing too lyrical about a piece of art or a beautiful view, for crying at sentimental movies, or for overreacting (his word) to his "little indiscretion" (also his words).

"Please, Becky," Genna said with a valiant attempt to keep her voice even, "Let's enjoy your visit. I know you think I should come home, and I probably will eventually. I doubt the French government will let me stay forever. But as I said, I'm not planning to leave for at least another three months. I've made a few friends and my book is going well. I can't remember the last time I enjoyed writing a book so much."

"Friends? What friends?" Becky said the word like it was something dredged from the mud at the bottom of the Seine.

"I've met some great people at my French class, especially Marsha. She's a few years older than you. She and I have been out for lunch quite a few times. Her French is much better than mine and she's been helping me practice."

"Where's she from?"

"Colorado."

"She's American?"

"Yes, Becky. The last time I checked, Colorado was in the United States."

"Hmm. Who else have you met?"

Genna told her about Denise and Tessa from England and taciturn Helmut from Munich.

"And the Aussie?"

"His name is Bill Turner, which you already know."

"Yes, but how did you meet *him*? It can't be that easy to pick up strange men, even in Paris."

"I didn't pick him up. I fell down in front of the Starbucks where his son works. Tyler rescued me, we got to talking, I started dropping by to say hello, and a few weeks ago when his dad arrived from Sydney, Tyler asked me to show him around Paris."

"You fell in front of Starbucks?"

"Yes."

"How?"

"If you must know, Becky, I slipped in a mound of dog shit."

"And this Tyler guy saved you."

"He helped me up and then brought me a coffee."

"Does his dad know you're married?"

"He knows I'm separated."

"You're not separated."

"What do you call it, Becky? A break?"

"I don't know what to call it. But I don't like the sound of *separated*."

"How about *divorced*?"

"You're not getting divorced."

"I'm not?"

"Dad said you'd be like this."

"Like what?"

"Kind of bitter, if you want the truth." Becky's voice softened and she reached across the table for Genna's hand. "Don't worry, Mom. I understand if you're having some sort of midlife crisis, and I can even understand why you came to Paris. But it can't last forever. Dad needs you back."

"Dad will be fine without me."

"He won't. He isn't. Since you left, he's been miserable. You should see him, Mom. He's pathetic. Remember how he used to get kind of irritable sometimes?"

Irritable? Try petulant and cranky. Give him a few more years and he'd morph into one of those grouchy old men who rattled on about how the world has never been the same since Jimi Hendrix died and eight-track tapes became obsolete.

"I'm not going back to him, Becky. Sorry."

"But Dad's really mellowed. Every time I call, he's kind of quiet and despondent, like he can't figure out what to do without you. It's as if he's lost himself."

Genna flashed back to a trip that she and Drew had taken together to the west coast of Vancouver Island a few months before they bought the house. They'd strolled along the endless sand beach. The setting sun flamed across the Pacific Ocean, rolling to the horizon to cover half the globe. Genna remembered feeling like the luckiest woman in the world.

Then her mind flashed forward, and she saw him the way he'd looked that afternoon when she'd come home early from her book tour.

"Forget it," she said. "I'm sorry your father's missing me, but I'm not ready to come home." She dropped some money on the table and stood up. "And I might never be ready, Becky. So, please, stop pushing me. It's a beautiful day, so how about we take a walk to the Luxembourg Gardens. Do you remember how much you and Michael enjoyed going there when you were kids?"

Becky looked like she'd prefer to keep up the assault. Genna could see how determined Becky was to force her into a tearful reunion with Drew. And her daughter was the last person to run from a challenge.

Genna couldn't imagine where Becky got her determination from.

"Okay, Mom," she said. "Let's drop it for now."

Genna led the way out of the café and down Rue Bonaparte past the Église Saint-Sulpice. She reminded Becky of how she loved the lions spouting water from the fountain in front of the church.

"I was twelve, Mom." But Becky slowed her pace and allowed the slightest of smiles to lighten her expression.

"Saint-Sulpice is such a lovely old church. It's on my list for next week."

"You and your lists!" Becky said, shaking her head, but Genna recognized a hint of affection in her daughter's exasperation.

That was a good sign.

They walked from Saint-Sulpice toward the Luxembourg Gardens without talking, but at least now Genna felt it was a friendly silence as opposed to a cessation of hostilities while the opposing forces regrouped.

Luxembourg Gardens had been one of Genna's favorite places in Paris ever since she and Drew brought the kids there fifteen years ago. Both Becky and Michael went wild over the playground, a creative conglomeration of equipment for sliding, swinging, hanging, and spinning. A fence enclosed the entire area, which was guarded by a grumpy man who collected an entrance fee. A soft, cushiony rubber pad blanketed the ground, reassuring parents watching their children. Outside the fence, a row of plastic chairs faced the playground so the adults could relax in comfort, sipping cappuccinos from the nearby concession and chatting with their neighbors.

It was all so civilized.

Genna and Drew spent many hours watching the kids burn off energies tested by mornings spent touring the grand sights of Paris. More than once, they bought another hour of good behavior with the promise of a trip to the playground at the Luxembourg Gardens.

The Gardens had it all—a playground for children, a chess area and pétanque courts for old men, a palace for government offices, a circular pond for lovers to lounge around, formal gardens to stroll in, enough statues of naked people dotted around the landscape to keep the most determined classicist happy, and wide walkways for cycling, inline skating, strolling, and even horseback riding.

As they entered the gardens and started down the long thoroughfare flanked on both sides by deep green cypresses, Genna thought about what dish was robust enough to pair with the Luxembourg Gardens. A casserole immediately came to mind, something hearty and filling that contained whatever the creative cook decided to throw in.

"Pot-au-feu!"

"What?"

Becky's purse slid out of her hand, the contents scattering across the gravel. She and Genna spent the next several minutes scrabbling for lipsticks, pens, keys, loose change, gum wrappers, paperclips, and assorted bits of tattered paper.

"Don't you clean out your purse before you travel?" Genna asked as she chased a quarter into the flower bed. "There's no point bringing Canadian money to France."

"I didn't have time," Becky snapped. She held out her purse for Genna to dump in the handfuls of junk. "What was that you yelled?"

"I didn't yell."

"Whatever. It was something about pot, wasn't it?"

"Seriously?"

Becky shrugged. "Anything's possible. What did you say?"

"I got an idea for a recipe to pair with the gardens. Sometimes I blurt things out without thinking. I scared the *merde* out of a snooty French matron the other day when I came up behind her in the Place de la Concorde and said *madeleines* a little too loudly. You should have seen the look she gave me!"

"I can imagine. What's the recipe for the Luxembourg Gardens?"

"Pot au feu. It's a casserole dish with all sorts of ingredients— beef, pork, and chicken with vegetables and herbs. It's like this park—a mishmash that somehow just works."

They turned onto a wide avenue that bisected the entire length of the gardens. Ahead and to the right they glimpsed a whirl of movement in the children's playground, and to the left the large round pond glinted in the sunlight. Everywhere they looked they saw people—young and old, locals and tourists.

"I think you're on the right track," Becky said. "This place is a mixed bag of spaces and activities. No wonder I loved it when I was a kid." Suddenly, she grabbed Genna's hand and pulled her forward toward the playground. "Let's go see where Michael and I used to play!"

Genna again saw the determined little girl, her hair caught in a fuzzy elastic, her face set in concentration, one foot wearing a pink sock, the other a blue sock. Almost from the second she emerged, somewhat disgruntled, from Genna's womb, Becky had gone her own way. A favorite expression in the family was "Becky was just being Becky." That was the only explanation for behavior that never quite matched expectations. It wasn't that Becky was a poorly behaved child. But if there was a smooth road running parallel to a bumpy one, Becky always chose the bumpy road, and the rest of the family paid the price.

Becky was being Becky.

Genna and Becky spent the afternoon indulging in peaceful bouts of nostalgia that managed to avoid any mention of Drew. They also chatted about Michael and his thwarted attempts to secure a girlfriend who would put up with him and about Becky's work at the Museum of Anthropology on the campus of the University of British Columbia. Apparently, Becky was angling for a promotion. She even solicited Genna's advice about how to approach her boss.

That evening, Genna treated Becky to dinner at an upscale restaurant across the river in the first arrondissement. Genna usually confined herself to local bistros with relatively accessible prices, but she was feeling so grateful that Becky had spent most of the day in a good mood that she didn't hesitate to make a larger than usual inroad into her dwindling finances.

Big mistake.

First, Becky refused to drink, which put a cork in the conviviality quotient for the evening. Genna had ordered a full carafe of red wine while Becky was in the toilet and was obliged to drink all of it herself. As a result, by the time they were halfway through the entrée, Genna was as relaxed and expansive as Becky was tense. The wine so dissipated Genna's usual wariness around Becky that she told her about Marsha and Colin.

"You should do something. This Colin guy is taking advantage of her. You can't stand by and watch her ruin her life."

"Colin wouldn't be my choice for a husband, but if Marsha wants him, there's not much I can do. At least I introduced her to Pierre."

"Big deal! What's *he* going to do?"

"I believe he's advising her to protect herself, legally I mean."

"And yet she left with Colin after the meeting at Les Deux Magots? Have you heard from her since?"

"No."

"Have you even called her?"

"No." Genna took a generous gulp of wine in a desperate attempt to fend off the inevitable. Becky was spoiling for a fight, likely brought on by nutritional deprivation. She'd barely touched her roast duck, a culinary crime in Genna's opinion. The duck had been prepared to crackling perfection.

"The point is, Mom, that your friend needs help."

"What do you want me to do?"

Becky didn't appreciate that question. Even as a child, she'd hated being put on the spot. "We're not taking about me."

"I realize that, but you could stop attacking me for two minutes and cut me some slack. I'm not Marsha's mother."

"I'm not attacking you!" Becky did righteous indignation better than anyone Genna knew.

"I'm sure you don't mean to," Genna said in a heroic effort to be conciliatory when what she really wanted to do was take the slim white neck of her darling daughter between her hands and throttle her.

It was a damn good thing she loved her.

"You've got to take some *responsibility*, Mom."

Genna stared at Becky, openmouthed.

Responsibility?

"This whole running-off-to-Paris thing is so wrong. You know it is."

Genna took another gulp of wine. So, they were back to that. If she was to be raked over the coals, she might as well be drunk. "You're mad because I came to Paris."

"Not mad, exactly. *Disappointed* would be a better word."

Ouch. Another punch, this one to the lower abdomen.

"Disappointed how, exactly?" Genna asked, more than a touch of resentment creeping into her voice.

"You know what I mean," Becky said. "Everything was going along fine. You and Dad had your new house—your House with a View, right?"

"House with *the* View."

"Whatever. You wouldn't stop talking about that view as if it were the only house in West Vancouver with a water view."

"Well, it *is* a great view."

Becky rolled her eyes. "And Dad's business was doing well, and you had your cookbooks and . . ." Becky paused, her voice catching. "And then you took off for no reason."

"Is that what your father told you?"

"It's the truth."

"It's one version."

"You took off!" Becky said again.

"I let you and Michael know where I was going. Neither of you said anything."

"We didn't believe you'd actually leave."

"You saw where I was living in that awful basement suite. Did you think I'd want to stay there forever?"

"Of course not. We figured you'd move home. With Daddy." Becky glowered. "Where you belong."

"I belong with your father?"

"Stop twisting my words. You have to go home, Mom. You know you do."

"Do I?" The wine was fuzzing her brain. She took another swig in the fond hope she'd soon pass out.

Let Becky deal with that.

"Please, Mom, stop this act. You and Dad should be together. Enough is enough. You've proved you can survive on your own. Now go home."

"And live happily ever after?"

Becky had the grace to look mildly uncomfortable. "Something like that. You've been together almost thirty years. You don't just walk away from that."

"You think I should go back for another thirty years."

"Dad wants you back."

The spasm that squeezed her heart at Becky's words was either regret or indigestion. Genna wasn't sure which was worse. "Your father doesn't need me."

"He does!" Becky said with surprising vigor. She leaned forward, her elbows on the table. "He's a total mess. He's gained weight and he's not working. All he does is watch TV and eat pizza."

"He just misses my cooking."

"He misses *you*."

The urge to throttle her daughter again took hold. When did the world shift and the daughter became the mother?

Genna thought about their conversations after Becky had graduated from university and was working at a dull job that she hated but couldn't manage to quit. *Conversations* was the wrong word. More like *harangues* with Genna talking and Becky listening glumly, and with Becky as resentful of her mother's interference as Genna now was of hers. But Genna claimed the right of mother to coax Becky out of her slump. As a daughter, Becky didn't have the same right.

"Your father will survive," she said.

"Will you at least tell me when you plan to leave Paris?" Becky asked.

"I told you. I plan to stay until September. My financial guy thinks the time's almost right to sell the stocks, and I still have lots more work to do on the book."

"I'm sure you've taken enough notes by now, and anything you don't know, you can find on the internet. Every attraction in Paris has a website. You could finish the whole book without leaving Vancouver."

"*L'addition, s'il vous plâit,*" Genna said to the waiter who had floated over to the table. If she didn't leave the restaurant soon, she'd order a brandy, which considering her current state of inebriation would not be smart.

"*Oui, madame,*" he murmured.

"Stop it, Becky. I'm staying here for as long as I can and then I'll let you know what's next. In the meantime, can we at least try to have a good time? There's so much of Paris I want to show you."

Becky fumbled for her purse. "Whatever. I guess I wouldn't mind seeing the new anthropology museum. What's it called?"

"The Branly. I haven't been there yet."

Becky actually smiled. "Good. I'll go with you."

They left the restaurant, with Genna staggering slightly. All she wanted was her bed and some quiet.

"Can you make it, Mom?" Becky was suddenly a paragon of solicitude. She even took Genna's arm and let her lean against her while she hailed a taxi.

"I'm good."

"You drank a lot."

"I thought you'd join me." Genna's tongue had grown to enormous proportions and she couldn't swear to the crispness of her consonants.

Becky didn't reply as she steered Genna into the taxi and gave the direction to the driver in passable French. Genna slumped back and stared at the passing lights.

"You're such a good daughter."

"It's fine. We'll be home soon."

A wave of drunken affection swept over Genna. "I'm sorry, honey."

"I know."

Genna was never sure how Becky got her home and into bed. She woke the next morning with a pounding head and a creeping anxiety that she'd embarrassed herself rather more than usual. She rolled out of bed and crept into the living room. The couch was empty, and the sound of retching was coming from the bathroom. She grimaced at the injustice. Genna had drunk more than she should have, and yet poor Becky, who'd drunk nothing, sounded sick as a dog. She hoped Becky hadn't picked up a bug on the plane.

Becky healthy was a challenge. Becky sick would be a nightmare.

twenty-two

Bitter Chocolate Macarons

*Filled with Cointreau cream and sprinkled with
crystalized sugar*

Becky recovered from whatever had bothered her tummy, and she and Genna set off for the Musée du quai Branly in the late morning. The Branly was an architectural marvel, with a world-class collection of anthropological and ethnological displays from every corner of the globe. Genna wasn't convinced she'd find any connection to food, but if going there kept Becky from pestering her about Drew, then she was all for it.

After taking the Métro to Saint-Michel, they rode the clunky interurban to Quai Branly located across the street from the river and within sight of the Eiffel Tower. The cartoon colors and odd angles of the building both rejected and embraced the phalanx of traditional, gray-topped French apartment blocks rising behind it.

Genna's first impression of the interior of the Branly was of a dark sensuality, all curving walls painted in rich earth tones. They strolled past softly lit alcoves displaying artifacts from indigenous cultures on every continent—feathered headdresses from Borneo, Aboriginal rock paintings from the Australian outback, carved statues from Africa, and even a clutch of full-size totem poles from the First Nations people on the west coast of Canada.

Each exhibit was meticulously mounted and documented in French and English. Every few yards, an indent in the curving ocher wall led to a sheltered seat where visitors could watch a video describing the exhibits. A person could spend days in the humid dimness, absorbing volumes of new information.

Even Becky was silenced—and she worked at a museum that was itself no slouch in the exhibitions department. Ignoring Genna, she wandered from exhibit to exhibit, her eyes glazed with longing.

Genna lagged behind, giving herself over to the cocooning effect of the low lighting. Culture after culture rose from the gloom, their artifacts glowing softly under muted spotlights. She entered the Amazon area and paused in front of a magnificent feather headdress made of plant fibers, scarab beetles, monkey skin, and feathers.

Dark, rich, smooth.

Of course.

Mousse au chocolat.

Genna imagined each mouthful exploding across her tongue, bringing with it visions of plump cocoa beans in a steamy rain forest. While Becky continue to prowl past the exhibits, Genna found a comfortable dark corner—easy to do in the Branly—and pulled out her notebook and pen.

As a celebration of so-called primitive societies, the Musée du quai Branly shows us the complexity common to all human life. Whether a modern skyscraper or a soaring totem pole, the skills, creativity, and willpower required to design and build it is the same. No one who has gazed awestruck at an intricately carved exorcism mask from Sri Lanka or the complex geometric rugs woven by Berber tribeswomen could doubt that the objects on display in the Musée du quai Branly represent human ingenuity in all its diverse glory. Intrepid visitors glide from the Congo to the Sahara, across India and around

Polynesia, into the vast lands of Asia and on across the Pacific to the plains of North America and the secret jungles of Brazil.

A delicately constructed chocolate mousse should explode with flavor with the same intensity so richly captured in the Branly's dark passageways.

"Did you think of a dish for this place?"

It was a few seconds before Genna realized Becky was standing in front of her, hands on her hips, once more her briskly important self.

"I have."

"Are you going to tell me?"

"Nope."

"Mom!" Just enough of the fourteen-year-old Becky escaped to make them both laugh.

"You'll find out at the party. I think I'll put the Branly's contribution on the menu."

"Party? What party?"

Genna took her time standing up and stowing her pen and notebook. "I'm having a dinner party for some of the people I've met since coming to Paris."

"When?"

"A week from Saturday. Most of them are from my French class."

"I suppose you want me to help."

If there was such a thing as a graciousness gene, Becky had missed out on it.

"Not particularly. I've asked Tessa, the young woman from my class I told you about, to come early to help with the prep. I've been teaching her to cook. You're welcome to hang around, but you don't have to. You can just show up for dinner with everyone else. It'll be crowded, but everyone's keen to try my cooking."

"Will Bill be coming?"

"I'm inviting him."

"Your friend Marsha?"

"Of course."

"What about the awful boyfriend?"

"Probably. It's up to her."

"Pierre?"

"I don't think so. The party's for my friends from French class."

"Bill isn't in your French class," Becky said sharply.

The darkness of the museum suddenly felt oppressive rather than comforting, reminding Genna that the flip side of a chocolate mousse was its million-plus calories. Everything good had to have something not so good.

Just like daughters.

"I'm aware, Becky, but it's my party and I can invite whomever I like. Now let's get out of here."

Becky looked mutinous, but to Genna's relief, she kept quiet. As they walked in the direction of the Métro, Genna's phone rang.

"Please say you'll have dinner with me tonight."

Genna smiled. "Hi, Bill."

"Are you having a good time with your daughter?"

"I'm surviving." She glanced over at Becky who was scowling.

"Bring her with you. I'd like to get to know her better."

Did he realize what he was asking?

Becky had zero ability to hide her feelings, particularly negative feelings, a trait Genna had to admit Becky came by honestly. In a flash, Genna saw the three of them sipping wine in awkward silence — Becky glowering, Bill bewildered, Genna mortified.

She'd be better off staying home and waxing her bikini line.

"Sure, Bill, dinner sounds great and I'm sure Becky would love to join us."

Becky was shaking her head so vigorously that she missed seeing an elegant French matron walking her tiny dog behind her. With one step backward, Becky's heel caught little Fifi's hindquarters. The resulting squeal from both Madame and Fifi distracted Becky long enough to allow Genna to arrange to meet Bill at the Seine, across from the foot of Rue Bonaparte, at eight.

"Why did you tell him I'd come?" Becky asked once she reassured the outraged Madame that her dog would survive to get under the feet of hundreds more innocent pedestrians. Madame stalked off with Fifi scuttling behind her.

"He invited you, but you don't have to come."

"So, what am I supposed to do for dinner?"

"There's a place just around the corner from the apartment that sells great roast chicken and potatoes for takeout. Or there's pâté in the fridge. You could get a baguette and some cheese."

"You don't mind if I stay home?"

"Why should I? Bill can get to know you another time."

"But..."

"I don't mind, dear. Really." Genna was not above enjoying herself. Her prospects for the evening had brightened considerably. Either Becky stayed home so Genna could enjoy a tête-à-tête with Bill or she joined them and, because it was Becky's choice, she'd be, if not charming, at least tolerable.

"Okay, I'll come. That's what you want, isn't it?"

Genna suppressed a smile.

Once back in her apartment, Genna left Becky to recline on the couch under the *Odalisque* and took her steaming mug of tea into the bedroom. Thanks to Marsha's suggestions, she'd transformed her dreary cell with its sagging bed and yellowed wallpaper into a cozy nest. She'd replaced the musty and torn bedspread with a crisp turquoise duvet and scattered it with yellow and orange pillows. She'd also stapled a pale cream sheet over the hideous wallpaper and hung a blue sheet in front of the tall window.

The room now resembled a moonlit ocean cave, with her bed a drifting rowboat.

Genna lay down and imagined gentle ripples buoying her up, the air sharp with salt. Her drowsy thoughts turned naturally to Bill as she slipped into a nap that flowed gently into a warmly satisfying dream.

Strong arms held her close, her nostrils filled with a familiar scent—a scent she loved. She inhaled hints of male sweat mixed with plain soap and the dry, pungent smell of wood chips. She sighed as the arms tightened. Her body melted into the tangle of arms and legs wrapped around her. One strong hand, the tips of the fingers roughened, the veins on the back prominent, began a long, languorous stroke up the front of her body, first thighs, then into the crease where leg met belly, and on up over the smooth white skin across her midriff. A ragged breath signaled his desire, which more than anything made her melt. She drew him on top of her, enjoying his weight and her own power.

Gentle morphed into urgency. It was so familiar, so comfortable.

Genna felt whole, alive, loved.

Merde!

Her eyes flew open and she bolted upright. Lights exploded, shimmered, exploded again. She clutched her stomach, feeling like she wanted to be sick even as the force of her arousal still clung to her like hot silk.

What the hell was Drew doing in her sexy dream? Was her subconscious telling her to follow Becky back to Vancouver and her old life?

If so, then her subconscious could take a flying leap in front of a speeding Citroën.

By the time Genna rose trembling from the bed, it was time to get ready for her dinner date with Bill. Unfortunately, the chances of the evening ending in wild sex with a man who said "g'day" and by his own admission once trapped a crocodile (a small one, but still) were nil.

"You look nice."

Genna peered past Becky to the kitchen, thinking someone else was there. But, no, it was only Becky sitting at the table, her hair tousled from scrunching it with her hand while she concentrated, a habit from her childhood. Genna felt a sudden surge of love. Becky would always be opinionated and difficult. Yet Genna loved both her and Michael with a fierceness that would never be extinguished.

"Thank you." Genna kept her voice neutral to avoid betraying her sudden attack of maternal devotion. Becky would see it as weakness. Until she became a mother herself, Becky couldn't know how it felt to love with every cell of an expanding body.

"Are you working on something?"

"Just some research I'm doing for the museum. Aboriginal art." Becky closed her laptop and shuffled away her books, several of which sprouted fluorescent stickies. Genna moved forward for a closer look, but Becky whisked them off the table and into a large bag at her feet.

"As in Australia?"

"Yes, Mom. That's where they live." Becky stood and moved toward the bathroom, then paused a moment, turned back, picked up the bag, and took it with her.

As usual, Becky's brief spark of humanity was quickly snuffed out. Blink and you'd miss it, as Genna's father used to say on family trips driving through dusty interior towns with little more than a signpost, a Dairy Queen, and a used-car lot.

"We're meeting Bill in twenty minutes," Genna called to the closed door.

"I'll be ready," came the muffled reply.

Genna retrieved her own laptop from the coffee table and settled herself on the couch. The file containing the first draft of her book was open. She added a new page in the Dessert section for *Mousse au Chocolat Musée du quai Branly* and then updated the table of contents. The list of dishes and sites scrolled before her. A respectable collection of appetizers, salads, soups, entrées, and desserts were all matched with museums, monuments, artwork, and gardens.

Her two passions intertwined.

Genna searched for gaps. Her list of soups needed bolstering and her collection of gardens was thin. Paris had a marvelous assortment of green spaces, ranging from the majestic Bois du Boulogne to the perfect little Parc Monceau with its eighteenth-century follies and well-heeled occupants. Genna owed it to her readers to include as many as possible.

True to her word, five minutes before they had to leave, Becky presented herself in the living room, dressed in a yellow cotton dress that fit her slight curves to perfection.

"You look wonderful!" Genna exclaimed.

And she did. Although certainly not unattractive, Becky was not a great beauty. She was too spiky, too angular. Her habitual look of irritation soured otherwise even features, and she rarely made an effort to enhance nature. Yet there was something about Becky that Genna had never seen before—a kind of glow, as if she were standing beneath the arc of a rainbow.

"Thanks. I'm feeling better."

At just past eight, they stood at a railing overlooking the Seine. Cars swooshed along the Quai Anatole France behind them, the volume steady but lacking the frenetic energy of daytime traffic. The air smelled soft. Genna detected a slight tang of river water mixed with car exhaust and faintly, but enough to bring a smile to her face, the delicate aroma of flowers from the Tuileries Gardens across the river. She felt light and free and happy. It was almost June, she was in Paris, and in a few minutes, she was meeting an interesting man for dinner at a Paris restaurant redolent with garlic and butter and sizzling steak.

"Evening!" Bill boomed when he joined them at the railing. He wrapped one arm around Genna's shoulders and planted a kiss on her cheek and then turned and offered Becky a meaty paw. "Great to see you again, Becky. Enjoying Paris?"

Becky was not made of stone, although sometimes Genna wondered. By the time they were settled at one of the swishier restaurants on the Right Bank, Becky and Bill were embroiled in an earnest discussion about Aboriginal art.

Bill, it turned out, knew a lot about the subject and owned a large collection of art from all over Australia. He'd even met several of the artists. His knowledge about many of the styles exceeded even Becky's. She sat forward over her dinner, eyes shining as she questioned him about his collection and shared information about her research, even asking his opinion about specific cultures.

Although the evening ended with Genna going home with Becky instead of spending quality time in Bill's arms, she decided it had been a success. Bill had been charming and appeared to enjoy talking with Becky. And at one point, he'd slid his hand onto Genna's knee and squeezed. Desire had flared, stoked by her languid dream that afternoon.

She had to find a way to break free from Becky in the next week. How hard could that be?

twenty-three

Champagne Macarons
Glittering gold shells filled with sinfully rich
mascarpone cheese

The next morning, Genna awoke to the sound of retching. A rush of maternal concern surged past the parts of her brain dulled by rich food. She tapped on the bathroom door.

"Are you all right?"

She heard water running and then Becky's voice, more subdued than usual but still sharp. "I'm fine. Just give me a minute."

Genna backed away from the door and went into the kitchen to make breakfast. Becky must have eaten something the night before that had disagreed with her, although Genna couldn't imagine what. The meal had been incredible, even by Paris standards. The restaurant Bill had chosen sprinted so far out of Genna's league it might as well have been in Outer Mongolia.

With the *prix fixe* menu of one and fifty hundred euros per person, they had eaten, at one sitting, Genna's food budget for a week. But you gets what you pays for, as her grandfather used to say, and they'd certainly gotten.

Genna had started with a coquilles Saint Jacques that made her want to weep. The firm scallops peeped shyly from a parsley cream sauce that filled every crevice of her mouth with bursts of exquisite flavor. Her main course was a tenderly braised filet mignon, all thick and pink and fleshy, snuggled under a medley of sautéed wild mushrooms topped with Roquefort-spiked compound butter and caramelized garlic cloves. If she'd died at that moment, she would have died a happy woman. Dessert was a simple clafouti made with the rich red Guigne d'Annonay cherries from the Loire valley. Each spoonful tasted like a hot and hazy June day. Genna could almost hear the crickets chirping.

The hideously expensive wine Bill had ordered was one of the best Genna had ever tasted. Smooth and round and red, it burst across her palate with a dance and a song.

If Becky was feeling under the weather this morning, it was understandable. Although, come to think of it, Becky again hadn't drunk any wine. At the end of the evening, she'd been as clear-eyed and cynical as she'd been at the beginning, while Genna remembered feeling a touch on the giggly side.

Becky emerged from the bathroom. She walked slowly and Genna noticed a thin sheen of sweat on her face that made her look as if she'd been in a sauna.

"Are you sure you're okay?" she asked as Becky slumped onto the couch. "I hope you're not coming down with something."

The only reply was a slight groan as Becky eased herself into the horizontal position and covered herself with a blanket. Above the couch, the orange skin of the needlepoint *Odalisque* contrasted grotesquely with Becky's whitish-green pallor.

Genna wondered if it was the veal Becky had eaten the night before, although she couldn't imagine how anything served at a restaurant with two Michelin stars could make someone ill. Imagine the scandal!

Becky closed her eyes. "I'll be all right soon, Mom. Just an upset stomach."

"I'll make you some ginger tea." While Genna boiled the water, she considered including a veal recipe in her cookbook. A tasty *escalopes de veau en papillote* — morsels of tender veal cooked with herbs, wild mushrooms, and tomatoes steamed inside squares of parchment paper. The dish wasn't complicated to make and was always a hit. When guests opened the packages at the table, a cloud of savory steam filled the dining room and set the taste buds on overdrive.

Normally while writing *Eat Like a Parisian*, Genna let the Parisian site determine the matching dish, but there was no reason why she couldn't come up with the dish first. What would pair well with *escalopes de veau en papillote*? It needed to be something encased, something rich yet light. Something surprising. She glanced over at Becky who appeared to have gone back to sleep, her chest rising and falling softly. Best to let her rest. Genna could get some work done and then later hopefully Becky would feel well enough to go to the Musèe d'Orsay as they'd planned.

Genna went over to the table to find her laptop shoved to one side to make room for Becky's books and papers. She pushed them to the edge of the table and drew her laptop toward her.

What would go with the veal? A garden? A painting? One of the monuments she hadn't yet visited? She was running low on monuments. She'd included most of the biggies, and she didn't want to repeat herself. She visualized the *escalopes de veau en papillote*—its paper exterior opening to reveal the smooth veal center. The veal could be seasoned any number of ways, each version a different gustatory experience. Genna sat back in her chair and gazed up at the ancient ceiling. Beams blackened with age and decay bisected yellowing plaster that in some areas had peeled to reveal multicolored layers.

Layers, wrapping, nuggets of gold inside.

L'Opéra Bastille!

The controversial structure at the site of the old Bastille prison of revolutionary fame housed the famous Opéra national de Paris. Genna had walked by it just a few weeks ago and hadn't been able to come up with a match. The building was too new, too starkly modern, too nonorganic. And, yet, it had a complicated magnificence about it that could pair well with the veal. Both had deceptive exteriors that hid alluring interiors—the creamy smoothness of perfectly cooked veal and the ever-changing worlds of opera and ballet.

Perfect! As Genna placed her fingers on the keyboard, her elbow jostled one of Becky's books, which tumbled to the floor.

Sighing with irritation—she wanted to get her thoughts down before she forgot them—she bent down and picked up the book.

Becky opened her eyes, took one look at the book in Genna's hand, and burst into tears.

Becky? Tears? Was the world coming to an end?

Genna threw the book down and rushed across the room to take Becky in her arms. For a few seconds, Becky clung to Genna, sobs racking her body.

"Hey! It's okay. What's wrong?" The last time Becky had cried in her presence, she'd been fifteen years old and recovering from having her heart broken by Teddy Friars, the little worm.

As Genna waited for Becky to calm down and explain what had prompted such an unprecedented outburst, she noticed the book she'd dropped, lying open in the middle of the floor.

A full-page picture of a womb filled with a curled-up fetus was a glossy smudge of color against the drab brown carpet.

Oh. My. God.

twenty-four

Root Beer Macarons

Smooth and sweet as a summer day at the fair

Grandmother? She was going to be a grandmother! In an instant, Genna saw herself pushing a stroller along the seawall in West Vancouver, boring friends with endless photos, buying adorable clothes and educational toys, and contributing to a college fund.

"Mom?"

Genna felt her own joy fade when she saw the expression on Becky's face. Morning sickness had made her pale, but it wasn't morning sickness that was making her look so miserable.

"How do you feel about it?" That seemed the safest way to go. Getting all gushy and grandmotherly was probably not the wisest option at this critical juncture.

"I don't know!" Becky wailed. "I just don't know! At first, I was shocked, but that only lasted a few hours. Then I felt this, I don't know, incredible feeling of fullness, of, like, I can't describe it."

"Love?"

Becky managed a weak smile. "Yeah, I guess that's it. I feel like I'm living for a purpose now, that there's something bigger than me." She spread her palms across her flat belly. "I guess a lot bigger soon."

"Yes, there is that. But you have a while yet. What are you, two months?"

"Almost three." Becky couldn't manage to keep a note of pride out of her voice.

Genna relaxed. At least she knew her first grandchild was likely on its way to being born. Now she just needed to find out what was going on with the other half of the equation.

The father.

With an incredible effort of will, she stayed silent. Becky would let her know when she was ready.

"How about you tell me all about it while I make myself some breakfast," Genna said as she heaved herself off the couch, feeling suddenly ravenous. For her, food and highly emotional situations went together like butter and cream. She'd never been one of those people who stopped eating when the going got tough. She knew people who slimmed to mere wisps when life threw curve balls. Not Genna. Hours after Drew fell off the monogamy wagon, she ate a jumbo bag of taco chips washed down with a liter of root beer followed by a tub of butter brickle ice cream.

And she didn't even want to think about the multiple orders of take-out Chinese food.

She wondered if Drew already knew about the baby, and then realized she didn't care. Becoming a Grandma was all well and good, but as far as she was concerned, Grandpa could go fly a kite.

While Becky sat on the couch, Genna made herself an omelet. She cracked two perfect brown eggs that only days before had nestled beneath the butt of a well-fed Norman hen, then added a few tablespoons of cream, a handful of crumbled goat cheese fresh off a Provençal farm, a clove of chopped garlic, and a grind of black pepper. She picked up a fork and began beating the mixture into a froth.

"It's Rolf," Becky said.

Genna dropped the fork. It bounced across the floor, smearing the white tiles with a lurid yellow streak.

"Oh?"

Genna didn't know what else to say. It was crucial she hide her delight until she knew what Becky felt.

"We kind of got back to together."

"Obviously."

"Yeah, well, it was just once."

"Almost three months ago?"

"But it's not going to work out. He hasn't changed, and I guess I haven't either."

"You've changed now."

"True."

Genna retrieved the fork from the floor. Feeling truly famished after this latest bit of news, she heated the omelet pan, poured in the eggs and cheese, swished the mixture around a bit, and then threw in some prosciutto slices. Within seconds, the whole apartment smelled rich and eggy.

Becky ran for the toilet.

Poor lamb, Genna thought, as she tucked into her omelet. She remembered not being able to cook for three months when she was pregnant with Becky. Drew had eaten salads and cold meat from the deli counter and Genna had lived on soda crackers.

At the time, Genna had thought her pregnancy was stretching forever, but when she looked back, it felt as if the whole nine months had lasted only a few weeks. She smiled at the memory of the wonderful sense of peace she'd felt toward the end, when she sat Buddha-like on the couch and chatted with her unborn child. Genna wasn't to know then that she'd give birth to a bundle of arms and legs and energy that would grow past her into the woman now retching in her tiny Parisian toilet cubicle.

By the time Becky returned to the living room and again lowered herself to the couch, Genna had finished her omelet and was washing the dishes.

"Rolf doesn't know yet."

Genna left the kitchen and sat opposite Becky in the only other chair, a greasy-armed recliner that had not reclined since the sixties. "I guessed as much," she said. "Are you planning to tell him?"

"I should," she said. "What do you think?"

Becky and Rolf had been together for three years before breaking up about six months earlier, much to Genna's disappointment. Rolf was as laid-back as a man could be and still remain upright, but he had the ability no one in Becky's blood family had, which was to be Becky's anchor and her support. He tempered her cynicism with mildness and her volatility with steadfastness, and Genna was certain he loved Becky. Even more important, he was Becky's intellectual equal, which was no mean feat. Becky had scared off professors twice her age and left more than one young man bewildered and broken.

Genna sighed.

"Are you going to tell me what you think?" Becky asked.

"I'd rather not."

"But you have an opinion."

"I do. But what's important is what *you* think about the baby and about Rolf. Do you want him in your life?"

"I don't know."

"Do you still love him?"

Becky curled her fists into tight balls and said nothing.

Genna plowed on. "Do you want to bring up the baby alone?"

"Who says I'll keep the baby?" Becky asked, her usual truculence returning in a flash.

"Will you?"

Becky's shoulders slumped as she again placed her hand on her belly. Genna felt her throat constrict at the tenderness of that one gesture.

"Yes," she whispered, then looked up at Genna, tears in her eyes. "Of course, I will."

Genna crossed to the couch and wrapped her arms around Becky, who relaxed against her shoulder and wept. There would be many months to talk things through, and Genna had high hopes for Rolf.

But for now, all she could do was hold her daughter and her daughter's child in her arms.

* * *

By midmorning, Becky felt well enough to consider going to the Musée d'Orsay for an hour or two of art appreciation before lunch. Becky was sure her stomach would have quieted enough by that time to enjoy a nibble of something.

Bill called just as they were getting ready to leave the apartment.

"You two all right after last night?" he asked, his voice booming through Genna's phone, so Becky heard him from across the room. She rolled her eyes, but Genna could tell she was trying not to smile. She'd enjoyed the evening with Bill almost as much as Genna had.

"We're fine, Bill. What's up with you?" She moved into her bedroom.

"Would you be up for a walk tomorrow? Those gardens by the Louvre?"

"You mean the Tuileries?"

"Sounds like 'em. I thought I'd take in the Louvre first and then meet you afterward. I'm a bit of a slow coach in museums so don't mind if I don't ask you along."

Genna laughed. "I also prefer going to museums on my own. There's nothing worse than having to go at someone else's pace."

"Too right!"

"Today Becky and I are off to the Musée d'Orsay. She's feeling a bit under the weather and needs some cheering up."

"Oh?" The concern in his voice sounded genuine.

"It's nothing serious," she said, smiling to herself. Few things were more serious than starting a new life.

"Glad to hear it. What time works for you?"

"If Becky's up for it, I'll take her to the Cluny in the morning, but we should be through and have had lunch by two-ish. How about I meet you by the Louvre pyramid at three? We can have a walk through the gardens and then get a glass of wine or a coffee somewhere."

"What about Becky?"

"She'll probably want to go back to the apartment to rest," Genna said. "Let's just make it the two of us."

"I'll see you tomorrow at three, then. Oh, and Genna?"

"Yes?"

His voice dropped an octave. "I had a wonderful time last night."

"I did too, Bill. Magical."

"Well, that's all right, then. I'll see you tomorrow at three." Genna said goodbye and put down her phone. Then her knees buckled, and she collapsed onto the bed.

Merde!

She grinned up at the ceiling. The next twenty-four hours couldn't go fast enough.

* * *

Genna and Becky decided to walk along the river to the Musée d'Orsay, a twenty-minute amble over cool cobblestones. Genna was reminded of her first walk alongside the Seine to the Eiffel Tower just after she'd arrived in Paris, getting on for two months ago. She realized with a jolt that she'd left Vancouver not long after the conception of her first grandchild.

"I'll need a few more weeks to finish the book," Genna said suddenly.

"What was that?" Becky was distracted by a houseboat gliding by, its windows cheerful with purple and yellow petunias sprouting from painted pots.

"I need to finish the book before I go home," Genna repeated, feeling like the life she wanted for herself would paradoxically end just as her grandchild started kicking.

"Go home? I thought you wanted to stay in Paris."

"Well, yes, but things have changed now."

"You mean because of the baby."

"Yes, I mean because of the baby, Becky."

215

"Why should you come home just because I'm having a baby?" Becky looked truly bewildered.

"Don't you want me to come home?"

"For Dad's sake, maybe, but not for me. I might not even stay in Vancouver."

"You won't?"

The thought hadn't occurred to Genna. She'd just assumed Becky would keep working at the museum, have the baby, and then, well, she hadn't thought that far ahead. Genna wasn't ready to offer her services as a live-in babysitter, but she thought Becky would jump at the chance to have her mother close by.

"I don't know for sure where I'll be," Becky said, tears again filling her eyes. She flicked her head and concentrated again on the boats.

"You have to tell him."

"I know." Her voice was so small, so wretched, so un-Becky that Genna longed to take her in her arms again and stroke her head, just like she'd done when Becky was four and feeling jealous of her baby brother.

"Maybe I *want* to come home," Genna said after a few minutes.

"You don't," Becky said grinning through her tears. "If you decide to go home, do it for yourself. Please promise me you won't leave Paris out of some misguided sense of maternal duty."

"Get used to it, dear. It's what mothers do."

"I'm not the baby here."

"Unfortunately, love, you'll always be my baby. That will never change, no matter how many babies of your own you have." Genna patted Becky's arm and steered her toward the stairs leading up to the road. "But I promise I'll only come home because I want to."

The massive Musée d'Orsay rose along the left bank of the Seine, its origins as a railway station still visible in the glass domed roof and huge archways. Surprisingly for early June, the lineup at the entrance was short and moved swiftly. Genna and Becky entered the cool foyer and walked into the main hall with its grand open spaces, monumental sculptures, and golden light.

"Do you want to meet back here in an hour?"

"Let's stay together today," Becky said.

Genna just about fell down the first sweep of marble steps. "You're kidding!"

"I know, it's not our usual style," she said, "but let's just stroll along. I promise I won't go too slowly." Misinterpreting Genna's expression of disbelief, she said, "Unless you'd rather be alone to get inspired? I'm guessing there might be quite a few aspects of the museum you could incorporate into your book."

"I've been here a few times and already have something for *Le Déjeuner sur l'herbe* by Manet and a nice apple tart that goes with the great clock."

"How about the museum as a whole?"

"Not yet. But I'm sure something will come to me today. Don't worry. I'm just as likely to think of something with you as without."

"All right then. Let's go right to the fourth floor."

They followed the hordes to the fourth floor and began their reverential stroll through room after room of some of the greatest paintings of the nineteenth century—Manets, Monets, van Goghs, Renoirs, Cézannes. The colors, shapes, and textures whirled into one brilliant mass that always left Genna awestruck. When she was in a place like the Musée d'Orsay, she often thought the whole world would be at peace if only everyone took up painting. How could people have time to kill each other when they were busy swirling colors across a canvas?

Thus transported, Genna forgot for a few moments about Becky. When she turned to find her, she was invisible among the heaving masses of T-shirts and baseball caps. Genna stood in the center of the room and turned in a slow circle. Had Becky gone on into the next room? Was she still lingering in the last one? The crowds were so thick that she couldn't see either doorway.

The museum was huge. They could easily wander in circles for hours and never cross paths. She remembered the day Becky went missing from home. She'd been just five years old and as stubborn then as she was now. She'd lashed out at her little brother, and instead of going to her room as ordered, she'd walked out of the house and disappeared.

Twenty-two years later Genna could still dredge up the guilt as vivid as a slash of red blood across one of Monet's snow-covered haystacks. If she'd only been more vigilant, more understanding, less angry, her little girl would not have walked away. If something had happened to Becky, Genna doubted she'd have survived. Fortunately, she and Drew found Becky two hours later playing on a grass boulevard three streets away. She'd looked up and with the impatience of a child asked, "Where were you?" In her mind, she'd been lost and so had sat down to wait for her parents to find her, just as she'd been taught.

Would she do the same now?

Genna returned to the room she'd come from and stood in the center. The crowds flowed around her, like ball bearings scattering across the smooth wood floors, some people looking at the paintings, some reading, some snapping pictures, many yawning.

The recipe to pair with the Musée d'Orsay came to her just as she spotted Becky. She was stationed squarely in front of one of the most famous works in the museum, much to the frustration of several people around her who were holding their phones aloft to get square-on pictures.

Genna moved closer and almost laughed out loud. No wonder Becky was so captivated.

Called *Mère et enfant sur fond vert*, the pastel drawing by Mary Cassatt showed a mother holding a child of about six months. In the hands of a lesser artist, the subject could easily have been sentimentalized. But Cassatt's drawing provided an achingly intimate glimpse into the unfathomable love of a mother for her child—quiet, graceful, and as solid and immovable as granite.

Becky glanced sideways, noted Genna's presence, and then flicked her eyes back to the drawing. There was a softness about her stance that Genna had never seen before. Angular and athletic, Becky was a poster girl for strong, unselfconscious womanhood.

She made no apologies for who she was. With Becky, middle ground didn't exist.

And now she was about to take her first steps into the chaotic, complicated, messy, and glorious realm of motherhood.

Genna knew that Becky, like all first-time mothers, had no clue what she was in for. But like millions of women before her stretching back millennia, self-absorbed, opinionated Becky would make many mistakes and suffer agonies of uncertainty, but she would survive.

"I never appreciated Cassatt before," she murmured.

"I had you down as more of a van Gogh girl," Genna said. "All tortured swirls and bursts of hot energy."

Becky shook her head. "Probably more like Dalí."

Genna nodded. *"Metamorphosis of Narcissus?"*

Becky grinned. "Something like that."

"Ready to go?"

"How about lunch? I'm starved."

"That's what you get for skipping breakfast," Genna said as she led the way to the stairs.

"More like breakfast skipped me. How long does this bit last?"

"A few more weeks. By the fourth month, your tummy settles down and you start feeling pretty good. I remember loving that stage of my pregnancy with both you and Michael. You're big enough so people know you're pregnant and not just fat, but you're still compact enough to move around."

"And the last three months?" Becky asked as they left the museum and emerged into a sunny day.

"Don't ask!"

They walked to a bistro just a few blocks from the museum. Once they were seated, Genna said, "While you were mooning over the Mary Cassatt, I figured out a good dish to pair with the Musée d'Orsay."

"And?"

"Cassoulet!"

Becky looked blank.

"Come on! Don't you remember having the most amazing cassoulet when we went to Carcassonne?"

"I was twelve and I just wanted McDonald's."

"Oh yeah, I blocked that bit out. Well, anyway, cassoulet is a specialty of southwest France. Beans and garlic sausage and duck confit are layered and slow cooked."

"What's the tie-in with the Musée d'Orsay?"

"Beans."

"Excuse me?"

"I was watching all the people crowding into the galleries and I couldn't help thinking of them as so many ball bearings all rolling along together, one indistinguishable from the next. Then from there I went to beans — white haricot beans that are smooth and round and meaty. And from *there*, I thought of richness — the paintings, which led me to think of chunks of homemade garlic sausage and duck confit legs simmered in wild garlic and . . ."

"Stop!" Becky held up her hand. "I get the picture. The cassoulet mixes all kind of colors and textures with herbs and beans, just like the museum combines paintings and people."

"Exactly!" At this rate, they'd start wearing matching stretch pants and pink T-shirts with MOTHER on one and DAUGHTER on the other.

Becky shrugged. "It's okay, I guess."

Oh.

Genna changed the subject to one closer to Becky's heart. *Becky.*

"Have you told anyone else about the baby?" She wanted to add *like your father,* but resisted.

"No."

"And you didn't exactly *tell* me. When were you planning to, by the way?"

"There's hardly been time. I've been here less than a week, and you've kept me busy with relentless sightseeing."

"Hardly relentless."

"Whatever."

"You haven't answered my question. When were you going to tell me about the baby? Or maybe you weren't planning to tell me at all?"

"To be honest, I don't know. The trip was kind of last minute. I was due for a few weeks off between projects, and then Dad suggested I come over to see you. He even paid my airfare. You know he's worried sick about you, Mom."

"I doubt that."

"Come on, Mom, don't be so hard-hearted."

Genna refrained from saying that she wasn't the one keeping news of her baby from the father. And Rolf would make a great father. At thirty-one, just four years older than Becky, he was moving steadily up in his engineering firm. He was also good with money which Becky was not. He'd already purchased a small two-bedroom house in Kitsilano. One of the bedrooms would make a perfect nursery.

"Mom!"

"Huh?"

"You're not listening to me. I said you shouldn't be so hard-hearted."

"I'm not hard-hearted, Becky. That's the trouble."

Becky looked at her quizzically, and for a few moments, Genna considered telling her about her father's cheating. Maybe then she'd stop taking her father's side.

The waiter arrived with a large *salade Niçoise* for Genna and a wedge of spinach quiche for Becky, and the moment passed. Maybe it wasn't a good idea to disillusion Becky about her father. She'd been a daddy's girl all her life.

"Eat," Genna said.

"You can always depend on food to change the subject," Becky said, but with a smile that showed she wasn't as irritated with Genna as was her habit.

Motherhood really was agreeing with her daughter, Genna thought, as she speared a wrinkly, black olive and savored its rich Mediterranean saltiness.

221

twenty-five

Rose Macarons

Delicate pink shells filled with lavender-infused rose cream

"Don't take this the wrong way, love, but are you crazy?"

"Probably."

"Come here." Bill's large brown hand cupped Genna's shoulder and drew her close. They were sitting together on a sunny bench in the Tuileries. All around them lavish flower beds wafted their perfumes into the balmy air. The weight of his arm comforted her. He felt solid, like he'd never let her down.

She sighed deeply. "I want to do what's right."

"Then you need to do what feels right for you."

"What about Becky?"

"She'll be fine. That's one independent girl you've got there. I wouldn't fancy the chances of anyone getting in her way, even her mother."

"That's true. She's been her own girl since she was a baby."

"And didn't she tell you not to go home on account of her?"

"Well, of course she *said* that. But that doesn't mean she means it. Besides, it's my first grandchild. I want to be there."

"Last time I checked, planes were still flying over the Atlantic."

"The reality is that I'll have to go home in a few months anyway. My money's running low."

"You want to stay, don't you?"

"I love it here, even with my bad French and the high prices and always feeling like an outsider."

"It's a fine city."

"What would you do if you could stay in Paris past the six months?" Bill asked.

Genna drew away from him and sat up straight. "Promise you won't laugh?"

"Why would I laugh?"

"Because my idea is ridiculous."

"More ridiculous than giving up and going home because your perfectly capable and independent daughter is having a baby?"

"Good point. Okay, here goes. I want to start a small cooking school."

There, she'd said it. The idea had come to her the night before when she'd lain awake for hours, thinking about Becky and the baby and knowing that she really didn't want to go home.

"In Paris?"

"Of course, in Paris. I'd cater to tourists, mostly North Americans and Brits since my French is pretty limited."

"Aussies?"

"Sure, them too. Do you think they'd be interested in learning how to cook something other than shrimp?"

"You malign an entire continent."

"You'll survive. Am I totally crazy?"

"Yes."

"Bill!"

"You asked. And now may *I* ask what you plan to use for money, since you've said you're running low?"

She was surprised by his businesslike tone, although she shouldn't have been. The owner of ten branches of a landscaping company could probably navigate his way around a balance sheet.

"I'm still hoping Drew sells the house, plus I have some investments to cash in."

"That's your plan? You're expecting your husband to sell a house he's refused to budge from in over a year and who, from what I can gather, is still hoping you'll come through the front door and back into his arms? And as for cashing in your investments, have you looked at the markets lately?"

"My investment advisor said I could be looking at a fifteen percent return."

Bill snorted. Yes, he snorted like a bull elephant, shaking off pesky flies under the hot African sun. Genna didn't like the image of herself as a pesky fly.

"What's wrong?"

He waved away the question, and then with a visible effort to keep his voice neutral said, "Let's just say, for the sake of argument, that the house sells and your investments pay. Will it be enough?"

"I haven't crunched the numbers yet."

"Then do some crunching and tell me what you come up with."

"The house has gone up in value."

"*If* you can sell it."

Genna was not sure she liked Bill the businessman. Before her eyes, the blunt exterior hiding a heart of gold had hardened into a cold-blooded numbers man. She felt tears pricking at her eyes and looked down quickly.

"Do yourself a favor and crunch the numbers," he said, his tone softening. "You might have enough to get started, but you shouldn't do anything until you have the facts. How much does space cost in Paris? Where would you set up? How about permits? Marketing? Supplies? Those are just some of the things you need to consider."

"I know!" Genna's head flew up, her tone was sharper than she intended because his reality check was franker than she wanted. She preferred her version of *La Vie en Rose* where Drew sold the house and, weeks later, she was cooking for a steady stream of grateful foodies.

"I am sure of one thing," Bill said, his voice kind. "If anyone can figure things out, it's you." He stood and reached for her hand. "Now come on, let's enjoy the rest of our day. We can talk about business after you've had a chance to think things through."

Genna let him pull her to her feet. While part of her felt foolish for sharing her dream to offer cooking classes in Paris, the other part felt the tiniest bit heartened that Bill hadn't dismissed it out of hand.

He took her arm and veered onto the central path that led through the Tuileries toward the Champs-Élysées. They strolled through the gardens, his hand firmly encasing hers. The skin was calloused and soft at the same time, like he worked hard all day at his landscaping and then soaked his hands each night in freshly squeezed aloe vera. Did they have aloe vera in Australia?

More like essence of wombat or great white shark.

"I haven't figured out a dish to pair with the Tuileries yet," Genna said as they wandered past formal flower beds edged with military precision and filled with sweetly scented rose bushes in full bloom along with newly planted summer annuals in a riot of colors.

"No? I'd have thought it would be one of the easy ones."

"Why so?"

"There's so much abundance here!" Bill said. "These gardens are like a banquet for the eyes. You need a dish that looks as good as it tastes."

"All dishes should look as good as they taste. But I know what you mean. I need something bursting with textures and colors. I just have to pick the right ones."

"And you will."

As they wandered through the gardens, Genna focused on the flower beds.

Green leaves, deep brown soil rich with nutrients, flowers in deep pinks and purples, sunshine yellows, and dashing reds.

"*Salade Niçoise*," she said quietly.

"Explain."

"A *salade Niçoise* combines a banquet of tastes and textures—black olives and white tuna and yellow eggs and vivid green asparagus with steamed new potatoes on a bed of greens. Every bite is a new combination of salty and crunchy. Yes. *Salade Niçoise* it is! I just had one yesterday with Betsy and it was perfect. Thank you, Bill. You're a great muse."

"I'm glad we decided to meet here. These gardens are some of the best I've seen."

"I suppose you ought to know."

"Too right. It takes a helluva lot of planning to do what they've done. My hat's off to the master gardener."

"Do you miss it?" Genna asked.

"The landscaping business?"

"I don't mean the business part. I mean the flowers, the shrubs—all this." She swept her arm in an arc that took in a flowerbed filled with magenta zinnias.

"Some days," he admitted, "but there's precious few opportunities for gardening at the condo I moved into after Marjorie passed. I putter along with a few pots and such on the balcony, but other than that I'm pretty much out of it."

"Why couldn't you have bought a place with a garden? You don't strike me as the kind of man who would enjoy condo living."

"I considered it. But then Tyler and his sisters convinced me I should get something easy to take care of so I can spend a few years traveling the world and squandering their inheritance."

"How's it working out so far?"

"Well, I'd say I'm doing pretty bloody well. I found you on my first stop."

"Found me?"

Right in the middle of the smooth gravel pathway, Bill stepped in front of Genna. Before she had time to take an extra breath, he kissed her.

A long, comfortable kiss. A kiss that made her feel young and beautiful and desirable, like she hadn't felt for a very long time.

There was nothing else for her to do but melt. He could have lifted her up and had his way with her behind a naked statue and she wouldn't have said a word. She'd have been too busy moaning. *Oh là là là là.*

When they finally came up for air, the decision was made. They left the gardens, hopped into a taxi on the Rue de Rivoli, and minutes later were walking into the gilt and gold lobby of Bill's hotel on the Rue Saint-Honoré. If she were in any doubt that Bill Turner was seriously wealthy, the sumptuousness of the hotel was proof. She never realized there was so much cash to be made planting petunias.

His room was even more beautiful than the lobby. The thread count of the sheets was off the charts. Who knew that fiber woven by human hands could be so soft?

Fortunately, *soft* was not the word she'd use to describe what slid between those sheets and into her.

A few hours later, they were giggling like high school sweethearts and hungry enough to eat half of Paris.

"All right, my girl, what now?"

Genna stretched her arms over her head and enjoyed the admiring look on Bill's face as her breasts popped out from under the covers.

"Hungry?"

"Too right!"

"I'd better call Becky," she said. "She might wonder where I am."

"When did she expect you back?"

"I didn't say. She knew I was meeting you for a drink. She'll probably think we got held up."

"I suppose you could call it that," he said, grinning. He had nice teeth—white and straight against the brick red of his complexion.

"Shut up!" Genna stretched across him to extract her phone from her backpack. He reached down and slapped her bottom with enough force to send a delicious tremor through her entire body. Well, so much for Becky. By the time they surfaced again, the clock on the bedside table read nine, and she was more famished than she'd ever been in her life.

"We have *got* to eat!" Genna exclaimed, disengaging herself and jumping out of bed. "I can be ready in five minutes." Leaving him stretched out in blissful exhaustion on the bed, she hopped into the bathroom, paused to admire its gleaming porcelain, and then stepped into a pulsing hot shower. Every inch of her body vibrated with pleasure. She'd forgotten what it felt like to make love for hours on end. Come to think of it, had she ever known? Before Drew, she'd had little experience beyond the usual adolescent fumbling.

And even when she was first married, she and Drew had never had time for much more than the basics. Then the babies arrived and for almost thirty years, with the occasional exception, passion had taken a back seat to life.

And now, here was Bill Turner — big, blustery, and loud and all the way from Sydney, Australia. What was she to make of him? What did she expect to happen next?

She had no idea.

When Genna emerged from the bathroom, Bill was dressed and sitting on the edge of the bed, his phone clamped to one ear, his free hand making notes. "Not bloody likely," he growled. "I already told him no." His voice rose. "I'm not changing my mind."

He twisted around to see Genna standing in the bathroom doorway. "Hold on a sec." He held the phone to his chest and motioned to her clothes, which were strewn across the floor and furniture. "It's fine, love. I won't be a moment."

She picked up her clothes and scurried back to the bathroom. As the door closed behind her, she caught the words "home" and "flight."

Those were definitely not the words she wanted to hear so soon after having her nerve endings blown apart.

twenty-six

Peach Macarons
Roasted peach filling between pink and orange shells

Becky was asleep on the couch by the time Genna got home at eleven.

The last two hours of her evening had not measured up to the first hours, not by a long shot. She and Bill had barely spoken after they left the hotel in search of a meal. The good restaurants in the area were all closing, so they ducked into a café. A handful of glum-looking customers were finishing their coffees, and the young woman on duty scowled at them for making her put down her phone to take their orders. The menu looked like it had been printed in 1975, its edges brown and curled, smears of ancient sauces obscuring half the words. The typical café fare was listed: omelets, simple sandwiches, a few soups and salads, some pasta dishes, and a few entrées.

Genna ordered fillet of sole and was presented with a cracked plate containing a mound of limp green beans, a shriveled piece of fish buried under a gummy yellow sauce, and a puddle of scalloped potatoes the color of dirty wax. Bill opted for an omelet that after a few bites he declared inedible.

The meal passed in gloomy silence. Bill's responses to Genna's attempts at conversation were monosyllables at best, distracted grunts at worst. And this was the man who just hours before had transported her to heights of pleasure she hadn't known the human body capable of—particularly her human body.

They'd parted on the curb, Bill to walk back to his hotel and Genna to grab a taxi to take her across the river. He mumbled what sounded like an apology and then trudged into the Parisian night.

"Mom?" Becky's voice cut through the darkness. "You can turn on the light if you want. I'm not asleep."

Genna felt like their roles had suddenly reversed. She was the rebellious teenager coming home late after being up to no good with the captain of the rugby team, while Becky was the long-suffering mother trying hard to find the right mix of parental discipline and hip understanding.

"Your boyfriend dropped by."

"Who?"

"Sorry, I mean your *Parisian* boyfriend. It's so hard to keep track these days." She grinned at the look of horror on Genna's face. "Monsieur Leblanc, Mom."

"Pierre?" she asked alarmed.

"You mean from the *tabac*?"

"Yes. He's the one who gave you the key. Tall, handsome, early fifties, snappy dresser? And we're just friends, in case you're wondering."

"I wasn't wondering, and you're not even close. Try short, dark, and smelly."

"Ah! That would be Monsieur Leblanc, *le père*. He's my landlord."

"I gathered as much. I also gathered that he's quite an admirer of yours, or at least of your cooking. He was disappointed that you weren't home with a hot meal waiting."

Genna collapsed into the recliner and kicked off her shoes. "I forgot this was one of Monsieur's nights. He's been coming to dinner twice a week for a while now. He's not much of a conversationalist, but he does appreciate good food."

"You mean he just comes over and invites himself to dinner?"

"I don't mind. What did he say?"

"You mean when he got over his disappointment that you weren't greeting him at the door with a steaming pot of lobster bisque?"

Genna nodded.

"He wanted to know who I was, and when I told him, he just grunted and left. I got the feeling he wasn't happy you were entertaining guests."

"He wouldn't be. You might use three more watts of electricity."

"I kind of liked him."

"He scared me to death the first time I met him, but I have to say he's grown on me over the past few weeks. I can practice my French, and he doesn't groan when I mispronounce something. Also, he gives me tips about my recipes. His sainted *grand-mère*, who brought him up after his parents were killed in the War, was apparently a wonderful cook. Since my cookbook focusses on typical Parisian bistro fare, Monsieur is familiar with many of the recipes."

"He doesn't look like a gourmet."

"No, but he's a Frenchman, which means he has great respect for the affairs of the stomach. Also, I think he's lonely. His wife died a few years ago and Pierre's often busy. He's a lawyer, *un avocat*. Monsieur is very proud of him."

"You were out a long time. How's Bill?" The quick change of subject caught Genna off guard. She was hoping she'd get through the conversation without mentioning her evening.

"Fine."

"What did you do?"

"Nothing much."

Like laser beams, Becky's eyes bored into Genna. "You look different. Are you sure everything's okay?"

"Of course. I'm just tired." To underscore her point, Genna closed her eyes and slumped back in her chair in what she hoped was a convincing display of simple exhaustion brought on by nothing more than a long walk in the fresh air and too much wine at dinner. There was no way Becky would suspect anything. Children never suspected their parents of having a sex life.

"You slept with him."

Genna's eyes flew open. Becky should have been a spy for the Secret Service. No double agent would stand a chance against her.

Genna let a few beats go by. "Well, we didn't really sleep."

"Very funny. All right, then. You had sex."

"Yes, Becky. Your mother is a loose woman. Would you like details?"

"Yuck, of course not. But what about Dad?"

"What about him?"

"You're still married."

"As you keep reminding me. But it's way too late to talk about this. You need to get your sleep and I'm about ready to pass out."

"I'll bet you are." Becky grinned.

"Ha, ha." Genna pretended to be offended and stalked into her bedroom. As she shut the door, she heard Becky laughing, fully and delightfully.

* * *

The next morning, Genna and Becky studiously avoided any mention of the two topics uppermost in their minds.

"Today is my French class," Genna said after she'd eaten her breakfast and Becky had thrown up twice and was half lying on the couch, white-faced and exhausted. "Do you want to come with me and then go for lunch after? I could ask Marsha. You two should get to know each other."

"Why?"

"She's just a few years older than you and she likes art."

"Lots of people like art."

"Suit yourself. You'll meet her and the others at the party next week. I'm going for coffee across the street. Coming?"

"All right. It's not like I have anything better to do."

"Fine. I'm leaving in ten minutes."

"Fine." Becky affected her usual expression of bored unconcern, but nature proved too much for her. Her eyes bulged and her throat constricted and she darted back into to the toilet.

Genna heard retching, then silence as Becky recovered herself, then the flush of the toilet and finally the water running as she brushed her teeth.

Genna tapped on the door. "How about I meet you at the café in about fifteen minutes? That will give you time to get yourself together."

"Okay."

Becky couldn't have sounded more pathetic if she'd tried, and Genna knew Becky wasn't trying. She loathed being ill and saw it as a sign of weakness. Morning sickness was hard enough for anyone, but for Becky it was truly hell.

Genna grabbed her daypack and left the apartment, sprinting down the five flights of stairs to the street and along three blocks to the internet place. She would need to be quick to get the email off to Rolf and be back at Les Deux Magots in fifteen minutes, looking cool and unconcerned.

When she arrived, breathless, every computer in the small storefront was being used. "How long?" she demanded.

The attendant shrugged. He was the same guy from Texas whom Genna often spoke with after checking her email. "Probably ten minutes. Most of 'em just got here. Bad timing."

Genna paced restlessly. What did she think she was doing? Becky would murder her if she found out.

"Genna? That one's free now." The attendant jerked his head toward a computer just being vacated by a sweet-looking young woman no older than eighteen or nineteen, her cheeks wet with tears. Genna smiled sympathetically at her and then sat down at the computer and logged on.

* * *

"Where were you?" Becky asked when Genna arrived at the café to find her sitting at an outdoor table, sour-faced and fuming as she sipped the jasmine tea she'd grudgingly taken to drinking instead of coffee. "You told me to meet you in fifteen minutes and it's been at least half an hour."

"I just popped into the internet place down the street. I was hoping Nancy might have emailed."

"Did she?"

"No."

Becky gestured to the waiter and ordered Genna a café au lait. "Feeling better?"

"Marginally." She lapsed into moody silence.

Genna let her sulk as she relaxed with her coffee. Few activities were more relaxing than sitting at a marble-topped circular table at the side of a busy street on the Left Bank of Paris, sipping a foamy café au lait and watching the sun play across the facades of the surrounding buildings. How could she even think of leaving?

How could she find a way to stay?

Although she'd sworn not to let it ruin her day, Genna's mind turned to one of the emails she'd retrieved. It was from Jack, the financial advisor she'd hired to take care of the savings she'd extricated from her joint investments with Drew. Jack had indicated that judging on past performance, she could expect a 15 percent return on one of her short-term investments, maybe more. He'd purchased some surefire stocks that were bound to shoot up dramatically, probably within a few weeks and *definitely* by the time she needed to top up her bank account in June. Sure, the stocks were considered "high risk," if you wanted to use those words, but, honestly, that was just a figure of speech. *These* stocks were poised to go as high as Everest.

Genna couldn't lose.

But erosion wears down all mountains eventually, even Everest. When she read in Jack's email that the stocks had plummeted, she felt like she'd been kicked in the head. With the house still unsold and no money coming in from the investments,

Genna could not afford to stay in Paris. A half-strangled sob escaped her throat before she was able to grab it back. Becky's head whipped around.

"What's wrong?"

"Nothing."

"You're not worried about the baby?"

"No! Of course not. Why would I be? I'm thrilled about becoming a grandma. My only worry is how *you're* going to cope."

"I'll cope fine."

"I know, but I can't help worrying. Bringing up a child is not easy."

"Especially on your own. That's what you want to say."

"It's hard whichever way you slice it, but doing it on your own will have its challenges. I have to say that your father was good with you two when you were little. He wasn't keen on changing diapers, but he always made time to play with you."

"He was wonderful." Becky sighed.

Genna resisted the urge to remind Becky that she'd been the parent who went on school outings and shepherded her and her brother to piano lessons, dance lessons, swimming lessons, skating lessons, archery lessons, skiing lessons, Taekwondo meets, soccer practices, and soccer games (almost always in the rain). Becky had been an active child who rarely passed up the opportunity to cost Genna money. And as for Michael, he had a passion for every sport known to man or boy. It was a wonder she ever wrote one cookbook, never mind five, even if only a few yielded decent royalties.

Which brought her back to her financial troubles.

Damn.

"Yes, your father was a peach," she said. "Very caring."

To Genna's surprise, Becky reached over and placed her hand on her mother's. "I never said he was perfect, Mom. I know what he's like when he's in a bad mood."

"A pain in the ass?"

"Is that why you left him?"

"Not exactly."

"So?"

"Let's not talk about it." Genna glanced down at her watch. "*Merde!* Class starts in half an hour and we have to take two Métros to get there." She threw some euros on the table and stood up. "Come on, you're about to meet my friends."

On the Métro, Becky lapsed into her own thoughts, while Genna tried not to not think about her hollowed-out investments. Instead, she contemplated the stations whizzing by and wondered about finding a dish to pair with the Métro. Most large cities had subway systems, but there was something special about the Paris Métro, a sense of history in the old entranceways, their elaborate wrought iron green with age but still evoking the Belle Époque.

And the stations themselves often had a surprising amount of personality. The Louvre station displayed dramatically lit ancient art, and in the Concorde station, the text of the 1789 *Declaration of the Rights of Man and the Citizen* was set in tiles. The Cluny La Sorbonne station celebrated the writers of the Latin Quarter, and the Bastille station featured murals depicting scenes from the French Revolution. Another great thing about the Paris Métro was its price. Unlike the subways in most world capitals, the Paris Métro was ridiculously, gloriously cheap. For a couple of euros, it was possible to ride from one end of Paris to the other. A suitable recipe should be something frugal, and suitable for a quick weeknight dinner. Genna's mind flipped through possibilities. What dish could go with the Paris Métro?

Fast, cheap, efficient, but with a touch of whimsy, a sense of history. Pissaladière!

A round of flatbread was spread with caramelized onions and then studded with olives and crisscrossed with strips of anchovies reminiscent of tracks across the belly of Paris. Common in Provence, pissaladière was good peasant food, economical, easy to make, and fast to eat on the run.

"You're looking pleased with yourself," Becky said as the train rattled into Champs-Élysées Clemenceau and they rose to leave.

"I figured out another recipe for the book, one to go with the Métro."

"And?"

"Do you remember pissaladière, the flatbread from Provence? You and Michael ate a ton of it the summer we visited Nice."

"I remember," she said, laughing. "Michael got so sunburned that his little arms looked like glow sticks."

"Poor dear. He hated having to stay in the shade while you and your dad went swimming."

"And you sat under the umbrella and read cookbooks."

"I was in heaven!"

Becky smiled as they climbed the stairs out of the Métro onto the busy Champs- Élysées. "We had fun in those days, didn't we?"

"Of course, we did."

"So why did you leave?"

Genna stopped so suddenly in the middle of the sidewalk that the large tour group barreling down the street behind them was forced to split and flow around them. Their leader, holding a blue pennant aloft, threw Genna a dirty look as she passed.

"Please don't keep on at me as if I'm some kind of a villain. You know that any breakup involves two people."

"Dad says you left for no reason."

"Believe that if you want." Genna started walking again, quickly now since they were a few minutes late, and Mademoiselle was a real stickler for promptness. They'd be in for a long harangue in rapid French that would leave her stammering and red-faced.

"You can't keep running away!" Becky said.

"You're one to talk."

"That's totally different. Rolf and I don't have twenty-eight years of history."

"Not yet."

That silenced her. Becky contented herself with scowling as she followed Genna up the stairs to French class. Genna suddenly felt unsure about bringing her old life into her new life. Her Paris friends knew her only as Genna McGraw, the Canadian cookbook

237

author who spoke bad French and brought great treats. None of them except Marsha, and she only to a limited extent, knew anything about Genna's life as a wife and mother back in West Vancouver.

Genna needn't have worried. Becky knew how to be civilized when she chose, and she comported herself admirably throughout the class. Her French was better than Genna's, thanks to two summers spent in Québec when she was a teenager, and then a year working on her master's at Concordia University in Montréal. She was able to describe her job at the museum, her interests, and her travels with a respectable degree of grammatical precision. Her Québécois accent made poor Mademoiselle wince at times, but at least she didn't need to use the present tense in every sentence.

After class, Genna invited Marsha to lunch, but she declined with a shake of her head and a barely civil acknowledgment of Becky. Embarrassed, Genna hustled Becky down the stairs and into a tourist café on the Champs-Élysées.

"This place is awful," Becky said, throwing down the plasticized tourist menu that offered two choices of three-course lunches in four languages. They'd found a table outside under an awning and inches from the cars swishing past. Every other table was filled with tired-looking tourists. Genna had already heard Italian, Japanese, German, English, Chinese, Hindi, and Russian.

No French.

"I know, but let's eat something, and then we can decide what to do for the rest of the day."

Becky ordered the more expensive of the two lunches, which promised a slice of pâté, steak and *pommes frites*, and crème caramel. Genna opted for the cheaper one—*salade verte*, fettuccine, and a piece of gâteau. The first two courses, when they finally arrived in the hands of a sweating young woman who had forgotten how to smile, were spectacularly dreadful. Becky's steak lay comatose on the plate, its peculiar shade of brown making it look like a small brick soaked in mud. Genna's fettuccine consisted of slimy noodles glued together in a noxious fist. The conversation, or lack of it, matched the meal. Becky retreated into her own thoughts and Genna was preoccupied with comparing the food to the disastrous meal she'd shared with Bill the night before.

Would he call her again? Did she want him to? Hadn't all this angst about relationships been put to rest in high school?

Evidently not.

The doleful food and sparse conversation were interrupted by a sudden, fierce rainstorm. Genna and Becky forgot all about the demands of their stomachs in their frantic scramble for cover. The flimsy umbrella shading their table was no match for the monsoon. They were marooned in the middle of a waterfall so solid the buildings on the other side of the sidewalk turned into a blurred mass.

"This is insane!" Becky squealed when a bucketful of cold rainwater overflowed the edge of the umbrella and splashed down her back.

Their food was soon backstroking across their plates, the noodles from Genna's fettuccine oozing onto the slick table, and Becky's steak a canoe without a paddle.

"Let's make a run for it!" Genna said.

"You're kidding. We'll get soaked."

"We're already soaked."

Becky grinned and picked up her purse. The young server was huddling under an umbrella, miserably directing diners to make a dash across the flooded pavement into the restaurant to pay.

They sprinted across the sidewalk. The inside of the restaurant was a steam bath. Genna grabbed Becky's elbow to prevent her slipping on a puddle of rainwater dripping from the group of Spaniards in front of them. The last thing Becky needed was to slip and risk a miscarriage.

By the time they paid for lunches that neither of them had eaten, the rain had stopped — just stopped like God had turned off the tap. The sun flamed across the Champs-Élysées, and in seconds steam billowed from every surface.

"Amazing!" Becky said. They crossed to the pedestrian island. To the north rose the Arc de Triomphe bathed in a sun shaft that pierced the roiling clouds like a spotlight. She looked at Genna and grinned. "No wonder you love Paris, Mom. Look at that light!"

Trust Becky to be cheered up by a rainstorm.

* * *

By her second week in Paris, Becky had begun to loosen up. She allowed Genna to organize several outings and often looked like she was enjoying herself. They visited museums, spent an evening wandering the streets of Montmartre, and took a full-day tour to the palace at Fontainebleau. Unfortunately, Becky hadn't been able to enjoy that excursion since she'd spent most of it throwing up in public toilets. Already whippet thin, she was in danger of disappearing when she turned sideways. So far, Genna had not been able to detect even a hint of swelling in Becky's belly, although Becky had confided that her tiny breasts were starting to blossom, an occurrence that charmingly delighted her.

Genna saw Bill only once for a quick coffee while Becky was checking out one of the Gilbert Joseph bookstores on the Boulevard Saint-Michel. He hadn't been rude, exactly, but he'd been distracted, frowning several times. When she asked him what was wrong, he'd quickly changed the subject. By the time they'd finished their coffees, Genna was ready to sink under the table and become one with the cigarette butts.

Did Bill regret their romp under the million–thread count sheets? When they parted, he kissed her on the cheek and promised to call, then excused himself and lumbered off down the crowded street. Later, Genna poured her heart out to Nancy in an email. Nancy's reply the next morning was no surprise.

Genna!

You have *got* to stand up for yourself! This Bill guy is probably having cold feet. He's been a widower for only two years, right? He doesn't know what to do with you.

You must be clear. Let him know what you want out of the relationship. But don't scare him off. Suitable men aren't all that easy to find. I should know.

Keep me posted.

Love Nancy

Well, that was helpful. How should Genna know what she wanted out of the relationship? She and Bill barely *had* a relationship.

A bright spot in the week was Genna's preparations for the party on the upcoming Saturday. Becky was planning to return to Vancouver the Wednesday after, and Genna was beginning to think she'd be following her before long.

It was useless to put off the inevitable. She'd be out of money in a few weeks now that Jack had gambled her nest egg away, and she had to face the fact that Drew was never going to sell the House with the View without her there to make him.

And as Becky pointed out, she could easily finish the book at home, checking the internet if she forgot what something looked like. She wouldn't feel the sun on her face or hear the constant rumble of traffic or smell the damp old stone or taste the wind off the Seine, but who needed five senses? One would have to do, and that was that.

Everyone from class agreed to attend the party, including Mademoiselle Deville. So, with Marsha, Tessa and Denise, and Helmut, Genna had five people, six if Colin came. She'd seen Marsha outside of class only twice since Becky arrived and knew only that Marsha was back together with Colin. Tyler would also come, and she'd invited Bill, although she wasn't sure he'd show up. With herself and Becky, her apartment would be bursting.

Genna could hardly wait.

twenty-seven

Chestnut Macarons
Filled with Kahlua-chestnut puree

Five days before the party, Genna went online and bought her ticket back to Vancouver, then stopped by Monsieur Leblanc's dusty *tabac* to give him notice.

"*C'est un catastrophe!*" he wailed, hands like spotted claws massaging his skull in the dim light of the *tabac*. "You cook like an angel! You must not go."

"I have no choice, monsieur," Genna said as tears leaked down her cheeks. He started back in horror and then shepherded her around the counter and into the back room.

"Sit, *ma pauvre*," he said. "I close the shop. We talk."

The air in the back room tasted solid, as if for two hundred years it had stayed in the small space, absorbing smoke and cooking fumes until it became one rank mass. The only furnishings were an old, worn easy chair, one hard chair to which Monsieur led her, a bare table, a wall of bookshelves crammed with ancient paperbacks, most with their spines worn to the glue, and an enormous flat-screen television. Genna wondered if it had been a gift from Pierre. A single bulb lit the space, proving that Monsieur was as frugal with himself as he was with his tenant.

"I make tea," he said, crossing to the kitchen before stopping and looking back. "Or something stronger?" he asked hopefully.

"That would be fantastic!" Genna said, then, at his quizzical expression, switched to French. *"Mais oui, merci. Un verre de vin?"* A glass of wine?

"No, no, *non!*" he said in half English, half French. *"Pas de vin!"* He winked and grinned as he reached an arm around the kitchen door and produced a bottle of brandy. When she saw the label, she gasped appreciatively.

"Mais oui, ma pauvre," he said, pleased that she recognized the lengths to which he was prepared to go to cheer her up. *"Pour vous, le meilleur."* For you, the best. The bottle Monsieur brandished cost well over a hundred euros. Genna's taste buds stood at attention, the putrid air and her own despair forgotten.

Steak Diane flamed in brandy popped into her mind, but what to pair it with? She didn't think Monsieur's *tabac* would rank high on any tourist's list of Parisian must-sees. Her mental Rolodex of Parisian sites flipped open and as quickly slammed closed as Monsieur handed her a crystal brandy snifter, another anomaly in his dismal apartment. The heady aroma of the brandy invaded her sinuses. Who cared about a cookbook? She was about to be transported to nirvana.

Monsieur lowered his sparse frame into the easy chair and crossed his bony knees. *"Salut!"*

With suitably ecstatic and silent respect, he and Genna devoted their attention to their glasses. Few things are more enticing than the first swallow of a premium brandy. The startling smoothness, the warm glow, the sighing aftertaste. If heaven didn't serve Napoleon brandy, Genna wasn't going.

"So, *chérie*," he began after a suitable pause to acknowledge the brandy. "What makes you unhappy?"

"I told you. I must leave Paris."

"You do not like Paris?"

"I love Paris!"

"So why do you leave?"

"I must go home. I can't afford to stay any longer. My investments . . ."

"Ah!" he exclaimed. "Money? *L'argent?*"

"*Oui*. More like lack of money."

"*C'est dommage.*"

The tears welled up again. And before she had time to think better of it, she was pouring her heart out to Monsieur. He might not be the most salubrious of confidantes, but he did genuinely care about Genna, or at least about her cooking. She told him everything, about Becky and the baby, about Drew and her money troubles, about Bill, and even about her ridiculous dream to open a cooking school in Paris. He listened to it all with complete attention, only occasionally interrupting her to ask for clarification in French.

"You see, monsieur," she said, exhausted from her monologue. "I have no choice. Next week I return to Canada and you can rent the *appartement* again."

"But I do not want to rent it again."

"You'd get much more for it if you rented it by the night."

He shrugged.

"I won't forget how kind you've been."

He shrugged again and took a long, thoughtful mouthful of brandy. Genna attended to her own glass, feeling foolish that she'd unburdened herself. The man was only her temporary landlord. He didn't need to know her life story.

She finished her brandy, set the beautiful glass on the table, and stood.

"*Merci beaucoup, monsieur.* The brandy was incredible. *Incroyable.*"

He inclined his head. "*Bien sûr.*"

"I will bring the keys to you before I go, or should I take them back to the agency?"

He waved one gnarled hand. "What you wish."

"Well, *merci bien. Je pars maintenant.*"

Monsieur acknowledged her with a nod, but remained sitting, lost in thought and brandy fumes.

"*Au revoir,*" she said. He didn't reply. She left the room and walked through the darkened shop to the front door where she fumbled with the latch and then let herself out into the clear evening air. The breeze brought with it the luscious smell of roasting chicken from a nearby kiosk, crowded now with Parisians picking up their supper after a hard day's work at *le bureau*. The tears fell in earnest as she contemplated her prospects back home.

She'd have to return to the dingy suite in her cousin George's basement. He was twenty years older than she, a retired social worker who had never married. He'd taken Genna in when she needed a place to stay and would do so again without complaint. She and George had nothing in common except their grandmother. Even on a good day, his basement suite was uncomfortable, dank, and lonely.

But the price was right, and she had nowhere else to go.

Genna walked as far as the Boulevard Saint-Michel and turned north to the river, golden in the early-evening sun. Notre-Dame dominated the skyline to her right. She descended the stairs to the walkway by the river, her favorite place to go when the world started crashing in.

After walking west toward the Eiffel Tower for several minutes, Genna rounded a bend in the river past the Musée d'Orsay and glimpsed the dome of Les Invalides, under which lay the tomb of Napoleon. She hadn't yet visited Les Invalides. Although monuments to dead emperors left her cold, there was no denying the power of the place. Under Napoleon's rule, France's empire had extended as far as it ever would. Napoleon had also overhauled the legal system with the Napoleonic Code, set up government-run public schools, and created an efficient tax system. She should include his final resting place somewhere in her book.

In the back of her throat, Genna could still taste the last vestiges of Monsieur's brandy—Monsieur's *Napoleon* brandy. Right, of course. *Les Invalides Steak Diane Flambéed in Brandy*. Yes, that would do. And in the book, she'd include a dedication to Monsieur himself. His unwavering appreciation of her cooking had never failed to boost her confidence. Without Monsieur, she would not have considered including *Les Jardin des Plantes Leeks Braised in Wine* or *Les Halles Rabbit in Mustard Sauce*. Genna would always treasure her evenings with Monsieur, eating and drinking and talking about food.

The river glowed in the rays of the setting sun. What she was in love with, she reflected, was no man. She was in love with Paris — large, dirty, chaotic and enchanting Paris. It was just a city. But what a city!

She could live there forever.

The realization that living in Paris forever was never going to happen crashed in on her for the hundredth time that week. On Saturday, she would bid farewell to her new friends and less than a week later say *au revoir* to Paris to return home, low on cash and low on love, her self-esteem shattered.

Fuck.

Her phone rang, a delicate tinkling barely discernible above the sound of the river lapping against the stone embankment.

"Hello?"

"Mom?"

Her heart swelled as she sank onto a bench for once unoccupied by a couple in a clinch.

"Darling! Where are you?"

"I'm outside your apartment building. Where are *you*?"

* * *

"I can't believe you changed your email address and didn't tell me!" Michael marveled for what seemed like the tenth time that evening. He and his sister, who was still grumpy from the shock of having her little brother appear on their doorstep, sat opposite Genna in a bistro on Rue Saint Benoît about a block from the apartment. She loved both her children equally, but there was something about her little boy, her golden Michael, that always made her smile.

"Knock it off, Michael. Mom already said she was sorry." Becky glowered at her mother. "She's been *busy*."

Genna ignored Becky and sat forward. "So, what are your plans, darling?" Tall and tanned with tousled hair and a grin that had been melting Genna's heart since he was a toddler, Michael would have no trouble turning the heads of the Parisian girls. He lounged back in his chair like a friendly panther, all soft paws and coiled muscles. Becky, on the other hand, radiated tension. Her slight, compact frame, so like her father's, vibrated with indignation. Her hair and complexion matched her brother's, but in every other respect they were completely different. A stranger would never guess they were brother and sister.

But Genna had the stretch marks to prove they were.

"I'll hang out here in Paris with you for a few weeks, Mom. Okay?"

"Not really," snapped Becky before Genna had a chance to reply. "Did you not notice a distinct lack of beds in Mom's place? She's got the bedroom and I'm on the couch. Where do you plan to sleep?"

"I'm fine on the floor until you leave. Then I'll take the couch. No problem."

Becky looked mutinous.

"I might head south, pick up work crewing on a sailboat. I gotta keep myself busy until the winter."

"And then what?"

"I'll head to the Alps and get work there. Some of the European ski resorts are pretty amazing."

"Well, yes, the Alps are rather known for their ski resorts," Genna said.

Irony was lost on Michael. "Are you cool with me staying?"

"Of course, dear, but I'm leaving Paris next Thursday."

"Oh?"

"She's going home," Becky said. "Tell him, Mom."

"Genna sighed. "I'm afraid your timing is a bit off. But you're welcome to stay until I leave. And on Saturday, you can meet my Paris friends."

"You've made friends here?"

"A few. Two of them are around your age."

"Wow! Sounds like you've been having a good time."

"You could say that," Genna said.

"So why are you going home?"

"It's time. Now, tell us what you've been up to the past few months."

Michael accepted her nonexplanation with his usual ease and spent the rest of the meal entertaining his mother and sister with stories about his exploits up at Whistler, several of which made Genna cringe. The boy must have a guardian angel watching over him. If his stories were to be believed, he'd wriggled out of more close calls in six months than most people experienced in a lifetime. While he and Genna killed a bottle of the house red, Becky remained as tightly wound as ever. If Michael wondered why his sister wasn't drinking, he didn't ask.

They never mentioned the giant elephant in the bistro—their father.

twenty-eight

Strawberry Macarons
*Delicate pink shells filled with a simple vanilla
buttercream*

On the day of the party, Genna awoke at dawn, stepped over her sleeping son on her way to the kitchen, retrieved her notebook, and returned to bed. She adored preparing to cook for a crowd. A constant bustle of activity would fill the hours between now and the arrival of her guests—shopping at the market for the freshest ingredients, preparing each dish, setting the table, choosing the right flowers. It was like a dance that increased in intensity the closer she came to welcoming the guests and serving the food.

And the menu! It was a work of art if she did say it herself. She'd decided against making bouillabaisse for the main course, opting instead for salmon stuffed with shrimp. The weather had grown hotter, and the thick Mediterranean soup was more suited to frosty winter nights. When the guests arrived, they'd enjoy canapés garnished with spreads including *tapenade noire* made from black olives, *caviar d'aubergine*, *anchoïade*, and grapes stuffed with a variety of goat cheeses. Tessa was in charge of the canapés. She'd been over for a few cooking lessons since the night she and Denise came to dinner and was proving herself a willing apprentice. She had an innate sense of how flavors blended.

The canapés were paired in the book with the Centre Pompidou because their variety reminded Genna of the embarrassment of modern riches at the Pompidou. She could have created a recipe to pair with each of a dozen or more paintings, but then her readers would need a forklift to heft the cookbook onto their kitchen counters.

Genna decided to let nothing get in the way of her enjoyment of her last dinner party in Paris. She closed her notebook, threw back the covers, and pulled on her sweatpants and a tattered T-shirt, her favorite outfit for a day of intense cooking. When she tiptoed back into the living room, Becky was already stirring, getting ready for her first meeting of the day with the toilet bowl. She wouldn't be much help.

Thank goodness she could depend on Michael. She prodded his solid body with her toe. "Morning, sweetheart. Up."

"Go 'way."

"Ten minutes." She went into the kitchen and started laying out serving dishes and utensils.

"Morning, Becky."

Becky didn't answer as she stumbled across Michael on her way to the bathroom. He popped his head up and looked after her. "What's with her?" he asked as the unmistakable sounds of retching seeped through the thin bathroom door.

"Probably ate something that disagreed with her."

"She didn't drink anything last night and she barely touched her food."

"Maybe she's coming down with something."

"That's too bad, especially today when you're having your big party." Michael lay back on his pillow and stared up at the ceiling. "I hope it's not catching."

"I doubt that."

"Uh-oh!" he exclaimed. He reached under the couch and pulled out a copy of *So You're Pregnant . . . What Now?*

"So that's it!" He looked over at his mother with wonder in his eyes. "I'm going to be an uncle?"

"Don't ask me. It's up to Becky to tell you."

A few minutes later when Becky emerged shakily from the bathroom, Michael was ready for her. He leaped out of his sleeping bag and launched himself across the room, enfolding her in a bone-crushing embrace.

"Hey, sis! Congratulations! You'll make an amazing mom."

It wasn't often Genna saw Becky nonplussed, but this was one of those times. She stood rigid in her brother's embrace, her eyes wide with a mixture of terror and anger.

"Mom!"

It was astonishing how much venom she was able to inject into that one word.

"I didn't say anything!"

"Naw. Mom's okay," Michael said. "I figured it out on my own. The throwing up and this book were kind of a giveaway." He held it up. "Don't look at me like that, Becks. I think it's great." He grinned at her. "Where's Rolf?"

That was most definitely *not* the right thing to say. Becky flinched as if she'd been slapped, then struggled out of Michael's arms and flopped onto the couch, her eyes brimming with tears.

"Crap!" Michael said as he went to sit next to her. Clumsily, he put an arm around her and let her head fall on his shoulder. "Hey, come on. Everything's going to be fine. I'll help. I promise. I'll be the kid's favorite uncle."

"You'll be his only uncle."

"Yeah, well, no competition."

Genna watched the two of them from the archway leading to the kitchen. They were good kids. A surge of love engulfed her. Being a mother had one wonderful advantage over being a wife. It lasted forever.

Slowly, Becky let her brother defrost her. Even as children, Michael had been the only one in the family able to get uptight, on-edge Becky to relax. Genna remembered a time when Becky was eleven, her skinny little body as brittle as a matchstick. One stiff wind would shatter her. Someone at school had taunted her for being the top of her class in everything. Even as a child, Becky had been an awesome overachiever. The taunting might have made some children cry, but not Becky. She'd stomped around the house, a dervish of prepubescent fury. Drew hadn't been home and all Genna could do was get out of her way. Then sunny little Michael had strolled into the house.

He grabbed his sister's bony arm and pulled her onto the floor, tickling her until her howls of fury turned to howls of laughter. Why hadn't Genna thought of that? Although if Genna had tried to wrestle little Becky to the ground for a tickling match, she'd have lost an eye. Only Michael could get away with it.

Becky adored Michael. He was the only living thing she truly adored, a situation that was about to change, Genna thought happily.

The buzzer for the downstairs door interrupted the charming filial scene.

"That's Tessa," Genna said, hanging up the phone. "You'd better get dressed, Michael. She's shy enough as it is without you parading around in your skivvies."

"Sure, Mom." Michael strode into the bathroom, trailing clothes from his bursting backpack, leaving his sister looking calmer than Genna had seen her since she arrived in Paris.

Moments later, they heard the shower followed by the off-key tones of Michael singing an old Beatles tune.

"'Let It Be,'" Genna said in response to Becky's quizzical expression. "Although I admit it's hard to tell. Might be 'Help!'"

"Either way, how appropriate," Becky snorted, but her smile lingered. "I don't have much choice but to let it be, and I sure as hell will need help."

"Sounds like you're feeling better." Becky looked marginally less green, more of a light aqua beige.

"A bit," she said. "Maybe I'll be able to eat some of your lovely meal tonight."

Lovely meal? The presence of her brother really was mellowing Becky. Genna heard a quiet knock on the door.

"It's open!"

Dark brown arms, hair still hiding most of her face, and a slight body clad in a tight yellow T-shirt and red skinny jeans entered the apartment. Tessa peered at Becky, nodded, then scuttled toward the kitchen.

When she was halfway across the living room, Michael emerged from the hallway leading to the bathroom, his bottom half barely covered by a towel, his muscles rippling. Poor Tessa didn't stand a chance.

As she collided with Michael, the towel slipped alarmingly, before being caught in time by one lean hand while the other hand wrapped around Tessa's waist to prevent her falling. Michael blinked in surprise and held on a little longer than necessary. When he released her and stepped back, grinning, Tessa looked ready to faint.

The electricity crackling through the room could power a small city for a week.

"Hi!" Michael said. "You must be Tessa."

And then a startling thing happened. Tessa, who always wore an expression of surly dread, looked straight into Michael's eyes and smiled. Her entire face was lit from within. The effect was stunning and did not go unnoticed by Michael. Genna got the feeling that she and Becky could drop through the floor and neither Tessa nor Michael would miss them.

Becky broke the spell by heaving herself off the couch and pushing past them on her way to the bathroom. For once her pace was measured, which indicated she was heading there for normal purposes rather than to throw up.

"Get dressed, Michael! Tessa is here to help Mom with the party."

"I can help too." As Michael headed toward the bedroom to put some clothes on, he winked at Tessa, who giggled before joining Genna in the kitchen.

"We need to get to the market to pick up the fish and the produce. Here's the list." Genna held it out to Tessa, but before she could take it, Michael reemerged from the bedroom dressed in jeans and a T-shirt, looking even more gorgeous then he had half-naked. He crossed the living room in three strides and plucked the paper from Genna's hand.

"You stay here and get started on the prep, Mom. Tessa and I will do the shopping. Have you got some money?"

Tessa looked like she'd just discovered that Santa Claus did indeed exist. Genna would have to be a heartless brute to deprive her of Michael's company for an hour. And she rather liked seeing her Michael with Tessa. His kindness and good nature would bring her out of her shell, and there was an intensity about her that would appeal to Michael. They'd be hopelessly impractical, but Genna had married practical, and looking back, she wasn't so sure it had been the wisest thing she ever did, although at least it had produced Michael and Becky.

As usual, she was getting a little ahead of herself. Michael and Tessa had known each other for five minutes. It was a trifle early to start picking out her mother-of-the-groom outfit.

"Here's a hundred euros. Whatever you don't need for food, spend on a few bottles of wine. Most people will bring some, but we can always use more. Something white, preferably from the southwest, to go with the salmon. And make sure the strawberries are local."

"You got it. See you later."

Genna was confident that Michael would get everything on the list and that it would be the best quality available. Like all naturally gifted cooks, he had an uncanny ability to pick good ingredients. And if there was something on the list he couldn't find, he'd substitute something equally good. It was a shame he had no desire to pursue a career as a chef.

"It looks like Michael has made another conquest," Becky said as she appeared from the bathroom. "He's incorrigible."

"He certainly works fast. Tessa's young, but I think she's perfectly able to handle Michael."

"Let's hope so. You don't need *two* grandchildren."

Genna ignored the comment. "Are you up to helping me today?"

"Do you need my help?"

"I can always use an extra pair of hands on the day of a dinner party."

"This place is a mess."

"Yes, and most of the stuff belongs to you. Start by packing it back into your suitcase and shoving it all in my bedroom. Then you can tackle the bathroom and do the vacuuming. Oh, and there's the flowers to buy and arrange. Do you want to figure out what would go with the menu?"

"Leave it to me, Mom. I've read *The Feasting Gardener*. It's my favorite."

"You have a favorite? I didn't think you'd read any of my books."

"I haven't read all of them, but Rolf loves them and was forever cooking your recipes. I kind of started absorbing them by association." She stopped. "Why did I think of Rolf?"

"Considering he's the father of your unborn child, it's hardly surprising he'd occasionally find his way into your thoughts."

"I promised myself I'd put him out of my mind. If we were meant to be together, we already would be. I'm not going to impose my baby on him."

"It's his baby too."

"I'm the one having it!" Becky hovered one hand protectively over her belly. "And if I told him, I know he'd want to get back together."

"And that would be the worst thing in the universe. Imagine! Pledging your troth to a man who adores you and would probably lie down in the street in front of a speeding bus if it would do you any good. You'd be a fool to let him anywhere near you."

"Stop taking his side!"

"I'm not taking anyone's side. I'm telling you the truth, which you well know. Now, stop stalling and start cleaning. In about ten hours, this place is going to be awash in hungry people."

Genna walked over to the bookshelf where, in addition to the threadbare paperbacks and old guidebooks, was a small stack of CD's. She picked them up and handed them to Becky. "You can pick the music."

Becky grudgingly took the stack and shuffled through it. She put an ABBA CD into the player, smiling when *Dancing Queen* came on.

"Excellent choice," Genna said. "Now get to work."

To the accompaniment of 1970s disco, Genna settled into her day-of-a-dinner-party-groove. Everything would be perfect. Tomorrow, she'd start dismantling the apartment and packing up her cooking gear to go back to where she came from.

But today was for Paris.

twenty-nine

Peppermint Macarons
Zesty green and white striped shells with a rum filling

Becky finished tidying and left in search of flowers. Genna glanced at the little clock above the stove. If Michael and Tessa didn't get back soon, her finely crafted party prep schedule would be in serious jeopardy.

The phone rang, signaling the presence of someone down on the street wanting to enter the building. Both Michael and Becky had the combination to open the front door and Genna wasn't expecting anyone else. Had Bill come to explain his absence over the past week? In spite of herself, Genna's heartbeat quickened. She wished she could be one of those cool and collected women who went through life like a Teflon frying pan—nothing ruffling them, nothing bad sticking to them.

"You're six hours early!" Genna exclaimed to the tinny voice at the other end of the line. But she pressed the button to open the door and waited on the landing. In a few minutes, the sound of puffing heralded the arrival of Denise, her hair coiffed into a shiny helmet, her fleshy arms and shoulders quivering as she rounded the last twist of the circular staircase.

"I know, I know, I'm sorry to disturb you today," Denise said, bustling into the apartment. "You're probably frantically busy."

"Not terribly. Your daughter and my son went off hours ago to buy the food and they aren't back yet. They probably stopped for a coffee."

Or a quick bit of heavy petting by the river.

"Your son?"

"He arrived unexpectedly yesterday. But don't worry. He'll take good care of Tessa."

"Not worried," she said. It'll do her good to spend some time with someone of the male persuasion. Does your son like to cook?"

"Yes. My daughter can't tell the difference between bacon and ham, never mind how to put them together in a quiche, but Michael, my son, has been helping me in the kitchen since he was old enough for solid food."

"Then they'll have something in common," Denise said.

"Please," Genna said, remembering her manners. "Sit down. Can I get you anything? Cup of tea?"

"I'm fine, thanks." Denise perched on the edge of the couch. "I bring you a proposition and I want you to know up front that I won't be offended if you say no."

Genna's mind blanked. Was it something to do with Tessa? Did Denise want her to help get Tessa into chef school? Or did she want her to train Tessa herself?

"What's on your mind? And I can't imagine I'll say no whatever it is."

"All right, then," she said. "Do you remember I said I worked in TV before Tessa and I came to Paris?"

"I remember."

"My boss is Jason MacQuarrie. He's a TV producer?"

"Yes?"

"He puts programs together, reality shows and such. House hunters, renovation shows, living abroad, that sort of thing."

Genna nodded politely. "Okay."

What did this have to do with her?

"And cooking shows! You see?"

"See what?"

She rolled her eyes. "Your book," she said. "You passed out a bunch of the pages in class last week?"

"Yes?"

"I overnighted them to Jason."

"What?"

"The pages of your book! By courier. To London."

Dimly, a strange scenario drifted into the outer reaches of Genna's mind.

Her cookbook, Denise's TV producer boss, reality shows . . .

Her head snapped up.

"You're kidding!"

"Absolutely not!" Denise cried. "Jason *loved* what he read and can't wait to see the finished book. He said the concept of marrying recipes to Paris sites was—oh bollocks, hold on a sec."

Genna clamped her lips together, every nerve in her body taut with an excitement she didn't dare trust. Denise rummaged through her enormous purse, spreading its contents across the coffee table. An Eiffel Tower paperweight, a heavy sweater, two toothbrushes and a box of dental floss, a makeup bag the size of a laptop computer, a water bottle, a tin of peppermints, and three squashed Mars bars tumbled out before Denise produced her phone and scrolled through her messages.

"Right. Here it is." She cleared her throat, and swelled her generous bosom, clad today in skin tight purple spandex.

"Intriguing!" she said. "Yes, that's it. He says your cookbook idea is *intriguing* and he wants to talk to you about doing a show."

"You mean a cooking show?"

"Yes! Like the ones them celebrity chefs do? Jamie Oliver and that rude bloke?"

"Gordon Ramsay?"

"That's the one." Denise grinned. "I told Jason you'd be first rate on TV. People would want to watch you cook. You don't look all posh. You look normal."

In a flash, Genna saw bright lights and bustling crews, heard the call of a director for quiet on the set. Would they want her to go to England? Or could she stay in Paris? How? A million questions bubbled up.

"When?" she asked.

* * *

Denise took off shortly after answering as many of Genna's questions as she could, leaving Genna feeling like she'd been punched in the stomach by something soft and exceedingly pleasant.

Michael and Tessa arrived home a few minutes later and heard with the equanimity of youth the news of Genna's impending television stardom.

"I think it's brilliant, Genna! You on the telly! You'll be great."

"Good for you, Mom. You're the best cooking teacher I've ever had."

"I'm the only cooking teacher you've ever had," Genna said. "But this Jason guy just wants to meet me. Nothing's settled."

"He'll love you," Tessa said.

Genna smiled at the two of them, gratified they hadn't dismissed the prospect as absurd, which it clearly was. She moved in a daze from counter to sink to stove, her hands chopping and dicing and gathering, her mind flying forward to her meeting with Jason MacQuarrie, executive producer of Swan Productions, a company based outside London that specialized in developing reality shows—travel, home decorating, child-minding—and cooking. Many of Swan's shows were syndicated and sold worldwide. Genna recognized the names of some of the ones that had made it to North America.

In three weeks, she'd fly to London, meet Jason, and then . . .

The knife she was using to slice the strawberries slipped, narrowly missing her thumb.

"Shit!" she yelled, so loudly that Tessa dropped the pan of cold water she was moving from the sink to the stove to boil. A demure row of tomatoes lined up neatly on the counter awaited the plunge into boiling water to remove their skins. Even in her distraction, Genna had to admire the precise incisions Tessa had made in each tomato to remove the cores. Tessa had a brilliant career ahead of her if she was prepared to work hard.

"What's wrong? Are you hurt?" Tessa was so concerned that she forgot to be shy.

Genna waved her away. "No, I'm fine. Sorry." She bent down to clean up the water.

"I'll get it. You go sit down."

"What's all the noise about?" Michael asked, coming in from the bathroom. "You look awful, Mom. What happened?"

Genna slumped onto the couch. "I just realized that I'm going home next Thursday." She glanced up at Michael. "Denise has arranged for me to meet Jason next week, but I won't be here."

"Exchange your ticket," Michael said.

"It's nonrefundable."

"That sucks."

No kidding.

Suddenly, Genna had to get out of her apartment. Nothing made sense. She was preparing to leave a place she loved, give up a shot at the career of her dreams, and turn her back on any chance of romance.

For what? To go back to living in a dingy basement suite? In what universe did that make sense? The one in which she had no money.

Bingo.

Dreams didn't come true without solid financing.

It didn't matter how much she loved Paris. The brutal truth was that she'd be flat broke within a month. If she left Paris, she'd have enough to get settled into George's basement suite and feed herself for a few more weeks. Then, she'd be out knocking on doors for a teaching job at a second-rate cooking school for a few bucks more than minimum wage.

She stood up. "I've got to get out of here for a while. Can you manage?"

"No problem."

Genna left the party preparations in the capable hands of Michael and Tessa and set off down the stairway. She needed a long walk down by the river. At the bottom of the stairs, the sun pouring into the cobbled courtyard blinded her. Squinting, she crossed to the shadowed entrance area bounded by the heavy blue door that led to the Rue Bonaparte. With the door closed, she heard only the muted swish of passing cars, punctuated by the rumble and rattle of an occasional bus.

She was still several feet from the door when a thin slit of light sliced the dark, silhouetting a large black form in the open doorway. A few seconds later, the door banged shut, leaving Genna alone in the darkness with the looming presence. Her head told her she was safe. The sun-drenched courtyard was a few steps behind her. Most of the windows overlooking the courtyard were propped open to let in the hot June air. Help would come quickly if she yelled.

She started forward, meaning to edge past the body now almost filling the confined space. She needed only a few seconds to get to the door.

Her nostrils filled with the scent of Ivory soap overlaid with the sharp organic smell that had been her constant companion for most of her adult life.

"Hello?"

Genna stumbled backwards into the courtyard. A man emerged from the shadows, kicking a small suitcase in front of him.

"I thought that was you. Why's it so dark in this entryway? They should have a light."

"Drew? What the hell are you doing here?" Genna stared at him, the gap between them half a meter and eight thousand kilometers. "And how did you get in?"

"Michael."

"Oh. Well, I guess you'd better come up." She turned and crossed back over the courtyard to the stairs. She climbed quickly in a futile attempt to get as far ahead of him as possible — so far that he'd never catch up.

Fat chance.

"Hey! Not so fast!"

She sped up, thankful that all her walking around Paris had strengthened her legs. Drew on the other hand looked much pudgier than when she'd last seen him, his hair longer and grayer.

"It was a horrible flight," Drew said as he rounded the last turn of the stairway, his breath coming in gasps. "The food was garbage and I couldn't get an aisle seat."

She crossed her arms and stared down at him. "Why did you come?"

He reached the landing and leaned against the window, sweat glistening on his pale skin. "Christ, Gen, couldn't you have gotten a place with an elevator?"

"Too expensive. Why did you come?" she repeated.

"To see you, of course. It's not as if I wanted to visit Paris again. You know I never liked it here."

"As you've said, many times."

"I've been emailing you for weeks. You never replied."

"I had nothing to say to you." She turned to the door.

"But Becky said you'd want to see me."

Genna froze. For a moment, she imagined pushing him off the narrow landing, sending him hurtling down the twisting staircase, his head bumping the wall, his legs collapsing beneath him, skewed at impossible angles, the bones shattered.

She took a deep breath and held it for a few minutes before slowly letting it out. She might be pissed off, but she wasn't ready to kill him — yet. Her daughter, on the other hand, was quite another story. It was a good thing she was pregnant.

"*Becky* called you?"

"Of course, she did," he said, steadying himself against the narrow railing. "She told me you'd be happy to see me, that you wanted to come home, but that you needed me to show up and convince you. You've had your adventure or whatever you want to call running off to Paris to find yourself. It's time for you to come home so we can get our lives back in order."

"I seem to remember *you* were the one who screwed up our lives in the first place."

"One mistake, Gen. That's all it was. Aren't I entitled to one mistake?"

"No."

Genna pushed open the door to the apartment. She heard Michael and Tessa clattering around the kitchen. They were so young, so vulnerable. Would they get together and then in thirty years be like she and Drew — two strangers so hurt and broken they weren't able to climb a twisty Parisian staircase together without breaking into a fight?

"Dad!" Michael emerged from the kitchen, wiping his hands on a tea towel, a daub of flour on his nose. Genna's heart lurched. At least she still had Michael, even if he was only on loan until some woman stole his heart and made Genna share.

Damn her.

Drew leaned his suitcase next to the couch and gave his son a one-armed hug. "I'm here to get your mom."

"You could have saved yourself the airfare," Michael laughed. "Mom's already bought her ticket home."

And now Genna would need to kill both her children.

As if on cue, Becky bustled into the apartment, her arms overflowing with cut flowers. "You made it," she said flatly, moving forward and proffering her cheek to Drew for a quick kiss. "Like Michael said, you needn't have bothered. I was planning to email you."

"Great." Drew flopped onto the couch, then twisted and looked up at the needlepoint reproduction of the *Odalisque*. "That's hideous!"

"I happen to like it!" Genna snapped. All three members of her family stared at her like she'd gone mad.

"You said you hated it," Becky said.

"She's grown on me." Genna looked fondly at the face of the *Odalisque*. Even the garish colored wools used to fill in her shape were not enough to obliterate the mastery of the original work. Old Ingres knew what he was about when he painted his nude to appear so unashamed, so in control, challenging viewers to find fault with her for what she did, for confusing what she did with who she was.

Genna could learn something from her.

thirty

Salted Caramel Macarons
Filled with whipped cream and candied almonds

"So here we all are together in Paris again," Drew said. He settled himself on the couch and crossed his legs, beaming at his family and looking so smug Genna felt like smashing the *Odalisque* over his head. "It's just like the old days."

"Hardly."

"Lighten up, Gen. How about we all go out for a meal tonight? Somewhere nice. You must know some great places."

"She can't go out." The voice was so quiet that for a moment no one realized whom it belonged to. Michael reacted first. He led Tessa forward from the kitchen.

"This is Tessa, Dad," he said. "She's Mom's friend from her French class. We're helping Mom cook for tonight."

"It's a party," Becky said. "Mom's invited everyone she knows in Paris."

"You know people in Paris?"

"No, Drew," Genna said. "I'm such a loser, who'd want to be friends with me?"

"I didn't mean that. You always twist my words."

"I do not!"

"Give me a break. You take everything I say the wrong way. I didn't mean that you couldn't make friends. I was just surprised you've met people. You've only been in Paris a few weeks."

"I've been here almost three months—and it's not been long enough."

"What's *that* supposed to mean?"

They squared off, ready to rumble. Drew sat on the couch. Genna stood next to the table. The expressions on the faces of the others in the room ran the gamut from disgust (Becky) to bemusement (Michael) to embarrassment (Tessa).

"It looks like you two need to be alone," Michael said. "Lots to talk about. Come on, Tessa, Becky, let's go get some coffee. The prep's in good shape, Mom. Another hour should do it." He glanced at the clock. "We'll be back by six, which should leave lots of time before everyone arrives. It's eight, right?"

Genna nodded, wishing she could prevent them from leaving her alone with her husband. At the same time, she was grateful for Michael's tact. Although the baby of the family, he was the only one showing any shred of maturity.

Part of her wanted them to leave as quickly as possible. The other part desperately needed them to stay and act as human buffers between her and Drew. What could he possibly say to get her back? He was gazing around the room, his expression maddeningly complacent. He thought he'd won, that Michael's slip about her going home proved that her escape to Paris had crash-landed.

Michael planted a light kiss on her cheek and squeezed her hand. Tessa nodded at her shyly, while Becky frowned and followed them out the door. Genna wanted to be angry with Becky for telling her father to come to Paris. How dared she? But when she noticed how Becky was moving slower than she normally did, one hand unconsciously resting on her stomach to protect its precious cargo, she hadn't the heart. Her daughter may be misguided, but she wasn't mean. She probably thought getting Drew to come over was the right thing to do.

If only she'd take care of her own love life instead of interfering in her parents'. Would she ever give her pride a rest long enough to contact Rolf? He deserved the truth.

The door slammed, leaving her alone with Drew—the love of her youth, the companion of her middle age, the father of her children.

Was that as far as it went?

"Sit down, Genna," Drew said. "You look like you're ready to bolt out the door."

"I wish I could."

"You're still mad. Are you ever going to get over it?"

"Why should I?"

"Isn't it obvious?"

"No."

"Can you please just sit down? I'm getting a crick in my neck looking up at you."

"Fine." She sat down so hard on one of the wooden kitchen chairs that it creaked.

"I see French food agrees with you."

She stiffened.

"I'm kidding!" he said. "Cut me a break. I've been on a plane for ten hours."

"I never asked you to come."

"Yes, you've made that painfully obvious."

"Did you expect me to welcome you with open arms?"

"Becky said that if I came to Paris, you'd probably go back with me." He looked at her with such a pleading expression that a few of the iron bolts encasing a distant corner of her heart loosened.

"Becky had no business interfering."

"The truth is I was about to come anyway. Becky's email just speeded things along."

"You were? Why?"

"Because I want you to come home, of course!"

"You heard Michael. I *am* coming home."

"To me?"

"No."

"You don't mean it. Come on, Gen, I know you."

"Maybe I've changed."

Had she?

"People don't change because they spend a few months hanging out in Paris."

"My French is better."

"Good for you. Look, I'm glad—really, I am—that you've had this time in Paris. I know how much you love the place and how you've always wanted to do the cooking here."

The cooking.

He always made what she did sound trivial. Oh sure, he sometimes bragged about her to his clients, but the truth was that Drew truly believed that he was the one who did the real work in the family. Genna's cookbooks, even when they brought in money, were frills.

Drew leaned forward, hands on his knees. "Becky told me you've almost finished the first draft of your book, and now I hear you've bought a ticket home. Let's put this last year behind us. I know you love Paris, so I'm willing to spend a few days here with you enjoying the sights. Then we can fly home together."

"You want to go *sightseeing* with me?"

"Well, not right now. I'm pretty exhausted." He looked around the living room. "Is that the door to the bedroom?"

She nodded.

"How about I have a bit of a rest and then we can go out for dinner?"

"I told you already. I'm expecting ten people in two hours. And besides, you can't stay here."

"Why not?"

"There's no room. Becky has the couch and Michael's on the floor."

"How about the bedroom?"

"That's where I sleep."

"Yeah, I figured that." He grinned and she saw a ghost of the young man she'd once loved, the man who had married her and lived with her through two children, five books, three houses, and one affair.

Right, that was the kicker. The bolts around her heart tightened again. She saw herself at home in the House with the View, living with Drew, everything back to normal. Then she saw herself standing before their front door, terrified to open it for fear she'd again step into her home and sense the presence of another woman taking her place.

No. Never again.

"You can get a hotel."

"But . . ."

"Oh, and you might be interested to know that a man I've been seeing is coming to the party tonight."

"Seeing?"

"Yes, Drew, as in dating."

"You're dating?"

"That's so hard to believe? Since you say you want me back, you must acknowledge the slim chance that another man in the universe might find me attractive."

The shocked expression on Drew's face almost made up for his betrayal.

Almost.

"Who is he?" Drew's voice came out as a strangled whisper.

"I didn't need a blow-by-blow account about *your* bit on the side."

"She wasn't a bit on the side!"

"What was she then? The main course? Dessert? An appetizer?"

"Do you have to reduce everything to food?"

"It's what I do. You don't have to put up with it."

"But Michael said you already booked your flight home. That means this dating thing can't be serious."

"That's not the point," Genna said. Not for the world would she admit that she hadn't heard from Bill for days. She wasn't even sure he was coming to the party. "Anyway, I don't have time to talk about it right now."

"Bad timing. I get it. I know how you get when you're expecting guests."

Angry as she was, Genna couldn't deny that Drew was right about one thing. During the last few hours before guests were due, she morphed into Genghis Khan on steroids, barking orders to every family member within earshot. Over the years, both Drew and Becky had learned to absent themselves from the house until minutes before the guests arrived. Only Michael, bless his even-keeled soul, was able to keep Genna from self-immolation on the altar of entertaining.

What she'd written in *The Comfy Entertainer* bore no resemblance to her own reality.

Never let your guests see you sweat! They have come to your home to enjoy your cooking and your company. You want them to feel as if every minute of your day leading up to their arrival has been filled with pleasure.

"Are you sure I can't stay here? I'm really tired."

Ignoring him, she stood and walked into the kitchen. Michael had left everything in perfect order, the platters lined up on the counter, each one laden with all the ingredients needed for the meal. The shrimp and salmon were in the refrigerator, along with the individual ramekins of Quai Branly chocolate mousse.

"Where am I supposed to go?"

"There are plenty of boutiquey hotels in the neighborhood," she called. "Look them up on your phone."

"*Boutiquey*? And you know I don't have a Smartphone."

She leaned against the arched entryway leading into the kitchen, her arms crossed. "Small places, quaint, not super posh."

"But not cheap."

"Not in this neighborhood, but there are a few that are probably around three hundred a night, which isn't too bad for Paris. You can get Michael to help you find something."

"Three hundred dollars a night? You're kidding."

"Three hundred *euros*. And breakfast is extra. Or look for something in a cheaper part of the city. Most of the budget chains are out on the *périphérique* about fifteen Métro stops south of here."

"You seriously expect me to lug my suitcase fifteen stops and stay in some budget hellhole in the middle of nowhere?"

She shrugged and went back to her preparations. The salted caramel-infused cream puffs inspired by Sacré Coeur needed sprinkling with shaved dark chocolate and it was almost time to decant the wine.

Drew came to stand in the entryway. "How long am I supposed to stay in a hotel?"

"Until you leave Paris, or were you planning to do some traveling around France first?"

"I'm not planning to travel around France or anywhere else. I came to get you and take you home."

Genna glanced up at the clock. Eighty minutes to zero hour. She took her phone out of her pocket and called Michael.

He answered on the first ring.

"On my way, Mom. It's showtime."

Genna smiled. Her son was a splendid young man if she did say it herself, worth two of his father. A hurricane could blow up in the middle of Rue Bonaparte and Michael would calmly get everyone under cover and then stand at the door to watch the wind rip up the cobblestones.

"Gen?"

"Good-bye, Drew. We can talk tomorrow."

Drew retreated to the middle of the living room, looking lost. Never had she spoken so indifferently to him. She'd always been the one who made things better, who paved the way for him and for the family. When they traveled, she found nice places to stay and decent restaurants, made sure they took flights and trains at reasonable times, researched sightseeing options, and soothed hurt feelings.

The door opened and Michael walked in, trailed by Tessa looking starstruck and Becky, who threw herself onto the couch and kicked off her shoes. Genna looked from Michael to Becky. She needed Michael in the kitchen, not helping his father find a hotel. Becky, on the other hand, was hopeless in the kitchen, and it was her fault her father had come to Paris in the first place.

"Becky?"

She looked up, a hint of defiance on her face. "Yeah?"

"Help your dad find a place to stay in the neighborhood. Phone the Hôtel Saint-Germain-des-Prés down the street, and if that's full, try the Grand Hôtel De l'Univers on Rue Grégoire-de-Tours. It's not far."

"Why can't Dad stay here?"

Genna shot her a look dangerous enough to quell even Becky.

"Oh, right." Apparently, Becky had figured out that if Bill Turner showed up, it might not be a great idea for her mother's husband to be in the same room as her mother's new lover.

"Come on, Dad," she said. "Mom's about to start cooking and you know how she gets before guests arrive. Let's leave Michael and Tessa to deal with her." She took out her phone and started scrolling for hotels. "It shouldn't take long to find something."

To Genna's relief, Drew picked up his suitcase and resignedly followed Becky out the door.

Progress.

thirty-one

Pistachio Macarons
Sweet and salty with a tangy Greek yogurt filling

"Right!" Genna said as soon as the door closed behind them. "Let's go. Tessa, you do the salad. Here's the bowl. Michael, put on the rice and then help me with the sauce for the main course. We have an hour." She extracted the two trays of canapés from the fridge. "These look amazing."

"Tessa's got the knack, for sure," Michael said.

"She does. Did she tell you she's thinking of applying to chef school?"

"Yeah." Michael reached across the tiny kitchen and laid one hand on Tessa's shoulder. He held it there for a few seconds, long enough to send a visible shudder through Tessa. Considering they'd met only that morning, things were moving fast.

But the clock was ticking, and this was no time to contemplate Michael's love life.

"Where are the chives?" Genna demanded as she surveyed the plate of ingredients for the main course.

"I substituted shallots. The market didn't have any."

"They'll need sautéing first. And what about a garnish? I need something green."

"You have time, Mom. And here, I found some Italian parsley. Tessa can chop some for the garnish when she finishes the salad."

"Lemons?"

"In the fridge. You can zest them now."

"Oh."

With a start, Genna realized that Michael was in control of the situation. The tables had turned. Her son was a man, and her daughter would soon be a mother.

Genna turned to hide the tears pricking her eyelids. She felt as if she'd taken the first tentative step on the slippery slope to old age, alone with nothing but memories and the hope that her children and their children wouldn't forget about her, stashed away in a cottage somewhere, her only companions stray cats.

She didn't even like cats.

"I put the pistachios into the oven already for roasting," she said. "Tessa can chop them when they come out and sprinkle them on the mousse."

"Good," Michael said. "Move away from the stove and I'll get started on the sauce."

She opened the fridge and extracted a large bowl of deep pink and glistening salmon fillets marinating in olive oil and herbs, laid them on a large broiler pan, then unwrapped a bulging packet of cooked Atlantic shrimp, each one large, plump, and red-veined. She popped one into her mouth. The firm texture between her teeth held a hint of the sea.

Perfect.

Michael glanced at the shrimp. "Good thing Dad's not here."

Genna grinned. "Yeah, well, I must admit I've been indulging in lots of seafood since I came to Paris." The salmon she planned to serve was Shrimp-Stuffed Salmon, which she had paired with the Denon Wing of the Louvre. The deep red of the walls of the galleries displaying the works of all the great Italian painters, including the *Mona Lisa*, were exhibited resembled the firm, rich flesh of a perfectly cooked salmon filet. Each flake was a different masterpiece.

Fifteen minutes to go. She laid five shrimp in the middle of each salmon fillet, then rolled them into a tight package secured with two small skewers. At 8:30, she'd pop the fillets under the grill so they were ready to serve promptly at 8:45, which would give the guests time to assemble and enjoy drinks and appetizers. She put the broiler pan back into the fridge and turned to survey the rest of the preparations.

"All done, Mom." Michael grinned. "You don't need to freak out."

"I never freak out."

"Yeah, sure. You're always the picture of serenity before guests arrive. I still remember the time you brandished a meat cleaver at Dad."

"I did not!"

"You know you did. He should have taken the hint then."

"That's not fair, Michael!" But she laughed. "He hadn't done anything that bad back then."

"What do you mean?"

Merde.

"Nothing, dear. You're sure everything's ready?"

Michael looked at her curiously before turning back to the counter. "Tessa will toss the salad just before we serve. The rice is ready to go on at eight. I'll take care of it so you can be with your guests. The vegetables can go into the oven now. We can take them out before the salmon goes in. And the appetizers are ready to put out on the bar. We'll do that now." He and Tessa whisked the plates off the counter and onto the bar that separated the kitchen from the living room.

Genna checked that the glasses, plates, and flatware were ready on the table. She would serve buffet style since the table wouldn't accommodate ten people. The living room looked as clean and inviting as it could, considering the heavy, dark furniture, and the needlepoint *Odalisque*. Genna wondered if the apartment had ever hosted so many people at one time.

The phone rang, signaling the arrival of the first guests. While Michael activated the door to let them in, Genna dashed into the bedroom to change. She had four minutes, the time it took a reasonably fit person to climb the five flights of stairs to her apartment. She stripped to her underwear, ripped a skirt from the ancient wardrobe, pulled it over sweaty thighs, then slipped into her green top, the same one she'd worn on her outing to Versailles with Pierre Leblanc. A quick dab of lipstick and a brush through her hair made her as presentable as could be expected, considering her prep day had been interrupted by Drew's arrival. It was just like him to show up at the most inconvenient time. She wondered who would arrive first and rather suspected it would be Marsha. Hopefully, she'd left Colin at home.

"Hi, Genna!"

"Tyler! I'm so glad you came." It was all Genna could do to focus on him and not peer around him to see if his father was with him.

He wasn't.

Tyler held out a bottle of wine from Château Coujan in Languedoc-Roussillon that must have cost at least ninety euros. "Dad sent this along. He'll be here in a while. Business stuff."

"Oh. Thank you. This looks terrific." Genna took the bottle of wine and carried it reverentially to the kitchen. Bill was coming after all. Did that mean he was still interested? Did she care? The shiver running the length of her spine told her that, yes, she did.

She returned to the living room and helped Tyler to a drink, then introduced him to Michael. "Tyler, this is my son, Michael. He's a skier."

"G'day," Tyler said, holding out a hand. "I'm mostly a surfer when I'm not in art school."

Marsha, with Colin in tow, arrived next. He was looking as supercilious and bored as ever. Genna fixed him a drink and settled him in one of the chairs facing the *Odalisque*.

"Everything looks wonderful!" Marsha cooed as she accepted a glass of white wine and sat next to Colin. The *Odalisque* wouldn't offend her. The first time she'd seen it, she'd burst out laughing and declared it the most gloriously kitsch piece she'd ever seen. She *loved* it.

Next to arrive was Denise, followed by Mademoiselle Deville and Helmut. They were holding hands, which must've meant Helmut had finally gotten up the courage to see her outside of class.

Only Bill and Becky were missing.

Tessa emerged from the kitchen, balancing a plate of canapés. She flashed a wide smile, then looked down, shyly accepting the compliments of the guests.

"Did Genna teach you how to make this?" Denise asked, holding up a round of bread fried in butter and garlic and topped with tapenade, parsley and toasted slivered almonds. She popped it into her mouth and chewed cautiously. "You know, this is first rate." She looked up at Tessa. "You like cooking, don't you?"

"Yes, Mum."

"She's a natural," Michael said as he joined Tessa. Before Denise could object, he slid a few more hors d'oeuvres onto her plate. "You can't tell me she didn't get her knack for cooking from you."

Denise smirked, and within minutes she was telling Michael all about her job in television and her stay in Paris. Meanwhile, Tessa continued to serve the guests, only occasionally casting furtive glances back at her mother and Michael. Genna wouldn't be surprised if Michael had Denise asking where to sign Tessa up for chef school by the time they were ready to serve the main course.

"These are rather tasty," Colin said to Genna, surprise oozing between the cracks of his plummy accent. "Your little helper is to be congratulated."

"Thanks. She's got a lot of potential."

"Evidently. Where did you say she was from? Birmingham?"

"Reading. Close to where you're from, I believe?" Marsha had already told Genna that Colin hailed from a council estate near Basingstoke, down the river from Reading on the western outskirts of London and had gone to the local comprehensive school. He was about as close to being upper class as Genna was and must have worked extraordinarily hard to get his marbles-in-the-mouth accent.

"Yes, quite." He took another handful from the plate Tessa was passing around, and then turned to talk with Marsha, who was chatting with Mademoiselle in French. Colin looked comically discomfited as he gloomily munched his canapés.

Genna wondered what had happened regarding the apartment. Marsha was looking more relaxed since their meeting with Pierre. Hopefully, she'd find an opportunity to get an update.

Tyler ambled over to Marsha and Mademoiselle and joined in their conversation. Hmm. Tyler might be a bit young, but he was kindhearted and easy to get along with. Marsha could do worse.

Like Colin, for instance.

Genna settled herself on the couch next to Helmut, confident that everyone had a drink, and that Tessa had the appetizers well in hand. The assembled company looked comfortable and, except for Colin, seemed to be enjoying themselves.

"You have a nice place here," Helmut said. "It is old, no?"

"Not that old. Early nineteenth century, I think, although the foundations are much older than that. Saint-Germain is one of the most ancient districts in Paris."

"Ja." Helmut sipped his wine and looked longingly across the room at Mademoiselle Deville. As usual, she was dressed with the impeccable attention to detail all French women appeared to possess as a birthright. Soft leather pumps the color of old weathered stone complemented the delicate blue of her dress, a simple shirtwaist that fitted her compact body to perfection. No wonder Helmut couldn't keep his eyes off her.

"She is beautiful," Genna said.

"Ja." But this time he looked at Genna and smiled. "I am a lucky man."

"You are. What are your plans now that you've finished our course?"

"My company, it will keep me here for a while, I think. They like that I have now a French girlfriend." He returned her grin. "But before I go back to work, Thérèse and I, we are going to the south for a little *vacance*."

"How lovely! Where?"

"Somewhere in Provence I am thinking. I am looking on the internet for a nice place to take her. Do you know any?"

Genna had been to Provence only once and with Drew and the kids in tow. The notion of going there as a couple to enjoy long, sunny days steeped in the smell of lavender and with the sound of cicadas a constant thrumming was captivating.

A flutter of excitement took over the pit of her stomach at the prospect of Bill's imminent arrival. Tyler had said his father would be about half an hour late, and that half hour was almost up. Bill would have to arrive soon if Genna was to see him before disappearing into the kitchen to assemble the main course.

The intercom phone rang. She answered it expecting to hear Bill's wide vowels boom into her ear.

"Gen?"

Her stomach contracted at the sharpness of his tone. "What's wrong? Where's Becky?"

"Just let me in, please."

Everyone stopped talking to stare at her. Her cheeks flamed. She pressed the button that activated the front door and hung up the phone.

"You okay, Mom?"

"It's your dad. He's coming up."

"Is Becky with him?"

"I don't know." Drew had sounded upset. Had something happened to Becky? She flung open the door and peered down the winding staircase, impatient now to see the top of his head emerge around the final turn. She had a sudden memory of putting her arms around Drew and kissing the top of his head as he sat at the computer back home. She remembered the feeling of complete trust, the certainty that she'd be kissing the top of his head for decades to come.

A sob caught in her throat. Damn him. But at that moment she wanted to see him more than anyone in the world. Finally, she heard his breath coming in short gasps. "Where's Becky?" she called when he reached the fourth-floor landing.

He looked up, puzzled by the panic in her voice. "I left her in the lobby of the hotel. She wanted to use the Wi-Fi to send an email." He climbed the rest of the way to the fifth floor. "It's okay, Gen. We had a bit of a father-daughter chat. She told me about the baby, and I convinced her to email Rolf."

Genna closed the door so her guests wouldn't hear them, although she wouldn't be surprised if they were all straining forward to catch every word. And no wonder. Genna's life had become a soap opera.

"You sounded like something was wrong."

"Nope. All good."

"Then why are you here? I told you I'm having a party."

"I'm hungry and I didn't think you'd mind. You always say the more guests the better and you know how much I hate airplane food. You can introduce me to all your Paris friends."

"Fine." Genna stood aside to let him in, then after introducing him, left him seated next to Denise while she went to prepare the main course. She didn't have time to indulge her anger.

That would come later.

In the kitchen, Michael withdrew the pan of roasted vegetables bubbling with oil and redolent with roasted garlic, onions, and thyme. "Put in the salmon and I'll coordinate the rest."

Genna slipped the salmon into the oven and turned on the broiler. Five minutes on each side should do it. She kept the door ajar to watch the progress. The key to broiling fish was split-second timing. A minute too long resulted in dry, overcooked fish; a few minutes too little and the inside of the roll would be raw and weeping.

"Ready, Michael?" Genna asked when she was sure the salmon was done.

"I got your back, Mom. Let's do this."

Together, they arranged the serving dishes on the table.

"Dinner's ready!" Genna announced, turning to the room. "The plates are here on the bar. Please serve yourselves."

For a few minutes, all was chaos as everyone surged forward. Drew was last in line. Genna slid a serving of salmon onto his plate and glared at him. "Enjoy."

"Thanks, Gen. It looks good."

Well, of course it looks good.

Genna filled her own plate, then looked around the room for a place to sit. The only vacant spot was next to Drew on the couch.

He looked up and smiled as she crossed the room. "This pilaf's amazing."

"Michael made it," she said shortly. Engaging in dinnertime chitchat with Drew was the last thing she wanted to do. She turned slightly away from him and watched people enjoying their first bites. A comfortable silence fell over the room, punctuated occasionally by murmurs of appreciation.

So preoccupied was she with enjoying the scene that she didn't see the forkful of shrimp and salmon making its way into Drew's mouth until it was too late.

"Stop!"

Drew looked at her curiously as he chewed. "What?"

"It's shrimp."

The look on Drew's face would have been comical if the situation wasn't so serious. His eyes bulged as involuntarily he swallowed. "Shrimp?"

"It was stuffed into the salmon. I'm so sorry. I didn't even think."

"Shrimp?" he repeated. "You served me shrimp?"

Genna felt a flicker of annoyance. No matter how angry she was at him, she didn't intend to put his life in danger. But that is exactly what she'd done. Drew was so allergic to shrimp that even the smallest morsel of it on his plate was enough to constrict his throat and swell his skin with painful hives. A whole mouthful would cause his throat to contract. Already his eyes were watering and the skin on the back of his hands was becoming inflamed.

"Where's your EpiPen?"

"At the hotel. Can't breathe. Hurry!"

Forks clattered to plates and a babble of voices filled the room. Everyone wanted to help; no one had the faintest idea how.

"Mademoiselle! Please, call an ambulance."

This was no time to fool around with language-school French. Genna thanked the stars for Thérèse Deville, the only French person in the room. She sprang out of her chair, teetered for a moment on her high heels, and then, helped by Helmut, found her phone and began the call.

Meanwhile, Michael got Drew up and walked him around in circles. His breath was becoming more labored. The ambulance had better be quick. Was one mouthful of shrimp enough to kill him?

"Let's get him down the stairs," she said. "We can meet the ambulance people on the street."

"Good idea."

Genna and Michael each took an arm and led Drew out to the landing. His hand was clammy, like he'd dipped it into a pot of fish scales. His head lolled onto her shoulder. "Help me, Gen," he whispered. "I can't do without you."

She gripped his arm harder, steadying him as he descended the steep staircase. They made it to the second floor when the door leading from the bottom of the stairs to the courtyard opened.

"Good Lord!"

Drew looked blearily down the stairs at the ruddy face of Bill Turner, who was hurrying toward them.

"He looks ghastly! What happened?"

"Dad's had an allergic reaction," Michael said. "We're getting him to an ambulance."

"Your dad?"

Bill glanced up at Genna who mouthed "*It's Drew.*"

"Right! Hold on a sec." Bill reached into his jacket pocket and extracted a thin cylinder. "Looks like your dad and I have something in common," he said, handing the cylinder to Michael. "I'm horribly allergic to bee stings—never go anywhere without my EpiPen."

Michael plunged the needle into his father's thigh. Seconds later, Drew sank to the floor of the landing and leaned his head against the cool stone wall. His ragged breathing slowed, and the angry red hives began to recede.

"You'll be feeling crook for a while," Bill said, patting his arm. "But it's nothing a bit of rest won't cure."

"Sure. Thanks." The color was seeping back into Drew's cheeks, but he still looked shaky.

"I'm Bill Turner," Bill said. "A friend of Genna's."

"A friend?"

Bill shrugged and glanced at Genna. He smiled contritely. She took his smile as an apology and returned it with a smile of her own.

Even in his weakened state, Drew couldn't miss the significance of the exchange. He opened his mouth and then closed it again. Genna had an overwhelming urge to laugh. Here was her husband languishing on the tiny landing of a stairwell in a Parisian apartment building while a few steps below him stood her lover. Now that Drew was no longer inches away from death, she wasn't above finding the situation amusing. She'd never been the kind of woman who men fell over. She'd slept with three men in her life and 66.66 percent of them were now within spitting distance of each other.

A commotion at the bottom of the stairs signaled the arrival of the paramedics. Thérèse tottered down to the crowded landing.

"He is okay now?"

Genna told her about Bill's EpiPen. "Would you mind?" She pointed down the stairs at the two paramedics.

"*Ah, oui. Bien sûr.* I will talk with them. They will understand."

She let forth a barrage of French too quick for Genna to follow. One of the paramedics climbed the two flights and examined Drew. He declared him out of danger and then admonished him for not carrying his own EpiPen. Drew smiled and nodded. His French had never progressed beyond Grade 8.

"You'd better come back up," Genna said after the paramedics left.

"I'm sorry about your party," Drew mumbled.

"And I'm sorry I gave you shrimp."

"You all right, mate?" Bill asked as he helped Drew to his feet.

"Sure. Thanks. I can make it from here." He shook off Bill's hand and gripped the railing, before turning to look at Genna. "I shouldn't have come."

"No, you shouldn't have."

She stood still while he started up the stairs.

Bill leaned over and whispered, "How are you?"

"Not good."

Suddenly, she felt unbearably tired. How did femme fatales manage it? Two men were two too many for her. All she wanted was to sink into a very hot, very deep bath perfumed with jasmine and rose petals.

Bill followed Drew up the stairs. She climbed more slowly.

"Hey, Mom!"

The voice behind her belonged to Becky but it sounded more like a Becky clone who had taken happy pills.

Becky reached her mother, then peered around Genna in time to see her father disappear into the apartment followed by Bill Turner. Her eyes widened. "Bill's here too?"

"Yep."

"Does Dad know about him?"

"Yep—and Bill just saved his life." Genna described what happened.

Becky threw back her head and laughed. "You're joking!"

"Wish I was."

"Your lover saved your husband's life?"

"Yes, Becky, I see the irony."

"But that's hilarious!" She smiled a smile so radiant that Genna was bathed in an emotion she'd never experienced from her eldest child.

Joy.

"I take it you've heard from Rolf?"

"We talked on the phone. I was just about to email him when I got an email from *him*."

"Oh?" Genna tried hard to keep her tone neutral. Fortunately, Becky was so preoccupied with her own excitement that she didn't notice anything unusual about her mother's voice.

"He told me that he loves me and that he wants to get back together. And that's before he even knew about the baby. He didn't say he loved me because I'm pregnant."

Genna was one hundred percent sure that Rolf loved Becky with all his heart. She also knew that he'd already learned Becky was pregnant because Genna had told him. She should be stripped of her maternal stripes and made to spend the rest of her life eating low-fat cheese. But when she looked at her daughter's face glowing with excitement, Genna could not repent.

"Telling someone in an email that he's about to be a father is a bit cold," Becky was saying. "So, I phoned him. It was about nine in the morning back home, and he was having his coffee and reading the newspaper."

"What did he say?" Genna wondered if the Academy awarded Oscars for *Best Performance by a Mother Pretending That She Hadn't Interfered in Her Daughter's Life.*

"He was over the moon, Mom. Really over the moon."

Genna turned quickly to hide the tears starting to form in her eyes. She didn't care what anyone thought. She'd never regret that she'd given Rolf the heads up about the baby, so long as he never told Becky. If he did, Genna would stand zero chance of ever seeing her grandchild.

While Becky laughed and told Genna all about her conversation, she half-turned so she could listen while gazing at her Parisian view from the small window off the landing. The evening sky was turning a dusky pink rose while long rays of sunlight played across the stone facade of Notre-Dame.

My God, she would miss this place.

"I'm happy for you," Genna said when Becky finished telling her all about what she said and what Rolf said, and that the upshot was they'd give it a go and that she wanted to return home as soon as possible.

"Thanks, Mom."

Becky stepped forward and hugged Genna—something she hadn't done voluntarily or with any emotion since she was eight.

"You're going to have a wonderful life together," Genna whispered into her daughter's hair. "He's a lucky man."

"Thanks, Mom, but I think I'm the lucky one," Becky said as she stepped back. "I've been a bit of an idiot."

"Hormones. You can use them as an excuse for all sorts of wild behavior until the baby's born and for many months afterwards. They cover a multitude of sins."

"I'll keep that in mind. Come on, we should get back to your guests. They must be wondering where you disappeared to."

As Genna followed Becky back into the apartment, she wondered how she'd survive the next few hours.

thirty-two

Cotton Candy Macarons

Hot pink and sweet with a whipped cream filling

"I was just enjoying a very nice conversation with your man," Denise said an hour later as she sat down next to Genna and handed her another glass of wine.

"Which one?" Genna asked before she could stop herself.

Denise glanced sideways at her before answering. "Ah, your husband. Drew, is it? He seems a nice bloke."

"He can be."

"I told him all about how Jason wants to talk with you about doing a cooking show."

"About that, Denise. I forgot to mention this morning that I'm going home Thursday. I won't be able to meet with your boss in London."

"No worries," Denise grinned. "Jason will be happy to chat with you on the phone. If he thinks you've got potential, he'll arrange to get you over to England. Drew thought it was a great opportunity."

"He did?"

"Course. He's very proud of you."

"Pardon?"

"Proud of you," Denise said slowly and distinctly. She leaned forward so they were head-to-head and whispered, "To tell you the truth, it's not easy to get a word in edgewise when he starts going on about you—how you've written so many cookbooks and are such a fantastic cook and all. I see what he means. Your meal was marvelous."

"Thank you. But I can't take all the credit. Tessa was a huge help. I only need to tell her how to do something once. You should be proud, too."

"That doesn't sound like my Tessa, but I'm glad she's found something she likes to do. Maybe I'll look into this cooking school lark when we get home."

"I think that would be a great idea. And in the end, we don't get much of a say in what they do." She nodded across the room at Becky, who was chatting with Marsha. "All you can hope for is that every so often they let you in on their lives."

"When's she due?"

Genna looked at Denise in surprise. "How did you know?"

"Well, it's obvious. Just look at her."

Denise was right. Becky appeared lit from within. Her skin glowed and her tanned arms cradled her stomach. Genna was reminded of the Mary Cassatt drawing in the Musée d'Orsay that had caught Becky's attention.

"*Clafouti!*"

"Beg pardon?"

"It's a dessert. Super basic, only egg custard and fruit—plums or cherries usually. Clafouti is one of the simplest and homiest French desserts."

"So?"

Genna shook her head. "Sorry. I was thinking about including it in my book. Looking at Becky reminded me of a drawing by Mary Cassatt that we saw the other day at the Musée d'Orsay of a mother holding her child, and that got me thinking of the type of dessert a busy French mother would make for her children. Something sweet and yet nutritious. Clafouti!"

"Sounds lovely." Denise sipped her wine thoughtfully. "You're lucky, you know, to have a husband like Drew. I don't think I've ever met a man so proud of his wife. If he were mine, I'd hang onto him."

"You would?"

"No question. He's besotted with you, and that's remarkable after all the years you've been together."

Besotted was hardly the word Genna would use to describe Drew's feelings for her. He was sitting across the room next to Colin, who had almost licked his plate clean even as he affected a look of total boredom. Drew, on the other hand, looked pale and sad. She caught his eye. He nodded and smiled tentatively, as if testing the waters and hoping to find them warm.

Genna's heart wobbled. He used to look at her like that when they were at parties and trapped in dull conversations on opposite sides of the room. The look asked "Is it time to go home yet?"

She was tempted to nod in response like she'd always done. Within weeks, they could be together again in the House with the View. When they'd first moved in and gotten settled, they'd shared so many laughs, lingering on the deck at the end of every day to watch the dusk sweep across the view. They were so proud of themselves for buying their dream house.

Could they go back to their old lives—Drew in his workshop sanding wood things, Genna in her kitchen testing recipes, year after year, growing old, familiar, easy?

"All I have to do is forgive him." Genna said under her breath, then glanced sheepishly over at Denise who was smiling sympathetically. "Sorry, I was thinking out loud."

"I've learned the hard way that the only place you get to by holding a grudge is alone."

"I'm hardly holding a grudge."

"Something's got your knickers in a twist."

Genna laughed. "It's not *my* knickers that were the problem."

"Ah," Denise nodded. "They're all the same. My advice, since you didn't ask for it, is to get over it and go back to him. I wish I'd forgiven mine when I had the chance. I didn't, and now look at me."

"Why? What's wrong?"

"Nothing you'd see for looking," Denise said cheerfully, "but I've got no illusions about my future. Tessa will be gone before long, and I'll have to shift for myself."

"You might meet someone."

"I tell you what," she said, grinning, "You patch things up with your husband over there, and I'll take up with the hunky Aussie." She winked and nodded toward Bill, who was talking to Michael. From the gestures that Bill was using to make his point, Genna gathered they were discussing surfing and the endless opportunities down under to catch the perfect wave.

"He *is* rather hunky, isn't he?"

"I wouldn't say no."

Genna took another sip of wine. "I didn't."

There was a short pause and then they both burst out laughing. Genna relaxed back into her chair. Whatever the future held, she couldn't do anything about it right that minute in a roomful of half-tipsy, well-fed friends and family.

She drained her glass. Perhaps the best she could hope for in life was a succession of evenings with interesting people, great food, and excellent wine.

Except that there was more to life than good food. There was pain and commitment and hope and forgiveness. She looked again at Drew and then at Bill. She remembered an evening almost thirty years ago—the only other time she'd been in a room with two men who had both been her lovers. Like now, one had been Drew. And the other?

Gary Grenville.

Ah, now there was a guy she hadn't thought about in years. Gary Grenville with his rock-hard butt and piercing green eyes that could make her knees shake with one glance.

And yet she'd chosen Drew. Sensible, even-keeled, self-centered Drew.

What would her life have been like if she'd chosen wild man Gary, with his guitar, a thick leather strap circling the muscular wrist of his strumming hand, and an empty wallet?

"Mom?"

Genna looked up to see Michael crossing the room toward her. At least one thing was certain. If she hadn't chosen Drew, she wouldn't have had Michael and Becky, and that would have been a tragedy. She rose to meet her son.

"Dessert?"

"That's what I was thinking." Michael took his mother's empty glass and steered her toward the kitchen. "Help me put it together."

Once through the archway and into the kitchen, Michael turned on her. "Okay," he whispered. "What's going on?"

Uh-oh. Either Becky had spilled the beans or Michael had just figured it out. Either way, Genna imagined that from his point of view, the presence of his dad at one end of the room and his mother's boyfriend at the other end might give even Michael pause. After all, it wasn't that many years ago when Michael had promised he'd never find a girl as nice as his mom. Of course, he'd been six at the time, but Genna still cherished the memory.

"I never invited your dad."

"That's your defense?" he asked.

"I'm not on trial."

"No, but honestly, Mom, this isn't right. I mean, how do you think Dad feels? Does he know?"

"He knows."

Michael looked taken aback at her matter-of-fact tone.

"That doesn't bother you?"

"Your dad can hardly object." Genna didn't elaborate. Michael wasn't exactly a choir boy. He'd figure it out.

"What are you two doing in here?" Becky breezed through the archway. "Getting dessert, I hope. I'm still hungry."

"You ate two helpings of the salmon."

Becky ignored her brother. "Can I help, Mom? What do you need?"

Genna felt like she'd stepped into an alternate universe where aliens had kidnapped her children and switched their personalities. Sunny little Michael, her golden boy, scowled at her, while spiky Becky glowed with goodwill and happiness.

"Mom's having an affair!" Michael blurted.

"You only just figured *that* out? Can you blame her?"

"What do you mean?"

"Ask Dad."

"Ask Dad what?"

"Honestly, Michael, if you were any dimmer, you'd be comatose. About *his* affair. Why do you think Mom came to Paris in the first place?"

"Dad had an affair?"

"Like it's a big secret."

"You knew?" Genna asked.

"Not at first," Becky admitted. "I thought you were just being selfish when you left. And Dad played the poor bereft-husband act very well."

"How did you find out?"

"His girlfriend emailed me yesterday."

In her tiny kitchen, Genna stood inches from her children. She could reach out and touch both of them, hold them close like she had when they'd been her babies.

"His girlfriend?" Genna sputtered. "Who?"

"I'm not sure you want to know, Mom."

"Tell me." Genna's voice grew stronger.

"Yeah, Becky. Who? What are you talking about?"

Becky leaned forward so her mouth was close to her brother's ear and hissed, "I'm talking about the woman our father's been bonking, or at least he was until a few days ago when he decided to come to Paris to try and get Mom back."

"Tell me who she is." Genna said evenly.

Becky placed one hand on her arm. "This isn't the best time. Let Michael get the dessert ready, and I'll help you with your guests. Once we get this party wrapped up, we can talk."

Genna never did know how she made it through the rest of the evening. She emerged from the kitchen miraculously dry-eyed and determined to finish her last dinner party in Paris with style. She circulated from person to person, proffering desserts, refilling glasses, joking, laughing. Her only concession to the gaping hole in her heart was that she bypassed Drew each time she circulated with the wine.

She should have known he'd been lying, the bastard. He'd sworn up and down that his *mistake*, as he called it, had happened just the once.

* * *

Sixteen Months Earlier

Genna was about to leave her hotel room in Seattle to go to the final event on her book tour when the phone rang. It was her publisher telling her that the signing had been canceled and she was free to catch an earlier flight home.

She almost wept with relief. After a seven-day whirlwind of presentations at bookstores in ten cities from San Diego to Seattle, she was beyond exhausted. All she wanted to do was get home as quickly as possible, feel Drew's arms around her, and then sit with him in front of the big picture window in their new living room and watch the sun go down.

Genna quickly packed her suitcase and grabbed a taxi to Sea-Tac Airport, where she was able to change her flight to one that left twenty minutes after she cleared security. Drew would be thrilled to see her back a day early. She wouldn't call to let him know. It would be more fun to surprise him.

Genna couldn't wait to unpack the last of the boxes and get busy on some holiday baking. Neither of the kids could make it home that year, which bothered Genna less than she'd expected. Instead of spending half the day in the kitchen, she planned to spend their first Christmas in the new house sitting by the fire, sherries in hand, chatting about all the projects they wanted to do over the winter. At least one room didn't need any work at all—the kitchen.

Genna closed her eyes against a bit of turbulence on the short flight and visualized her new kitchen. It had a wraparound bar and a panoramic view of Georgia Straight and the islands, along with a brand new six-burner gas cooktop and convection oven. The stove had been an extravagance they could ill afford, but Drew had insisted she have it. He said he'd figure out some way to write it off on their taxes. Sometimes he really could be incredibly thoughtful. She smiled with contentment.

At Vancouver Airport, she took the shuttle to the long-term parking lot and drove north through downtown Vancouver. The December afternoon sparkled. A surge of happiness coursed through her as she crossed the Lions Gate Bridge that spanned the narrows between Stanley Park and West Vancouver. Directly ahead, a fresh snowfall dusted the North Shore mountains, and the waters of English Bay to her left shone as blue as the sky arching above.

It was a perfect west coast winter day.

Genna turned into her driveway, lined on both sides with mature rhododendrons that in May would burst into vibrant pinks and purples and reds. Their house was in an older area of West Vancouver where the homes were relatively modest compared to the multimillion-dollar mansions crusting the flank of the mountain behind. Genna hadn't met any of their new neighbors yet. She made a mental note to reach out over the holidays. Maybe she would invite a few of them for drinks on Boxing Day.

Genna parked the car and got out, leaving her suitcase in the trunk for Drew to retrieve later. She walked around the side of the house to the back door and paused to enjoy the view. It was December 21, the shortest day of the year. At just past three o'clock, the winter sun was already sinking in the west, washing the ocean with undulations of gold. Away in the distance, the mountains of Vancouver Island provided a bulwark against the full might of the Pacific Ocean. Genna sighed happily.

Home.

Smiling, she opened the back door and walked into the kitchen.

"Hey!" she called. "I'm back!"

Instead of the shout of pleased surprise she expected, Genna heard a door upstairs slam and heavy steps coming down the stairs.

"Drew?" She walked through to the living room.

"Gen?"

She turned, her heart lifting at the sound of his voice. And then she saw him, and her life changed forever.

Drew reached the bottom of the stairs and walked toward her, his face ashen with guilt, one hand stretched out and the other gripping a pink towel wrapped around his naked waist.

Pink — the color of innocence, the sweet side of the color red. Pink was for romance and friendship, for little girls (although not Becky) and for cotton candy.

"You weren't supposed to come home until tomorrow," Drew said.

Genna turned and fled.

* * *

Sixteen months later in a tiny Parisian apartment full of new friends, Genna had just discovered that his *girlfriend* was emailing her daughter.

Never had Genna wished with more fervor for an evening to end.

A few minutes past ten, Thérèse stood and proposed a toast in French to what she called her *meilleure classe de l'année* — her best class of the year. She rattled on about Marsha, her *élève étoile*, her star pupil, and gave a nod to Denise and Tessa. She thanked Genna for all the times she'd brought food to class. Finally, she turned to

Helmut and spoke with such Gallic rapidity and passion there wasn't a person in the room who doubted what the two of them planned for the rest of their evening.

Around eleven, everyone began making noises about going. Thérèse and Helmut left first amid a flurry of double-cheeked kisses and shouted *au revoirs*. Tyler and his father left next, but not before Bill drew Genna aside and out of earshot of Drew.

"Let's get together tomorrow," he whispered. "We need to sort a few things out."

"I'm still going home, no matter what happens with Drew. I'm broke, Bill. You know that."

"That's what we need to talk about."

"I'm not taking money from you, if that's what you're suggesting."

"Wouldn't dream of it, love," he said. "But . . ." Whatever he planned to say was lost as Colin swept him toward the door.

"Lovely evening," Colin murmured as he passed. "Really quite stunning."

It was all Genna could do not to smash his arrogant face into the door jamb. But she restrained herself for the sake of Marsha, who followed in his wake. She folded Genna in a hearty embrace and kissed both of her cheeks in a giggling parody of Thérèse. Of all Genna's guests, Marsha appeared to have enjoyed herself the most. She'd spent the evening talking with Tyler, and then with Thérèse and Bill, much to the dismay of Colin. While he'd glowered in the corner, she'd glowed with animation.

"I got the contract to decorate Pierre's place," she said.

"And Colin?"

"We've figured things out. Pierre's been helpful there too. I'll tell you all about it in a few days."

"I'm leaving Thursday."

"No! Well, don't leave before we've talked." Marsha leaned forward again. "And I have to say that your Bill is a peach. I had a great, long chat with him about you."

"What did he say?"

Too late. Marsha let Colin usher her out the door, leaving Genna to wonder what Bill was playing at.

Becky came forward with her father. He looked about ready to pass out from jet leg, too much wine, and the lingering effects of his allergic reaction. Having just spent an evening sharing a crowded living room with his wife's lover might also have been a factor.

"'Night, Gen," he slurred. "Great party. You're amazing."

He swayed toward her, his lips just grazing her cheek before she had a chance to step back. Then the strong arms of his son appeared out of nowhere to straighten him up and steer him out the door.

"Got him, Mom," Michael said. "Becky and I will get him back to the hotel. We'll see you later."

Denise and Tessa followed them, and suddenly Genna was alone. The sound of feet descending the stairs receded and the quiet pressed in on her. She sank onto the couch.

"I don't want to go home!" she wailed to the empty room. "I don't want my old life back."

So now what was she going to do?

thirty-three

Apricot Macarons
Filled with cardamon and apricot jam

The answer came at precisely 10:16 the following morning. Genna
knew it was 10:16 because she looked at the digital clock next to her
bed when the pounding woke her up. She waited for Michael or
Becky to open the door.

Silence.

"Becky!" she yelled. "The door!"

More silence. Michael was perfectly capable of sleeping
through the noise. As a teenager, he'd been known to sleep through
Genna vacuuming under his bed. Becky, on the other hand, had the
ears of a dolphin. When she was a child, she sensed when her
parents were even thinking of sex, never mind having it. Genna
couldn't count the number of times Becky's slight, jammies-clad
figure appeared at the bedroom door, teddy in tow, to ask for water
or to report a bad dream when Genna was seconds from climaxing.

Genna lay in bed a few minutes longer. Perhaps Becky was in
the bathroom, a not-unlikely assumption, given her condition. The
pounding continued.

Damn.

She slid out of bed and fumbled for her robe. In the living room,
the curtains were still drawn, but the beddings from the floor and

couch were folded neatly in one corner. Genna reached the door and yanked it open.

"*Eh bien!* Finally! I am sorry if I awakened you, but I could not wait."

Genna stepped aside to let Pierre into the apartment. He looked dreadful, as if he hadn't slept for days. In his hollow cheeks and gray stubble, she saw the first hints of how one day he'd look like Monsieur.

"What's happened? Please, sit down. I'll make coffee."

"*Oui, le café. Merci.*" He slumped onto the couch. "*Désolé.* I come only now from *l'hôpital.*"

Genna almost dropped the cup she was rinsing. Hospital? Instantly, she constructed an elaborate scenario in which Michael or Becky or both lay dying or dead in a French emergency room. Before either or both expired, one of them had managed to croak out Pierre Leblanc's phone number with precise instructions on how he should contact Genna.

And then she came to her senses.

"Your father?" She abandoned the cup and went to sit next to Pierre on the couch.

"*Oui.*" He closed his eyes. A tear rolled down one cheek. "Last Thursday he, how do you say, took a turn for the worse. I found him on the floor behind the counter at the *tabac*. He'd had a stroke."

"Oh, Pierre, why didn't you call me?"

"You had your daughter with you. I did not want to intrude."

"But your father and I have become such good friends. I'm happy to help any way I can. What's the prognosis? May I see him?"

Pierre shook his head. "There is no prognosis, as you say. My father . . ." His voice broke. "Papa . . . He died yesterday."

Genna didn't want to believe it. Monsieur? Dead? How was that possible when only a few days ago they'd sipped Napoleon brandy and she'd poured her heart out to him? She'd intended to invite him to share a farewell dinner of *Coq au Vin Parc Monceau*. He would have liked that.

"I'm so sorry, Pierre. I'll miss him."

Pierre nodded miserably. Genna remembered the day Monsieur first arrived at her door, shrouded in a miasma of Gauloises and garlic. She could not have anticipated he'd become her most devoted and informed critic—and one with a remarkable level of gustatory refinement. He was able to tell her the precise origin in the French countryside of the flecks of sausage meat studding one of her quiches. He could probably name the farm, or even the pig, although perhaps that was a long shot, even for Monsieur.

Back home, Drew had eaten everything she put in front of him without compliment or complaint. As a tester, he was hopeless. Michael was a dependable tester, but he'd moved out two years ago. Becky was as hopeless as her father. Her version of a gourmet meal was a stalk of celery and a latte.

And then Monsieur had come into her life in the city of her dreams, and she'd reached new heights with her cooking. Thanks to him, the *Île de la Cité Rainbow Trout* dissolved on the tongue with a hint of lime as unexpected and as welcome as a flash rainstorm at the height of summer. And Genna's *Montmartre Moules à la Marinière* exploded with the flavors of the sea blended with white wine, butter, shallots, and parsley. The combined tastes were so intense she could close her eyes and be transported to a beach lounger in Nice.

A sob caught in Genna's throat and she squeezed Pierre's hand. "What can I do?"

"There is nothing to be done right now. But we need to talk about the *appartement*." Pierre sat up straighter and wiped his palms across his wet cheeks.

"I'm leaving Paris soon. Thursday."

"I know. Papa called me not long after you left him last week and told me. But you cannot leave now."

"I don't want to go, but my money's almost run out. I booked my ticket a few days ago."

"But you must cancel it!"

"Non-refundable," Genna said.

Hadn't she been through this before? Why did everyone think she could cancel her ticket and eat the cost? Did she look like Oprah?

"*Pfft!* A few hundred euros, no? You cannot go."

"Why not?" Genna let Pierre's crack about a few hundred euros go. The ticket had cost eight hundred euros, which was about half the money she had left. He seemed to have forgotten that she wasn't a fancy French *avocat* with a vintage Peugeot and a home in the South of France.

"Because of the *appartement*."

"I'm sorry, did you need more notice? I understood the agreement was week to week. Since I told your father last Tuesday, I presumed there would be no problem."

Was it not a bit unseemly to be haggling about the rental agreement with poor Monsieur barely cold?

"You do not understand," Pierre said, withdrawing his hand from hers. "The *appartement* is yours."

She was floating in a dead space as quiet and dark as a black hole.

"Geneviève?"

Still silence. The world and all its problems disappeared. She was nothing and nobody.

And everything.

"Geneviève?"

Genna tumbled back to earth, landing with a sharp thud that left her shaken and elated. There's no way she'd heard what she'd just heard. Pierre's English was excellent, but he must have mixed up his pronouns. The apartment couldn't be *hers*.

"My father was very fond of you."

"And I of him. We both loved good food."

"I think he saw in you a younger version of his beloved *grand-mère*, who made the *Odalisque*." He tilted his head back to view the hideous wool stitches upside down. "Yes, I know, it is an abomination, but my father had it fixed to the wall so it could not be taken down."

"I know. I tried to remove it the day I moved in."

"Understandable," Pierre said, smiling sadly. "But she has brought you good luck, no?"

"Has she?" Genna stared up at the *Odalisque*'s turban and fan—exotic touches that gave her nakedness context, reminders of a life spent in luxury and despair. Whatever she thought Pierre meant about the apartment couldn't possibly be true. She wouldn't embarrass herself by saying what she thought she'd heard.

"Tagine," she said quietly. There was something fitting about the idea for a dish to pair with the *Odalisque* coming so soon after hearing about Monsieur's death. Genna was sure he'd have approved.

"Pardon?"

"Tagine—the funnel-shaped dish they use to cook food in Morocco?"

"*Ah, oui.* I know tagine. I think it is because of my *maman's* lamb tagine that I am here."

"How so?"

"Papa said he fell in love with my mother's cooking first and with her second. She was the only person he ever met who could cook a lamb tagine like his *grand-mère*. It was one of her specialties. But what does this have to do with the *appartement*?"

"I've just decided what dish to pair with *Le Grande Odalisque*," Genna said. "I'm sorry. Now is not the time to be talking about food."

Pierre shrugged. "We have always time for food. Tell me about the tagine."

"Moroccan lamb tagine cooked with spices and dried apricots and nuts."

"And served with couscous?"

"*Naturellement!*"

"And how does it relate to *L'Odalisque*?"

Genna pulled Pierre to his feet and together they contemplated *Grand-mère* Leblanc's creation right side up.

"Yes," Pierre said. "I see it. The exotic and the familiar are joined."

"Exactly." A quiet desolation stole over her as she realized that *Lamb Tagine à La Grande Odalisque by Ingres* would be the final recipe for *Eat Like a Parisian*.

"Will you keep it?" Pierre asked.

"Keep what?"

"*L'Odalisque*," he said. "It is dreadful, but Papa would hate to see it go."

"Why would it go?"

"But you do not like it. Did you not try to take it down?"

"Yes, that's true." Genna turned her back on the needlepoint and sank onto the couch.

"Don't you *want* to stay in Paris?" Pierre asked, bewildered.

"Of course, I want to stay in Paris. But, as I told you, I must go home now."

"But you will come back."

"In a few years."

"Oh no, *non*. You cannot wait that long. There will be some delay for the paperwork to go through, but no more than a few months. These things are not completed quickly in any country, but especially not in France."

"I'm sorry, what paperwork?"

"You are not understanding me, *chère* Geneviève," Pierre said. "Perhaps I do not make myself clear." He shook his head. "These last few days have not been easy."

"I'm sure they haven't," Genna said sympathetically.

"Papa wanted you to own the *appartement*," Pierre said. "He told me the day after your visit. Then, when I checked his papers after his death, I found he had already visited an *avocat* and changed his will. *La volonté.* Once my father made up his mind about something, he never wasted time. He liked you and wanted you to stay in the *appartement* rent-free until his death and then to inherit it. Of course, poor Papa did not believe his death would come so soon."

"Your father left the apartment to me?"

"*Oui.* That is what I have been trying to tell you."

And at that precise moment the door crashed open and in tumbled Genna's family — all three of them.

thirty-four

Coconut Macarons
Filled with shredded, toasted coconut in a cashew cream

"Well, *obviously* you'll sell it," Drew said as soon as Pierre left. "It's got to be worth a small fortune in this neighborhood. I was looking at the properties in the window of a real estate agency down the street and, wow, a studio apartment fetches a million euros. As for this place" — he gazed around appraisingly — "it's a bit worn and in need of renovation, but how big did you say it was?"

"About eighty square meters," Genna said tightly. She stood in the entryway to the kitchen, her arms crossed and jaw tight.

"That's about, what, eight hundred and fifty square feet? Even back home that's a pretty good size for a one-bedroom. I figure we're looking at one and a half million, maybe two! Think about it, Gen! We could use the money to pay off the house and still have plenty left over. You'd never need to write another cookbook!"

If Drew were any more pleased with himself, he'd shine as brightly as the floodlit Parisian cityscape on a clear night.

"Are you okay, Mom?" Michael asked. "You look kinda pale."

"Well, of course she's pale," Becky snapped. "It's not every day you inherit an apartment in Paris. It's all right to be shell-shocked, Mom," she said. "You don't have to make a decision right now."

"Decision?" Drew said. "What decision? There's nothing to decide except how fast we can get the paperwork through. We've hit the jackpot, family!"

"No, Drew. *We* have not hit the jackpot. I've lost a dear friend, and now I need to decide what I want to do."

"Well, sure, that's too bad about Monsieur," Drew said, "but he was ancient, wasn't he? And it sounds like you kept him well fed up to the end."

Genna looked at her family and felt more alone than she'd ever felt in her life, even in her first days in Paris. Monsieur's generosity had left her bereft. She would miss his twice-weekly visits. Thanks to him, she'd written her best book yet.

Drew began pacing the perimeter of the living room, measuring the proportions with his carpenter's eyes.

"Please stop."

Drew paused midstride. "I'm working out some ideas for renovations. You know, it might be better to fix the place up before we put it on the market. We'd get a much better price. And we've got to convert it into a two-bedroom."

"I'm not selling."

"Don't be stupid, Gen," he said as he continued pacing. "You're upset. Have a glass of wine."

"It's eleven o'clock in the morning."

"Oh, right." He spread his arms out to measure the width of the doorway leading to the bedroom.

Genna tightened her arms across her chest. "I'm not selling."

He glanced back at her. "You're being ridiculous. You can't stay in Paris."

"Why not?"

Drew sighed theatrically and flopped on to a chair next to the table. "Well, for one thing, I doubt the French government will let you stay here indefinitely, and for another, you belong at home."

"What home?"

"Our home, with me."

"You're forgetting something, Dad."

Drew turned to look at Becky, who was sitting on the couch. Her glare finally penetrated his jubilation about soaring Parisian real estate prices.

"You can't expect Mom to go running back to you after what you've put her through."

"But I thought you *wanted* your mom and me to get back together."

"That's before I checked my email the other day."

Genna held her breath. So *now* was the time Becky chose to identify her father's girlfriend? She sure had a flawless sense of timing.

"What are you talking about, Becky? What email?"

"The one from Nancy."

Whoa.

For the second time that morning, Genna felt cast adrift in a dark universe—no up, no down, nothing to grasp hold off, nothing to believe in. She braced herself against the entryway to keep herself upright and stared at Drew. With every atom of her being she willed him to deny it. Nancy was her friend, had been her support when Genna's world had gone sideways. She'd never betray her.

"What about Nancy?" Drew asked, his voice pitched an octave higher than normal.

"You mean the Nancy you've been friends with for years, Mom?" Michael asked. "Jonathon's mother?"

"Yes," Genna and Becky said together without looking at Michael.

"*She's* who Dad had an affair with?"

"Apparently," said Genna.

"Only it's not in the past tense," Becky said. "According to Nancy, you left her high and dry, Dad, to come and see Mom. She's pretty upset."

"God knows why," Genna said turning away. "She can have him."

"Gen!" Drew's voice now sounded high *and* strangled, which was just as well since it saved Genna the trouble of strangling him herself. "It's not like that. Yes, Nancy and I got together, but I never meant it to last. It was all her idea. She came over to the house to see you that day. You weren't home and so it just, well, happened."

"But you kept seeing each other," Becky said.

"Only after your Mom left for Paris. I mean, she'd left. What was I supposed to do?" Drew walked toward Genna. "You wouldn't reply to my emails and Nancy kept coming over. It wasn't *my* fault."

Typical Drew. Nothing was ever his fault.

"Why did you really come to Paris, Drew?" Genna asked.

"We've been through this already." He looked around at Becky and Michael, who were staring at him as if he'd grown horns. "How about we go for a walk? The kids don't need to hear this."

"Oh, I'm sure the kids are fascinated."

"I already said I was sorry about ten thousand times. What more can I do?"

"Nothing," Genna said. "You can do nothing, Drew. Go home and take up with Nancy or anyone else who'll have you."

"What about the house?"

Trust Drew to pivot to real estate.

"Sell it."

Michael stepped in. "I think you should go now, Dad," he said. "I'll walk you to your hotel." He guided his father toward the door and then looked back at his mother. "I'm meeting meet Tessa over by Notre-Dame in a while. Maybe we could do dinner later?"

"That would be good."

Drew's face had gone gray, and Genna saw him as the old man he'd become. They were supposed to have grown old together—neither of them noticing the wrinkles and the creaks. They'd be one of those couples who still held hands and laughed at private jokes. When one died, the other would die soon after of a broken heart. That was the plan. That was what Genna had signed up for.

Merde.

Drew looked back at Genna with eyes that for the first time appeared truly sorry. Genna didn't think he'd believed she would leave him for good, and she realized that she hadn't either. In the far recesses of her mind, she'd still considered Drew her safety net.

And now that safety net was walking out of her Paris apartment. The next time they met, there'd be no more pleading, no more talk of getting back together. They would fill the dead space between them with lawyers and contracts and bank accounts.

"I'm sorry, Becky," Genna said when the door closed behind Michael and Drew.

"You had no choice, Mom. He brought it on himself. I hope you aren't mad at me for telling you."

"I'm not mad at you, although I guess I'd have preferred not to know it was Nancy because now I've lost a friend *and* a husband. I'm just sorry your child won't have two grandparents."

Becky laughed. "The baby will still have both of you—just not at the same time. I'm not letting Dad off the hook. I'm pissed at him now, but we'll see plenty of each other. He's still my father."

"Pregnancy has sure mellowed you."

"Are you saying I wasn't mellow before?"

"Oh well, I wouldn't, um . . ."

"It's fine, Mom. I know how I get sometimes, and I can't guarantee I won't get like that again. But for now"—she patted her stomach—"I feel so damn happy. I only wish Rolf were here."

"You'll see him soon."

"He's meeting me at the airport. We have a lot to talk about, but I think everything's going to work out."

"Rolf's a good man."

"Like Dad was when you married him?"

"You and Rolf are more mature than we were. I was only twenty-two when I married your father and I didn't know what to expect. And now I *know* what I was missing."

Becky dimpled. "Because of Bill?"

Genna paused, embarrassed. Discussing her sex life with her daughter, even her grown-up, pregnant daughter, seemed vaguely indecent. "He's got a few moves that are new to me."

"Mother!"

"You asked!"

"Okay, okay, too much information!" Becky laughed. "What now?"

"I'm not sure. Suddenly, I have all these options. I have a place to live in Paris and I should be able to borrow enough money to tide me over until your father sells the house. Pierre said he'd work something out with the bank."

"Rolf and I can help get the house cleaned up and back on the market."

"That would be great."

"And then if your phone interview goes well with the guy in London, you can fly back in the fall to do the cooking show. Michael thinks you should do it and I agree."

"I haven't even talked to the guy yet. Do you think I have what it takes?"

"I think the question you should ask is do *you* think you have what it takes."

"I want to try."

"Excellent! And if things don't go the way you hope, what have you lost? You have an apartment in Paris and you can start another book. You have plenty of options."

Genna smiled at her daughter. "I'll miss you."

"You can come home anytime to visit the baby."

"What about Michael?"

"Michael can take care of himself. Besides, he plans to stay in Europe, at least until the spring. You'll probably see him more here than you would at home."

"You're saying that no one will miss me."

"Stop fishing, Mom." Becky went into the kitchen. "What have you got to eat?"

"I gather you're feeling better."

"Yeah, all of a sudden I want to eat everything in sight which is so not like me."

"Have some yogurt with fruit."

Genna got up and joined Becky in the kitchen where she extracted a jar from the cupboard. "And here, sprinkle on some of this toasted coconut. It adds a nice flavor."

"Thanks. Maybe now I'm going to be a mom I should learn how to cook."

"Well, you're eating for two now."

Becky grinned. "I know. Oh, and I forgot to tell you that I changed my flight. I leave tomorrow."

"You wouldn't want to give your ticket to your dad, would you?"

"Non-transferable. You'll have to put up with him for another week at least. He's booked to go home on the fifteenth."

"I'm still flying home on Thursday so I can get things organized before I move back here."

Becky brought her bowl into the living room and sat cross-legged on the couch. "And so you're leaving Dad all alone in Paris with nothing to do for six more days? He'll go ballistic."

Genna shrugged. "Not my problem."

"More importantly, what are you planning to do about Bill?"

"Didn't you say I was managing well on my own?"

"Yes, but that doesn't mean you need to join a convent. When a hunky Aussie with money comes knocking, you owe it to yourself to answer."

"Becky!"

"Come on, Mom, I saw how he was looking at you last night."

"He said he wanted to meet with me today."

"When?"

"We didn't set a time."

"Do you want me to call for you?" Becky put down her bowl and picked up Genna's phone from the coffee table, her fingers curled over the keypad.

Laughing, Genna grabbed the phone and dialed.

thirty-five

Red Grape Macarons
*Filled with grape jelly and topped with roasted
macadamia nuts*

They met in the middle of the Pont des Arts.

Just as they had on the day they'd visited Sainte-Chapelle, Genna and Bill stood side by side and contemplated the view of Notre-Dame. Massive white clouds puffed high into the blue sky and the sun sparkled off the Seine. The air caressed their skin like a warm bath—a perfect June day in Paris.

"I'm sorry I've neglected you this past week," Bill said.

"You're here now."

Bill placed his large hand over Genna's on the railing in front of them. She kept her gaze on the view while her heart did a quick shimmy.

"Do you remember that phone call I got the night we, ah . . . ?"

"Yes."

"Right, well, it was my business partner back home. He told me the offer for the business had fallen through."

"I thought you said you'd already sold your business."

"Not quite. When I left for Europe, the sale was in progress, but at the last minute, the silly bugger backed out."

"I'm sorry." Below them on the river, a *bateau-mouche* glided by, the top bristling with tourists. Genna waved. Several of them waved back.

So, Bill's coldness hadn't had anything to do with her.

That was good. Right?

"His financing fell through, and my partner discovered he had a history of shady dealings with some wineries out near Adelaide, adulterating the wines with inferior grapes, that sort of thing. Fraud charges were pending. We're well out of it, I can tell you. But the upshot is that when I found out the business hadn't been sold, I started wondering if I want to sell it at all."

"Do you?" She turned to face him.

"No." He grinned. "No, I don't. This traveling lark is fine for a while, but it turns out I'm not ready to retire yet. I miss working."

"I understand that."

"I was hoping you would." Bill put his arm around her and pulled her close. "I'm guessing you saw Drew this morning?"

She nodded, the image of Drew pacing the perimeter of the living room fresh in her mind. His absolute confidence in his right to be there and to share in Monsieur's legacy had infuriated her.

"He's still alive, if that's what you mean."

"Aye, well, serving him shrimp was an accident." He smiled down at her. "It wasn't your fault."

"No, but ..." Genna paused, not sure if she wanted to be completely honest with Bill. After all, how well did she really know him? And why did her knees still keep going rubbery? On the other hand, what did she have to lose at this point by being honest? He'd be returning to Sydney soon and she to Vancouver. The most she could hope for was another romp between the one-thousand–thread-count sheets at the Rue Saint-Honoré hotel.

There were worse fates.

"When I was worried that he might die, there was a moment when I wished I'd forgiven him when I had the chance." Genna looked up at Bill. To her surprise, his jaw tightened.

"I know how you feel."

"You do?"

"I talk about my life with Marjorie like it was perfect and all, but things weren't always right between us." He scowled. "Not by a mile."

"You mean?" Genna pulled back.

Bill too?

What was *wrong* with men?

"Aye. I do."

Without a word, Genna turned and started walking back the way she'd come. She blinked away tears. Bill wasn't worth it. Drew wasn't worth it. She was *so* much better on her own.

Bill caught up with her at the top of the staircase leading to the walkway bordering the Seine.

"Genna! Please, listen to me."

She stopped, keeping her gaze focused on the river flowing under the bridge.

"Please," Bill said.

Against her better judgment, Genna let Bill take her hand and together they descended the staircase and found a free bench.

"Are you sure you can't forgive Drew?"

"Did Marjorie forgive *you*?" Genna hated the hurt in her voice, but clearly, she'd been wrong to trust this man. If he cheated on the sainted Marjorie, whom he'd adored, then he'd do the same to her. She started to rise.

"Ah, no," Bill said catching her hand. "It was the other way around."

"Oh." Genna sat back down. "You're kidding."

"I wish. And, yeah, I won't pretend it was easy." Bill shook his head. "Not by a long chalk. But in the end, I couldn't chuck everything we'd built together—the kids, the business, our lives—just because she'd made a mistake. And as it turned out, my Marjorie and I only got another five years." His eyes filled with tears.

"I'm sorry."

"I know, love."

In silence, they watched another boat glide past, this one heading west in the direction of the Eiffel Tower, the symbol of Paris that so many Parisians had loathed when it was first built. And now could any of them imagine Paris without it?

"Last night, I found out that Drew's still at it," Genna said. "Becky told me. Do you still think I should forgive him?"

"That's not for me to say."

Genna closed her eyes and let her head fall onto Bill's shoulder, more relieved than she cared to admit that he'd been the injured party and not Marjorie.

"I guess you're going back to Sydney soon," she said finally.

"I am."

"For good?"

"Depends."

"On what?"

Gently, he stroked her cheek, then leaned forward so his lips were inches from hers. "On you. Would you consider coming back with me?"

Her heart did a backflip followed by a full double pike with a twist.

And then her phone rang.

Bill nodded at Genna's bag. "Go on. I'm not going anywhere yet."

"Hello?"

"Genna!"

Drew *never* called her Genna. A dart of fear lanced her heart. "What's wrong?"

"It's Michael. He's had an accident."

thirty-six

Spiced Chai Macarons
Redolent with ginger, nutmeg, cinnamon, and cloves

Genna found Tessa at the entrance to the emergency department at the Hôpital Saint-Louis on the Right Bank. She was crying. Genna enfolded her in a hug, her worst fears returning. Drew had given her the name of the hospital and told her to hurry. But before he'd had a chance to give her details about Michael's condition, the doctor had arrived, and he'd ended the call.

Bill had wanted to come with her, but Genna said no. It was too much. Too soon. He made her promise to call him and then helped her up the stairs to the road and hailed a taxi. She barely had time to thank him before the taxi, understanding the urgency of Bill's shouted directions—even if they were in English—roared off toward the hospital.

Paris flashed past, a blur of browns and grays. She hadn't even told Bill about the apartment. Would it make a difference to any chance they had of a future together? How could any of that matter now?

She found Tessa waiting for her outside Emergency. She fell into Genna's arms, her slight body trembling.

"What happened? Can I see him?"

Tessa sniffed and pulled back. "I think they took him for X-rays."

"Where's Drew?" The one thing she knew beyond any doubt was that Drew loved his children as much as she did. And now she wanted to see him more than anyone, to have him reassure her, to tell her that Michael was fine. To hear him call her Gen again.

"I'll take you to him." Tessa led the way into the emergency department. "They've been dead kind here," she said. "I've called Mum."

"What happened?"

"We were near Notre-Dame and Michael wanted to show me his rollerblading. He borrowed skates from some bloke, and he was really good. Then something happened, I don't know what, but he was going superfast and then he fell really bad. Hurt his leg. And hit his head."

"His head? Genna's mind instantly ran to concussion. Her darling, sunny Michael with the gleam in his eyes dimmed. Her heart squeezed with anguish.

As soon as she entered the small waiting room, Drew gathered her in his arms.

"Hey, Gen. Shhh. It's okay. The doctor said she'd be back soon. He's banged up, but it's not critical."

Relief weakened her knees, making her feel as if every bone in her body had suddenly liquefied. If Drew hadn't been holding her up, she'd have sunk to the floor.

"Come on," Drew said. "Sit here and we'll wait to talk to the doctor. Thank God she speaks English."

Genna nodded. That was a blessing. Her French wasn't even close to being good enough to converse with a doctor about concussions and broken legs.

Gently, he led her to a chair. "Here, I got you a hot drink." He picked up a paper cup from the side table.

She took a sip and smiled in spite of herself. "Chai. You remembered."

"Of course."

After Michael was born, Genna had been ill for several months. The nanny they'd hired to help out was a recent immigrant from India. Every day she made Genna chai tea with hot milk. Over the years, chai became a family go-to whenever anyone was sick.

As Genna inhaled the comforting spiciness of the drink, she fought back tears. "He's going to be all right, isn't he?"

Drew nodded and put his arm around Genna, his touch her lifeline back to normalcy. "'Course he is. Our boy's indestructible, right?"

How many times had they argued about Michael and his wild ways—his love of speed and risk, his cheerful belief in his own immortality?

"Monsieur Watson? Madame?"

Broad faced and stout, Dr. Monique Ng smiled reassuringly, her eyes sympathetic. She pulled a chair around to face Genna and Drew. Tessa stood near the door to keep an eye out for her mother.

"Your son is going to make a complete recovery. He is very lucky," she said.

Genna leaned forward, all her focus on the doctor. The terror was starting to recede, replaced by a profound gratitude to this comfortable, capable-looking woman whom she instinctively trusted.

"He has fractured his left leg. But the break, it is not severe." Dr. Ng spoke slowly, her English precise. "And his concussion, it is fortunately mild."

"May we see him?"

"*Bien sûr.* He is on the painkillers, but he is still awake. We have set his leg and want him to stay two days in *l'hôpital.*"

Genna slumped back in the plastic chair. Michael would be fine. Would he be able to travel home with her on Thursday? Probably not. He'd have to fly home with his father, and then stay at the new house. There was plenty of room.

She imagined cooking his favorite dishes, spoiling him rotten like she had after he'd broken his arm jumping off the swings when he was eight. And while he recovered, he could help her finish *Eat*

Like a Parisian. Maybe she'd even convince him to go back to school. She knew of at least two excellent culinary programs in Vancouver.

Everything was going to be fine.

"Will he be able to ski?" Drew asked, fear making his voice too loud for the small space. Genna put her hand on his arm to calm him, a gesture she'd made so often before. He glanced down and immediately softened his tone. "He loves to ski."

"*Oui.* I think so, yes. It is good that now is not time for skiing, no? By winter, he will be fine."

Dr. Ng stood. Genna kept hold of Drew's arm as together they rose and took turns shaking the doctor's hand.

"Come on, Gen. Let's go see our boy."

"This way." The doctor led them back into the corridor. "Turn left at the end of this hallway." She consulted her clipboard. "*Vingt-deux.*" She looked up. "He is in room twenty-two."

"Thank you so much. *Merci.*"

"You are most welcome." She set off in the opposite direction, leaving Genna alone with Drew.

"Well, that's a relief," Drew said.

Now that she was certain Michael was out of danger, Genna pulled away from Drew and set off down the hall. All she wanted was to see her son.

"Do you think Michael had the sense to get travel insurance?" Drew asked, coming alongside her.

Typical Drew. Always thinking about money.

Her anger returned in full force. "He's not an idiot."

"No, but he's young. He might have forgotten, and then we'll be on the hook for his medical bills."

"Tough."

Without waiting to hear more, Genna entered the hospital room to find Michael lying on his back with his leg elevated. His eyes were open but bleary with painkillers, his skin pale under what remained of his spring-skiing tan.

"Hey, Mom, Dad." Languidly, he held out one hand for Genna to take. "Sorry I scared you."

"Don't worry about it, son." Drew came to stand next to Genna. "We'll have you home in no time. The doctor says you'll be fine."

Michael nodded, then winced. "Yeah." He looked from Genna to Drew. "You two all right?"

"We're fine, darling," Genna said. "You just focus on getting better." She moved to the other side of the bed, away from Drew. "The doctor says you need to stay here for a couple of nights."

She pushed the hair off his forehead like she had countless times when he was a little boy. Without looking at Drew she said, "Call Becky."

Drew patted his son's hand. "Sure. I'll be right back."

Michael watched his father leave the room and then carefully turned his head to look at Genna. "It's okay, Mom. I don't need you to pretend everything's fine for my sake. I'm feeling pretty banged up, I won't lie. But I'm not a kid anymore. You guys do what you need to do."

"We'll always be here for you."

"I know."

Genna leaned forward and kissed his forehead. "I love you, son."

He smiled weakly, her sunny Michael, the child of her heart. "Me too, Mom."

thirty-seven

Passion Fruit Macarons
Filled with papaya cream flavored with Grand Marnier

"He'll be okay, Becky. You know Michael."

The next morning while Becky packed, Genna bustled around her kitchen, pulling ingredients out of the fridge and cupboards, planning ways to use up the food before she left Paris.

"I do," Becky said, "but I still hate leaving while he's in hospital."

"It's only for another day, and then he'll go home with your dad next week. We'll have lots of chances to get together. I won't be coming back to Paris until September."

"Will you see Nancy?"

Genna laughed. "Not bloody likely, as Bill would say. At least now I understand why she was so keen on me coming here."

"Which has turned out to be the best thing you've done in years."

Genna turned to look at her daughter. "You think so?"

"Don't you? You're a lot more confident than you used to be. It's like now you know you can manage on your own."

"You don't think I knew that before?"

"I love him and everything because he's my father, but to be honest, Mom, you've always been pretty dependent on Dad. He kind of took you for granted. When was the last time he told you that you look good?"

Genna laughed. Why did daughters have to be so perceptive? "Point taken."

"And aside from acknowledging that you're also a decent cook, did he ever tell you how amazingly capable you are?"

"Ah, no."

"I rest my case! Now, tell me what's up with Bill."

"He asked me to come to Sydney with him."

"Whoa! That's big. What did you say?"

"I didn't have a chance to say anything. Right after he asked me, your dad called about Michael."

"Talk about timing!"

Genna laughed, then glanced at the clock on the wall in the kitchen. "I'm supposed to meet him across the street in about ten minutes."

"You look excited, Mom." Becky paused and peered more closely at Genna. "Even with all this business with Michael, you look happy."

Genna landed a quick kiss on Becky's cheek and received a hug in return. "Thanks, dear. I'll be back in plenty of time to say goodbye before you leave for the airport."

"Don't rush on my account!"

Genna descended to the street and found a table outside at Les Deux Magots. She ordered a café crème, and then called the waiter back and asked him to bring her two boules of her favorite *fruit de la passion* ice cream. She felt like celebrating.

A few minutes later, she spied Bill's chunky form rounding the corner in front of the church. Following him was a short, compact body — the body of a former cheerleader.

Make that squad captain.

"Marsha! What are you doing here?"

Marsha plopped herself down opposite Genna and gave her a two-cheeked kiss. "*Bonjour!* How's Michael?"

"Good and already bored. He gets out of hospital tomorrow. Tessa's barely left his side. She postponed going back to England."

"Wow! I wonder what Denise thinks of that."

"She's decided that the path of least resistance is her best bet. Besides, Michael's going home with Drew next week so it's not like he'll have time to do too much damage. And Tessa can take care of herself"

"True. I have to say you're looking amazing, Genna. Did Bill spill the beans on the phone?" She glared at him. "I told you to wait for me."

Bill dragged a spindly chair next to Genna and sat down. "Of course, I didn't tell her." He drew back and surveyed Genna. "You do look good, love." With one meaty paw, he patted Genna's knee. The electrical charge vibrated up her thigh to a region somewhat more sensitive than her quads.

"You may have noticed Bill and me talking at your party the other night," Marsha began.

"I did."

"We were talking about how you've *got* to find a way to stay in Paris and open your cooking school."

What with the excitement with Michael, Genna had still not told Bill about Monsieur's *appartement*. She leaned forward. "But . . ." Marsha held up one hand. "No, Genna. You're not to say anything until we're finished. I know you think it's impossible, but Bill and I think we've found a way."

"But . . ."

"Genna!"

"Just listen to her, love," said Bill, again patting her knee. This time the electrical charge made her gasp. She cooled down with a spoonful of the ice cream. Tangy, smooth, hints of citrus— marvelous.

"You remember the enormous kitchen in my new apartment?" Marsha asked.

"Of course. It's incredible."

Marsha flashed a triumphant smile at Bill. "Told you! Anyway, I was telling Bill about how I think it would make a great location for your cooking classes. You could keep them low-key to start. Four or five people, maybe. Then, if those classes worked out—and they will—you could find a bigger venue. In the meantime, you could build a clientele and it wouldn't cost you a euro." She sat back in her chair, grinning. "What do you think?"

"Um . . ."

"Don't answer yet!" she said. "Bill also has a proposition."

"I'd like to invest in your idea," he said. "I could make it a loan to help you with marketing and start-up costs, or you could consider it an investment in return for a percentage of the business."

"Okay."

"Okay what?" Bill asked.

"I accept."

Clearly, neither of them had expected her to agree so quickly.

"We figured you'd object because of, you know, the money," Marsha said. "Bill told me you were dead set against taking any money from him. What changed your mind?"

"I'm still dead set against taking any money, although I appreciate the offer of a loan, at least for a few months. No, what I've been trying to tell you is that I'm coming back to Paris after all."

"Did the house sell?" Marsha asked.

"No, but it will. But that's not the reason." Genna told them about Monsieur and the apartment.

"Oh dear, I'm so sorry," Marsha said, patting Genna's hand. "You were fond of him, weren't you?"

"Very."

"Why didn't you tell me yesterday?" Bill asked.

Genna shrugged. "I never got the chance."

"No, I suppose not. Well, this puts a new spin on things," Bill said. "I guess our offer isn't as game-changing as we thought."

"I still really appreciate it. I think Marsha's apartment would be perfect for my first cooking school. As you say, I'd start small, and then if I get to host the cooking show in London, I could build a bit of a following. It's possible, isn't it?"

"Absolutely!" Marsha laughed.

"But what does Colin think about having strangers in his apartment?"

"He hates the idea, but he's at work during the day and I told him I wanted to help you out and that he could go along with the plan or not. And guess what?"

"He's going along with it."

"Yes!"

"And the wedding?"

"Plans are on hold for a while. Colin still wants us to get married in September, but I've decided I'm not ready yet. I have Pierre's job now, and he's promised to recommend me to some of his friends. And if it's meant to be, it will be. I'm not going to push it."

"Good girl!" Genna squeezed Marsha's hand. "If Colin's the one, he'll wait for you."

"I hope so." Marsha pushed back her chair. "I promised Colin I'd help him with the packing this afternoon. We're moving into the new place next Saturday. Can we get together later in the week?"

"Let's try for tomorrow. I'm leaving Thursday, remember."

"Right! OK, I'll call you." Marsha hugged Genna and then dashed across Rue Bonaparte on her way to the Saint-Germain-des-Prés Métro.

"She's lovely," Bill said as he watched Marsha go.

"It's too bad she's chosen Colin, but I guess he must have some good points. I'm glad to see she's standing up for herself."

"And you are too."

"Hmm?"

"I'm presuming your decision to return to Paris means that things definitely are over between you and Drew. Michael's accident didn't change anything?"

"It almost did." Genna reached for Bill's hand. "For about two seconds, I imagined us all living together in the new house, me taking care of Michael, everything going back to the way it was."

"Could it?"

She shook her head. "No." She stroked the back of Bill's hand with two fingers. "I realize now that what Drew and I have isn't strong enough to survive what he did. It's not like with you and Marjorie."

"I'm sorry."

"Me too, but I'm learning that the only thing I can really depend upon in this life is myself."

Bill was silent for a while, his gaze fixed on their intertwined hands. Finally, he looked up at her. "Do you remember what I asked you before Drew called about Michael? About coming home to Sydney with me?"

"But what about my cooking school? You said you wanted to finance it."

"I do, if that's what you want, but I'm asking if you'd consider an alternative. You could set up a cooking school in Sydney. We don't all eat crocodile steaks for tea."

For a few glorious seconds, Genna saw herself testing recipes in an airy, sunny kitchen overlooking Sydney Harbor, and having Bill to wake up to every morning. And then she saw the other path— the one where she pursued her own dreams, but she did so on her own terms.

"I can't, Bill."

"I thought that's what you'd say. And I get it. But I don't want this to be the end, do you?"

"No."

"Good. You go home, get yourself sorted, and then we'll see what happens. I'm not inclined to let you out of my life, Genna McGraw. Not for a good long while yet."

The backflip with a full double pike and twist sliced neatly into the deep end of the pool.

"I'm happy to hear it."

Genna set down her spoon and nestled into Bill's arms, feeling comfortable and safe and, above all, free. The waiter glided by and tucked a scrap of paper under the ashtray. He glanced at Genna, a ghost of a smile lightening his usual indifference. She winked at him and mouthed *merci*.

He looked startled, and then his smile widened. "*De rien, madame.*"

It is nothing.

Genna wasn't so sure about that. Young and chic she was not, but she was in Paris, and she'd have Bill to herself for a little while longer.

epilogue

Eight months later, a tiny hand grasped one of Genna's fingers and squeezed with such force she winced.

"She's a strong one," her father said proudly. "What do you think, Grandma?"

Gemma smiled at the sound of her new name. She bent over little Sonia Josephine—two months old today—and kissed her smooth forehead. The baby gazed back, her eyes bright and clear. Genna looked into them and saw the wisdom of the ages. If Sonia could talk, what stories could she tell of the galaxies and worlds she'd visited before arriving here on Earth and into her grandmother's arms?

While the baby had been growing inside her mother, Genna had been busy creating a life she could never have imagined a year earlier. The renovations to transform Monsieur's *appartement* into an airy two-bedroom haven would be completed by the time Genna returned to Paris by way of Australia. Bill had promised to take her camping in the outback and to barbeque all the shrimp she could eat.

In the fall, she had shot the first ten episodes of *Cooking with Genna* in London. The first few had already aired in the UK and early reviews were positive. *Eat Like a Parisian* was published in time to enjoy brisk Christmas sales, and Genna was hard at work on *Natural Goodness for Happy Cooks*, her seventh cookbook.

Her social circle in Paris was expanding along with the small cooking school she ran from Marsha's apartment—now Colin-free. To Genna's relief, Colin had finally succeeded in turning Marsha against him. He'd returned to England and was not missed. And thanks to Pierre's connections, Marsha's new design company was flourishing, as was Marsha.

At a college in South London, Tessa was earning top marks in her first year of culinary studies while Denise continued working for Jason MacQuarrie. And as for Michael, he was fully recovered and spending his winter in Austria, skiing and waiting tables, although he had mentioned once or twice to his mother that following Tessa to culinary school wasn't beyond the realm of possibility.

Genna lived in hope.

The House with the View in West Vancouver sold for a reasonable price, and so far as Genna knew, Drew was getting on with his life. Whether it was with or without Nancy did not concern her, and she never asked her children for details.

"She's beautiful," Genna murmured. Across the room, Becky sat with her feet curled under her in a rocking chair, a fuzzy pink baby blanket in her lap. For the first time in her life, she looked completely and utterly contented.

The baby reached out a pudgy hand.

Genna caught and held it. "Welcome to the world, Sonia Josephine," she whispered. "Grandma's here."

parisian sites
and bistro dishes

Are you feeling hungry after reading *Love Among the Recipes*? If you're now inspired to make macarons, you'll find hundreds of amazing recipes and taste combinations online, and following is the list of the Parisian sites Genna visited along with the bistro dishes she included in *Eat Like a Parisian*.

Visit me at www.carolcram.com for links to the recipes and sites.

Arc de Triomphe: Braised Lamb Shanks with Caramelized Onions
Cassat's *Mère et enfant sur fond vert,* **Musée d'Orsay:** Clafouti
Denon Wing, Musée Louvre: Shrimp-Stuffed Salmon
Eiffel Tower: Steak Haché et Frites
Great clock, Musée d'Orsay: Apple Tart
Greek and Roman Antiquities, Musée Louvre: Country loaf of bread studded with walnuts and figs
Île de la Cité: Rainbow Trout
Ingres' *La Grande Odalisque,* **Musée Louvre:** Tagine and Couscous
L'abbaye de Saint-Germain-des-Prés: French Onion Soup

L'Opéra Bastille: Veal cutlets in parchment (Escalopes de veau en papillote)
Lady & the Unicorn Tapestries in the Musée de Cluny (Musée national du Moyen Âge): Duck Confit
Les Halles: Rabbit in Mustard Sauce
Les Invalides: Steak Diane Flambéed in Brandy
Les Jardin des Plantes: Leeks Braised in Wine
Luxembourg Gardens: Pot-au-feu
Monet's Gardens at Giverny: Asparagus Soufflé
Monet's *Les Nymphéas*, Musée de L'Orangerie: Vichyssoise
Montmartre: Moules à la Marinière
Musée d'Orsay: Cassoulet
Musée Delacroix: Bœuf Bourguignon
Musée du quai Branly: Chocolate Mousse
Musée Picasso: Bouillabaisse
Musée Rodin: Crème Brûlée.
Notre-Dame: Lemon Sole
Parc Buttes Charmont: Chicken & 40 Cloves of Garlic
Parc de la Villette: Pork Terrine with Roasted Red Peppers and Hazelnuts
Parc Monceau: Coq Au Vin
Paris Métro: Pissaladière
Place de la Concorde: Madeleines
Place du Tertre: Macarons
Pompidou Centre: Canapés: Tapenade Noire, Caviar d'Aubergine, Anchoïade, and Grapes Stuffed with Goat Cheese
Rose Window, Notre-Dame Cathedral: Strawberry Tart
Sainte-Chapelle: Pavlova with Strawberries, Raspberries and Blueberries
Stravinsky Fountain, Centre Pompidou: Fruit Flan
Tour Saint-Jacques: Homemade Sausages
Tuileries Gardens: Salade Niçoise
Versailles: Caesar Salad

acknowledgments

Thank you to Pam Conrad and Rachel Bunin who read and provided great comments on the novel. I've worked with both these wonderful editors for many years in my other life as a textbook author and am so grateful for their enthusiasm and support. I'm also thrilled and humbled by the thoughtful feedback from fellow authors Edythe Anstey Hanen, Martin Lake, Amy Maroney, Patricia Sands, and Cathleen With, and from other beta readers including Elizabeth Petrie who corrected the French, Becky Dawson who also advised me about the food, Brunilda Musikant and Julia Simpson.

Thank you also to my intrepid launch team that included Belle Ami, Margo Arel, Paula Butterfield, Kate Coffey, Stephanie Cowell, MT Cozzola, Becky Dawson, Adriana Diaz, Jennifer Duffy, Maggie Humm, Jacqueline Massey, Julie McCarrin, Patricia Morrisroe, Liza Nash Taylor, Barbara Quick, Diane Romain, and Susan Steggall.

A huge thank you to Paul D. Zablocki for his insightful and much-appreciated copy edit and proofread, and to Bailey McGinn for her fabulous cover design.

And now the biggest thank-you of all to Stephanie Williams, my BFF since kindergarten and an amazing editor, proofreader, advisor, confidante, supporter, cheerleader, and all-round awesome friend. I am deeply indebted to her and so grateful to have her in my life.

Finally, as always, I owe everything in my world to my family—my most excellent daughter, Julia Simpson; my incredible mom, Ruby Cram; and my partner of over thirty-five years and my daily support and love, Gregg Simpson.

about the author

Photo: © Heather Pennell

Carol M. Cram loves the arts, food, travel, and writing novels about people who follow their passions.

She writes about women in the arts in her three award-winning novels of historical fiction, *The Towers of Tuscany* (Lake Union Publishing, 2014), *A Woman of Note* (Lake Union Publishing, 2015) and *The Muse of Fire* (Kindle Press & New Arcadia Publishing, 2018) and matches her travel-inspired vignettes with pastel drawings created by her husband, Canadian artist Gregg Simpson, in *Pastel & Pen: Travels in Europe* (New Arcadia Publishing, 2019). In *Love Among the Recipes* (New Arcadia Publishing, 2020), a woman searches for new passions amid the sights and tastes of Paris.

Carol also expresses her enthusiasm for the written word, the arts, and travel on *Artsy Traveler* (www.artsytraveler.com) and *Art In Fiction* (www.artinfiction.com) and on the Art In Fiction Podcast where she chats with authors who write novels inspired by the arts.

She also teaches writing courses and mentors new authors—one of her favorite things to do.

Carol has written over sixty bestselling college textbooks in computer applications and communications for Cengage Learning and was on faculty at Capilano University in North Vancouver for two over decades. She holds an MA in Drama from the University of Toronto and an MBA from Heriot Watt University in Edinburgh. She lives with her husband, painter Gregg Simpson, on beautiful Bowen Island near Vancouver, BC, where she also teaches Nia, a holistic dance/fitness practice.